BINARY STAR

Clif Mason

Copyright 2000 by Clif Mason
All rights reserved. No part of this book may be reproduced in any form without written permission from the publishers, except by a reviewer who may quote brief passages in a review to be printed in a newspaper or magazine.

First printing

ISBN: 1-893162-70-2
PUBLISHED BY AMERICA HOUSE BOOK PUBLISHERS
www.publishamerica.com
Baltimore

Printed in the United States of America

For Laurie
whose love made this book about love possible

I would like to express my deep respect for and gratitude to the Lakota people, for their profound story of the White Buffalo--without which the spiritual dimension of this novel would have been grievously diminished.

I would also like to make grateful acknowledgment of the Council for the International Exchange of Scholars for a Fulbright Fellowship to Rwanda, Africa, during which earlier versions of some chapters of this book were written.

so close that your hand on my chest is my hand,
so close that your eyes close as I fall asleep.

Pablo Neruda

Lovers don't finally meet somewhere.
They're in each other all along.

Jelaluddin Rumi

And that love is a kelson of the creation . . .

Walt Whitman

PROLOGUE

There is a water that is night and dream. The moon bows out upon it in a silky curve; the stars fall into it like rain. Its waves roll successively in, fall back forever into memory. Storms boil up there of a sudden, sullen and rancorous, in a sky without distance. Or peace lies soft as a cloud across the water, in all directions.

Islanding out of the night, like dawn, this past, this lambent dream. Endless anamnesis--this calling to mind, ever and ever again, as we call after departed friends, wishing them to return. Remembrance has its secret charm, its private scintillance. Yet there is, too, art's rare sorcery to be reckoned with, changes that linger, superimposed on the real, like gold leaf. And last, there is the future's sure, if unspoken, promise--that there will be other times, other people, other places, which likewise will exist at first purely for themselves, then for memory, and finally for art's transmuting alchemy.

* * * * * * *

On a hot, humid, grasshopper-thick day late in the month of August 1805, the two supremely competent explorers sent by President Jefferson to chart the lands contained in his new Louisiana Purchase marched overland with ten men from the juncture of the Red Earth and Missouri rivers to a tall hill that jutted alone above the prairie, several miles to the north. The Yankton Sioux called it Spirit Mound. It was, they said, inhabited by tiny spirit men--not more than a foot tall, but with big heads, like gourds--whose bows were very powerful and could shoot arrows with deadly accuracy over a distance of a mile or more. The two captains, being of an inquisitive but nonetheless skeptical frame of mind, had thought this so-called Spirit Mound too intriguing a phenomenon to pass unexamined. Thus, despite the heat and humidity--so intense their shirts were wet through after a single mile's tramp; they felt as if they were walking in a ground cloud--the swarms of gnats, and the grasshoppers that flew about like popping corn before their every step, they marched on.

When they were two and a half miles away from Spirit Mound and were beginning to doubt the wisdom of such a time-consuming and sweat-productive foray into "local superstition," a strange and most unaccountable thing happened when they were still far enough away not to be able to see the prominence because of the shorter intervening hills. A white buffalo of massive size, its boss shagged out as if for winter, its huge, inward-curved black horns gleaming like obsidian in the bright sunlight, walked unhurriedly up the Mound on the north side, the tall bluestem grass parting before its big black nose and bending to trail beneath its belly. It stepped without breaking stride around gopher holes and a patch or two of prickly pear cactus. The buffalo, whose hide was the color of unbleached muslin, stopped at the very center of the hill's crest, snorted and rolled, flattening the grass and rearranging several of the red ant mounds there--causing commotion both above and below ground--and then walked straight off the Mound into the air some eighty or ninety yards and disappeared. It was as if a small white cloud had suddenly dissipated, without discernible cause.

An hour later, the two tired but somewhat bemused captains and their men stood atop the mound. After so many days in the river valley, they were exceedingly pleased with the prospect, happy to be able to see such a considerable distance--south, past the Red Earth River, all the way to the hills on the other side of the Missouri, and far out onto the prairie on the other sides. As they walked leisurely about, they commented on how rich the mostly flat land looked.

They had seen their first buffalo and had eaten their first buffalo meat a few days earlier. They had felt quite a child's wonderment, almost awe, at the bison's size and power and what they thought of as its nobility. Glancing to the north, they saw several small, scattered groups many miles away. They noted some odd holes, perhaps, they speculated, the result of rodent excavations, and they observed the flattened grass and the displaced sand of the anthills. But they found the wallow of a single buffalo (most likely an old cow too slow to keep up with the others) of little interest. And when one of them (history has not recorded which) was suddenly bitten by a red ant that had crawled up one of his pantlegs, they started hastily back to the river, more than a little disgusted with themselves for not accomplishing more the past several hours, but worse, parched, lightheaded from thirst, having neglected to have brought water with them.

As they walked along--the grasshoppers jumping about (they seemed in their armor more to them like little machines than living things), sweat rilling into their eyes without stop, no matter how many times they wiped them with their sleeves--yes, as they walked along, the high curiosity of the morning faded, like the color from old clothes, into late afternoon apathy. They had seen no tiny archers with big heads, and after another hour's march across the prairie, they no longer cared. At sunset they arrived at their white pirogue, lashed to a sixty-foot cottonwood tree, and, not being able to help themselves, drank so much of the brown river water that their stomachs protruded and ached. They camped a mile or so upstream on the Missouri, knowing that the next day they would catch up to their big boat, which had pushed on ahead. They slept the sleep of the exhausted, unheedful of coyote calls and the unevenness of the ground whereon they made their bed.

* * * * * * *

Fifty-four years later, the town of Red Earth was built below the bluff on the north side of the Red Earth River--two miles from the place Lewis and Clark had tied up their pirogue. One morning in early December of that year, 1859, shortly before daybreak, a large white buffalo trudged calmly, steadily southwards across the prairie, through snow up to its knees, its warm breath steaming from its nose. Just moments before dawn, it reached the edge of the bluff above the few cabins of Red Earth. It rolled, making a sizable depression in the snow, then walked straight off the bluff, several hundred yards out into the air, stopping right over the cabins of the small settlement. Most of the town's inhabitants were just rising and one man had stepped outside to relieve himself. But neither he nor anyone else chanced to look up and see the sun's first light break in glints off the huge buffalo's black horns, like the sparks shed by struck flints. The white beast vanished, a marvelous brightness gone from the frosty air. By ten o'clock the sunshine was replaced by thick, sludge-gray clouds, and by eleven it was snowing heavily--large wet flakes that fell soundlessly through the still air. It snowed all afternoon and most of the night. By sunrise next day, the tracks of the buffalo and all trace of its rollings had been buried under an immaculate robe of snow, which was a far more glistening, more eye-smarting white than the buffalo's hide.

* * * * * * *

And no one saw the white buffalo walk placidly out of the west, right down the main street of the town, a few hours after midnight one April morning a hundred years later, its black hooves clicking unheard on the asphalt. The town had been relocated to the top of the bluff--all its citizenry, that is, but a few stalwarts, or fools, depending on one's perspective--after a flood had washed away most of the original town. The buffalo paused under the stoplight at First and Main, pawed, rolled several times, then began to walk into the dark, down the First Street hill, toward the Bottom, as the part of the town below the bluff was now called. There was one last streetlight, about a hundred yards down. Under it the buffalo disappeared, its white bulk melting instantly into the foggy air.

Not ten minutes later, a police cruiser drove down First Street and proceeded on a green light through the intersection with Main and straight down that same hill to the stop sign at its bottom, where the cop decided to turn right. He had just had a cup of coffee and was feeling good for that time of his shift. The whole night passed without anything worthy of remark, and after a bowl of cereal at the small table in his apartment the next morning, he slept, both untroubled and unexalted by any dreams.

* * * * * * *

The buffalo's visitations, not restricted to Red Earth and its environs, were almost always unseen, save by various holy men, children, poets, lovers, and madmen and -women.

Part I

October 1969

Chapter 1
Wolfram Kohles

They walked down a dark, still street in the university town of Red Earth, in late October. Judith Larkin, her brother Nick, her roommate Val Burroughs, and Bill Matthews, Nick's roommate. The cold night air was tinged with the smell of leaf-fires and over-ripe brown windfall apples, which lay, decomposing by the score on the ground beneath denuded, spidery trees. Hundreds of others yet hung from the boughs, like long-forgotten Christmas balls. Judith stepped on an apple, and it crushed mushily under the sole of her boot. The four friends were on their way to Banks' Bar to hear the blues-rock guitarist and singer they'd been hearing about all week: Wolfram Kohles. His hands were rumored to move so fast they disappeared in a blur, as if one's eyes had suddenly teared up. Two friends, Mike Red Horse and Bruce Baker, had gone earlier to save some tables up front.

Nick hadn't wanted to go out, but Judith had forced him, saying she was tired of his moping around, mooning over a girl who'd dumped him eight months before. Nick hadn't cut his wavy black-brown hair since the end of basketball season the year before, and it now obscured the white head and part of the wings and breast feathers of the eagle (clutching olive branches in the talons of both feet), embroidered on the backside of his jean jacket. His mother Lena had done the finely detailed embroidery the previous spring to try to boost Nick's spirits. Though she worked full-time as a teacher, Lena spent her free time doing the things that she had always done and loved--and had inspired the twins to love, to one degree or another--gardening, quilting, knitting, embroidery, drawing, and jewelry making.

Judith's hair was slightly longer than her brother's but cut identically. The siblings both stood eleven inches above five feet, and most people could not tell the difference between them, especially not if Judith wore a loose-fitting coat or jacket. They were frequently mistaken for each other. The likelihood of such errors occurring was greatly increased by their epicene features and by the fact that the twins had markedly similar tastes in clothes. Without planning to, they often managed to dress alike. This night, for example, they'd both chosen-- without consulting each other--black knee-high boots, Levis, and blue work shirts. Instead of a jean jacket, however, Judith wore a black leather jacket, the zippers of which gleamed under the streetlights, like silver scars.

The sky was overcast, the moon shining soft as the dust on a moth's wings behind the low gray clouds, veined with black ore. The air's incisors bit, and the fitful breeze brought blood to their cheeks. Judith liked the wood frame houses they passed, perhaps because they reminded her of the farmhouse she and Nick had spent the happiest years of their childhoods in. Most of these houses were thirty or forty years old, though some were much older. They were two- and three-stories tall, gabled, and roofed with asphalt shingles. Most had front porches, some had porches that wrapped around one side or the other, and better than half were painted white.

They were comfortable houses, with that lived-in feel. They had large, well-lit rooms and tall ceilings, earth-colored braided rugs or wall-to-wall plush carpeting, black rubber runners or carpeting on the stairways, laundry chutes and attics, green plants standing in clay and varicolored plastic pots of all sizes--in the windows, on end tables, and suspended on knotted ropes--and the skeletal silver saplings of TV antennae sprouting from their roofs. A fair number of these houses had been broken up into apartments and rooms to rent to college students.

Judith hoped to rent a room in one of those houses the next year, when she'd be able to move off-campus. She particularly liked a corner house a couple of blocks back, often walking out of her way to look at it. The house was huge--three and a half stories--and possessed a variety of different shapes and kinds of windows--hexagonal, round, diamond-shaped, and oval, with ordinary and stained glass. It also had a big balcony that curved around both sides on the second floor, above the first floor porch. The spindles of its porch and balcony railings were elegantly carved as antique furniture legs. In structure and ornamentation the house reminded her of old Mississippi steamboats.

After they were carded, they pulled open the plate glass door and entered. As they made their way down the length of the bar to the downstairs stairway that led to the stage where the band was to perform, their nostrils were assaulted by the smells of cigarette smoke and ash, beer (spilled, stale, and fresh-poured, froth-headed), pizza (a back room held two ovens), and more beer. As they were walking through the crowd downstairs toward the two tables Mike and Bruce had already pulled together up front and saved for them, they got sudden intense whiffs of perfume, deodorant, and cologne. After the band's first set, by which time the room temperature had risen ten degrees or more from the sheer number of bodies stuffed into the room (to say nothing of the number of people dancing), they would smell sweat and body salt.

"So, Nick, I see Judith succeeded in dragging your ass down here?" Mike asked. Mike Red Horse now wore his hair--the black of crow feathers--parted in the middle and pulled back into a ponytail.

"Let's just say she can be very persuasive when she wants to be."

"I told him he either came with us," Judith said, "or he'd have to find another ride home at Thanksgiving."

"But Nick owns half the car," Bruce said. The most one could say about Bruce Baker's long straight hair was that it was no more ill becoming to his haphazard features than short hair had been.

"Except that Nick lost his keys, so he's dependent on me for a ride."

"Yes," Val said, raising a fist, "real women's power!"

The room was long and rectangular and its walnut-paneled walls were undecorated except for the occasional townhouse-style wall light or neon beer sign. Oddly, the Pabst Blue Ribbon, Michelob, and Budweiser signs were darkened, their usually garish competition to assuage the masses' unendingly parched throats precluded by pulled plugs. The cramped stage stood against the rear wall, separated by the band's lights from a small dance floor. A drum kit was set up in the center rear of the stage. A bass guitar rested on a stand in front of the drums, flanked by a Yamaha organ on one side, and, directly in front of the twins' tables, a Fender Stratocaster and a Gibson acoustic guitar (modified for electric amplification). The other tables, arranged around a square-shaped dance area in the middle, were filling up fast.

The audience was an incongruous mixture of well barbered and coiffed fraternity and sorority kids and a good share of the longhairs from a twenty-five mile radius (many of whom lived communally in rented farmhouses--old, poorly insulated, and all too often, ramshackle). A bar built into the area under the stairs sold soda and tap beer by the pitcher and glass. To get bottled beer, one had to visit the bar upstairs. Mike and Bruce had already bought two pitchers, but since neither Judith nor Nick drank (something that stretched back to some murky event from their childhoods and which their friends had long since ceased to question), Nick left to buy them two sodas.

"Wolfram Kohles and Body Count," Bill read off the center of the bass drum. "Where're these guys from, anyway?"

"They're a local band," Judith said.

"Jesus, is that what you got us down here for, Judith, a local band? Maybe next time I'll ask a few more questions," Bruce said.

"Bruce, you could ask as many questions as you wanted and it still wouldn't help!" Judith shot back.

"I thought this bar booked bands from places like Denver, Chicago, and Minneapolis," Mike said.

"Beaver Madness played here last week," Val said. "They're from Chicago."

"From what I hear, this band is really tight," Judith said. "People say they won't be local for long."

"And Wolfram Kohles is supposed to be hot stuff," Val said.

"You hope," Bruce said.

"I meant as a guitar player," Val said.

"Sure you did," Nick said, setting a 7 Up in front of his sister and another at his place next to her.

"So what kind of name is Wolfram, anyway?" Bill asked.

"Isn't that an element on the periodic table?" Nick asked.

"Of course, the periodic table. Everyone goes *there* to find their kids' names," Bill said.

"It's probably just a stage name," Val said.

"Yeah, who'd name their kid Wolfram?" Mike said.

"Look who's talkin'," Bruce said, socking his adoptive brother on the shoulder. "What was your great-grandfather's handle . . . Red-Horse-Who-Runs-Away-Over-The-Darkening-Prairie-Hills, or something like that?"

"Yeah, you white guys are just jealous," Mike said.

The door opened on the left side of the stage--a door not to a dressing room, as one might have expected, but to an alley behind the bar. Four musicians stepped through. The wiry drummer, with the thin, straight, shoulder-length blond hair, peeled off his windbreaker, settled onto his seat, thumped the bass drum twice with his foot pedal, picked up his sticks, twirled them like tiny batons, did a roll on the snare drum, ending with quick hi-hat taps. He wore a sleeveless royal blue T-shirt, faded jeans, and red low-top tennis shoes. The short, chunky organ player, with long, thick, curly brown hair bulging out from his head, switched on his Yamaha, randomly fingered several chords, then raced through some riffs.

The bass player was a tall black guy, built as solidly as a wall of concrete blocks, dressed in black denim pants, an American flag shirt, black high-tops, and a scarlet cloth headband that cinched in a burgeoning Afro. He picked up his bass from its stand as if it were no heavier than an umbrella, spun it along its vertical axis, and slipped the strap over his head so the bass' neck faced his right. A surprise: he was left-handed. He skimmed with such nonchalant grace through several scales that it seemed as if playing the bass were under the control of his autonomic nervous system, like breathing.

Wolfram Kohles unzipped and slipped off his Army fatigue jacket, and moved with quiet speed to his Stratocaster. He picked it up and slung the strap over his head in one motion. The wide brown leather strap was incised with a three-inch-square design that was repeated down its whole length--a set of scimitar-curved lines that, after a moment's study, were recognized as the conflation of his initials, the right bar of the W making the spine of the K. Kohles had straight chestnut-brown hair that hung down past his shoulder bones. He was six feet tall--six inches shorter than his bassist–and had the build of an erstwhile gymnast. He wore Army camouflage pants, black combat boots, a sleeveless olive T-shirt, tight enough that one could see the outline of the dog tags that hung from the beadchain around his neck. Kohles played several licks, made micro-adjustments to his amp knobs, checked his wah-wah pedal, checked the band's simple light array that he controlled with a foot switch, and clicked on his microphone. He scanned the crowd, his handsome, beardless face earnest as a shotgun with the safety off.

Kohles lifted his right hand straight out to a level with his shoulder and all the lights in the house went off. Gasps from all sides; random giggles; stillness. But for scattered cigarettes, the room was black as a cave. A soft drum roll rising slowly to a crescendo, ending with a cymbal crash, allowed to linger in the air a moment, then stilled. Bass, drums, and organ began a soft, somber lament in G, twelve bars repeated in endless refrain.

Kohles spoke clearly, his baritone voice rich-timbered and resonant:

"And I saw askant the armies,
I saw as in noiseless dreams hundreds of battle-flags,
Borne through the smoke of the battles and pierc'd with missiles, I saw them, [his voice rising, carrying in its tone pain, chaos, madness, and hopeless anger]
And carried hither and yon through the smoke, and torn and bloody,
And at last but a few shreds left on the staffs, (and all in silence),
And the staffs all splintered and broken. [this last line practically spit out with disgust]
I saw battle-corpses, myriads of them,
And the white skeletons of young men, I saw them,
I saw the debris and debris of all the slain soldiers of the war, [fury and the helplessness of loss]
But I saw they were not as was thought,
They themselves were fully at rest, they suffered not,
The living remain'd and suffer'd, the mother suffer'd,
And the wife and the child and the musing comrade suffer'd,
And the armies that remain'd suffer'd. [these last lines softly, with heartbroken resignation]".

A long minute of silence followed. The stage lights snapped back on, then just enough of the room lights to enable people not to stumble on their trips to bar and bathrooms. Applause, whistles, a "right on" or two.

"Walt Whitman wrote that after his service as a nurse in the Civil War," Kohles said. "My war was fought in another country, and it's still being fought there. And day after day the death toll rises, on both sides. I want you to know I have also seen battle corpses. I have also seen the myriads of the dead--and of those still living, but dying. Young bodies laid open by bullets, by land mines, by shrapnel, bodies jerking, impaled on pain's steel spikes, lifeblood saturating their uniforms, running freely out onto the tall coarse grass flattened beneath them, spilling out onto the brown, ever-absorbing soil of the planet, until it can be staunched. I have heard their screams and their breathless, choking voices begging for help, for anything to stop the pain. I have watched helplessly as they slipped into shock, and I have held them until their ragged, gurgling breathing stopped and their bodies sank loose against my own and their souls vanished from their eyes. And when they were lifted away, their life's blood remained on my uniform and on my hands. On these very hands." He held up both hands, palms forward, at chest level. "And I have seen them zipped into plastic body bags and carried off in smooth, steady flight above the broken mirrors of the rice fields--in choppers, whose bubbles signaled in the sun like heliographs. And I have seen their flag-draped metal coffins loaded onto the big cargo planes--line upon line of them . . . And somehow--I couldn't tell you how--I survived, with my own body intact. Whether it was by chance or providence, I couldn't tell you. I survived to come and stand before you and tell you what I've seen. And I'll tell you one final thing. Whitman was right. It is the living who remain who suffer. It is the families, the comrades, the buddies, and yes, it is the armies that remain that suffer."

Kohles paused an instant, during which no one dared breathe. "But I don't suppose you people came here for a funeral. How about if we do a little rockin' and rollin' for you?" Kohles and the bassist pitched gleefully into the opening bars of "Sunshine of Your Love." The crowd broke into applause. Kohles played with effortless speed and precision, all the while singing with conviction of his confident anticipation of lovemaking. There was no one in the room who did not feel his love hunger.

Judith had felt her blood start when the lights went off and Kohles' voice broke forth, sudden as an artillery shell. From that moment she was alone in the dark room with Kohles and his band. On the song's break, Kohles held the Stratocaster out from him and played with eyes closed. Judith saw notes spray off the guitar and spin into the air about her head, hundreds of asteroids, dozens of comets, trapped by the force field of a star far greater than they were. She watched them whiz by, dazzled by their flaring colors, flashing fire. At song's clanging guitar ending, she refused to relinquish the music, but held it still orbiting in her mind as applause, whistles, and cheers erupted from all sides.

"Thank you . . . thank you," Kohles said, nodding his gratitude to the audience. "Glad you liked that. Here's another Cream song you'll recognize. Truth is, they only covered it. It was written by Robert Johnson, the greatest of all the Delta bluesmen." Guitar, bass, and organ flung themselves full tilt into "Crossroads," like thoroughbreds leaping from a standing rest into a gallop.

Kohles' guitar breaks this time were like stars exploding into super nova, bursting out around Judith in engulfing, vaporizing fire. But she emerged unscathed, save for a moment or two of stertorous breathing. On the second break, the organ, which had been playing behind Kohles, suddenly soared out with its own scorching lead. How could it not melt the cable to the amp, short out the wires, melt the very keys off the board? Kohles played behind and around him for a time and then they began to trade leads, alternately burning all the air out of the room, until a space opened between them and the bassist came sawing through, with a riff consisting of scores of rabbit punches and a dozen bludgeoning blows. Then caresses soft as satin, rich as honey, all up and down the fretless neck of the bass. Then a screaming dive from lacerating heights to sonorous, punishing, plangent depths, and the drummer came sputtering forward with slashing sprays on the snare, tom-toms, and the two big floor toms, bass drumbeats bouncing all the while off the four walls. Cymbals screamed as if in pain, tom-tom beats chopped sound into a thousand staccato bits, the bass heartbeat fused them, and the tom-toms chopped them into bits again. Then all four musicians came together, like separate molten streams meeting in one great, red-orange-glowing blues-rock river for the song's last chorus. This time when the song ended the crowd broke into a shockwave of applause, punctuated by whoops, whistles, and hollers. Everyone at Judith's table was making a commotion, but she clapped weakly. Her arms felt powerless, as if she'd been awakened suddenly from deep sleep.

"You liked that, huh?" Kohles looked wonderingly at the smiling faces. "We'll do another Robert Johnson for you later on. But for now, let me introduce the band. On drums, please acknowledge that most capable of stickmen, Mr. Ken Carrothers." Kohles turned, right hand pointing, halfway toward Carrothers, whose bow consisted of raising himself a few inches off his seat and tilting slightly forward. Applause and cheers.

"On organ, the onetime child prodigy, who cut his teeth on Chopin and Rachmaninoff, give a big hand to Mr. Larry Hutson." Hutson did a half-bow, his hand making an elegant flourish in front of him. Another burst in the continuous clapping and cheering.

"And finally, our bassist extraordinaire, and my oldest and closest friend in this world, the man who's been with me from kindergarten through the rain forests of the Mekong Delta, a big hand if you please for this giant of a man, Mr. Howard Reynolds." An eardrum-shattering whistle and tremendous applause.

"And now we're going to change the mood a little. Here's something you've been hearing on the radio."

Foot-pedal cymbals, one-two, one-two, cowbell beats, maracas, then the guitar melody line to "Down on the Corner." Whoops of pleasure from all over the room. Kohles began to sing, with plenty of John Fogergty grit in his voice. Nick, who had become increasingly animated during the first two songs, turned to Bill and said, "I love this song!" People streamed onto the dance floor, limbs pulled into fluid motion by the music's irresistible propulsion.

And Judith was right there with Willie and the Poorboys, from beginning to end. The band didn't pause at all but bridged right into the slower pace of "Green River"--a sound that for Judith immediately opened the barroom out into the humid, mosquito-thick, hanging moss bayous of the lower Mississippi Delta; she could smell the riverbank, reeking of mud and decomposition--then into "Bad Moon Rising," that paean to apocalypse, imbued with superstition and dread (all to a backbeat rhythm), and finally into the barking guitar lead-in to "Proud Mary," which hymn to riverboat life Kohles and Body Count turned into a burn-the-house-down conclusion to the extended medley.

The crowd burst into tumultuous displays of gratitude. Sweaty dancers returned to their chairs. The temperature in the room had climbed at least five degrees.

"A quartet of Creedence songs for you. All you dancers keep it up. I like that. And as long as we're down in the Delta, here's a little something you may not know, but you should--a classic by Mr. Chester Burnett, A.K.A. Howlin' Wolf: 'My Country Sugar Mama.'"

The words had no sooner crossed Kohles' lips than Hutson did a trippingly light and airy version of the piano lead-in. Kohles shoveled a wheelbarrow full of gravel into his vocals. He couldn't match the rich, full rasp of the Wolf, but he could give the song's lusty double entendres enough passion to raise the room temperature another five degrees without anyone moving. When Kohles sang "I like my coffee in the morning, Crazy about my tea at night. If I don't get my sugar three times a day, ohhh, Darling, I don't feel right," Bruce whispered to Mike, "I'd be satisfied to get some sugar even once a day."

Mike chuckled. "Shit, you'd be lucky to get it once a year and you know it."

For the break, Kohles whipped a harmonica out of his pocket and wailed like an archangel enduring a crisis of hormonal frustration, plaintive notes, fairly dripping with lasciviousness. Judith was unaware that fine sweat beads had broken out on her brow.

Again, cheering, table-pounding outpourings of appreciation.

Kohles turned for a second and flashed a smile at Howard Reynolds, who smiled and nodded back at him from the heights. Kohles turned to his fans.

"All right! Nothing like a sexy song to heat up a room. Well, don't let your glasses steam over on these next two. Willie Dixon wrote 'em for the incomparable Muddy Waters."

Kohles raised his harmonica to his lips and all four musicians sailed languorously into "I Just Want To Make Love To You." After the first verse, guys broke into spontaneous cheers all over the room. When Kohles sang the second verse, "I don't want you to wash my clothes, I don't want you to keep our home, I don't want your money, too, I just want to make love to you, you, Love to you, love to you, love to you," every woman in the audience, Judith included, felt his voice go, a burning poker, straight into their blood. Couples on the dance floor held each other closer, pressed slowly into each other's bodies. Playing on the cinema of their closed eyes: falling peignoirs, dropping pants, the backwards slide onto the satin-sheeted bed, the smooth wet glide into oneness.

On the harmonica breaks between verses, Judith felt Kohles' melancholy, yearning notes as fingers touching, as a mouth kissing and kissing--and each kiss a hot compress to her flesh, a lingering, painless brand.

The musicians bridged straight into "Hoochie Coochie Man," and an element of urban Chicago comedy cooled the air just enough to forestall a saturnalia. Kohles slipped his harp into his pocket, returned to his guitar, and sang with good-humored fervor, "The gypsy told my mother before I was born, I got a boychild's comin', he's gonna be a son-of-a-gun. He's gonna make pretty womens jump and shout. Then the world wanta know what this all about," and the crowd relaxed and awaited his every phrase. After the penultimate verse, Kohles and his band did a long break, each one soloing in searing fashion. When they came together again and arrived, with the inexorable force of an avalanche, once more at the melody line, cheers and clapping sprang forth spontaneously from all sides.

At the end, as the waves of the ovation took him off his feet and washed him out to sea, only to roll him back billowingly to shore again, Kohles said, gesturing toward each musician in turn, "Mr. Ken Carrothers, Mr. Larry Hutson, and Mr. Howard Reynolds!" Each nodded, smiling, as his name was called. "And me, that boychild the gypsy woman told of, the seventh son, the hoochie coochie man himself! We're going to take a short break now. Just long enough for you to recharge those pitchers and test the plumbing."

The house lights came on and Kohles and his band exited through the same the door they had entered by, Carrothers propping it open with a brick as he left. The chilly October air flowed, a benison, into the smoky room.

Chapter 2
Blues Bacchanalia

"Well, you were right, Judith," Bruce said after she returned from the women's room, "This isn't your typical local band."

"I'm always right , Bruce," Judith said.

"I can't believe how fast Kohles was," Val said, "It was like listening to Clapton.'"

"And how about those classic blues covers?" Nick said.

"Yeah, talk about your earthy lyrics," Mike said, "those old blues guys knew how to get down and dirty."

"Evidently it impressed the chicks here tonight," Bruce said.

"Give me a break," Judith said. "You guys were salivating like dogs sniffing after a bitch in heat."

"I was referring, Judith, to those women who grabbed their jackets and purses and scooted out that stage door," Bruce pointed at the door, "after the band."

"When did that happen?" Judith asked.

"Right after you two left for the john."

"That is where you guys went, isn't it, Judith?" Bruce needled her.

"Up yours, Bruce."

"Whoa," Mike said. "Better watch out, brother, you're on her bad side tonight."

"Some days," Nick said, smiling, "there isn't any other side."

Judith coolly sipped her soda, not dignifying this with a response.

* * * * * * *

Kohles opened his second set with Hendrix's "If 6 Was 9"--his interpretation had the almost airborne abandon, the unstoppable force, of a runaway semi--and he ended it with a demonically inspired, fifteen-minute version of Hendrix's "Voodoo Chile," both of which songs gave him and the band a chance for even more virtuoso displays than in the first set. In between, Kohles played half a dozen of his own compositions--hell-bent rock and mournful blues songs that covered everything from his war experiences (one haunting song, "Land Mine

Blues," was about watching a buddy die after losing the better part of both legs to a mine) to that perpetual rock theme, life on the road, to his hard luck in love. It seemed that the man whose singing put others into such a lather had a tough time inspiring long-lasting love in his women--at least if his songs were to be believed.

Throughout Kohles played with perfect ease--as if the Stratocaster were a part of his own body, another of his limbs--and a reckless, risk-everything-and-tomorrow-be-damned attitude. He stood on tiptoes, scrinched his eyes closed, brought the guitar neck up close to his head, and vibratoed the blue notes, squeezing and wringing out tormented shrieks and keening sobs. He played his Stratocaster straight out from his pelvis--pumping his fretting hand up and down the neck-- in front of his face (even playing with his teeth, like Jimi), and behind his back; he gyrated it around his body, wrenching feedback (like the groans of those suffering the Inquisition's rack) from his amp.

Judith had never heard anyone play a guitar like that. Half of those sounds she had never imagined existed. And his showmanship. The man seemed as much at home playing a demonically complicated guitar solo in front of this crowd as an ordinary person would be sitting in a recliner and reading the newspaper. She had never seen anyone so perfectly self-possessed. By the time the band was ready for its second break, she'd decided what she was going to do.

* * * * * * *

Not to seem overly obvious, Judith went upstairs and exited the front door of the bar and then walked around the block and up the alley to where she saw people gathered around a VW Microbus, with a long covered trailer behind. She heard laughter, a mingling of voices. Judith tried to look as if she just happened to be out for a stroll and had randomly chosen to walk down that alley.

As soon as she got close enough to be seen clearly from the bus, Wolfram--who was in the front passenger seat, smoking a cigarette and talking through his open window to the young women gathered at his door--called to her over their heads.

"Hey, hey, pretty miss, if you're looking for me, I'm right here."

Judith stopped, she had to take the challenge. "Why do you think I'd be looking for you?" she asked, an arch smile on her face.

"Hey now, no call to be unfriendly. Come on over and say hello to Wolfram. That's better. Ladies, clear a space, please, let the woman through. Say, you're a tall one, aren't you. Man, I like those boots, and that jacket, too."

Howard Reynolds was sitting in the driver's seat of the bus. He lifted a beer bottle, took a long swig. Through the open side door, Ken Carrothers and Larry Hutson could be seen. The glowing ends of cigarettes arced toward their faces. A couple of guys stood on the other side of the bus, talking to Reynolds. More than a dozen women stood on this side.

"I know you," Wolfram said, playfully. "You were sittin' at the table down in front."

The other women, seeing that Wolfram' focus had shifted entirely, edged away. Judith suddenly saw a gray/white mist steam up and encircle the two of them, obnubilating them, till they stood alone, like Zeus and a paramour, in some Hellenic mountain bower. All sounds disappeared but the sounds of their voices.

"Yeah, I was."

"And there was this guy sitting there, too, who looked just like you."

"My twin brother."

"You know, I had an idea you might say that." He chuckled. "Say, you can clear something I've always wondered about. Is it true that twins sometimes dream the same dreams?"

"Identical twins do. Fraternal twins don't."

"And that's what you and your brother are, right, fraternal twins?"

"That's right. But Nick and I used to have the same dreams a lot."

"Not any more?"

"Oh, once in a long while. It's happened less and less as we've gotten older."

"So you've grown further apart as you've gotten older?"

"Something like that."

"How's that sit with you?"

"The truth?"

"Ain't got time for nothin' else?"

Were those grapevines that raced, tendriling up the sides and along the VW's roof? Was it the radio aerial that spiked up into that sixty-foot pine? What were those birds singing in its branches?

"OK, I hate it."

"That bad, huh?"

"When we were kids, up till about the age of six or seven, it was almost as if we were one person."

"Kinda like one soul in two bodies."

"That's right. But after we started school, we got different friends, and we began to move apart--very slowly, very subtly, but apart."

"How did that feel?"

"It was painful--extremely painful--especially once we became teenagers. We didn't want it to happen, but I really don't think there was any way we could've prevented it."

"It was meant to be?"

"Yeah, I think so. But that doesn't make it any easier."

"You mean now?"

"It still hurts. He's my brother and I see him every day, but somehow it's like I've lost someone very precious to me."

"You don't think maybe it's necessary? So you can each become your own persons, that sort of thing?"

"It might be easier for me to accept that if I thought being an individual was such a great thing to be."

"Whoa, you don't believe in individualism?" Wolfram's smile and the merry look in his eyes showed that he was half-joking. "Without that, how'd anybody ever discover who they really are."

"But what if 'who we really are' is really part of a far greater whole, part of an intricate network of others? Say, all the people in your town or city--maybe all the people in your country, or even beyond?"

"Sounds like a stretch."

"I know it sounds stupid, but I don't think it is. And if it is true, then what would it mean to sever ourselves from all those thousands and millions of threads that connect us all--like the strands of a great invisible spider web?"

"The Oversoul, huh?"

"I suppose."

Wolfram turned toward Reynolds. "So, Howard, what do you say about all this?"

Vines whistled away, birds flew off, tree shrank--pop!--into aerial, mist vanished, as if sucked away by some vast, invisible vacuum cleaner.

Howard laughed. "I think we'd better be for headin' back soon is what I think."

Wolfram turned back to the window. "He's right, break time's over. You can't let the crowd cool down too much. Otherwise, you have to build them up all over again. And it's a chore to do that three times in one night."

"You make it look easy."

"Thanks, uh," Wolfram slapped his forehead, "now don't I feel stupid. I didn't even ask you your name."

"Judith."

Wolfram opened the door and stepped out. "Wolfram," he said, extending his hand. They smiled at each other as they shook. He didn't immediately let her hand go. Reynolds, Hutson, and Carrothers climbed out of the bus and began walking toward the stage door. Wolfram and Judith followed, more slowly, still holding Judith's hand.

"So, Judith, what's your favorite band?"

"My brother's the one who's into rock. I'm more into . . ."

"Wait, let me guess--folk music. Am I right? Hah, I knew it!"

"How'd you know?"

Kohles laughed. "Just a wild hunch. And I'll bet you're *really* into folk--you know, everything from Woodie Guthrie and Josh White and The Weavers to Joan Baez and Ramblin' Jack Elliott and Odetta. No, don't stop me, I'm on a roll: Bob Dylan, Judy Collins, Joanie Mitchell, Tom Paxton, Ian and Sylvia, Leonard Cohen, Richard and Mimi Fariña, Arlo Guthrie. Who've I left out?"

"Carolyn Hester, Harry Belafonte, Miriam Makeba."

"That's right, and I'll bet you even like the Righteous Brothers--though a purist would never admit it."

"OK, but I also like the Beatles. That should count for something."

"Don't get me wrong, I like folk, too. I mean, the first thing I learned on the guitar after basic chords was the Etta Baker fingerpicking method. And I love Doc Watson. I mean I really love Doc Watson."

They'd reached the door. Wolfram paused.

"This set's our last for the night. You want to hang around afterwards? We could talk some more."

"Yeah, I'd like that."

"OK, till then, baby."

Wolfram leaned forward and kissed her, and then walked through the open door to his waiting band.

* * * * * * *

"Where'd you go?" Val asked. "I looked everywhere for you."

"Oh, just out to get some fresh air."

"Yeah, I'll bet she went out back to meet Wolfram Kohles," Bruce said.

"And what if she did?" Nick asked. He knew--without wondering how he knew--that that was exactly what Judith had done. "It's a free country, ain't it?"

Judith looked at Nick, surprised.

"Thanks, Nick."

"Don't mention it. Here," he said, sliding another glass of 7 Up towards her. "I thought you might like one of these."

"Thanks again."

At that moment, Wolfram, who had been re-tuning the D and high E strings and checking the amplification on his Gibson, clicked on his mic and said, "I told you we'd do another Robert Johnson song for you. This one's called 'Terraplane Blues.' If you haven't heard of a Terraplane before, it was a Hudson sedan made back in the thirties."

Wolfram duplicated the original Johnson lead-in and was joined by the rest of the band when he began to sing about how "lonesome" he felt to come home and find someone else had been driving his Terraplane for his woman in his absence. The song was sort of a Goldilocks and the Three Bears story, only about a car. When Wolfram hit the second verse, hamming up his sense of astonished discovery, the crowd laughed in appreciation of the running double entendre: "I'd said

I flash your lights, mama , your horn won't even blow/ [spoken]: Somebody's been runnin' my batteries down on this machine."

Wolfram kept to Johnson's percussive, almost flamenco-like blues accompaniment to the song's verses, but he and the band did four and five minute breaks between the verses, with Wolfram cutting loose, cranking his Gibson till it whined and yowled, whimpered, grieved, complained, and groaned. Everyone felt their blood run cold with mourning, felt ashes on their tongues, felt hearts stagger under fardels of pain and woeful, weepy lamentation. Wolfram's guitar ululated and screamed, squalled and howled with dolor, with the pain of betrayed love. Everyone who'd ever had their affections bruised and abused, who'd had a love smashed under a stupefying weight of lies and deceit, felt their chests ache, ache, ache, with a hurt worse than falling into a brazier of white-hot coals. Eyes teared up as Wolfram performed his suffering dirge for lost love, his jazz funeral for faithless love. When the whole room was on the verge of blubbering and bawling, Wolfram slipped oh-so-slickly back into the light, almost comic, staccato strumming and chording of the next verse.

When Wolfram sang the last lines--"I'm 'on' get deep down in this connection, hoo-well, keep on tanglin' with these wires, And when I mash down on your little starter, then your spark plug will give me fire--" and brought the song to closure, with a riff as graceful as a fleur-de-lis, the audience let forth with a typhoon of cheers and meaty, hand-slapping applause.

Wolfram looked down at Judith, saw her clapping and smiling, her lips slightly apart. He grinned, held her eyes a significant moment, looked away.

"I knew it," Bruce whispered to Nick. "What'd I tell you?"

Nick simply raised an index finger to his lips and softly, sibilantly shushed him.

Surprised murmurs raced like alternating current through the crowd. Ken Carrothers put down his sticks, Howard Reynolds replaced his bass on its stand, and he and Larry Hutson sat down on a couple of folding chairs on the left side of the stage. Wolfram pulled a stool up by his mic, clicked the lights to spot the stool, and climbed onto it with his Gibson.

"A few more acoustic numbers for you all. While we were out back in our bus during the last break, I met this beautiful girl who said she liked the Beatles and folk music. So I'd like to dedicate these next three songs to her."

Wolfram smiled down at Judith.

Nick gave his sister a raised eyebrow look. Val gave her a dig in the ribs and whispered, "Why didn't you invite me along, too?"

"This first song is one I'm sure you all know."

Wolfram did a straight-forward rendering of "Yesterday," restraining his guitar-work to the simple but elegantly melancholy backing that Paul McCartney had invented for the song. Wolfram sang the first verse alone, but during the refrain a few people began to sing along. More voices, ranging from bass to soprano, some wavering and reedy, some pure and full, joined in on the second verse. By the time Wolfram reached the last refrain and the song came to an end on a note of sad fatalism, the whole room was singing. Kohles repeated the melody line of the refrain one last time on his guitar and cheers and raucous applause broke out everywhere.

"You may recognize this next song, too. Dylan's 'Boots of Spanish Leather.'"

This ballad of fickle love was a surprising choice for Wolfram, but he sang, often with eyes closed, all nine slow verses, with a touching poignance of feeling. The two lovers' voices alternated, the woman offering, as she set sail, to send her lover a gift from the other side of the ocean (since she had no plans to return soon), the man saying he wanted no gifts, that he'd give up any riches just to have her. When the man finally received a fare-thee-well letter, he resigned himself to losing his love and wrote her back, asking her to give him the eponymous boots. It was a sad song about love's mutability, a not infrequent Dylan theme. The audience sat quietly, reflecting on the love's pathos. So taken up were they in thoughts of the wounding they had all suffered at the hands of hard-hearted lovers that they didn't even raise their glasses to drink. The last tristful guitar notes held in the air, echoed, and died totally away before the crowd could compose itself enough to applaud.

"There's nothing that hurts as much as unrequited love, is there? Sorry, didn't mean to make you weep in your beers. We can't have that.

Drink up. That's right, tip 'em, or they might just run me outa this joint. We've got to lighten things up a little before I bring the band back out here. So let's try this."

Wolfram dashed like a runaway horse into Doc Watson's adaptation of "Black Mountain Rag." Ninety seconds of utter fingerpicking jubilation and faster-than-fast virtuosity. Smiles sprang to lips, toes tapped, heads rocked in time. After the song's final waterfall spray of notes, the room broke into whistles, whoops, and table-pounding, floor-stomping applause.

"Thanks. Glad you all enjoyed that." Wolfram winked at Judith as he dismounted the stool. "Now let's bring back my buddies, my comrades in musical arms. Would you welcome again please, Ken Carrothers, Larry Hutson, and Mr. Howard Reynolds!"

Carrothers took up his sticks and Hutson and Reynolds stood up and took their places. Wolfram set his Gibson back on its stand and took up his Stratocaster.

"All right, are you ready to rock and roll?"

The audience shouted back "Yes!"

"I say, are you READY to ROCK AND ROLL?"

The audience screamed back "YES!"

"All right, then, we're gonna *do* it. And I want you folks up *dancin'*. I want to see that dance floor packed."

Wolfram jerked the neck of his guitar up and he and the band threw themselves into Led Zeppelin's recently released "Whole Lotta Love," as if they were flinging themselves headlong off a cliff. Howard and Wolfram faced each other and played the same pulsing, deep-bassed, pumping rhythm that propelled the boasting, swaggeringly phallic song like a turbine engine.

People flowed out onto the dance floor like water from a breaking dam, let music lift and impel hips, arms, and legs. At the end of the first break, after the individual solos they substituted for the original's feedback and vocal lust shrieks (held together by foot-pedal cymbal beats and bongoes), Wolfram flamed up like a Roman candle and exploded into Jimmy Page's bravura solo, which, ending, left the band once again at the portal of the thrusting main rhythm. Wolfram acknowledged the terrific applause at song's end, said, "OK, we're gonna keep it goin'." With that, he and Hutson started a sure-footed blues intro in E. Then the whole band skipped through the verses of a comic song by Wolfram about being down and out and trying to sell an old car. It was called "Old Buick Blues." The band took only brief breaks after the second and fourth verses, chastening their chops so as not to overwhelm the tune's light intentions. Wolfram was gratified to see everyone smiling throughout the song, and the band was pleased by the applause at the end.

Wolfram and Body Count slammed next through an anti-war song. Then Wolfram announced that the next song, "a little number we call 'Tomcat Blues,'" would be their last. He said he wanted everybody on their feet dancing.

"In the darkest part, in the darkest part of the night
I say, in the darkest part, in the darkest, darkest night.
Young Tom sets out, all bloody for a fight.

Tom goes down the alley, 'cross the railroad track.
Oh yeah, down the alley, 'cross the railroad track.
He's so mean and foolish, he don't look back."

The song told how Tom got distracted all of a sudden by a pretty pussycat he saw, how he prowled after her, how he got growled at by a dog, how he yowled from the back of his throat to get her attention. Wolfram sang of how the pretty pussy pranced and mewed and danced so slinkily, so hot-hot-hot, before him, and then how she led him on a long, hot chase (yeah, he got so-o-o hot); how he finally got her cornered someplace, and she was still coyly meowing, oh yeah, still meowing so sexily, and he was so-o-o hot, pacin' about on five legs--only to be disgraced when her hulking main squeeze stepped out of the shadows and ground him into catfood. He told how that other cat couldn'ta been any ordinary cat, but musta been a bobcat or a catamount or some crazy jaguar or leopard, or somethin', maybe some devil cat. He never knew because when he woke up again, all scratched and bit and black and blue, they were gone, plumb gone, and the only trace of their having been there was his own fur lyin' on the ground, was his own blood sprinkled on the ground. Oh my, young Tom learned a mighty big lesson that night, yes he did: if the pretty pussy don't come straight to you, then let her be, I say, let her be.

The song had a punchy rhythm and Wolfram's guitar lead was raunchy and driven. Everybody on the dance floor broke into a lather, writhing--arms and legs a jungle of lithe, snaking vines--pressing and moaning against each other. By verse three the temperature had risen ten degrees in the room, by verse five, twenty. After verse seven, the mercury shattered the thermometer behind the bar. The two bartenders swiftly filled pitchers of beer and people passed them hurriedly, sloshingly along a bucket brigade, until the last person flung the golden, foam-topped beer onto the sweat-drenched dancers. Instantly, steam burst into the air in hot clouds, like water spilled onto the white-glowing rocks of a sauna. The whole room heated up like a giant pressure cooker, and dancers began to slither, all slick and slippery, out of their soaked clothes. Shirts and sweaters slid to the floor, followed by shoes, socks, pants, skirts, underthings. Seeing that he stood on the brink of a bubbling, spark-and-ash-and-red-liquid-rock-spewing volcano, Wolfram slammed through the tenth and final verse.

The lights came on and one of the bartenders ran up and propped open the door, while the other took a fire extinguisher out from beneath the bar and began to spray down the naked dancers, who hadn't even noticed that the music had stopped. Nick led Bruce, Mike, Bill, and Val up the stairs in a near run. Fortunately, they had all kept their seats. Wolfram and his band quickly shut down and packed up what they had to take with them (they would be playing there again the next night) in the confusion and melee. Wolfram handed the case containing his Gibson to Ken Carrothers, took the case holding his Stratocaster in one hand and Judith by the other, and fled out the back door, to the safety of the Microbus.

Chapter 3
Body Count

After Wolfram had dropped off everyone else, he pulled the Microbus to the curb beside a big house.

"How does a late night bowl of chili sound, Judith? I never eat before a concert, so I'm well past starving and headed toward ravenous."

They got out and Judith realized where she was.

"You mean you live here?" she asked pointing at the big white frame house with the wrap-around balcony on the second floor, the one that looked like an old steamboat.

"Yeah. Why?"

"I love this house. I mean I go out of my way just to walk by it."

"Really?" Wolfram looked at the house as if to see what its attraction was.

"Yes! Which room is yours?"

"I rent the second floor."

"The whole floor?"

"You got it."

"So that balcony is yours?"

"Sure 'nough."

Judith began to run ahead, pulling Wolfram along. "Come on, show me. I want to see this place."

"OK, easy on the fingers, I'm coming."

Wolfram turned the key and led the way into the apartment, switching on the entryway light as he entered. "I hope this lives up to your expectations," he said. He switched on the living room and kitchen lights. The living room had ten-foot ceilings and its creamy white paint was faded. It was furnished with Goodwill furniture--a couch, two easy chairs, a loveseat--of some indeterminate gray-green color, a scarred maple coffee table, and a couple of end tables, supporting lamps that looked as if they might have been just the thing in the forties. The once beige rug showed the impress of the years, of the hundreds of thousands of footsteps it had suffered. The things that Wolfram had contributed to the decor, besides a small TV set with rabbit-ears, were rainbow-starburst tie-dyed curtains, an upright piano with several sheets of a composition in the making, a twelve-string Martin and a Gibson classical guitar (both on stands), a Fender bass guitar and amp, soprano and alto recorders, a Ugandan thumb piano, a dulcimer, a mouth harp, assorted harmonicas, a conga, castanets, a drum kit, a triangle, a silver trumpet and a golden trombone (on stands), a Lakota courting flute (carved from cedar into a mallard duck's head), assorted clutter (bank statements, bills, books--including *Leaves of Grass, Ulysses,* and *The Magic Mountain*--pens, paper, and a pile of Zap comics), and a top-of-the-line JVC turntable and amplifier, tall Pioneer speakers, and black metal racks of record albums.

"I can't believe it, you must have over a thousand records here."

"Oh yeah, easy."

"How do you ever find the one you want in all of this?" She gestured at the racks of albums.

"I've got a simple system, but it works."

Wolfram stepped up to the racks beside Judith.

"So what's the system?"

"Alphabetical--by type and then by artist."

"So these at the beginning here are blues."

"That's right."

"There must be hundreds of them . . . Blind Blake, Big Bill Broonzy, Paul Butterfield," she read, skipping randomly down, "Buddy Guy, John Lee Hooker, Lightnin' Hopkins, Son House, Elmore James--oh! here's Robert Johnson, who wrote that song about the Terraplane--Blind Lemon Jefferson, Albert King, B. B. King, Freddie King, Leadbelly, Little Milton, Little Walter, John Mayall." She skipped a whole rack. "Jimmy Reed, Bessie Smith . . ."

"Ah, Bessie's the best. They don't come any better. "

"Big Mama Thornton, T-Bone Walker, Muddy Waters, Sonny Boy Williamson, Howlin' Wolf . . . And now, look, Bach, Beethoven, Berlioz, Brahms . . ."

"Yeah, the classical stuff starts there."

Judith turned, looked at Wolfram inquisitively. "Somehow I never would have figured you for classical."

"Why not?"

"It just seems out of character somehow."

"Music's music. Classical is just what's held up the longest."

Judith stood a moment scanning the racks of opera and jazz and r & b and rock, and even Broadway musicals.

So, what do you want to listen to?" Wolfram asked.

"You're kidding. In the face of all this! No, you're going to have to pick something."

"OK, but you have to sit down and close your eyes."

She sat on the couch and Wolfram took the dust cover from the turntable, reached up, and lifted out an album. He slipped the sleeve, open end to the top, from the jacket, and the record from the sleeve. He placed the album on the turntable, wiped its shiny onyx surface with a cleaning brush, switched the power on, and adjusted the graphic equalizer controls.

"All right, here it comes. See what you think of this."

He switched the turntable control to ON. The needle arm rose and began its short horizontal swing.

Sonorous majesty on the trombone and lower strings, then violins, slow and quiet, then, a single violin clear and high, like a thin, pure flame. Judith opened her eyes.

After a minute Judith said, "Tell me, what is it?"

"'Scheherazade', by Rimsky-Korsakov."

"You mean, Scheherazade as in The Arabian Nights?"

"That's it. This movement is called 'The Sea and Sinbad's Ship'." Here, you can look at the liner notes if you want while I heat up the chili."

She heard the refrigerator open and close, heard Wolfram set something on the stove.

"It says here that the critics disliked it when it was first performed."

"Yeah, that happens a lot in the music biz. It happened to Berlioz's 'Symphonie Fantastique' and Stravinsky's 'Rite of Spring', too."

"It says Stravinsky was Rimsky-Korsakov's student."

"That's right."

The second movement was just beginning when Wolfram told her the chili was ready.

"Ah, cloth napkins and everything. And cornbread. I think I can get used to a man who cooks."

"Burgundy or rosé?"

"Sorry, I don't drink."

"Really? Now that's something you don't hear everyday."

"Well, it's true." She smiled.

"Is this a religious thing or something."

Judith chuckled. "Or something. It goes back to the summer when my brother and I were eight years old and we got really sick by going around at a party and drinking all these adult's beers. Our folks had finished harvesting their wheat crop that day and they were celebrating with the combine crew."

"So you grew up on a farm, then?"

"No, I can't really say I grew up on a farm."

"Why not?"

"We moved off the farm the next year and haven't gone back except for summers since. My parents lease out the land now. They get a percentage of the yearly crop."

"So you got really sick that once and haven't drunk anything since?"

"Yes, no . . . it's hard to explain."

Wolfram set a glass of ice water in front of her and sat down.

"It's all right. I've done my gig for the day, I have nothing but time."

"This chili's good. Hot, but good."

"Yeah, I like it on the spicy side. So, how about the rest of the story?"

"Really, I couldn't explain it, not so somebody else could understand it."

Wolfram leaned forward, planting elbows on the table, placing his chin on his hands. She saw herself diving into his eyes, the blue of tropical water.

"Judith, you're going to have to trust me."

"OK, remember how I said my brother and I used to have the same dreams?"

"Yeah."

"Well, we also knew what each other was thinking."

"That happens to lots of people."

"I don't mean when we were in the same room. We could be miles apart, even in separate states, and we would know exactly what the other was thinking. And not just words--images, too. Nick said once it was like the same movie playing in both our heads."

"OK, so that's a little unusual. What's it have to do with your not drinking?"

"I'm getting to that. That night, after supper, when everybody was sitting outside in lawn chairs, Nick and I went around begging drinks from people's beers. And whenever one of us took a drink from somebody's beer we both saw some scene from that person's life. We saw horrific things. Bill Burdette was the head combiner and we saw his baby son--it was awful."

Judith regained her composure. "Anyway, it was those terrible things we saw--no, it was more like we lived through them--it was all those brutal images, those ugly things we saw that made us sick, more than just the beer."

"How do you know what you were seeing was real? Know what I mean? How do you know you weren't just imagining the whole thing?"

"Both of us?"

"Well, you were--how old did you say, eight?--and you know how young kids can get to talking, exaggerating a little here, adding a little there--and before they're done, they've talked themselves into believing something pretty wild."

"No, it wasn't like that. What we saw had really happened to those
people."

"How do you know? Did you ever talk to them, ask them about those things?"

"No, after my mother found Nick and I throwing up--sorry--she and dad took us in the house and put us to bed and we never saw Big Bill or the other combiners again."

"Big Bill," Wolfram mumbled.

"What?"

"Nothing, just admiring his name."

"Well, he came by it honestly. He weighed over four hundred pounds."

"Yeah, that's one big guy."

"The Story of the Kalendar Prince" came to an end.

"Time to turn the record over." Wolfram stood up and took their empty bowls to the sink. "What do you think so far?"

"It's exotic. I can imagine the stories as I listen."

They walked back into the living room.

"I thought you'd like it. I've loved it since I was a kid."

"You mean you grew up listening to stuff like this."

"Didn't you?"

Judith smiled. "No, I don't think so," she said ironically. My mom and dad tended more toward Ray Charles and Sarah Vaughan, Nat King Cole and Johnny Mathis."

"Hey, they're all great, nothing to apologize for there."

Wolfram lifted the dust cover and flipped the album over. Hushed violins introduced the themes of "The Young Prince and the Young Princess."

"Want to see the balcony?"

Judith smiled archly. "That sounds like a proposition."

Wolfram breezed past the irony. "We can sit out on the swing. Best grab your jacket, though."

Wolfram opened the tall, faux French doors, let Judith walk ahead of him out into the dark. Wolfram left the doors open so they could hear the music. They sat down in the swing together and he took her hand in his. They pushed off, began to glide gently. The big elms in the front of the house towered above it. Their limbs shone, a more solid blackness, against the black sky.

"So, what kind of parents did you have, anyway, who listened to classical music?" she asked.

"My dad was a doctor, so we didn't see a lot of him. I mean, he was nice enough. He just wasn't around a whole lot. When he was home, though, we had to turn off the TV. All he wanted to hear was soothing music."

"Exactly the kind you don't play."

"I play some softer things."

"When did you decide you wanted to be a musician? In high school?"

"I can't remember a time when I didn't want to make music. I mean I used to drive my parents nuts, when I was three, four, five. I'd take all the pots and pans out of the kitchen cabinets and pound on them like drums. Then I'd get different kinds of glasses and bowls and I'd make a super marimba. My folks got me piano lessons just so I'd play something that sounded more like real music."

"Anyone else in your family play?"

"My mother played piano a little. And my grandpa, her father, played the accordion in a polka band, believe it or not."

"No."

"Yeah, in a group called Mel Swenson and his Watertown Polka Orchestra."

"Swenson was your mother's maiden name?"

"No, grandpa's name was Hugh Carter. During the week he managed a Gambles store. He picked up extra cash playing in Mel Swenson's band on weekends."

"When did you begin playing guitar?"

"After I first heard Chuck Berry on the radio. I just had to learn to make the sounds he was making."

"Chuck Berry, that doesn't sound like something your dad would have been too thrilled about."

"Not really, but my Mom liked Buddy Holly and Elvis. I begged and begged. My dad gave in after he found me one Saturday out in the garage, trying to stretch some picture wire over a two by four I'd nailed to a cigar box. He took me out and bought me a classical guitar and a couple of Mel Bay guitar books. I think he had Segovia in mind."

"So does he think you're wasting your talent playing rock music."

Wolfram laughed. "No, both my folks have been real supportive of my music. They've been behind everything I've done, except maybe dropping out of college. They weren't too happy about that."

"Is that how you ended up in Vietnam?"

"Here's the fourth movement. I like this one best." They listened a moment. "You know what I like most about this symphony?"

"What?"

"The lone violin that comes in a bit sadly but magically in each movement? That's Scheherazade, telling her stories."

"To keep from getting beheaded."

"That's right, trying to save her life each night. That's kind of how I see myself, too. Every night I have to throw myself into it full-bore, as if I was trying to save my life."

"What'd you do in Vietnam? How'd you keep yourself alive?"

"I could make something up, but really I think it was just pure chance."

"Was the war the way you describe it in your songs?"

"Well, the incident in 'Land Mine Blues' actually happened. One minute Tommy Nicolette was walking on point, the next he was flying through the air and his blood was spraying all over us. He weighed one eighty, and I tell you, that mine flung him into the air like he was a stuffed animal. Both his legs were blown off just below the knee, and he lay there in the road, spouting rivers from his stumps. He jerked at first; then his eyes went back in his head and he just lay there, kind of gasping for breath. He bled to death before a medic could get to him."

"I'm sorry, I know talking about it's probably the last thing you want to do."

"Most guys who come back don't want to talk about it. Howard's like that. We served in two different parts of the Mekong, and we saw each other only about every two months or so. He never wanted to talk about it when we got together. So we just listened to music, got high, and tried to forget where we were."

"Did you get high a lot?"

"Any time we weren't on patrol. Nobody got high on patrol. You had to be as clear-headed as possible." He paused. "I was scared the whole time I was in Nam. I lived in my eyes and in my ears."

"When did you get out?"

"Howard and I both got out eighteen months ago."

"And you came back and started your band again."

"Yeah, we picked up where we left off--except that now I talk and sing some about the war."

"You didn't do protest songs before?"

"You mean like 'Blowin' in the Wind'?"

"Yeah."

"No, I wasn't political at all before I got drafted." He snorted. "How's that for irony?"

"Are you going to take part in the Moratorium?"

"Yeah, the boys and I are gonna march, and the student government has hired us to play that night. How about you?"

"I'll be there. I've been working against the war for over a year?"

"While you were still in high school?"

"Yeah, we had a young minister who organized a couple of candle-light vigils. He also led one march. Lots of kids from the church participated."

"I bet I know how that went over."

"Yeah, he got transferred to a small town in Montana right after the march."

"What about your brother? Is he political?"

"Nick's against the war but he wasn't into anything serious during high school. "

"Let me guess. Sports and chicks--he was into sports and chicks."

"Well, one girl. Annie Thurston."

"Just one? So, they still together?"

"No, they broke up last Valentine's Day.

"Why's that?"

"Because he wouldn't marry her."

"What, was she pregnant?"

"No, she was just a whole lot more serious about things than he was."

"Didn't she think they were maybe just a little young?"

"From what Nick says, she thought because they'd been sleeping together for several months, they'd made a commitment to each other. I guess she was ready to act on that commitment."

"And he wasn't?"

"Not hardly."

"Jesus, if I'd married every girl I slept wi--sorry."

"Now you sound just like Nick and all his friends. What is it, a law or something that every guy's got to have this attitude?"

"Or something," Wolfram said, chuckling.

"What gets me is that if you turn them down, they throw all this free love crap at you."

"So you don't believe in free love?"

"Why would I? Why would any woman? I mean, there's nothing 'free' about it. There's always a price."

"A price!"

"Yes, and the woman's the one who pays it. Always."

"OK, you're saying that if you meet someone and you really turn each other on, you wouldn't go to bed with him?"

"Probably not."

Wolfram looked at her with incredulity. "Let me make sure I've got this straight. You like this guy and he likes you. And when he makes love to you, It feels good. No, it feels *really* good.

"OK, I've got the idea."

"You both have a good time, nobody gets hurt. And you're saying something's wrong with that?"

"A lot of the time, yes."

Wolfram's head began to spin and his belly began to ache. He saw he had misjudged things--badly.

"So, do you think everybody should be saving it for marriage, or something?"

"I swear this is *deja vu*. I've had this same conversation with my brother."

"Well, do you?"

"I don't know, maybe that is what I'm saying. I guess, yes. At least then you know you're going to be more than just a piece of meat to the guy."

Yes, he had badly misjudged. He was probably going to have to adjust his plans. Sinbad's ship had long since gone to pieces on the rock and the music had stopped.

"A piece of meat?"

"Damn straight. Most guys do whatever they have to do, say whatever they have to say, just to get you to get them off. It's like the name of your band--Body Count. They're just counting the bodies."

Wolfram winced. He saw the needle of his chances edging from slim to none.

"So, OK, I'll admit that some guys, hell, maybe most guys, are just out to get laid, at least at first. But what's wrong with that, if the woman wants it, too?"

"Just a one-nighter, a roll in the proverbial hay?"
"Yeah."
"Sounds pretty meaningless to me."
Wolfram sighed. "Judith, where did you get these ideas? From your minister? From your mother?"
"No, you can leave both of them out of it. When I was about fifteen, I took a long hard look at how guys were treating me and all the other girls I knew. I thought about what kind of relationship I wanted with a man in the future, and I asked myself the best way to go about getting it."
"Say, want to go in? It's getting kinda chilly out here."
"In more ways than one, huh?"
They stood up, still holding hands.
"Now Judith," he said playfully, "if you're going to read things into whatever I say, I don't see how this is ever going to work."
"So I'm right, then."
Wolfram laughed. "In spades."
They went in and he shut the doors behind them.
"So, Wolfram, what did you mean by 'this' just now?"
"What do you mean?"
"You said, 'I don't see how this is ever going to work.' What's 'this'?"
"You know. Us," he said, turning to face her and taking both her hands.
"Not sex?"
He lifted up both hands, palms up, as if declaring his innocence.
"Hey, only when you're ready."
"Are you sure a guitar god like you can wait for that?"
"I don't know." He chuckled. "Can't say I have much experience waiting."
"Yeah, I saw all your groupies tonight."
"Those weren't groupies."
"What would you call them?"
"Well, women, for one thing."
"Willing women," she said half-sarcastically.
He smiled. "Could be."

"Groupies, by any other name. What I'm trying to do, Wolfram, is keep from becoming just another one of those 'women' . . . but maybe that's what you thought I was."

"No, Judith, I knew from the first," he lied a little, "you were different."

"So you're not going to get upset if I say I'd better go now."

"No, I won't be mad . . . disappointed maybe, but not mad."

She walked to the door, turned. "So are you going to call me tomorrow . . . or is this it?"

"You know the answer to that." He took her in his arms and kissed her--long and deep.

"You sure you won't stay?" he asked in a husky whisper.

She smiled. "No, I think you've got to want me more."

He groaned. "I couldn't want anybody more than I want you right now."

She laughed, opening the door. "You will. Then we'll see."

She leaned forward, her jacket leather creaking, gave him a quick kiss, and started down the stairs.

* * * * * * *

Wolfram returned "Scheherazade" to its sleeve and cover. He removed an album from the racks. He pushed the volume up a couple of notches, set the needle down at the fourth song. Plaintive trombone intro, then--Bessie! Singing full-voiced, with rich soulful confidence and utter conviction: "Empty Bed Blues, Parts 1 & 2." Wolfram picked up the Martin twelve-string, sat on the edge of the loveseat, began to play along. As Bessie began to sing about the new man who'd left her (with "just a room and an empty bed"), yes, that coffee grinder with the "brand new grind," that "deep-sea diver, with a stroke that can't go wrong," Wolfram closed his eyes and played inside and around the trombone, piano, and muted trumpet accompaniment. He cranked the Martin, made it lament, weep and wail.

He opened the doors to the balcony, stepped outside. His twelve-string moaned and whimpered, whined and screamed into the black-clouded night. Bessie sang, Wolfram closed his eyes and his guitar sobbed. And when Bessie's song was done, Wolfram played on alone, his guitar aching, sobbing, anguishing into the darkness.

Up the street, at the edge of the university campus, Judith stopped, looked back toward Wolfram's apartment. She saw the elms in front of his house uproot themselves, shake muscular, big-barked trunks, and heave great bulging roots--big as anacondas, as fire hoses-- up in tumult from the lawn. Hundreds and hundreds of smaller roots whipped and whistled and snaked up. Hard black earthen boulders and thousands of dirt clods, marble to softball size, rained everywhere. Judith saw the massive elms begin to dance, slowly, elegantly, sorrowfully, before the lone guitarist. A score of others up and down the street wrenched themselves free and did the same, as did oaks and maples, pines and spruce, cherry and apple trees. Ashes and willows and honey locusts, shrubs and hedges. Bessie sang, Wolfram played, and all those denuded trees and bushes danced--ever so mournfully, yes, with such forlornness, with such deep, irrevocable loss--in the dark, in the moonless, black-clouded night.

Part II

December 1950 - July 1959

Chapter 4
The Exploded House

Though she issued the first by moments, engored and screeching, they may as well have both been birthed at the same tolling of the nine o'clock hour. Born out of one darkness and into another. Together, as if they were two parts, two limbs, of one creature, two freshly sundered halves of one whole. And he screeched as lustily as she--as if knowing not birth and emergence, but only the surgical shock of severance, the amputation, though living, of half himself. For they had been even as one flesh, one will, one feeling, and now they were two, split down the center, sliced beyond restoring or repair by some new cold blade of self, some keen-honed knife of aloneness. And they screamed in protest.

What a change when they lay, one at a time--warm, milk-narcotized, little half smiles curling up the ends of their mouths--against their mother Lena's breasts. What a change when they slept afterwards, on stomachs, snuggled close in adjoining hospital cribs, two little humped slugs on immaculate sheets. It would have been impossible to discern then where one differed from the other, so much did one's face--in baby fat, fine features, and dusky, pupil-dark eyes--mirror the other's.

* * * * * * *

Nick and Judith slept and woke, cried for food, relieved themselves, and cried again at the discomfort--all at the same times (never more than a few minutes apart). They turned over front to back, crawled, spoke their first words, and walked, and caught a ball, all within an hour of each other, often, it seemed to Lena and Roger, their startled parents, almost simultaneously.

And when separated, they inevitably put up such a caterwauling, sobbing, and wailing (stubbornly unassuageable until reunited) that, after a time, Roger and Lena, out of practicality and respect for their own nervous balance, simply chose not to remove one from the other.

* * * * * * *

It was not long after the twins' births that the confused parents began to notice even more strange signs of sympathetic connection between them. They moved their heads at the same time to notice a mobile, a second before Lena lifted her hand to touch it into motion. When one discovered something new--about a toy, a piece of furniture, or Randy and Mandy, the two orange housecats--the other instantly got up and came to look, without being called. And not long after they started talking--chattering away, garrulous as cockatiels --they began casually completing each other's sentences. They did it so smoothly, with such nonchalant, perfect synchronicity--never overlapping or abutting words up against the other--that Lena said to Roger, "I swear, they're not just finishing each other's sentences, they're finishing each other's thoughts."

* * * * * * *

The wind had snow in its throat and ice in its heart. It flew straight out of the Canadian Arctic and flung itself, bluff and blustery, against the house, was rebuffed, and screamed past the windows, a wounded cougar. It yowled, hissed, swirled away, subsiding to a dead, sub-zero stillness. There was no moon or stars. There was only the cold black funeral of the February sky.

The wind ripped demented through the shelterbelt trees, whipping denuded branches up like the hands of drowning victims. It socked, smash, against the boards of outbuildings, granaries, and barn, knocking the breath out of them. It slashed pitiless through bushes and shrubs and sang like a fire's shrieking chorus through the wind-charger tower beside the house. Smoke streaked out in a white line from the chimney and then dissipated into sheer air, vanished--as if the wind had translated it from this world to some other.

Like that wind, death came, startling and strange, into Nick and Judiths life that winter of their seventh year. It was like profoundly original music heard for the first time. Nick lay asleep beneath a blanket and a thick quilt, his head sunk in profile into the pillow, like a rock half-buried in pasture earth. Judith lay on her back, arms up by her head, in her matching twin-bed (they had been bunkbeds when the twins were young enough to sleep in the same room) in her bedroom on the first floor of the farmhouse.

Outside, the bleak ash of first daylight began to smudge the black, cloud-embanked sky. Roger Larkin sat at the Formica table in the kitchen, pulling on his combat boots, still highly polished, though he had been out of the Air Force for three years. Roger was a slender man, large-boned but lean, six feet tall. Roger wet the frayed ends of the faded black laces, thinned them to a slick point with his lips, and poked them through the eyelets. Sometimes they snagged, and with some irritation, he stopped to re-wet the ends. He frowned at the taste of dust and of something else, the original dye perhaps. For the hundredth time, at least, he thought he ought to buy some new laces one of these days. His long, well-manicured fingers (Lena often said it wasn't hard to fall in love with a man with such beautiful hands) swiftly wrapped the laces once around, crossed them, pulled them tight, and tied them into slim, drooping bows.

Roger sat up in his chair, arched his back to get the kinks out. He sipped from his coffee cup, bearing the name and logo of the local Farmer's Co-op. He slid a square, lime-green, Depression-ware honeycomb dish over to his plate, lifted off the lid, slathered a knife-blade of honey onto the final piece of buttered toast on his plate (all that remained of the blueberry pancakes and bacon breakfast he and Lena had eaten), and replaced the lid. Life size, bi-winged honeybees and stylized, five-petal flowers were raised on the top and sides of the dish, and a conical hive rose breast-like from the center of each side. The knob on top showed the imperfection of its making in a cluster of tiny air bubbles, like those frozen in winter ice.

Roger heard Lena's bath water running into the eagle-claw bathtub, behind the bathroom door. He imagined his naked, willowy wife slipping into the water, steaming hot (as she liked it) and so deep that after she got in, water ran for a minute out of the three oval overflow holes. Just as his pants began to feel uncomfortably tight, the shrieking of the wind reminded him of what he had ahead of him. He ate his toast, thinking about what he had to do that Saturday morning before he left for work at their laundromat in town: feed and water the twenty cows in the barn, feed and water the sixty chickens in the chicken-house, and take the tractor out of the machine shed and plow the four inches of snow that had fallen last night out of his driveway. The county plow hadn't been down either of the roads that crossed at the northeast corner of his shelterbelt, but with the chains on his pickup, he'd be able to make it the two-and-a-half miles to the highway, and then on into town. The forecast was for more snow--throughout the morning and afternoon and into the evening. Roger finished his toast and washed the crumbs in his mouth and throat down with the last of his coffee. Sighing, he stood up, walked into the living room, took his parka and gloves from the coat closet, and went out to do his chores.

* * * * * * *

Lena called Nick and Judith shortly after eight, telling them to get up and come look at the new snow. The sky had cleared, the sun had come out (though she knew it wouldn't last), and the fresh snow was eye-blindingly bright. Roger had left at seven-thirty for town, and she had fixed more pancakes and bacon for the kids. She was just stirring a can of frozen orange concentrate into a pitcher of water when they came into the kitchen, looking like creatures of flame in their red and yellow pajamas.

The twins took the two glasses of orange juice Lena had poured and walked down the short hall, past the bathroom, and opened the door to the dining room. It was a large room, with a ten-foot ceiling and hard-wood floor, covered with a violet faux-Persian rug (that matched the one in the adjoining living room). A long, heavy walnut table that sat six stood on elegantly tapered legs before the three long windows on the west wall. A long walnut bureau, containing, in its various drawers, Lena and Roger's wedding china, the silver Lena had inherited from her grandmother, the family's photograph albums and dozens of loose photographs, and Lena's and Roger's 45-, 331/3-, and 78-rpm records, took up most of the south wall between the windows and the glass door (with its own set of white curtains) to the onetime sun porch, now Roger and Lena's bedroom.

Lena had hung several Japanese paintings--bought while Roger was on R & R in Tokyo during the Korean War--in the dining and living rooms. These were mostly country scenes in different seasons. The twins loved to stare at those paintings, imagining they were making their way up those winter mountains (that fell so precipitously down to the raging white river below), or that they were walking at dusk across that bridge over that mysterious gorge, with the river lying so serenely below, or that they had entered any of a number of other scenes.

When they stared at these paintings, Nick and Judith would sit trance-like, their eyes glassy, their pulse and respirations slowing. They would see themselves in the paintings, struggling through snow up mountain paths or sitting in a garden hung with dim lanterns, listening to the birds sing in the dusky shadows of the trees. They could sit side by side in two tall-backed walnut chairs and speechlessly immerse themselves in a painting, simultaneously living out long, complicated tales of love and betrayal and war and reconciliation and peace and renewal of love that, truth to be told, resembled the plots of movies they had seen. This was one of their favorite activities and was always good for whiling away a spare hour. Often they would leave the story suspended at some critical juncture, as in Saturday matinee serials, and pick it up hours or days or even weeks later, exactly where they had left off.

Lena brought in their plates, butter, and syrup, carrying it all like a truckstop waitress, spread out along her forearms. "It's Saturday, so what should we do today?"

"Let's go sledding," Judith said.

"It's supposed to snow all day. I think we might want to stay inside."

"Wyethowmes," Nick said, starting to speak with several pieces of blueberry pancake in his mouth.

"Swallow first, Nick!"

He did. "I said, why don't we make papier-maché animals? We haven't done that in almost a year."

"I don't know, are you sure?"

"Yes!" the twins said together.

"We won't be able to finish in a day or two, you know. Last time it took us a whole week."

"We don't care," the twins said together.

"OK, I guess we can get the shapes sculpted and put the first coats of paper on today. We'll have to let them dry before we can add some more paper."

"And when we're all done for today, you have to tell us one of your special stories," Nick said.

"Now which ones would those be?" Lena asked.

"You know," Judith said, "the ones that fly us off to different places."

Lena raised her eyebrows. "Oh, really, one of those. I'm not sure I know any stories like that."

"Sure you do," Nick said. "All of your stories are like that."

"We'll see. One thing at a time."

* * * * * * *

Nick and Judith loved to do any kind of artwork with their mother because every time, without fail, something marvelous happened. Lena always acted as if everything was normal, as if whatever prodigy was taking place was perfectly natural. It was almost as if she simply didn't see the astonishing things that Judith and Nick saw. But how could that be?

Later that morning, Lena, dressed in old jeans, a green sweatshirt, green socks, and white tennis shoes, and the twins, dressed identically in red flannel shirts, slim-cut Wrangler jeans, and western boots, sat at the dining room table, which Lena had protected with old newspapers. They'd twisted coat hangers and other pieces of wire, sometimes using a pair of yellow-handled pliers, into the shapes of a long-necked giraffe (Nick's), an Arabian horse (Judith's), and an elephant and a Bengal tiger (Lena's). They had torn half a month's newspapers into long strips, had made paste (with that smell that decades later would always, like the waxy smell of Crayolas, bring back childhood to the grown twins), and had started to cover the big wire frames when the animals began to shift about under their hands.

The animals grew each time they placed another pasty strip of newsprint on their metal skeleton--they stretched, shivered, and twitched. Bones acquired mass and extension under hide, muscles took on definition and flexed, rippling. The wet strips became leathery hide and scales and fur. Nick's giraffe, horned and spotted, shot up from two to fifteen feet, the ceiling flying upwards before it, like a huge elevator. The giraffe craned its head up and snatched a mouthful of leaves off the group of acacia trees that had sprung up out of the wall as it slid back into a rolling, tall-grassed, termite-hilled savannah. Judith's Arabian grew fast to a height at which she could not see over its back; a wall fell back into a riding ring, and it began to prance and trot around it, its hooves printing the dirt and raising swirls of dust. The other walls melted into the humid mists of dense trees and bushes, vines and flowers, as Lena's animals plodded noisily and strode silently through a jungle.

* * * * * * *

It began to snow again before Lena and the twins had finished putting the first coats of paper on the wire frames of their animals. The snow fell softly at first--big parachuting flakes like cottonwood seeds. Then the flakes became smaller and fell harder as the wind picked up. About one that afternoon, Judith stood before one of the several tall, narrow windows in his parents' bedroom. Without his turning his head, or speaking, or signaling with his hands, Nick, who had been lying on the floor, coloring, appeared, soft and still as a shadow, at her side. Outside, the wind threw fists of snow against the house and the trees-- and there, not five feet from the windows, on a low branch of the Chinese elm, was perched a big crow. It was at least twice the size of a robin and shone black as anthracite. Its head was tucked so deeply under its left wing that it looked as if it had been beheaded. The twins stood absolutely still, breathing shallowly.

Judith whispered, "Go and . . ."

". . .get Mom," Nick said, leaving his side silently as a cloud. Nick reappeared, leading Lena by the hand. When Lena saw the bird, she said "Oh!" in a hushed voice. The three of them stood together a minute at the windows, marveling at the bird.

Judith whispered, "Mom, do you think you . . ."

"could catch it?" Nick said. "We could train it . . ."

" . . .to talk," Judith finished, looking up earnestly at Lena.

"Oh, I could never catch it."

"Sure you could," Judith said. "With its head tucked under its wing like that, it wouldn't see you."

"And with all the wind, it would never hear you," Nick said.

"All you have to do is sneak up and grab its legs . . ." Judith said.

" . . .and then stuff it in a cardboard box," Nick said.

Reluctantly, Lena began to put on her boots, black leather gloves, black scarf, and blue hooded parka. As she did so, Nick ran to the basement to get a box. Directly before the wooden steps was the furnace, white-jacketed in insulation so it looked like a huge unwieldy papier-maché sculpture itself, its four burly white limbs sprawling squid-like out of its top. To the right of the steps, back in the dim part of the basement (because its sixty-watt bulb was left half unscrewed), were the window screens, labeled and numbered and stacked against the concrete wall. To the left rear, murky for the same reason, were two floor-to-ceiling shelves of canned goods, representing hours of his mother's hot, steamy work in an un-airconditioned kitchen last summer. Tomatoes, string beans, wax beans, peas, carrots, and beets swam in the fuliginous waters of rubber-sealed Mason jars, as did three or four types of pickles. There were also dozens of pint jars of jellies--strawberry, wild Oregon grape, mint, blackberry, chokecherry, and most exotic, tart gooseberry, the gray-green of Russian olive leaves.

On other shelves, in the lit part of the basement, Nick saw many boxes of things. He quickly saw the size he judged would be about right and divested it of its contents: sewing patterns; material cut, pieced, and pinned; and material uncut--work waiting for his mother's spare hour, as work ever did. Hearing Lena, who'd just put on her overshoes, turn the knob of the kitchen door--opening on three steps leading down to the small landing from which one could either descend to the basement or pass out the side door--hearing his mother, Nick ran up the steps and handed her the box. She noted its label, sighed, shook her head, and went out.

From separate windows, Judith and Nick saw Lena come around the house, grimacing, face into the furious wind, wading through the snow drifts. She held the box against her chest so the wind wouldn't catch it and scare the crow. She nodded toward her children, smiled behind the scarf at the excited looks on their faces. She slowed her steps, watching the big crow intently as she approached it, as if she could will it into motionlessness by the power of her stare. She had no idea why she was doing this, except that it fit her notions of motherhood to attempt such things.

Lena set the box down on the snow, gripping it between her feet. Slowly, as if caught in cinematic slow motion, she extended her right hand soundlessly toward the crow. Inside, Nick and Judith held their breaths. She was but an inch or two from its legs when somehow it became aware of danger, withdrew its head from beneath its wing, saw her, and flew--all in one sudden motion--shaking snow from the branch it had perched on. It flapped away and disappeared into the storm. Secretly relieved, Lena turned to mouth the word "sorry" to the twins' disappointed faces, then retraced her steps through the drifts to the back door.

They couldn't decide later over hot chocolate what exactly had alerted the crow. Their mother said she had been as silent as possible. She speculated that the bird had been able to see her hand from under its wing. But Nick and Judith couldn't accept that explanation. They couldn't adjust to the fact that their mother had not succeeded, so keenly had they envisioned themselves as owners of the crow: training it to ride on their shoulders, to talk, to return from free flight to a perch on their hands. Many a time that winter they replayed the scene in their minds. They didn't talk about it, but they each knew what the other was doing. They watched as their mother's hand drew near the big black bird. Usually the crow took flight just as Lena was about to grasp its legs, but sometimes she was able to seize it--and, struggling with it as it shot its wings full-spread, back-thrusting and -pumping, and snaked its head around to peck at her gloved hands, struggling with it, she managed to force it into the box and, quick, close its flaps, while at the windows they jumped up cheering and clapping.

Years later, one day when the twins, then seniors in high school, were sitting with Lena at the kitchen table in their house in the town of Lebeau (an hour's drive south of their farm), Judith asked her mother if she remembered the time she had almost caught a wild crow for them, but Lena said, "Oh, Judith, catch a crow? You've gotta be kidding. Why would I ever try to catch a crow?" Judith and Nick insisted the incident had really happened and they described, in their unique antiphonal fashion, the event, in all the tender detail it had assumed in their imaginations. They tried several times, each time emphasizing different things--her blue parka, the cardboard box (Nick was sure it had the name of some breakfast cereal on it), how the gusting wind threw snow into her face, how she oh-so-slowly reached with her black-gloved hands toward the crow's tough reptilian legs, how it flung itself in a burst of feathers into the air and in seconds disappeared, black, between white bursts of snow. But no matter how well they told the story, Lena was not able to recall the crow. They looked at each other: We know it happened; it's still happening.

* * * * * * *

Later that afternoon, as the snow tapered off and the wind subsided somewhat, Lena sat slouched in the middle of the violet couch in the living room, with her feet propped up on the coffee-table, reading the book she had checked out of the town library the day before. The twins came out of Judith's room, where they had been playing a card game, and asked if she would tell them the story she had promised. Lena sat up, closed her book, laid it on the couch beside her.

"All right, I'll tell you a story from this book I'm reading."

"What's the book?" Nick asked

"*Black Elk Speaks.* It's the story of a holy man of the Lakota people. They were the Indians who lived here for hundreds of years before the white man came."

"This story doesn't have cavalry in it and a big battle, does it?" Judith asked.

Lena laughed. "No, it's not like that at all. Come on and sit by me. I'm sure you'll like it."

Nick sat down on one side of Lena and Judith on the other.

"Now this story took place a long, long time ago. One summer day two men were out by themselves, looking for buffalo for the tribe. As they were standing in the tall grass on a tall hill, they saw something slowly coming toward them from far away. As it got closer, they saw that it was a woman."

Living in their mother's clear, entrancing voice, the twins were there, on that hill, in that grass, where crickets chirped and ants crawled.

"One of the men wanted to do bad things to the woman, but the other one said he shouldn't be thinking those kind of thoughts, that this woman was sacred. When the woman got closer, they could see that she was young and very beautiful. She wore a white buckskin dress and had long beautiful black hair.

"Seeing how pretty she was, the evil man wanted even more to do bad things to her. She let him come close to her and then suddenly they were both covered by a white cloud. When the cloud disappeared, the bad man was lying on the ground, a skeleton."

The twins gasped, clearly seeing the white clean-picked bones.

"The woman sent the good man back to his people to tell them to build a big teepee for her in the nation's center. They built it and waited for her in it. She appeared, singing a beautiful song. A white cloud came out of her mouth, and it smelled good to the people.

"She gave the tribe's chief a special pipe. A buffalo calf was carved on one side and twelve eagle feathers hung from it. She told the people that the pipe would bring them many good things. Then she walked out of the village, and as she was walking away, she became a white buffalo. It began to run and before long they couldn't see it."

Nick and Judith loved this story and for months afterwards they would ask Lena to tell it. They particularly liked the parts where the evil man was turned into a skeleton and where the woman changed into the white buffalo. Whenever Lena told them the story, they would become very still, the room would fall away, and they would be standing on a big hill in the Dakota prairie.

* * * * * * *

When Roger turned into his drive, shadows were growing long in the shelterbelt trees, gathering, softening the angular lines of their naked branches. He walked into the house, a dark look on his face. He stepped into the living room, where Lena was sitting with the kids on the couch. One look at Roger's face, and Lena sent the kids into Judith's room to play, with the door closed.

"Roger, what's wrong?"

"You haven't heard?"

"No, what?"

Roger sat down next to her. "The Andrews farmhouse blew up this morning."

"Oh my God! Were they . . ."

"Yes, they were all inside, Gene and Linda and the two kids."

Lena took one of Roger's hands, held it between hers.

"How did it happen?"

"A gas leak in the basement. They figure that somebody switched on the basement light early this morning, the spark touched off the gas, and, bang, the whole house blew up."

"Oh no. And I just saw Linda and the kids yesterday in town. She was shopping and she came into the laundromat to say hi to Gene's sister, Mary."

Roger had gone to high school with Gene, but they had never been close friends, never much more than acquaintances really. The Andrews farm was five miles north of town, far enough away from the Larkin farm that the two families saw each other only in town.

"Did they recover the bodies?"

"Yes, they took them to the Burkholder Mortuary in town."

"Oh, Roger, they were such nice people. The kids weren't even school age yet."

"You know, this could happen to anybody. All the farms around here use propane."

The twins flung themselves out of Judith's door. "Dad, our house isn't going to blow up, is it?" they asked, looking worried.

They leaped into Roger's lap. "No, our house isn't going to blow up. We're perfectly safe here." He hugged them.

"Dad, can we go look at that house?" Judith asked.

"Oh, honey, we couldn't do that," Lena said.

"No, it's all right, Lena. I was going to suggest that we might drive over and take a look, just to see what kind of damage the explosion did to the house."

"I don't know, Roger, do you think it's the right thing to do?"

"Yeah, it'll be OK. I talked to a lot of people in town who were going to drive out to take a look."

"That's it, then," Judith said, "we're going."

* * * * * * *

It was dusk when the Larkins parked their pickup on a graveled county road a hundred yards down from the Andrews place. Thirty or forty other cars and pickups were parked along the road and in the pulloff to the house. That day's fresh snow had been turned to a dirty slush on the road and in the driveway by vehicle and foot traffic. The four of them, holding hands in one solemn chain, walked down to the yard of the house, where small pockets of people stood, looking, pointing, and talking.

The devastation of the house was complete. Nothing remained except the foundation, which was smothered in heaps of blackened rubble, still smoking in places. Debris had been flung out nearly a hundred feet in all directions. Nick and Judith were speechless before the sight. The yard looked like an annex of the city dump. Board fragments; twisted hunks of plumbing; pieces of insulation; dented pots and pans; shattered crockery and china; hundreds of articles of clothing lying every which way (as if dozens of people had disrobed in the snow and left their clothes lying wherever they fell); a disemboweled radio; a mangled sewing machine; cookbooks and murder mysteries, absent half their leaves--pages flipping, fluttering in the small ghosts of wind; a couch split in half, spilling stuffing and springs; an easychair, lying on its side, gashed in a score of places; dressers that looked as if they had been attacked with sledge hammers; a movie magazine, half its glossy cover ripped off, the jagged tear running through a star's famous name, which could still be recognized from the "Eliz" and "Ta" remaining; wooden chair legs, fractured and broken; a scarred tabletop, permanently missing its two leaves; smashed flower pots; a brass lamp that had come through unscathed, including its shade and light bulb; shredded curtains; mattresses that looked as if they'd been shot by a cannon; ripped sheets; torn blankets; a shotgun barrel, the stock, trigger guard, and trigger amputated; poker chips; a battered toy firetruck; a round-topped refrigerator, with no door and a huge dent in one side; a Raggedy Andy doll, looking like a war veteran, with its left arm missing and its right leg cut off below the knee; plastic animals from a farm set; wooden blocks, some with their bright red, blue, green, and white paint scuffed and chipped, some sheared in half; and stuffed animals--a Teddy bear, one ear sliced off, a lion missing both its button

eyes, a cat that would never be white again, a parrot whose long hooked
fabric beak was split and splayed.

It was the stuffed animals the twins thought about the most as they piled into the cab of the pickup between Lena and Roger for the drive home. The last of the sun's rays had died and their headlights were weak against the dark. Before they had gone two miles, it began to snow, heavily. Roger had to slow down as flakes flew fiercely into the windshield. They gleamed, from the road and its ditches, millions of quartz facets, or sequins.

The four of them rode without speaking. Judith and Nick thought about the stuffed animals and about the children, aged two and four, who would never play with them ever again. They could not get that thought out of their heads: Those two kids were gone, just gone, forever. Their lives were over. Nick and Judith would never see them again. That was what death was--people vanishing out of one's life for good. And it wasn't as if those peoples' lives continued elsewhere, in some other city or country. It wasn't as if they had gone on vacation or moved. No, they had simply ceased to exist. The twins did not have to look at each other to know they were thinking the same thing: A whole family had died; they had suddenly stopped living. Somehow, one could know this, could know it absolutely, and still not have a chance of understanding it.

As the pickup, like a good workhorse, trudged up a steep hill a mile and a half from their home, Nick and Judith suddenly saw a huge form appear at the farthest edge of the headlights, a great beast. Its hide was gleaming white, as if thousands and thousands of snowflakes had congregated and fused to create it. It did not move, and as the pickup bore down upon it, it brightened and then, in a flash bright as summer lightning, disappeared. They drove right through the empty space where it had stood. If it had been a cow or a deer, they could not have escaped hitting it.

From their unchanged faces, the twins knew their parents had seen nothing. In the silent cab, lit only by the dim wattage of the dashlight, Nick took Judith's hand in his and squeezed. She squeezed back. They still had their mother and father and they still had each other, to hold off the darkness. And somewhere out in the world, out in the snow and wind, was this big shaggy white buffalo, with two round black eyes and two inward-curved black horns. They felt more than thought that it represented a power beyond anything they could know or imagine.

Chapter 5
Crows And Toads

The next summer crows were everywhere. No one could explain it, but for some reason after the eggs had hatched out that spring and the baby birds had fledged and flown from the nest, crows cluttered the skies, cawing raucously, flocks casting great shadows on the ground, like fast-drifting, fairweather clouds. They perched on the fences, lined up like black ninepins. They perched on the gently looping strands of electric lines.

One day early in June, Nick and Judith were walking down the fenced-in lane that ran between the county road and a hundred-acre, pale green wheat field, the quarter mile down to the pasture, when they saw two crows come winging over the wheat and swoop up to land side-by-side on one of the electric wires over their heads. Evidently not caring for their first perch, the crows hopped a few feet down the wire, looking like buffoonish highwire artists, and then up onto a transformer box. They swivel-jerked their heads left and right, looking around. They cocked their heads at an outrageous angle so they could each get a good one-eyed look at the twins, who had stopped walking and were watching the show, grins on their faces. Suddenly the two crows touched black beaks and the twins heard a sizzling jolt, a lighting bolt in miniature, and the two crows were knocked straight backwards off the box. They plummeted to the ditch, stone dead.

Judith and Nick climbed through the barbed wire fence and found the two birds lying in a tall bunch of wild oats. The smell of singed feathers and charred flesh hung in the air around the two crows, which lay on the ground in that slack, unnaturally loose way that lifeless things have. The bright sunlight gave their feathers a purplish sheen. The twins were half afraid to touch the crows at first, thinking they might get shocked by some residual charge stored in their bodies.

Judith pulled out a wild oat stalk and diffidently poked one of the crows on its plump breast. She poked the other on the back. It seemed safe. Nick picked up one bird by its black feet and Judith the other by its tailfeathers. The twins dangled the birds in front of them and commented on how heavy they were. They noticed that the eyes of both birds had shut at the instant of death. They carried the birds--held out away from their bodies, and thus all the heavier--all the way to the turnoff from the road to the pasture. Unfortunately for them, the approach was nearly at the other end of the pasture, and their seven-year-old arms were sore and tired before they could lay their burdens down--inside the culvert under the turnoff. There was nothing else in the culvert but dirt and some thin, dry, papery snakeskin. They considered this a respectable burial for two good-time-loving, clownish crows who had died before their time, almost certainly not knowing what had hit them.

* * * * * * *

The shelterbelt that formed a right angle around the Larkins' house and barn and outbuildings was filled with crows all day and night. The mourning doves, robins, blackbirds, starlings, and sparrows were not nearly as numerous in the elms and hackberries and ash and spruce trees as they had been in past years. They had been scared off by the crows, who had laid claim to the trees that spring. Squatter's rights, the crows said, and what smaller bird had ever won a land fight with a crow?

The twins knew there had been fewer of the other birds' nests that spring because they had personally climbed every climbable tree in the shelterbelt and looked into every nest. Their father had long ago told them never to touch an egg or a baby bird, and they were scrupulously careful never to do so. If they found a baby bird lying, cheeping, on the ground, they ran back to the house to get a pair of rubber gloves from the cabinet under the kitchen sink, before picking up the bird and placing it tenderly back in the nest. That solution to the forlorn baby bird problem had been proposed in a moment of true inspiration by their mother a couple of summers before and the twins had embraced it, to Lena's great relief, enthusiastically.

Besides driving out many of the regular migrating birds, forcing them to find other homes, the crows were objectionable because of their constant garrulous, tone-deaf, utterly charmless chattering. Nothing if not gregarious, the crows always found something to gossip and backbite about, always found some paltry, threadbare excuse for noisy roistering, some picayune matter to squabble over for hours at a time, never reaching an amicable resolution of their differences. The shelterbelt had always been full of birdsong, not all of it lyrical, but compared to the crows' tuneless cacophony, it had been a Bach cantata.

Roger Larkin, who had a rich, full, sweet baritone voice and who had sung in choirs in church, in high school, and in his one year of college, took powerful exception to the ceaseless clamor of the crows, both on aesthetic and on personal nervous grounds. Whenever he saw his neighbors or stopped for a moment to visit with friends in town (he didn't go to town nearly as much since he and Lena had sold their laundromat--an eighteen-month business venture that had given them headache after headache and had not made nearly the net profits they had hoped), the talk inevitably turned--or returned--to the crows. The birds had appeared like a literal black plague and had infected the whole county. Everybody complained about them but nobody knew how to get rid of them. At least not successfully.

The crows had proven as hard to get rid of as gophers, as hard to eliminate as bindweed or Canada thistles. All manner of methods, ranging from the lamebrained to the ingenious, had been attempted. The Wilcoxes, who lived a quarter mile north, had sent their ten kids out several times a day with pots and pans and big stirring spoons, to run up and down the shelterbelt rows, banging away. They had, of course, scared what little wits they had out of the smaller, more desirable birds, while the crows had just sat in the trees' upper branches, shifting their black heads up, down, sideways, right, left, trying to figure out what these half-fledged humans could be up to now. They had seen people do strange things before, but this just about beat all. This was worth studying. Maybe something had gone wrong with the water in their cistern (a rat might have fallen in and drowned). Maybe they had eaten some of the wrong kind of mushrooms. Maybe they had sunstroke. Whatever it was, they were acting even loonier than coyotes--and that was about as loony as it got.

The Schneiders, whose farm was a mile south of the Larkins, had rigged an elaborate sprinkler system in their trees (made possible by their deep hardwater well), and early one morning had turned on the water full force. It looked as if their trees had suddenly all sprung leaks. Of course, it had scared the little birds silly. They had decamped so fast, and it had been so hard to navigate through the geysers of water, that some of them had brained themselves, flying smack into the branches and trunks of trees they ordinarily knew like their own pinfeathers. And the crows? They had nearly fallen off their limbs laughing. This was unbelievably droll. How had these humans known they wanted a birdbath? The crows flew in and out of the water, like kids running through a sprinkler. They landed on the ground and hopped under and all around the water sprays, craning their necks up and ruffling and shaking their black feathers, loving the sousing, giddy with the fun they were having in their own private water park.

The Schumacher brothers, Henry and Pete, who lived alone a mile and a half northwest of the Larkins, had determined on a simpler but decidedly more sinister course of action. They bought a few bushels of poison pellets from the Co-op in town and scattered them all through their trees. Within a few days the walkways between the trees were littered with the bodies of smaller birds. The Schumacher shelterbelt looked like the scene of some avian war or some other grievous catastrophe. But not a single crow lay dead between the trees. They hadn't been about to eat those pellets--and especially not after the little birds had begun to drop--to sway listlessly, loose their claws, and slip from their perches, unable to fly back.

Walter Van Aarsdel, whose farm was a quarter mile west of the country school, which was a mile due west of the Larkins, at an intersection of two county roads, had come up with the most original, albeit the goofiest, idea to deal with the crow invasion. He bought a truckload of boards at Miller's Lumber Yard in town, and for three weeks he and his two teenage sons, Gary and Bill, measured and sawed and hammered, totally neglecting all of their fieldwork.

When they were done, a line of twelve-foot-tall windmills lay at thirty-foot intervals, making a smaller angle inside the larger angle of their shelterbelt. Walter and his sons had purposely left each completed windmill lying on its back on the ground. They didn't set any of them up until they were finished with all of them. Walter had been confident that the steady movement of the windmills' blades, like the propellers of a row of DC-3s, would scare the bejesus out of the crows. They didn't want to give the crows the opportunity to get used to the movements of the windmills. They wanted them to get the full effect, all at once.

Then one breezy afternoon they set up all of the windmills and stood back to watch the crow exodus. But nothing happened. Some of the windmills' vanes turned languorously a half turn or so, but most of them remained stubbornly motionless. Frustrated, Walter ran down the line of windmills, shoving the blades for all he was worth--as if he were pushing a line of merry-go-rounds--thinking if he just got them started, they would spin and spin under the power of the winds. But one by one they turned slower and slower, until friction dragged them to a stop. It was then that Walter realized his enormous error. The windmills were inside the shelterbelt--which was, naturally, doing its job and stopping most of the wind. He took off his Farmers' Co-op ballcap, slammed it to the ground, and stormed back to the house, where he proceeded to drink can after can of Schlitz, until he passed out in his living room.

The next day Walter and Gary and Bill took their big truck and moved the windmills (the blades of which were lined with crows, who thought these were the best things they'd seen since the invention of trees) one at a time to the other side of the shelterbelt. Once again they waited till they had them all lying in their places on the ground and then they set them all up as fast as they could. It was a fairly windy day and the windmills turned smartly. Walter and his boys stood admiring their cleverness.

But the crows' eyelids began to droop, and, bored out of their skulls, they fell asleep on their branches. The whole shelterbelt of crows dozed. What did crows, who had ridden flailing, threshing tree limbs in thunderstorms, with windgusts up to a hundred miles an hour-- what did they care about a row of wooden things that moved in the wind? Walter fished a blue bandanna out of his right coveralls pocket, wiped the tears from his eyes and walked, stoop-shouldered, head lowered, in ignominious defeat, through the trees and over to his tractor. He connected it to his plow and drove straight out to his nearest field of summer fallow, where he worked till after nightfall.

* * * * * * *

Nick had not given up his hope of capturing a crow and keeping it as a pet, of training it to talk and do tricks. No, his desire was all the stronger now that their whole county had turned into a veritable crow sanctuary. Still thinking about his mother Lena's attempt the previous winter to catch a crow during a snowstorm and put it in a box, he went to the basement and again dumped out the contents of Trix box (the patterns and sewing his mother had carefully replaced the last time he had done this, deeming it the most suitable size heaviness of the available boxes.

He set it up on the ground in the center of the windcharger tower--erected by his grandfather and his father as a means of generating electricity and storing it in large batteries in the basement of the house, but now used only to support a big television antenna, giving them exceptional reception on the single channel they received. He propped it on a Y-shaped stick, tied to thirty feet of extra clothesline he'd found in the basement. He pulled on the line, testing the trap, several times. Each time it worked perfectly.

Nick dug in the refrigerator, selected a variety of leftovers (meatloaf, scalloped potatoes, green beans, and beets) and salad makings (his mother had, at his request, looked up crows in an encyclopedia at the town library and found out that they ate any and everything they could scavenge), and placed them on a plate in what he thought might be an attractive arrangement to a crow. He took the crow feast out to his trap, where he slipped it under the box. Testing, he pulled on the line again. It worked flawlessly. It was a guaranteed crow-catcher.

Then he went over to the end of the clothesline, behind the trunk of the Chinese elm outside the sun porch of the house. Since there were crows in the elm tree and in the line of hackberries that ran along the west and south sides of the yard, and since there were at least three dozen crows on the bars of the windcharger tower, Nick expected almost immediate results. He squatted down, his hands gripping the line, and stared at the box--for ten minutes, fifteen. Feeling his legs start to cramp up, he lay down on his stomach on the grass, being careful not to relax his grip on the line. Twenty-five minutes, thirty. The crows evidenced no interest in the free meal awaiting them under the cardboard box.

After forty-five minutes, Nick got up and walked over to the box, made sure the food was well placed under it (he moved the plate slightly and rotated it a quarter turn), re-set the stick (though it had already been very effectively set), and re-traced the line all the way back to the elm tree, making sure it was straight and taut. He lay down for another fifteen minutes, thirty. His mother called him in for lunch. He ignored her. Five minutes later she called again, telling him if he didn't come he was going to spend the rest of the day in his room. Exasperated (adults just didn't understand the first thing about a serious matter like crow-catching), he got to his feet and started toward the house. He hadn't gone ten feet before he ran back and yanked the line, pulling the stick out from under the box. No crow was going to get a free meal in his trap if he could help it.

As soon as lunch was over, he and Judith ran out and re-set his trap. Judith wanted to hold the line, but he refused to let her. He wasn't about to let his sister horn in on his glory when he captured his crow. For the next thirty minutes he had to keep telling her to shush, that no crow would fly down to eat from the trap if she kept yapping like that. Finally, calling the trap a silly, lamebrained idea, Judith went back into the house to play with the cats Randy and Mandy. (They, however, were not to be found, since Mandy was in season and Randy was busy living up to his name.) She contented herself with reading *Black Beauty*, one of her favorite books. She found it easy to imagine herself as the young boy hero.

Nick paid Judith's insults no mind; he knew she was just jealous because he had been the one to think of the trap. The day was warm and after another half hour sweat began to run down Nick's forehead and into his eyes, even though he was lying in the shade. He wiped the sweat away with one hand, keeping the other on the line. A daddy longlegs crawled, unbeknownst to Nick, up the side of his shirt and then up his back. It paused on his shoulder, considered the possibilities, and then began crawling down his right arm. When it reached flesh, Nick jerked his arm up, yanking the line and springing the trap. Realizing what he'd done, Nick sighed and shook his head.

Doggedly, he got up to re-set the trap once more time. He had not lain on the ground under the elm another half hour before a foraging red ant found the calf of his left leg in its way and bit it. Nick jumped up, slapping at his leg--in the process simultaneously clearing the ant's path of its obstruction and springing the trap once again. Nick decided that was it. He took the box and the plate of food into the house, flinging the box into the basement as he entered the side door and dumping the plate's scraps into the garbage can in the kitchen. He set the plate in the sink and went off to see what Judith had found to do.

Lying in bed that night, Nick, still determined, devised a new strategy. After breakfast the next morning, he took the clothesline he'd used the day before, tied a loop in one end, and, climbing up the metal ladder to the first level of the windcharger tower, carefully crept out to the middle of the crossbar facing the elm tree and laid his snare. Then, line in hand, he climbed up to the first horizontal branch of the elm (plenty big to hold him), and sat down on it.

As soon as a crow landed on the bar, he would jerk the line, closing the loop tight on its feet--and he would have himself a crow. Nick sat, lay, squatted, and kneeled on that branch all morning, not counting bathroom and lemonade breaks. Crows flew on and off of the windcharger tower, some landing on the first level, some on the bar he was watching so eagerly, but none came closer than two feet to his snare, which they appeared not to notice (did not deign to notice?). This time when Lena called him for lunch, he didn't dawdle. He was happy to get out of the tree.

That afternoon Nick was back at his post, though, patiently concentrating on the snare. Ninety minutes went by; he shifted position several times. It was hot again and sweat ran down his brow and trickled from his armpit down his side. He wiped the sweat out of his eyes and lay on his stomach on the branch. Ten minutes passed, fifteen.

Nick was about to give up and go in when an old crow came flying from the shelterbelt toward the tower. Seeing the number of crows already perching on the top bars, it made for first level. Would it land on his bar? Would it land in his snare? Would it? Would it? Yes! It did! Nick yanked for all he was worth on the clothesline and promptly spun right out of the tree and onto his back on the ground--at the same time jerking the big crow off the bar and onto the ground, not twenty feet away, and causing nearly three score of crows to evacuate the tower simultaneously. Nick wanted to get up, but he couldn't. He'd had the breath knocked out of him and it was a scary minute before he could breathe again. He got up, a bit dazed--only to notice the old crow succeed in freeing its legs from the snare and fling itself into the air, flapping fast back toward the shelterbelt.

"Damn," Nick swore (as he'd heard his father do in similar circumstances of crushing defeat), "I almost had him." He kicked uselessly at the grass and walked to the end of the clothesline, where he found two pitch-black crow feathers lying in the grass--his only reward for two days of trying. Nick looked up at the deserted crossbars of the tower. He had to admit failure. Even if the birds came back that afternoon, even if he could figure a way of keeping himself from falling out of the tree, he doubted the snare on the tower would work a second time. The crows were far too smart for that. He would have to give it up until he could think of a better plan.

* * * * * * *

It had been a wet June and the last week of the month it had rained nearly every day. The alfalfa grew by inches; the wheat grew tall and green, the oats tall and darker green. The corn approached knee-high. New growth appeared on the yard and shelterbelt trees--twiggy and paler green than the rest of the leaves. The tomatoes, cucumbers, corn, carrots, potatoes, peppers, beans, beets, broccoli and other vegetables in Lena's half-acre garden (running from the road to the chicken house, between the driveway and the shelterbelt) grew fast, as if rainwater were the sole substance of such plants.

Of course, the weeds grew, too--plantain, crabgrass, chickweed, wild buckwheat, witchgrass, velvetleaf, yellow foxtail, giant foxtail, and panicgrass. Lena worked in the garden an hour or two a day, hoeing weeds, and she could not keep up. Having worked hard to bring the garden along this far, having already harvested peas, onions, radishes, and lettuce, she felt bad that she could not keep her real garden as clean as the picture of a garden she carried in her head. She imagined the weeds elbowing in, like kids shoving into a line, and sucking all the minerals, nutrients, and water right out of the soil, causing the vegetables to wither, turn brown, and die.

A huge puddle--over twenty feet across at its widest part--had formed at the corner where the driveway turned around the yard and continued southwards, between the house and the barnyard, past the long white propane tank (which looked like something that ought to be attached to a submarine) then bowing back toward the road and into the lane that ran down to the pasture. The puddle did not dry up very quickly because it was shaded the first half of the day by an ash that stood at that corner of the yard. The driveway was muddy and showed tractor and pickup tracks, which would later harden into ruts. Luckily, there was a big grassy triangle between their yard's woven-wire fence and the driveway, so Roger and Lena could park their vehicles without getting stuck.

After supper that Saturday, in a fifteen-minute interval between showers, Roger left for town to buy a three-months-premature birthday present for Lena, making the excuse that he had to pick up some things from the hardware store before it closed. Roger had stopped at Ben Vogel's Mobil station to fill his pickup the day before and Ben had showed him a sixteen-gauge pump shotgun he had decided to sell. Roger admired the well cared for, shiny-as-new gun. He asked Ben how much he wanted for it; Ben said forty dollars. Roger loved pheasant hunting and, as Lena had said she wanted to try it next fall, he told Ben he would think about it. He wanted the gun but he hadn't subtracted his checkbook in nearly a week, so he didn't know if he could afford it or not. Saturday afternoon he'd discovered he could.

Roger stopped at the station first, but the teenage kid working that night said Ben had gone home. Ben lived alone in a bungalow on Maple Street, half a mile away. He brought out the gun again and let Roger look at it. Ben knew Roger was going to buy it, but he offered Roger a beer and sat patiently on an overstuffed chair in his living room as Roger convinced himself--breaking the shotgun open and holding it up to the ceiling light, to see from one end to the other, trying the pump action, putting the stock up to his shoulder, swinging the gun as if he were following a bird, sighting down the barrel.

****

Lena watched TV while the twins played concentration with a deck of cards. Beside each of them was a small glass of milk and a saucer of peanut butter cookies. Earlier Lena had let them help her make the cookies (which she had regretted when Nick had knocked an open five-pound bag of sugar off the kitchen counter and onto the floor, spilling a third of it). The twins finished their game (Judith victorious) and they came over and sat down by Lena on the couch, one on each side, as they did when she read them stories. They lay their heads against her and watched the last fifteen minutes of "The Lawrence Welk Show."

As the Champagne Musicmakers played and the show's credits rolled, Nick jumped up, saying, "It sounds like the rain's stopping," and ran to switch on the front porch light and look out the screen door. "Yep, it is. Mom, can we go outside?"

"Nick, it's all wet out there. You'll come back in covered with mud from head to toe, I know it."

"Aw, come on, Mom," Judith pleaded, "let us go. Please."

"Mom, why don't you go with us?" Nick suggested.

"Yeah," Judith said, "then you can make sure we don't get muddy."

"Oh, all right, let's go. But you have to come in when I say to, OK?"

They readily agreed and the three of them walked out the front door and out onto the lawn. The twins wore thongs and the rain-wet grass was cool on their toes and the tops of their feet. Lena's white tennis shoes were soaked through before she'd gone twenty steps. Light gleamed from the front and back porchlights and the far brighter yardlight, mounted on the garage, suffusing the black-clouded June night with a soft, misty light. The deep green, heart-shaped leaves of the big purple lilac on the east end of the sun porch dripped and shone darkly. The short, usually dull-green leaves of the bridal veil bushes along the front of the house were wet and glimmery. Rainwater rilled off the leaves of the ash and the two apple trees along the fence on the north side of the yard and glittered on the leaves of the caragena hedge that ran the length of the east side of the yard. Everywhere along the fence wires and gates were sparks, shines, shimmers.

"Mom, what's making that splashing noise in the big puddle?" Judith asked.

They heard splishes and splashes, and as they got closer, they saw the water was full of rings and movement.

"It's toads!" Lena said.

"Oh, Mom, they're everywhere!" Nick half-shouted, opening the gate and running with Judith--tiny toads springing from their path--to the edge of the puddle. Lena followed and stood beside the twins who were squatting, looking at all the toads hopping in and out of the water and all around in the grass.

"Mom, isn't it wonderful!" Judith said.

"They must have been lying dormant in the ground, and all the rain woke them up," Lena said.

Judith and Nick caught two little toads in the grass and ran over and held them up for Lena to see.

They walked around the puddle, toads flying in all directions before them. Nick and Judith were shocked to see their mother walk right out to the middle of the puddle, and bend down and swirl the water with her hands, shooing the toads, and laughing. This was the mother who didn't want them to get muddy? But the twins didn't waste time puzzling this out. They waded after her into the puddle, which at its deepest rose halfway up their shins. The three of them chased toads through the water for the next ten minutes, laughing and giggling.

They heard a vehicle come down the county road from the east and saw its headlights as it crested a hill. No, there were two vehicles. A couple of minutes later, Roger and Ben Vogel parked their pickups on the grass beside the Larkins' Nash Rambler.

"Lena, what are you and the kids doing out there?" Roger asked, walking toward them. He was genuinely surprised but a little too loud. He and Ben must have tipped back a few.

"Roger, where've you been. You left here three hours ago to 'get a few things' from the hardware store?" Lena walked out of the puddle and dried her hands on her Bermuda shorts. "The hardware store must sell Hamms now. Isn't that your brand, Ben?"

Her voice was pitched somewhere between a complaint and a chuckle. Roger loved her when she was like this.

"That's right," Ben said, laughing. He looked around, his eyes saying that he couldn't quite grasp what he was seeing. "Jesus, the toads out here are thicker'n hoppers in July."

Roger looked about, too. "This is amazing. There wasn't a single toad out here when I went to town." He turned back to Lena. "Now, Lena, let me explain. I tell you, you're going to love this."

"Oh I am, am I, " she said mock-chucking her husband under the chin, trying hard to keep from laughing. "Well, this had better be good. Damned good."

Roger took both her hands and held them in his own. "Come on over to the pickup. I've got something to show you. Sort of an early birthday present?"

At the pickup, Roger made Lena close her eyes. He opened the cab, took out a gun case, unzipped it, and slipped out the sixteen gauge.

"OK, you can look now."

"A gun? You got me a rifle?"

Roger laughed. "It's not a rifle, Lena. It's a shotgun."

"Roger, what the hell am I going to do with a shotgun?"

"Don't you remember? You wanted to go pheasant hunting with me in the fall."

"I said that, did I? I must have been trying to be nice."

"Well, for the next four months you and I are going to practice shooting skeet, and then when pheasant season starts at the end of October, we're going to go hunting. You're going to love it."

"Sure, Roger, and you can take a quilting class with me. I'm sure you'll love that."

"Now, come on, Lena, you can be a better sport than that. Trust me, you're going to love hunting."

"OK, Roger, but I'm putting you on warning. I'm still expecting a real birthday present."

"Whatever you say, Lena. Here, don't you want to hold it?" He held the shotgun out to her.

Lena accepted the gun. In the dim light by the truck, the stock and pump were dark brown as petrified wood and the barrel was black, with little sparkles streaking up and down its length. She held the gun up to her right shoulder.

"Doesn't it hurt when you shoot it?"

"Just a little kick. Hardly noticeable. It won't hurt at all."

"Not if you keep it tight against your shoulder," Ben said. "If you don't, it'll feel like a mule kicked you."

"You'd know about that, would you, Ben?" Lena asked.

Ben laughed. "Shit yes, I've been kicked by lots of mules. Just ask anybody. I'm famous for it."

Roger reached into the cab, took a box of shells off the seat. Lena handed him back the gun and he loaded half a dozen shells into it. He pumped one into the chamber.

"OK, Lena, now hold it tight against your shoulder. That's right. Point it up in that air that way." Lena aimed over the tops of the shelterbelt trees. "Put your finger on the trigger. Now, don't jerk the trigger to fire, just slowly squeeze it."

Blam. The gunshot echoed back from the buildings. Nick and Judith had been chasing toads in the puddle and they hadn't paid much attention to what their parents had been talking about. But when the shotgun went off, they jumped a foot straight up, then ran over to find out what was going on.

"Good job, Lena, you did that just right," Roger said.

"Yeah, I'll bet you scared some crows half to death," Ben said. "You do have crows in those trees, don't you?"

"Is the Pope Catholic?" Roger said. "Watch it, kids, this gun is loaded."

"Oh, Dad, can I shoot it?" Judith asked.

"Let me, Dad, let me," Nick begged.

"Maybe in a few years."

"But you let Mom shoot it."

"Well, she's a lot bigger than you guys."

"That's right, guns are dangerous things," Lena said.

"Then why did you buy it, Dad?" Judith asked.

"So your mama can go hunting with me."

"What are you going to hunt?" Nick asked.

"Pheasants. But right now we're going to go shoot us some crows."

"What?" Lena exclaimed. "Just how many beers did you have, Roger?"

"Can we come? Can we come?" the twins begged excitedly.

"Nope, you kids stay here. Catch yourselves a few more toads. Those crows are real wicked birds. No telling what they'll do once we start shooting them. It's best if you guys stay over here where it's safe."

"That's right," Ben said, "and if you hear us screaming out in the trees, you run for the house and shut all the doors and windows." Ben was carrying a fresh six-pack. The beer must have been for first-aid.

"OK, Lena, let's go blast us some crows," Roger said.

They walked down the path that ran between the garage and the barn on one side and the chicken house and a pyramidal stack of bales on the other. They stepped into the shelterbelt trees.

Apprehensively, the twins watched them vanish into the dark of the trees. After a couple of minutes they heard a shotgun blast. They listened keenly and heard more shots, then a silence.

"Dad's reloading," Nick said.

"How can they see any crows to shoot them?"

"I don't know. Big people must have a way to do that."

They heard another blam. A pause, then, blam, blam. It went on like that for half an hour, as the twins watched the trees (seeing nothing) and waited. Sometimes laughter followed the blasts, so the twins figured their parents were winning the war with the crows.

When Roger, Lena, and Ben reappeared around the edge of the garage, Nick and Judith went running up to them. No Hamms were in sight.

"Dad, did you kill all the crows?" Nick asked

"I think a few of the sneakier ones got away, but we got most of them. Wouldn't you say so, Lena?"

She laughed. "You bet, Roger."

They all walked toward the house. "What did you do with all the dead ones?" Judith asked. "How come you didn't bring any back with you?"

"No need to, Judith," Roger said. "Crows are nasty eating."

"That's right, just awful," Ben said, chuckling. "You can't get worse eating than a crow. We buried them all in one big mound."

"Ben, let's have us a beer," Roger said. "That crow-killing works up a powerful thirst."

"You got it," Ben said.

"And you kids, it's time for bed now," Lena said.

The twins complained halfheartedly. But they knew they'd already been allowed to stay up much longer than usual. As they fell asleep, they
heard the three adults laughing in the kitchen, where they sat around the Formica table with their beers.

****

Early the next morning, before breakfast, Judith and Nick got dressed and ran out to the shelterbelt. They wanted to see the big mound where the crows were buried. They ran down every row of trees and even checked the ditch between the shelterbelt and the road, but nowhere did they find the crow burial mound. They noticed that there were still lots of crows in the trees. It was hard to say if there were as many as yesterday, but there were a lot. They figured most of them must be newcomers, fresh recruits, who hadn't heard about the big massacre.

When Judith asked their father the location of the mound at breakfast, he laughed and said, "Judith, honey, you didn't really think we killed all those birds, did you?"

"Well, Dad, that's what you said."

"I was just joking, Judith. All we did was scare them a little while we tried out your mom's new gun."

Nick felt both happy that they crows had not been shot and disappointed that he and Judith had been fooled so badly. He consoled himself the rest of the morning by chasing toads and planning how he was going to capture a crow and train it.

****

The next fall and winter, while the Larkin family was living in a tiny trailer in Red Earth, where Roger and Lena were going back to college, the crows began mysteriously to diminish in numbers in the area around their farm. And when the Larkins returned the following May, only a handful of crows haunted their trees. All of the smaller birds had returned. The crow invasion was over.

The toads were gone, too, but hard ruts, several inches deep, remained in the driveway where the big puddle had been. As long as Nick and Judith lived on the farm, they never saw a similar explosion of toads, never in fact saw more than a random toad or two, hopping through the grass or the garden. But the memory of wading after the hundreds and hundreds of toads in the puddle that night with their mother, as rain drops glistened on the grassblades and along the strands of the woven-wire fence and dripped from the leaves of the trees and bushes--that memory would stay in their brains, magical and mysterious, the rest of their lives.

Chapter 6
Big Bill Burdette

The last Saturday in July of Nick and Judith's eighth year, the combiners nervously anticipated by their father arrived at the farm, like some traveling summer theater troupe that gave performances in public parks, using a flatbed truck for a stage. Roger was anxious to get his wheat out of his fields and to the Erickson Bros. Elevator in town before the price, which had climbed to $2.25 a bushel, fell, or before his near-thirty-bushel-an-acre crop got hailed out. Only thirty miles away, farmers had lost crops to hail the previous two weeks. Roger worried because he hadn't bought hail insurance.

But the combiners had come--the same ones Roger had hired the last three years--had worked their way north from Oklahoma, through Kansas and Nebraska first, had worked their way methodically and inexorably northwards on a journey that would take them through the rest of the Dakotas and well up into Saskatchewan. Big Bill Burdette's group had parked their weather-beaten, dull silver, twenty-five-foot trailers in an empty lot shared by several combine crews.

Nick and Judith had ridden along with their father several days before, when he'd driven in to hire Bill. Knowing he would be in the fields from daylight till dusk, they arrived late in the evening, leaving the car next to Bill's two dusty Dodge pickups, which still gave off heat from the long day in the fields, and his blue '55 Buick, with the dented left door and the giant fins. Bill had parked his three trailers under a shady stand of ninety-foot cottonwoods. The trees were still releasing their tiny seed parachutes, and once-snowy cottonwood seeds were trampled everywhere into the dirt of the lot.

As he and his sister jumped out of the cab of his father's dark green '49 Ford pickup, Nick noticed that not far away some other combiners had put a red-and-white '56 Chevy with a badly cracked windshield up on blocks and were working on it. Two men lay on their backs under the car and a thirteen- or fourteen-year-old kid was on his knees, leaning over and shining a flashlight on the problem site. He drifted a bit and one of them yelled at him to get that goddamned light back where they were working and keep it there.

As Big Bill opened the screen door and put his weight on the trailer's extended metal step, the twins saw his cowboy-booted foot depress the step a couple of inches. Domenico Modugno's "*Nel Blue Dipinto Di Blu*," better known as "*Volare*"--the song that had won not long before the first-ever Grammy for best record--floated out from a radio inside and the smell of fried chicken, American fries, sweet corn, cornbread, and buttermilk biscuits filled the air. Big Bill shifted his sweating, half-empty bottle of Budweiser from his right to his left hand, extended the right, vice-gripped Roger's hand, and gave it a jolting shake, a shake that sent visible tremors across Roger's shoulderblades.

"I'd been expecting you, Roger," Bill drawled, making the name sound like rajah. "The missus had begun to wonder if maybe you'd hired somebody else this year, but I said, 'nope, you jes wait, Roger'll be stopping by any time now.' And here you are. And look, you brought the mites along, too. I swear you two younguns look so much alike, if your sister didn't have longer hair, little brother, nobody'd be able to tell you apart, not even your mama."

All this time Bill had been jerking Roger's arm up and down as if he were pumping water from a well, and Roger had been trying to say a simple hello. At last, as Bill relinquished his hand, Roger said, "It's good to see you, too, Bill."

Then Bill was off again, talking in his *basso profundo* voice that rolled up out of his massive girth and poured from the distant height of his wide, ever-smiling mouth, smashing down on the people below him like an avalanche of boulders. He was called Big Bill for good reason. In his underwear Bill stood an even six-five and pushed the scales up over four fifty. Bill didn't weigh himself with any frequency, but when he did, someone else had to read the scale for him because his belly, the product of many thousands of bottles and cans and glasses of beer and his wife LilyAnn's high-caloric cooking, prevented him from seeing it. Bill wore a cream-colored straw cowboy hat, a royal blue western-cut shirt, Lee jeans, and a two-inch-wide leather belt, with BIG BILL carved in the back and with a huge silver buckle in the shape of a Texas longhorn in the front.

Blubber rolled over the buckle like mud sliding down a saturated hill, like floodwaters thrusting over a collapsing dam. Bill had the bulge of the Buddha, no, rather, of Bacchus, of Falstaff. The belt and buckle had been a Christmas gift from LilyAnn two years before, and Bill wore it with bottomless pride. Bill's size fourteen-double E brown boots were intricately sculpted, sides, back, and front, with white diamonds, whorls, and rococo loops. Bill loved those boots more than some men love their wives, and he kept them polished to the reflectiveness of a barroom mirror.

Sandwiching in words wherever he could--praying Bill would pause for breath--Roger managed to hire Bill and his crew to harvest three fields of winter wheat. In the process, he'd had to go inside and say hello to LilyAnn and Bill's four boys, Johnny, Jimmy, Jeremy, and Jasper--all younger than the twins but big for their ages and as wild in their play as young bobcats. He'd had to fend off an invitation to supper--"I tell you, Roger, you ain't lived till you've tasted LilyAnn's fried chicken. And those buttermilk biscuits of hers just melt in your mouth. I swear, eating one of her meals is like going to heaven. Better, by God, because you don't have to die first." Bill chortled, then said he already had several jobs lined up ahead of Roger, but he'd be out in three days.

* * * * * * *

Bill and his crew pulled two big flatbed trucks, a gleaming red International Harvester combine chained to the back of each, two GMC grain trucks, also painted barn red (with gold, whiskery wheat head designs painted on their sides and back), and a pickup down into the stubblefield across the road from the Larkin farmhouse. They backed one truck at a time up to the approach and drove the combines off onto the gravel county road. Sixty yards to the south they turned down an approach that led into a hundred-acre field on the Larkins' side of the road.

Wearing his straw hat and green-lensed sunglasses, Bill looked like a god atop the number one combine. In him the huge machine had found its predestined driver, a driver that was its match in physical power, energy, and endurance--though he'd had to replace the standard seat with a wider, heavy-duty steel seat (and a double thick cushion), guaranteed to support a weight of up to five hundred pounds. His combine's well-honed blades cut a twelve-foot swath into the yellow-gold wheat, masticated it, sprayed the seeds into the hopper, and spewed the chaff out the rear.

Ray Donovan, Bill's right-hand man for many years, and at twenty-eight the oldest of his crew (and the only other married man), drove the number two combine, cutting the next swath in, several hundred yards behind Bill. When one of them had a hopper full, either Billy Joe Campbell, all of nineteen, or Eddy Stewart, eighteen, drove a red grain truck up alongside, the spout was lowered from the combine, and a shower of gold-orange wheat seeds flew into the back of the truck, making a conical pile. After the grain started to get deep, either Bobby Murphy or Jimmy Baines, both seventeen, would jump into the back with grain shovels and scoop and spread the grain out as it rained in. While their machines were being emptied, Bill and Ray took swigs of ice water from gallon jugs (often Bill pulled a can of Budweiser from the ice of a small cooler and guzzled it down), and, when the need arose, walked behind their combines to urinate--though later in the day they were more likely just to step a few paces away and turn their backs. When a truck was filled, Roger rode with it into town to the elevator to sell his grain, and the other truck took over in the field.

Roger would make that ten-mile trip to the elevator several times that day, sometimes taking one of the twins with him. Only the building anticipation of the big check at the end kept him from an awful boredom. There was, after all, only so much a person could talk about with either Billy Joe or Eddy, who were considerably more terse in their speech than Bill. Their summer working for Bill (a subject soon exhausted), their girlfriends (or lack thereof), the glories of their days tearing up the gridiron in high school, and what they planned to do with their earnings when they got back home to Oklahoma (buy better cars, of course)--that about did it for conversation with Billy Joe and Eddy.

Bill and Ray kept their combines steadily chewing great mouthfuls of the blond wheat. They took no breaks other than those few moments when their hoppers were being emptied. If Bill got hungry, and he did at least once an hour, he grabbed one of the ham sandwiches LilyAnn had prepared for him or a package of Snoballs or a package of pretzels or beer nuts and gulped it down. Nick was amazed once to see Bill pop a whole Snoball into his mouth.

Promptly at noon, LilyAnn and Ruth Sanders (who earnestly told everyone she was Ruth Donovan, Ray's wife, and who kept her hands in motion or in her pockets as much as possible when talking to people so as not to be asked why she wore no wedding ring) wheeled Bill's blue Buick and his other pickup into the field and drove over to the truck to wait for Bill and Ray to finish their rounds. Bill's boys immediately jumped out of the pickup and ran over and climbed into the back of the grain truck. They tromped around in the wheat, grabbed handfuls, let it cascade through their fingers, then lay back and began to cover themselves in wheat.

Roger had always thought that LilyAnn looked like a woman who had once been a wild girl, but one who had fallen into some good luck. She stood five-four, had a head full of long blond curls, wore a rose-crimson shirt with the first three buttons undone, revealing the pale, shapely curve of her breasts, white shorts tight enough to appear to have been painted on her, and red sandals. Her long scarlet fingernails matched her earrings, shirt, and sandals. She wore a trace of rouge and bright carmine lipstick. Her thin arching eyebrows were, on second look, not real but drawn on with an eyebrow pencil. The diamond wedding ring on her left ring finger looked heavy enough to build muscles. She wore a floppy straw hat and black-framed, blue-lensed sunglasses, to protect her fair skin and eyes from the sunlight.

In two big picnic baskets in the back seat, LilyAnn and Ruth had packed a lunch of hot roast beef, fresh potato salad and cole slaw, sweet and dill pickles, steamed green beans slick with melted butter, hot cornbread biscuits, iced tea, and a choice of desserts--sourcream-raisin pie or chocolate cake. The two women shook out two blue-and-white checked tablecloths and laid them on the wheat stubble. They quickly laid out the food and called the men over. Roger ate with them (he had warned Lena that Bill would be mortally offended if Roger refused the invitation to break bread with him and his crew) and he was astounded at how fast the ample larder vanished into the voracious maws of the threshers. Roger had been raised in a small family so the experience of grabbing for food before it disappeared was new.

Bill was never unappreciative when it came to food, so throughout the meal he effusively praised LilyAnn's cooking--"I swear, LilyAnn, you have simply outdone yourself here. I don't believe I've ever tasted roast beef this tender before," or "Don't this cornbread just have the most perfect texture, Ray? I mean LilyAnn's cornbread is always superior, but this here is perfection itself," or "LilyAnn, this chocolate cake is truly one of God's greatest gifts to mortal man. I mean, you boys better praise your Maker for the bounty of a piece of cake like this--say, honey, why don't you slip another piece on my plate here--no, that big one over there,"--and he ended with a statement of sustained praise, just before he lit up a Winston, pulled the tab on a Budweiser, and relaxed into postprandial bliss.

Roger wasn't sure what puzzled him more, how Bill could eat so much so fast and still keep up an almost unbroken panegyric to LilyAnn's culinary talents and patter of smalltalk about the morning's work--"This field's looking mighty good, Roger, ain't that so, Ray? I swear this is about the purtiest little hundred-acre wheatfield I've seen since Kansas, wouldn't you say that's so, Billy Joe? Just look how thick it is and how big those heads are, Eddy. You see that? I don't even have to ask Roger here how it's lookin' at the elevator. If I know one thing in this wide world it's a wheatfield, and I'd say this is a twenty-seven, twenty-eight bushel-an-acre field, if I've ever seen one"--or, just as amazing, how LilyAnn could have single-handedly prepared all that fine food in a kitchen no bigger than a good-size closet back in Bill's trailer (Ruth's main job was to watch the boys and keep them from underfoot). Roger did his part to praise the food, too, as did all the members of the crew and Bill's four boys (though, admittedly, none of them with the eloquence or at the length of Bill), not out of mere politeness, but because it truly was toothsome.

After the last of Bill's eulogies to the lunch subsided, Roger, happy with the way the crop was looking and feeling like he should do something to respond in kind to Bill's generosity, invited Bill and his whole troupe to barbecue steaks and hamburgers at the house that night--not neglecting to mention that he'd also pick up a couple of cases of Bill's favorite brew on the next trip to town. Of course, Bill insisted that the meal be potluck (though he never used that exact word) and that LilyAnn help Lena prepare it. LilyAnn was markedly enthusiastic about the idea, perhaps because it would mean that for one night at least she would have someone to help her in her labors (and in a real kitchen! with a full-size oven!), but also because it would mean some real feminine companionship for a change. Ruth never seemed to have much to say, so Roger imagined LilyAnn's life on the road must be a fairly lonely one. It was agreed, then, grilled steaks that night at the Larkins'.

* * * * * * *

Big Bill and his crew finished in the fields late that afternoon. They loaded up and drove their machinery back into town, showered, changed clothes, and were back at the Larkin farm by quarter after six. Roger had just touched match to his pyramids of lighter-fluid-doused charcoal briquettes--one in the round grill that stood on its tripod of thin aluminum legs and one in the hibachi--and was watching the initial high flarings of yellow-orange subside to a quivering blue-yellow flame that clung lambently to the coals, when Bill's two pickups pulled in and parked next to his Buick.

"Roger, I don't see any steaks on those grills of yours yet. How long before we put on the feedbag?"

"We weren't sure when you'd get here, Bill, but the women have everything just about ready in the kitchen. And when this charcoal gets hot, we'll see about firing up those steaks."

"Well, in that case, direct me to where I might find that Budweiser you bought with the money from that fine crop of wheat we harvested today. After a long day in the field, baking on that combine in ninety-degree heat, I need me a few gallons of something cold."

Roger suspected Bill had already made a good half-gallon or better start on quenching his thirst.

"It's in the blue ice chest over by the picnic table, Bill." Roger motioned toward the table. "It's jampacked with cans, just waiting for you."

"You see there, Ray? You see, this Eddy and Billy Joe? This man knows how to receive a guest. I tell you, Jimmy and Bobby, he knows that God invented beer for a reason. And that reason was for the solace and pleasure of hard-working men like you and me."

Roger led Bill and Ray and the boys over to the chest and pulled each of them out a beer, even the seventeen-year-olds. He knew Bill wouldn't care and he figured they'd earned it. He took one out for himself and closed the metal lid. There were the sounds of seven tabs being pulled, of assorted swigs and gurgles, of seven sighs of satisfaction.

LilyAnn and Lena had washed the long redwood picnic table, laid two white cloths over it, and set it with places for the adults and the teenagers. Two card tables (one borrowed by Lena from the Wilcoxes) had been set up nearby and places laid for each of the six Larkin and Burdette kids--who were playing statue by the swing-and-slide-set at the other end of the yard. LilyAnn and Ruth brought out trays of sweet, dill, and butter pickles, black and green olives, pickled beets, celery and carrot sticks, cucumber slices (edges trimmed so they looked like little sprockets), deviled eggs, juice-dripping tomato slices, cherry tomatoes, onion slices, and bottles of catsup, mayonnaise, mustard, and sweet relish and arranged them in the middle of the big table, where gravy boats of French, thousand island, and Italian dressing (recently poured from bottles), little bowls of homemade onion and garlic dip, big bowls of potato chips and pretzels, salt and pepper shakers, butter dishes, and pint canning jars of wild Oregon grape, raspberry, and chokecherry jelly were already to be found.

"Ah, now, don't this look good?" Bill said, as he made for the food, moving gracefully as a panther and surprisingly quickly for such a big man. He snatched up four cherry tomatoes and two deviled eggs and popped them into his mouth before anyone could blink.

"Bill, you keep your paws off this food, you hear?" LilyAnn chided.

"Aw, sugar, I was just takin' a little taste. And I do say, those eggs are dee-licious! Did you make those?"

"No, Lena did. And don't think you can bribe me with flattery. You just wait till everything's ready before you begin."

"What's a couple little deviled eggs, LilyAnn?"

"You know perfectly well, if we let you, you'd have this whole table licked bare before supper even got started."

"She's got you there, boss," Ray interjected, laughing. The boys nodded at each other in agreement.

"You guys ain't s'posed to take her side!" Bill complained. "This hurts, I tell you, this hurts. I'd expected greater loyalty from my hand-picked crew."

"Bill, the lady's done nailed you to the wall," Billy Joe said, scarcely able to suppress a giggle.

"She's got you dead to rights this time," Eddy said. Nods and chuckles said this was the consensus. Bill took a long swallow of beer.

"OK, boys," LilyAnn said, "I'm trusting you to keep him away from this food while Ruthie and I go back inside and help Lena finish up."

* * * * * * *

The dinner was truly extraordinary. T-bone and sirloin steaks, ten whole chickens, hamburgers, hot dogs, and catfish and walleye pike filets; mashed potatoes (peeled, cut up, boiled and mashed, since neither Lena nor LilyAnn ever made instant), hashbrowns, cooked peas and pearl onions, green and wax beans, sweet corn, asparagus, and broccoli with cheese sauce; potato salad, cole slaw, and three-bean and tossed salads; sourdough and buttermilk biscuits and cornbread. To drink there was milk and ice tea and beer. For dessert they had strawberry shortcake, buried in fresh-made whipped cream, chocolate cake, blueberry and apple pie a la mode, and tart gooseberry pie for the adventurous.

During the dinner, everyone kept up a happy chatter, but afterwards, as Big Bill and LilyAnn smoked their Winstons, Ray his Camels, and Ruth her Salems, they all sank into a satisfied torpor. For a time nobody spoke; even the kids sat still at the card tables in their tall, hardbacked walnut chairs, brought out from the dining room. Then Bill began to speak, and since no one else had the energy to talk, they all turned their heads and listened to him.

"Roger, did I ever tell you the story of the time me and my combine got picked up by a big twister? No? You kids give a listen. You'll like this story. It was years ago and we had made it nearly all the way through Kansas, almost up to the Nebraska border. We were working for a farmer name of Eldon Brinley, who had two full sections of land and half of it in wheat.

"The afternoon of our second day in Brinley's fields, we were harvesting fast as we could because thunderstorms were forecast for late afternoon. Around three o'clock a whole line of clouds appeared in the west and we knew we were going to have a race on our hands to finish the field we were working on. All you had to do was look at those clouds and you knew they were mean. They were an ugly gray, the color of a dead fish, and they were all streaked-like with black, the color of axle grease.

"We burned through those fields faster'n a prairie fire, and we'd no sooner dumped our hoppers than we were back again blazin' away. But those ugly clouds, they kept comin' and buildin' upwards and solidifyin' themselves, until they were all one massive connected wall of stormcloud.

"There had been a decent breeze but all at once it up and died. It just came to a sudden halt, stopped right there in the middle of the field as if it had slammed smack up against some invisible building. It was eerie, I mean to tell you. Then the air, which had been kind of a dirty-water gray, turned this sickly green color, the color of one of those really awful bruises. It was the weirdest weather I ever saw. We ran those combines just as fast as their engines could propel them through the field. It was going to be close.

"Then this cold wind came up real hard, and fast, and furious. It was like a giant dam of wind had broken, and the winds backed up for miles behind that dam had all come swooshing down through the breach. The first blast of that chilly wind ripped the hat and sunglasses right off my head and purt near knocked me off my combine. I never did find that hat, I might add, and it was a particular favorite of mine. But I just gripped the wheel of that combine hard as I could--I mean I was white-knuckling it--and kept it headed down the edge of the wheat. My hair was blowing straight back from my head and my shirt was shivering in the wind. I was determined to beat that storm.

"All of a sudden, there it was, three hundred yards in front of me. It was as if the bottom of that gray-black wall of cloud had just torn out and dangled down like a tail, wobbled a bit, and then righted itself and stood up--as a hundred-foot-tall tornado. Now I'm what most people would call a big man, and I drive a big machine, but that twister was really big. It made me feel small, and I'd never felt small before in my life.

"I turned my combine hard right and made for the edge of the field, thinking maybe it would come straight ahead and I could dodge it--kind of like faking out a linebacker in football. But it didn't go straight. No, it leaned and staggered like it was drunk, and then it jumped and hopped around like a saddle bronc in a rodeo, no, more like a Brahma bull . . . you know, real strong and mean and scary. One minute it was behind me, the next minute ahead of me.

"And the noise of that thing. You ain't never heard nothing like it, I can tell you. People say it's like a freight train, and it is, but that ain't the half of it. It's like ten freight trains, each one bearing right down on you and no way you can escape--maybe from one, but not from all ten. The noise of that twister alone was like to make me wet my pants. I was 'most paralyzed with fear. I couldn't take my eyes off that tornado, not to save my life. I didn't even know what I was doin' any more.

"It was no more than twenty yards away when it just stooped-like down toward me. The noise got deafening, and then my machine and I began to tip and it was like we kind of floated a second, and then that twister swallered us. I tell you, it just up and ate us whole, like one of those giant pythons from South America. It was like I was flyin' in an airplane, or more like flyin' in a helicopter. At least what I think it would be like flyin' in a helicopter, since I ain't never had the chance to go up in one of those yet. I couldn't see nothing at all. I couldn't tell which way was up, down, right, or left. There was nothin' but ferocious black wind everywhere. It felt so smothery I could hardly get my breath. Now I wasn't thinkin' about time at all, so I can't tell you how much time passed. But it was more than a little, I tell you.

"Then bang,"--Bill slapped the picnic table hard and everybody jumped--"my machine and I were set down, and before I knew what was happening, that twister leaped back up into the cloud, just leaped up, as if it had been sucked back up through some big straw you couldn't see.

"I was on some section-line road, and it was pouring rain. It was a real gullywasher, as if the sky were this big tarp full of water that someone'd come along and sliced a hole in. I didn't recognize the land at all. I had no idea where that twister might have taken me. So I just drove my combine down that muddy road, slippin' and slidin', doing my best not to get stuck, until I came to a farm. I pulled in, got down, my legs still kind of rubbery, and knocked on the door. I had to knock and knock before somebody finally came up out of the basement to answer it. First thing I wanted to know was where I was.

"This farmer asked me whose place I was lookin' for. I said the Eldon Brinley place, figurin' it must be just a piece down the road. They said, 'why, Good God, man, you're really lost. That's ten miles to the westa here. And what are you doin' out in this weather anyway. Don't you know there's tornadoes around?"

Bill broke up at that. Everyone else laughed too. Bill laughed so hard tears came to his eyes. He tried to talk through his laughing, but he couldn't, and when he finally regained enough control to try again, his voice was high-pitched and unsteady. "That's what he said." Bill laughed, caught himself up short. "That's what he said, 'Don't you know there's tornadoes around?'" Bill cracked up again.

After a bit, he said, looking right at Nick and Judith, "And that's the story of how I flew ten miles in a twister. And every word of that story's the God's truth. Say, LilyAnn, would you snag me another of those Buds? Tellin' that story, my mouth has got all dry."

LilyAnn got Bill a beer from the blue chest, and as she handed it to him, said, "Bill, why don't you tell them about the time you almost got hit by a meteor?"

Bill took a long guzzle from the Bud, set it down, and was off again. And that story was followed by the one in which Bill's car--the red Buick he'd had before the current one--had been struck by lightning. And that one had been followed by the time Bill had been visiting one of his brothers up in Alaska and had got caught in an earthquake his first night there. Bill's stories all appeared to have a common theme: how he kept getting himself caught up in natural disasters that would humble even a big man like himself. Bill was a better performer than any tent preacher, and he had everyone with him the whole way through every story. The twins thought he was about the best entertainment they'd had in a good while. They wondered if maybe their dad couldn't adopt Bill--and his family too, of course. Couldn't very well leave them out.

By the time Bill stopped for a breather, it had been dark for a good half hour. The night was absolutely clear and the Milky Way was spread out like a banner overhead. The twins got one of their dad's blue wool Air Force blankets and laid it out in the middle of the yard. They lay down on it with Bill's boys and studied the stars.

"See that big star there." Nick pointed to the edge of the sky. "That's Vega. It's in the constellation Lyra."

"How do you know that?" seven-year-old Jeremy asked.

"My dad taught me. He was a pilot in the Air Force during the Korean War, and he knows about jet planes and constellations and the moon, and all kinds of things."

"All our dad ever taught us was the big and little dippers," six-year-old Jimmy said.

"Well, that's a start," Nick said.

"That's the big dipper right up there," Johnny said. At four, he was proud of his smattering of astronomical knowledge.

"Where?" Jasper asked. Only three, he hadn't been properly educated yet.

"Right there, dummy," Johnny said, "the one that looks like a dipper."

"See those five bright stars that kind of form a 'W'? That's Cassiopeia," Judith said.

"Did she say that right, Nick?" Jimmy asked.

"Yep."

Jimmy turned and looked at Judith as if he was having an epiphany. "Man, she must be smart."

"Yeah, I guess," Nick said. "Now, see that spidery bunch of stars just down and to the right of Cassiopeia? That's Andromeda."

After a long while of staring up at the lustrous spillway of stars, Judith and Nick began to see the stars wink and swirl and waltz, and they began to feel their thoughts waltz and swirl as well, until they thought they were up and the stars were down, and then the twins were free-falling toward them, ever and forever toward them. There was only so much of that one could take, however, without getting vertigo, so the twins got up to see what the adults were doing.

* * * * * * *

Nick and Judith slipped unobtrusively--easy in the dark--between the two loose but distinct circles of lawnchairs, one composed of adults, the other of teenagers. Big Bill was sitting in one of the wooden dining room chairs because there was not a lawn chair made that could support him. Everyone was drinking.

"May I taste your beer, Billy Joe?" Judith asked quietly.

"Sure, sweetheart, you take as much as you want."

Judith did and she saw, in a way that had nothing to do with mere eyesight, a tall, muscular man with a ring scar on his right cheek. He had a pack of cigarettes rolled up in the left sleeve of his white T-shirt, and on that arm's biceps he had a war eagle tattoo. He was in the bedroom of a small house and he was yelling at a woman with long, stringy brown hair. He backhanded her, whack, and then slapped her fast back the other way. He punched her hard several times in the face and chest, and blood spurted from her nose and trickled from a break in her bottom lip. She dropped to the floor and the man, calling her a "whore" and a "bitch" and other names, kicked her twice, once in the belly and once in the ribs before Billy Joe, three years younger than he was now, flung open the door and came running at the man, yelling, "You sonofabitch, you leave her alone."

Billy Joe swung at the man, but he sidestepped easily and hit Billy Joe in the stomach, doubling him over. He uppercut the boy and laid him out next to his mother. He kicked her twice more in the ribs, lurched a bit, regained his balance, and then, as he was leaving, kicked the boy in the kidneys. He walked out of the room and out of the house, leaving the front door wide open. Without knowing how she knew, Judith knew the man was not Billy Joe's father, that he was in fact a man who had picked up Billy Joe's mother in a honkeytonk earlier that same night. Judith also knew they'd never seen him again.

Nick took a long glug from Eddy's beer and he saw Eddy driving an ancient John Deere tractor, its once bright corn-green paint faded and dirty, the tracks of its big back tires worn down, its little front tires nearly bald. Eddy was maybe fourteen. He wore torn-and-patched blue jeans and a sweat-stained straw hat with frayed edges, but no shirt. He was pulling a disc through a forty-acre field, his six-year-old sister Janey standing at his left side, holding with one hand onto the headlight mounted on the fender. Behind them, the big round blades of the disc sliced through the brown weedy earth, leaving a rich black path behind. Eddy was singing Elvis' "Love Me Tender," singing it loudly so Janey could hear over the racket of the engine. He was looking at her and singing, and she was smiling.

Then the tractor jolted hard, the front tires bounced up like a horse rearing at the sight of a snake, and Eddy lost control of the steering wheel. The little tires clumped down on the other side of the big rock and the left rear tire struck it. That side instantly rose up, and, laboring, the tractor began to crawl up over it. Janey lost her grip and fell backwards, screaming. Eddy reached for her, missed, yanked the emergency brake and jammed the foot brake to the floor. The tractor stopped, but not in time.

Judith asked Ruth if she could have a sip of her beer and, without saying a word, Ruth held it out. Judith drank several big swallows, saw naked, sweaty bodies writhing together in a lumpy double bed of a down-on-its-luck motel in the middle of Kansas, writhing like the snakes on a caduceus. The sheets were soaked; the worn-out bedsprings whined and screaked to their rhythm, faster, faster, till the man, Ray, cried out as if his chest had been cut open and his heart removed, and he collapsed for the third time upon Ruth, who gasped and hugged him tight. They had met earlier in the evening when Ray had eaten at the diner she waitressed in. That had been about three weeks before they arrived at the Larkin farm.

Nick begged Ray for a drink, and Ray said, "Finish it, kid." His can was more than a third full. Nick saw nothing but blackness, blackness deep and cold as space--space without stars. Ray felt annoyance at Ruth's often embarrassing ignorance, irritation at her silliness, at her quirky little habits and ways, vexation at her childlike dependency, resentment at her increasing possessiveness, bitterness at her manifest stupidity (why hadn't he seen it before?), fear that Bill or LilyAnn or one of the boys might tell her that he was married, anxiety that she might do something crazy, like call up his wife, anger that she should have put him in this position. He had to get rid of her. He'd been a fool to let her stay with him this long. They were leaving in the morning. He'd wait till they were ready to hit the road, then tell her straight out she wasn't coming. He'd get in his flatbed truck and drive off. It was easy. He'd done it plenty of times before.

Judith stood for a moment beside LilyAnn's chair, listening to her give Lena the recipe for her sourcream-raisin pie. When Lena started to talk, Judith touched LilyAnn's arm and asked softly if she could have a sip of her beer. Equally softly, LilyAnn said, "You go right ahead, honey," and turned back to Lena. Judith was surprised to find the can warm and nearly full. Judith took drink after drink, saw a pregnant LilyAnn seven-and-a-half years before, when she was nearly eighteen, three years younger than Bill.

LilyAnn had just carried a washtub half-full of boiling water from her kitchen stove out onto the thin grass of her back yard. A hatchet rested on a chopping block a few feet away. She grabbed up one of the hens pecking in the dirt a few paces away, laid it on the block, and with one quick, expert stroke, severed head from body. She stood back, and while the dead chicken raced off through the yard, blood fountaining from its neck, calmly went after another hen. In just a few minutes she had eight dead chickens soaking in the steaming washtub to loosen their feathers, to make plucking easier. The smell of scorched feathers hung in the air already ripe with blood. She and Bill were expecting his parents and two brothers any time, and she wanted to barbecue those chickens for supper.

The phone rang and LilyAnn went inside to answer it. Half a minute after she'd gone in, fifteen-month-old Bill Jr. toddled out through the screen door, waddle-walked right over to the tub, leaned over to look at the strange chickens floating there, and fell in. A minute later, LilyAnn stepped outside and screamed at the sight of her scalded boy.

Nick waited a bit for Big Bill to stop talking, so he could ask for a drink from his beer, but deciding Bill wasn't going to stop any time soon and thinking Bill wouldn't miss it, he picked up Bill's half-full can and walked off with it. He saw Bill, dressed in a black suit, get down on one knee beside a freshly dug grave, cup a handful of dirt in his meaty hand and drop it onto a tiny casket. Bill bent his chin down to his chest as if he were about to pray, but instead, he broke into an uncontrollable sobbing. LilyAnn came forward, pressed his head against her waist, then took him by one hand, lifted him up, and led him away.

A shifting kaleidoscope of bars and package stores; solitary boozing in his living room, in his kitchen, on his porch, in his car, walking down dark country roads; drinking with family and friends on any and every occasion, whether anyone else was drinking or not; drinking double or triple what anyone else drank when they were. And always LilyAnn to help him out of his clothes and put him to bed, or to put a pillow under his head and cover him with a blanket when he passed out on the couch.

* * * * * * *

Lena walked around the side of the house, looking for the twins, and saw them on all fours, throwing up in the grass. "Roger!" she called, alarmed. When he appeared, she was holding the twins in her arms and dabbing at their mouths with a handkerchief.
"Roger, these kids are drunk!"
"What? Drunk? You're kidding."
But she wasn't. What Lena didn't know, of course, was that it was more the incomprehensible, involuntary torrent of images they'd had to swallow than the alcohol they'd imbibed that had made them sick.

* * * * * * *

The next morning Lena got the twins up early, fed them, made them take baths and dress up, and then she drove them into town for Sunday school. Roger and Lena had been at best hit-or-miss church attenders, but this summer Lena had taken the twins every week for a special series of Sunday school lessons. This was the final Sunday, and every child who'd attended the whole series was supposed to receive a certificate. She was determined that Nick and Judith would get their certificates. She warned the kids, under pain of death, not to say a single word about getting drunk the night before.

After the classes, Lena waited in their Rambler at the curb, as dozens of kids poured out of the church. Well-dressed parents were standing in groups all up and down the walk, waiting for their kids. There were the twins. They saw Lena and ran, clutching fancy pieces of paper in their hands, toward the car. Lena reached over and opened the door for them.

"Mom," they shouted together, about five feet from the car, "we were good! We didn't tell anyone we got drunk last night!"

Face burning as if she were too close to a furnace, Lena started the car, extended her arm like a vaudeville hook and swept the twins in. She reached past them, shut the door, slammed the Rambler into gear, and screeched her tires driving off. Neither Lena nor the twins ever set foot in that church again.

Nor did they ever see Big Bill or his family again. A week after leaving the Larkin farm, the truck Bill was driving (with his combine on the back) was struck by a train at an out-of-the-way rail crossing in North Dakota. Wreckage was strewn across the flat land for more than four hundred yards. The sun burned down from a cloudless sky; visibility could not have been better. The county coroner noted in his report--though he did not tell this to the hard-grieving but beautiful blond widow--that Bill had twice the legal limit of alcohol in his blood.

Long before the news of the terrible wreck got back to their farm, Judith and Nick knew what had happened. They realized, in fact, that Bill was dead the very instant the giant brake-screaching black locomotive smashed into the driver's side of his big red truck, caving in the door as if it was made of balsa wood, knocking the rig on its side and dragging it, wrecked combine and all, down the tracks. Bill had faced his last disaster.

Nick and Judith had run to the barn, climbed into a dark hole between hale bales, and cried for an hour, cried until they were drained dry of tears and hay dust scratched at their red eyes. They wept not only for Bill, not only for his wife LilyAnn and his four children, but also for themselves. For they knew that after their drunken harvest and the death of Big Bill, the world would never again be quite what it had once been for them. They knew they now inhabited some obscure, confused land, some dark, mysterious land the other side of simple childhood.

Part III

June 1970

Chapter 7
"A Hard Rain's A Gonna Fall"

In Nick's nineteen years he had never seen anything quite the like of Elizabeth Prescott, as she came gliding toward him, astride her green, three-speed Schwinn, down that wide sidewalk that ran along the northern edge of the campus, into sight and into his life.

Elizabeth's hair was long and auburn and, in the anarchistic fashion of those times, was frizzed out, making her look as if she had been struck by lightning. As she leaned into the breeze of her going, her hair blew like streamers, snapping, shedding sparks in the midday sun like a fireworks fountain. Nick saw a bright-charged nimbus about her head, a cloud of tiny lightnings.

Nick found two things peculiar about Elizabeth that day. First, that on a hot, humid afternoon she was wearing a red, popcorn-pattern wool sweater. And second, that propped on her shoulders, directly back of her head, squinting out through its small, almost human hands--its little arms making a strange victory chaplet--sat a raccoon.

Jon Arbalest, the tall renegade at Nick's side and one of the principle provocateurs of the University's protest rally over the shootings of four students at Kent State the month before, had waved to Elizabeth when she'd first come into sight. She swept down toward them, feet poised at the level, gears clicking in a manic staccato, and braked to a stop before Jon, slipping her sandaled feet off the pedals and placing them on the sidewalk. Without thinking, Nick smiled a smile that might have melted a long eve of January icicles--but that did not melt her. No, it merely haloed tenderly about her, flickered briefly in the air, and died away. Nick could only attribute it to lack of interest on her part.

Jon straightened himself and shifted his head, making a bit of a show of tossing his long lion's mane of blond curls behind him. He enjoyed the soft slap of his hair on his back and shoulders. Nick saw tight-braided yellow cables of hair shoot out twenty feet behind Jon and to both sides and anchor in the ground like tent ropes, pinioning him in a taut, intricate spiderweb. Then, zip, zip, zip, zip, and they'd retracted again. Jon stood two inches over six feet. He had a slim face, a high forehead, nearly invisible eyebrows, glittery, beryl-blue eyes that spoke more of seduction than sincerity, a skimpy mustache, and a spotty beard. It was evident that Jon not only knew this woman from some past from which Nick had been miserably excluded, but that he was ready to renew acquaintance.

Her hair! Nick thought, and since he had been reading Shelley, the simile, "Like the bright hair uplifted from the head of some fierce maenad," came to mind. Nick's sister Judith, who had in the last year taken up painting with fearsome passion, might have said that Elizabeth looked as if she had walked out of a Rossetti painting. Her brow was broad, her nose straight, her lips cupid-bowed and luscious. Nick saw himself meeting them with his own. Her eyes were hazel and so mutable in color and depth, they could suggest as much or as little as she wished, and at that moment, they were suggesting so little they might as well have been glass. She was two inches shorter than Nick.

"Elizabeth! How long's it been? A year?"

Elizabeth smiled coolly.

"About that, I guess, since I've lived here. I got back a few weeks ago." She added, "I'm taking a painting course at the University," to head off questions about the past.

The raccoon turned its head sideways, and Jon, bending his knees to lower himself to its height, turned his head sideways, too.

"I heard you were living in California."

"San Francisco."

Nick's ears tilted out, grew into bat ears: The San Francisco bands, especially the Dead and the Airplane, were his favorites.

"So, what was the scene like in Frisco? I'll bet there was lots of movement action there."

"There was a lot going on, but I was working. I didn't have much time for social activism."

"So, did you ever get to the Fillmore?"

She turned to Nick, smiled, extended her hand. "Hi, I'm Elizabeth Prescott."

Elizabeth had a firm grip. A brook trout broke surface in Nick's blood, dancing in a diamond spray atop the water. Before he could introduce himself, Jon blurted out, "Oh yeah, I forgot, this is Nick Larkin."

Nick offered her another incandescent smile.

Her smile was polite, no more. "Larkin? Like the British poet?"

"Yeah, I guess so." Nick was faltering, not having read his apparent namesake.

Jon bulldozed back in, "We're living on the same floor of the dorm this summer."

"Oh, not roommates, then?"

"No," Jon said, beating Nick out of the blocks, "we don't like each other well enough for that."

Jon grinned, meaning this as a joke, but Nick felt the blue-black, icy blade of truth in his words.

"In the summer," Nick leaped in--like a high jumper who's taken off on the wrong foot--explaining something too trivial to warrant explanation, "there's a lot of empty rooms in the dorms, so you can get a room to yourself for only a little more money."

Elizabeth nodded but Nick could see he was only a faint, peripheral blip on the weatherscreen of her afternoon.

"Elizabeth, you shoulda been here after Kent State," Jon said, playing his ace. "You'da loved it. I--"

"Yeah, I heard that you got everybody riled up enough to take over the Gym."

The ROTC Department had its offices, classrooms, storage cage, and target range on one end of the Blake Gymnasium.

Vanity stretched a grin on Jon's face. "Yeah, you should have seen it. It was beautiful. At the rally, we were hearing all these speeches telling us how horrified we should be and how we should recommit ourselves to the moral struggle to end the war--you know, the usual kind of bullshit, that everybody could feel good about agreeing with but that didn't ask anybody to actually do anything." He blazed right on, ignoring her look of disinterest. "So I got up and told them we ought to act, I mean, do something concrete to show that bastard Nixon our outrage. I said we had a physical symbol of the war machine right here on our own campus--the ROTC headquarters--and that we ought to march over right then and there and occupy the mother until the University agreed to abolish ROTC on this campus." Arbalest pronounced the dread military acronym so that it rhymed with Yahtzee.

"So, everybody got up and did just that, huh?"

"I wouldn't say quite everybody," Nick said, managing to dart into the conversation, like a pickpocket slipping through a crowded terminal.

"No, not everybody, Larkin, but at least half of those two thousand people got up off their asses and did something to show their disapproval of the war--most of them for the first time in their lives. It was the strongest statement of non-cooperation with the war we've ever seen on this campus."

"A bit warm, isn't it, for a sweater?" Nick asked.

Elizabeth looked down at her scarlet sweater and faded, patched, and embroidered jeans--a multi-colored chimera, a green Medusa, and a red Pegasus that looked like it had flown right off a Mobil sign--as if she had forgotten what she was wearing.

"Oh, it's to protect me from Heidegger's claws."

Jon frowned; he wanted to get back to bragging about his heroics at the Gym.

"Heidegger?" Nick asked.

"My raccoon. He likes to go riding with me, but I only took him once, for a *very short* ride, without something heavy on."

"You mean Heidegger, as in existential angst?" Nick asked.

"The same. It's sort of a family joke."

"You know," Jon said, "her father is Bill Prescott, the head of the Philosophy Department." Nick hadn't known. How could he have? "Remember, he spoke at the first Moratorium Day, and at the Kent State rally, too."

"I remember. He's an inspiring speaker." Nick immediately regretted
having said something so banal.

"Flattery's not necessary," Elizabeth said, smiling. "Actually, my dad's a phenomenologist, not an existentialist, but Heidegger's one of his real loves."

There was the slightest sear of battery acid around the edges of those last words, as if Elizabeth were not equally taken with the old master of our mortal anguish, or, perhaps, as if she resented the fact that over the years her father had sometimes seemed to spend more time with Kierkegaard, Heidegger, Husserl, Jaspers, and Sartre than he had with her sisters and her; or perhaps it was something else altogether.

"Heidegger's all right," Jon said, "but he's not exactly political."

"You can't say that," Elizabeth snapped back. "There are political implications to every new metaphysical position. A revolution in metaphysics is necessarily--"

"I'll take your word for it, Elizabeth," Jon said, chuckling. "I know better than to argue philosophy with you. So, where'd you get the raccoon, anyway?"

Jon was directing the conversation back to something not so likely to shift under his feet.

"Oh, our next door neighbor found a big female in his garage one night recently. And of course, being the sort of rigid, anti-natural person that he is, he shot her. But the next morning he found her two babies. He was all set to kill them too, but my sister Laura, who had heard him yelling at his wife to bring him his .22, came running over and begged him to let her have them. He didn't want to--he was convinced they'd get loose and ruin his garden--but she promised never to let them out of the house. They were so tiny Laura had to bottle-feed them at first. When I got back, Laura gave one to me."

"Looks like this one's flourished under your sister's care," Nick said.

"Yeah, he's a fat boy. Aren't you, Heidegger?" Elizabeth said, reaching a hand up to pat the raccoon. It turned its head, nipped playfully at her hand.

Jon, whose interest in Elizabeth had nothing remotely to do with raccoons, abruptly changed the subject again.

"Say, Elizabeth, what say you go with us to the big party out at the Freedom Farm tonight?"

Scarcely perceptibly, Elizabeth's eyes grew greenly cold. Nick felt chills run up his arms, saw frost emanating from Elizabeth's mouth as she breathed. She'd become a single, tall refrigeration coil.

"I guess I didn't hear about a party."

Elizabeth had just told a white lie.

"Well, now you have. How's about goin' with us?"

"Thanks, Jon, not this time."

"Come on, Elizabeth, there'll probably be people there that you haven't seen since you left last year."--Elizabeth's eyes grew colder; ice began to fringe them, thin, fragile shards of ice, as on ponds at winter's first onset.--"I'm sure everybody at the Farm would be really glad to see you again."

"That would be nice, but I can't. I've got work to do for class tomorrow."

"Come on, Elizabeth, you'll have to do better than that. Nick and I scored some Panama red from Jimmy Bowlegs earlier this week, and we saw Washington and Willow yesterday, and they said they'd laid in a stash of mescaline, hash, weed, and, get this, actual peyote buttons."

The perhaps scurrilous but universally employed nickname Washington derived from a time when one of his ex-girlfriends was asked to comment on the relative size of a part of his anatomy and she said, laughing, "Well, let's just say it isn't exactly the Washington Monument." The name Willow was occasioned by a time when the young man in question was sitting around with a circle of friends, smoking dope, and suddenly stood up, hung his arms out droopily from his shoulders and said, "Look at me, I'm a willow. I'm a weeping willow tree."

Elizabeth emitted a half laugh, shook her head no. "Sorry. Thanks, anyway."

There was a tone of bemusement in her voice and a fresh, greeny brightness in her eyes.

"You sure you won't reconsider now?" Jon cajoled. "You know, if you don't go, everybody's gonna think you went straight while you were out in California," he said, winking.

She grew measurably more reserved. "Will they? That would be quite the social stigma, wouldn't it. Why, I might even have to wear a scarlet 'S' on my chest."

They couldn't help it: Jon and Nick both looked reflexively at the place where her two braless breasts stood out against her sweater. Elizabeth wasn't quite melon-bosomed, but what they imagined beneath the red wool was sweet to contemplate.

"Guys, I've gotta go, Heidegger's getting restless."

It was true. The chubby, black-masked animal had been squirming around, causing her to readjust for him several times. She stepped forward on her right pedal, saying "Nice to meet you, Nick," as she started off. He caught the words, thrown like a newspaper over a paperboy's shoulder.

Jon and Nick said bye though they didn't want her to go. They stood watching her glide away, her raccoon behind her head, tail pendant. Nick thought of it as a sort of living Daniel Boone cap.

"Well, Jon, I think an objective view would have it that you struck out."

"Aw, she's just playing mind games with me. I'll call her up tonight and I'll bet you she changes her tune."

They turned and started up the sidewalk toward the dorm.

"Fat chance. I'd say she really doesn't want to go to any party."

"Nah, she's just being coy."

"Maybe it's the company."

"Speak for yourself, man. I've always had my pick of the chicks. There's never a shortage of your basic radical groupie."

"I don't know, somehow she didn't strike me as a radical groupie."

"Maybe not, Nick, but you oughta know that all chicks want the same thing."

"You sure about that? As I recall, you never got very far with my sister. Crashed and burned." He imitated with his right hand a plane falling out the sky, complete with sound effects. "At least that's what I heard."

Three sulfur butterflies, little shaped flames, flitted by, circling around and around each other in some aerial jazz dancing.

"Let me tell you, man, your sister is one twisted chick. I mean, whoever heard of a radical who doesn't believe in sex?"

"Oh, she believes in sex, just not outside of a long-term relationship."

"So, is that what she's got with that frigging guitar player--what's his name?--Wolfgang something."

"Wolfram Kohles. And I don't know anything about their sex life."

"I thought you twins knew everything about each other."

Nick laughed. "Not everything. Not by a long shot."

"Well, it doesn't make any sense. She told me she believes sex before marriage is a form of male dominance, or some such shit. And from what I heard, this guy had the chicks lined up for miles, just dying to rattle his bedsprings."

Nick smiled. "Yeah, that's about right."

"Think about it, Nick. This is a guy who could have it whenever he wanted--I mean, THREE TIMES A DAY, with THREE DIFFERENT CHICKS, if he wanted--and you're trying to tell me he's going to take some vow of celibacy just so he can date your sister?"

"Jon, would you try listening for once? I said I don't know a thing about their sex life."

They passed a system of metal water sprinklers; each sprinkler head was stuttering tchk-tchk-tchk-tchk as it revolved. Robins hopped through the wet grass, hunting for worms.

"Take it from me, man, if Judith isn't accommodating him, that Kohles guy is balling other chicks on the side. Shit, I bet he'd be balling other chicks even if he was banging Judith."

Nick stiffened, stopped dead, looked coldly straight into Arbalest's eyes.

"Hey, man, sorry, I forgot for a second she was your sister," he lied. "I didn't mean anything by it. Besides, we're talking man to man here, aren't we?"

Nick resumed walking, resigning himself to Arbalest's company until they got back to the dorm and he could get shed of him. Three iridescent-headed grackles flew across the sidewalk ten yards ahead of them.

"Anyway, like I said, I'll give Miss Elizabeth Prescott a call tonight, and you'll see how she comes around. She's just playing mind games with me."

"Yeah, we'll see."

* * * * * * *

They walked past the lounge area to the left of the front entrance. A couple were sitting on a couch, listening to the new *Woodstock* double album, which was playing on the console-style stereo. Santana was half-way through "Soul Sacrifice." They walked past the John

Crowfoot abstract expressionist painting, which looked out of place against the bright red brick wall by the stairs to the downstairs rec room. Crowfoot, one of the University's Indian students, had been dramatically successful in painting, with shows in Chicago, Santa Fe, and New York. Judith loved Crowfoot's work, though her own style of painting was very different. The passed the front desk where a radio was playing a heavily brassed Blood, Sweat, and Tears song and where a chunky guy with close-cropped, dishwater-blond hair was teasing two of the women's RAs. The fourplex was comprised of two men's and two women's dorms. The women at the desk were both dressed in white shorts and red university T-shirts; were were conventionally cute.

Arbalest whispered something about pre-political, opiated, future members of the bourgeoisie. Nick whispered that he doubted they were opiated. Arbalest laughed and they turned the corner past the mailboxes, opened the heavy metal door onto the first floor, turned right through another metal door into the non-air-conditioned concrete stairway, and began their ascent through the stifling air to the third floor. As they walked past the third-floor TV room, their tennis shoes making soft, padded noises on the all-weather, turquoise-red-and-yellow, diamond-patterned carpeting, they saw that the afternoon game shows had attracted an audience of almost ten--a fair number, considering there were only about sixty guys on the whole floor that summer. Nick and Jon peeked in but none of those sitting on the orange plastic chairs even looked up. "Talk about opiated," Nick said under his breath as they walked on. Arbalest said goodbye at his room mid-way down the hallway, just across from the two big, brightly lit shower rooms. Nick's room was the third from the last, on the right, across from an always empty study lounge.

Nick set his books down on the desk, turned and knelt at the cardboard Ajax box of records, flipped through, stopped at the album cover in soft-focus violet, cream, and blue: the album with Crosby, Stills, and Nash sitting on a dilapidated old couch in front of some anonymous frame house, a sloppy paint job around the window frame, a lime-green spray of palm frond in the upper left. He put the disc on the turntable, if something that unlatched and flipped down horizontal, without even detachable speakers, could rightly be called a turntable. The needle set down, a bit of crackling, then Stephen Stills' famous--

and for Nick always blood-quickening--acoustic guitar lead-in, joined by the bass on the repeat, to "Suite: Judy Blue Eyes."

A sweet melody line, even sweeter vocal harmonies, delicious guitar licks, and a tale of love's difficulties transformed a machine that was essentially cheap, factory-constructed junk into a conduit to the sound and sensibility of the time. It was CSN that came forth, but it might as easily have been The Beatles, The Stones, The Dead, The Mothers, Big Brother, or Dylan or Hendrix or Baez. Or Country Joe or Creedence or Quicksilver Messenger Service or Chicago or Grand Funk or Ten Years After or Cream or Jethro Tull or Traffic or Led Zeppelin. Or any of a hundred others.

The important thing was that for only the second time in history a generation was being defined by the radio and the record player. Music was not, and this was the mistake made by so many otherwise savvy parents, a mere background accompaniment, a mere soundtrack, to the times. No, music *was* the times. It shaped the way millions upon millions of young people would (and perhaps too often the things they could) perceive in the world about them--and how they felt about those things and about themselves. If the songs were sometimes soft-headed, sentimental, or unwarrantedly idealistic, they could be excused for the manner in which they were put across musically. And when the songs did attain to something akin to poetry, fusing words and melodic line in a sound that penetrated to the marrow of the moment, they spoke, in direct ways that people would not often let themselves speak, of their deepest, truest feelings of hope, fear, betrayal, or just plain joy in being alive. If an explanation is sought for why the sixties generation was so romantically confident that it could effect lasting social and political change in a world that, in reality, responded, as it always had, only to money, and to the power and influence that money brought--if an explanation is sought, one need only listen to the music.

But none of those things was on Nick's mind as he reclined on his bed, staring up at the posters on his walls: Phi Zappa Krappa (Frank Zappa sur la toilet), a pretentious psychedelic portrait of Dylan's face enclosed in a wheel of multi-limbed Hindu god figures, a black-and-white photo of Hendrix (looking a bit uncertain about just where he was), and a balloon-lettered Jefferson Airplane bill from the Fillmore

West. Nick was thinking about the young woman he had just met. Elizabeth Prescott.

Elizabeth. Did she always go by that? Not Liz, Lizzy, or Liza, Beth or Betty? What color were her eyes? Why haven't I met her before? She was in California--working. That doesn't sound like enough. Was there some other reason she left for California? And why did she come back? Jon thinks he's going to get into her pants, but she sees right through him. She didn't seem too interested in me, either, damn it. Still, I didn't get the feeling she had a boyfriend. What color were her eyes?

Nick got up and sat down in one of the bucket-shaped orange plastic chairs at the desk, or rather, the two work areas built between the closets of the normally two-man room. He punched the on-button of the fluorescent desk lamp, took down from the built-in bookshelf at the rear of the desk a half-empty box of hundred-sheet corrasable bond paper, began a letter to his best friend Bill Matthews.

24 June 1970

Dear Bill,

It's been almost a month since I've heard from you. Almost nothing is happening with the movement this summer. Most of the members of the People's Revolutionary Committee--you know, Kathleen Doyle's group--are still in town, and they're still meeting two or three times a week in the Student Union. But as you know, I don't get into their endless abstract arguments about Marx, Lenin, and Mao. For people who idolize Che Guevera, they seem to me like a pretty do-nothing group. These days they're talking about "organizing the farmers" and creating "a new, radical prairie populism," though none of them has ever been on a farm, or I'd be willing to bet, spent even ten minutes talking to a real-life farmer. If they had, they'd know there's about as much chance of converting farmers to a radical agenda as there is of Congress legalizing marijuana.

I remember vividly, as I'm sure you do as well, that when we marched down the Main Street of Red Earth the morning before we took the ROTC headquarters, a group of farmers stood out in front of the hardware store, dressed in bib overalls, jeans, and blue workshirts (their apparel their only connection with the marchers in the street), calling us Commies and long-haired hippie fairies and yelling at us to love America or leave it. I can't imagine any rational person trying to forge a radical coalition with those men. But then, I've never accused the members of the People's Revolutionary Committee of being rational.

In any case, this seems to be the summer of apathy. It's sometimes hard to believe that it's been less than two months since the shootings at Kent State. If this campus is representative, the peace movement is fatally disintegrating. Let's hope things pick up again this fall when everyone comes back to school. I can't help but feel, though, that ground is being lost here--and at a time when we should be doing so much more, not less. How can we ever hope to bring about peace if we take the summers off? I suppose there's something inherently undependable about a movement composed mostly of college students, people who have never had to assume any of life's major responsibilities. Listen to me. I sound exactly like my father. With all my friends gone except Judith, I've been hanging out with Jon Arbalest--yes, Red Earth's answer to Jerry Rubin--this summer. And what have we been doing, other than getting stoned with a perhaps symptomatic regularity? The answer, I'm ashamed to say, is not much.

Write and tell me how you're doing. Are you still planning to transfer to the U. of Minnesota this fall? Or will I have my old roommate back?

Nick

PS: On a different subject, I met someone interesting today, walking back to the dorm after lunch. Her name is Elizabeth Prescott, and she's the daughter of Bill Prescott, the Chairman of the Philosophy Department. When Arbalest and I met her, she was riding around on her bike, with her pet raccoon (yes, raccoon!) propped on her shoulders. She's intelligent and well-

read. Damn easy to look at, too. It's a longshot, but I may see her at a party tonight.

Nick prepared the letter for mailing. He'd drop it into the slot for outgoing mail the next time he went out.

He reached up to the second shelf, selected a black three-ring binder, the journal he'd begun keeping in the spring. He opened it to the end of the last entry--Monday's. He sighed, mentally castigated himself for not being able to adjust himself to the everyday journal habit. He wrote the date and began to write.

In first grade, Judith and I went to a country school a mile from our family's farmhouse. In the frigid November nights, in the interval between going to bed and that time just before I slipped without volition or awareness that I had made a step backwards from the airplane of wakefulness into sleep's endless, blank freefall, when, from the bed's warm center, I would extend my toes into the still-chilly corners for a touch of coolness, just a touch and then withdraw--in that interval I would wonder for the hundredth? thousandth? time in the past several months whether I were actually lying in my bed, or whether I were not still asleep, lying on a pile of bright jackets, in the cloakroom of our country schoolhouse, in warm September, merely dreaming that I was in bed. My toes would search the corners of the bed for a patch of still-cool sheet. I was about to step, without knowing I had stepped, into sleep's perfect oblivion.

It occurred in the gold-warm days of September's false summer. Judith and I attended a small white-painted country school a mile west of our farm. Across the gravel road just west of the school, a field of tall, yellowing corn ran in straight vertical rows down an incline to a point about six feet before a barbed wire fence. But the slope, covered with thick grass, wild oats, and foxtail barley, continued, through the fence and down into the ditch. The air was sunny, the sky pale blue. Mare's tail clouds whipped by high overhead. Looking during afternoon recess at the horizon's circle and then up at the sky, arcing roundly above, I imagined myself at the center of a blue cat's-eye marble, staring up at its soft-floating white patterns.

Judith and I and a half dozen other kids of different ages (eighteen students attended the school's eight grades) played at the edge of the cornfield. Two kids would hold the bottom strand of the barbed wire fence up, while one at a time the rest of us would slide down the incline on a big piece of cardboard, one of the top flaps of the box the school's new four-burner electric stove had come in. The older kids slid down first. When it was finally my turn, I started down the now smooth grass of the incline. But just as I reached the fence, Billy Vogel, who was holding up the wire with Janelle Meyers, lost his grip, and I took the wire--slap!--across the face, a steel barb missing my right eye by an eighth of an inch but leaving a cut from which welled bright arterial blood as soon as the barb exited.

I lay on the flattened grass, stunned. Blood ran in a crimson rivulet from the puncture site down the side of my head, discoloring my short, light brown hair. Judith, who had been next in line to go down, screamed my name, jumped-flew down to me, knelt and lifted my head to her chest, unconcerned about the blood that spotted her green jacket.

"I'll get Miss Thomas," Janelle said, and she ran off to get the teacher, who was playing Annie Annie Over with a bunch of kids at the school stable (a remnant of a Depression-era past in which kids actually rode horses and ponies to school) on the other side of the schoolgrounds.

Miss Thomas was a generous-spirited, enthusiastic woman in her late twenties, who had gone back to college eight years after she graduated from high school, had earned her two-year teacher's certificate, and had been hired the summer before (jubilation!) to teach at the school. Like most adults of a certain age, she thought herself incapable of surprise. Well, not quite. When little Janelle Meyers ran up and, though breathless, demanded that she "come quick," saying, with a hitherto unobserved dramatic passion, that Nick Larkin had "cut open his head on the barbed wire fence," and was "bleeding all over."

Ellen Thomas dropped the black-and-white volleyball she was holding, gasped, went pale, and ran as fast as she could--kids trailing after her like chicks scurrying after a hen--to the stricken first grader, me.

"Nick, are you OK?" Miss Thomas asked.

I was sitting up and leaning against Judith--or more exactly, I was submitting to being clutched by her. Judith answered the question before I could think what to say.

"Of course he's not OK. Don't you see he's been cut by the wire that stupid Billy Vogel dropped right in his face?"

Billy, a second grader, having already endured several like abuses of his character, had fled to the schoolhouse for sanctuary. I was still on the other side of the fence. Miss Thomas ignored Judith, pulled up the wire, and asked me to crawl through. She helped me stand up, asked Bobbie Snyder for his handkerchief, and pressed the blue-and-white, flower-printed bandanna to the weeping cut, staunching the bloodflow. I hoped privately that Bobbie had not already made use of the handkerchief.

Miss Thomas asked me if I felt dizzy and I said no. As she walked with me back to the schoolhouse, she kept the handkerchief pressed against the cut. Judith walked on the other side, holding my arm. Inside, Miss Thomas sat me down on a chair near the kitchen sink, wet the handkerchief (which was by then soaked through the middle with blood) and squeezed it out a few times, then dabbed at my cut and at the side of my head until she had cleaned all the dried blood away. She had me hold the wet handkerchief against the cut until she had retrieved her first aid kit from a drawer in her desk and removed from it hydrogen peroxide, cotton balls, a large square of gauze, and surgical tape.

Miss Thomas taped the gauze over the cut, but she knew it would need stitches. She called my mother in town at the laundromat she and my father had bought seven or eight months before to try to add to their income. Town was eleven miles away, so, after telling the kids to go back to their desks, Miss Thomas had me lie down on a pile of jackets in the cloakroom just off the single big classroom. Judith refused to go back to her desk, saying she couldn't leave me when I was hurt. She held one of my hands between hers.

I soon fell asleep, woke up only long enough to stumble out to the car with my mother and Judith (who insisted on accompanying us into town). I learned only later that, after turning off her mangle and retrieving my father--he was at his coffee break at the restaurant across the street--to watch the laundromat, Mom had practically screamed out to the school, driving the 65 mile per hour limit on the highway (though she usually drove a conservative 55), and driving a slightly reckless 50 on the gravel road.

I woke up when Mom angled the car into a space in front of Dr. Vincent's clinic. Though clear-headed, I had the weird feeling, as Mom checked in and sat down with Judith and me in the waiting room, that I was not really there--in town, in the clinic, in a chair between my sister and mother. I had this strange feeling that I was still in the school cloakroom's, lying asleep on brown and blue and green and red and yellow jackets, dreaming I had driven into town with Mom, dreaming she had checked me in, dreaming I was sitting there, waiting for the nurse to call my name and take me back to one of the rooms to have three stitches put in my head.

That night, as I lay in bed, trying to fall asleep, I could not stop thinking that I was not really there, in the farmhouse, in my bedroom on the second floor, lying between cool white sheets. No, I felt I was really still in that cloakroom, dreaming I was home in bed. In some way I could not begin to understand, I had become the school's cloakroom's permanent resident. And everything that had happened since I had fallen asleep on that motley pile of jackets? I had simply dreamed it, dreamed it all.

Nearly every night for months afterwards--long after my stitches were removed, leaving a thin, scarcely noticeable white line where the flesh had been rejoined, I would wonder if I was truly lying in my bed, or if I was not back in the cloakroom, dreaming I was lying in bed. I told absolutely no one about those disturbing thoughts.

But one November morning Judith said to me at breakfast, "Nick, I know what you've been thinking. But you're not in that room at school. That's stupid. You're here with me and you always will be." She smiled and I knew that she was right. Where else could I be but right there, at the Formica-topped breakfast table in the corner of the kitchen, eating a box of sweetened cereal (one of those variety pack boxes with the slits on the front, so you could eat the cereal right out of the box)? Yes, where else could I be but there, with Judith?

Nonetheless, that night, as I lay alone upstairs, staring up towards the sloping ceiling, my eyes not yet adapted enough to the dark to make out the shapes of the dresser and mirror, the antique rocker, or the table and chairs, my sister Judith became part of the general silence from downstairs and in that interval between sliding my feet between the cool sheets and freefalling out of the warm-sheeted bed into dreamless sleep, I could not help but wonder where I truly was. In that instant of doubt--was that not when my real life had stopped and my dream life had begun? Or at least when my dreams had so thoroughly interpenetrated my real life as to make one indistinguishable from the other? Would I ever make it completely, once and for all, back to my bed and my ongoing life? Or would I remain forever imprisoned outside of time, stopped in that narrow cloakroom, in the diffused light of mid-afternoon?

I don't know exactly when it occurred, but some time that winter I felt that eerie feeling for the last time. Until this morning. Today I woke up before my alarm went off and lay there in the twilight, not really thinking about anything. Suddenly I had the sensation of falling away from my room--or rather, of having the room dissolve about me--and finding myself lying once again on those red and blue and brown and green jackets, dreaming--dreaming everything that had happened to me since. It lasted a long, vertiginous moment and then I felt myself slamming hard down onto the bed, and, with a jolt, waking fully. Why, after all these years?

Nick closed the binder, capped his pen. He thought about re-starting the album, since he hadn't really heard any except the first song, but decided not to. He took a paperback copy of Manzoni's *The Betrothed* down from the shelf, lay down on his bed to read. He'd stayed up late the last several nights reading the book for the European novel course he was taking. He was enjoying the book, but an incidental comment the professor had made yesterday had really intrigued him.

At the end of class, after lecturing at some length on Manzoni's revisions of the novel, in which he had shifted from the eighteenth century Enlightenment philosophy to the democratic compassion of Romanticism, Dr. Harris had commented--actually it was more of a toss-off statement--that Lorenzo's entry into Milan and the subsequent bread riot was notably cinematic, as were many of the novel's other scenes--the abduction of Lucia by the Un-Named's men, Lorenzo's flight from Milan to Venice, the ravages of the plague in Milan, the evil Don Rodrigo's death by plague, and the much-belated marriage of Lucia and Lorenzo. He said that if Manzoni were alive today, he might not be writing novels at all, but instead, might be directing films. The tiny cottonwood seed of this idea had blown straight into the rich black topsoil of Nick's brain, and he had found himself watering it until it sprouted and sprung up, green, strong, and incredibly fast-growing.

Nick began to read but after a few minutes he re-placed his bookmark, closed the book, and laid it beside him on the bed. He turned his head a bit on the pillow, stared up intensely at the long blank white wall beside him, till everything else in the room dissolved into airy blankness and the wall began to shift and slide, melting before him. Then, as if cast up on the wall by a hidden projector, were himself and Judith and Roger and Lena arriving just before showtime at the Astro Theater to see *It's a Mad, Mad, Mad, Mad World*, and finding the house almost sold out and that the only four seats together were in the very front row. He had felt, until he'd got used to the perspective, as if the movie was taking place in his lap. How they laughed and laughed all through the film--it was so good to see his mother and father, who had been through some amount of financial hell over the years, laugh like that.

Lena said afterwards that the film was misnamed, in typical Hollywood fashion: the word "Mad" should have been replaced with "Greedy." Roger was a longtime Spencer Tracey fan, but on the way home that night he couldn't stop recalling the scene in which Jonathan Winters had destroyed a gas station with his bare hands; indeed, years afterwards, perhaps prompted by some improvisational bit on "The Jonathan Winters Show," he would ask, "Say, Nick, do you remember when he played that truck driver and he got so furious that he tore that gas station apart?" And Roger would laugh.

Direct cuts, flashing like slides being changed one after another by a silent control: their family attending, at various times, various theaters and drive-ins.

Direct cuts to some of the movies he had attended with his mother, movies, many of them musicals, that he saw, only in retrospect, all dealt with romance.

An iris closing and opening on he and Annie watching *2,001 A Space Odyssey* at the Griffin Theater, watching, in gap-mouthed astonishment, Kubrick's edits and Douglas Trumbull's special effects.

A wipe from left to right, leaving he and Annie watching Zefferelli's *Romeo and Juliet* at the Republic Theater. They'd actually stayed and watched the film a second time.

A wipe from right to left, and he and Bill Matthews watching *In Cold Blood*. An opposite wipe, and he, Bill, Bruce, and Mike were watching *The Dirty Dozen*. Another wipe, *Bonnie and Clyde*.

A fast series of superimpositions and dissolves as he and his father--both movie omnivores--watched *Citizen Kane* on TV. Roger said it was *the* story of the failure of the American dream. Nick watched so intently, he hardly dared blink. Then *On the Waterfront*, Roger's favorite film--something in Roger responded profoundly to that tragedy of working class individualism. While the rest of the country watched Johnny Carson, Nick and Roger watched old movies, dozens and scores of them--every imaginable type and genre.

More superimpositions and dissolves: films the whole family watched, ending with *The Wizard of Oz*--and Roger asking as the tornado sucked up Dorothy's house as handily as if it were a little Monopoly house, "Say, do you remember when Bill Burdette told that story about how that twister snatched up him and his combine and dropped him down ten miles away?"

And Judith and he saying with mock exasperation, "Yeah, Dad, we remember."

"That was the last time we saw Big Bill," Roger said, and then they all turned momentarily downcast, honoring the memory of the dead, sainted in family lore.

A montage sequence: films he had seen at the Student Union this past year, in the Thursday night film series--films by Weine, Murnau, Cocteau, Kurosawa, Bergman, Renoir, Truffaut, and Fellini.

Obnoxiously hard knocking at, then hammering on, his door. His last name called. Nick dazed, as if he'd just wakened in a strange place.

The projector flicker-stopped, sound running down, screen going dark.
The houselights snapped on; the screen became an ordinary dormitory wall.

He got up and answered the door.

"What the hell were you doing in here, Larkin, jacking off?"

"What's up, Jon?"

"Come on, I've had a great idea. I'll explain it to you as we go."

"Go where?"

"Never mind, just come on."

Nick sighed, picked up his green-lensed sunglasses, and went out the door with Jon. At the first floor, they took the hallway to the north side of the dorm complex, exited the glass doors, walked to Jon's '65 royal blue Impala in the parking lot. Jon unlocked the driver's side door and opened it to intense waves of heat. Grimacing, he got in and reached across to unlock the door for Nick.

"Dumb S.O.B. He must have been blitzed when he parked that thing," Nick complained, angling himself through the passenger-side door, which he could only open about a foot because a white '66 LTD had been parked well over the white line dividing the two spaces. "Jesus, it's hot in here. Why didn't you leave the windows cracked?"

"Quit bitching and roll your window down."

Jon started the engine, pulled the gearshift up the column into reverse, released the park brake, and backed out charily, so as not to scrape the LTD.

"OK, so what's the big scheme?" Nick asked as they turned right at the edge of the lot and started toward Jefferson Street, the name the two-lane highway assumed as it passed through the northern edge of Red Earth. This was four years before the highway by-pass was built that enabled truckers and others whose business lay further down the road to skim around the town without appreciably altering their speed.

"You remember when we were talking to Washington last week at Ted's Bar, and he told us about picking weed along the railroad tracks south of town?"

In the years after, Ted's would change hands and names several times, only to be resurrected in the eighties as an ice cream parlor, featuring thirty exotic flavors. The ice cream parlor's immaculate blue-and-white tile lay over the old wooden floor, the walls painted a brilliant white, the posters of banana splits and sundaes, the quaint, white-painted little metal tables and chairs, and the long banks of freezers, holding five-gallon containers of each flavor as well as such attractions as ice cream birthday cakes, ice cream and chocolate cookies shaped to look like trains or various animals--no, none of these niceties ever quite squelched the smell of beer and smoke, faint, but noticeable, distinctly so on hot summer days.

"Yeah, I remember. So?"

"All right, what I propose, Nick, is that we become our own suppliers."

"What?"

"You know, harvest our own dope."

"You're kidding."

"Not a bit."

"Local green?"

Arbalest took a right onto Jefferson.

"Give me a chance to explain, will you? You're always so narrow in your thinking, Nick. I mean, it's a wonder you're not in the dining room of some frat house, getting drunk, right now."

"Oh, Jesus, next you'll say--."

"Listen, Nick, listen. Washington told me how to cure local green so it comes out as potent as Mexican."

"Sure, Jon. Now I've heard everything. By the way, do you mind telling me where we're going?"

"For now, down to the Old Town bridge."

There were in fact two Old Town bridges over the Red Earth River. But Nick knew Jon meant the much older bridge, on the southwest side of town.

"Out to smoke some dope, huh?"

"You've got it, Jack."

"Nick, the name's Nick."

"Now listen. Here we are, two revolutionaries."

"Oh yeah," Nick said, ironically, "that's us, a couple of Young Trotskyites."

They passed Anthony's Restaurant. Two rednecks sat in a booth by the front window and behind them two cops sloshed down their coffee at the counter. Two blocks later, Jon turned left onto First Street.

"OK, now, smoking a little weed or dropping acid once in a while can in itself, at least in these oppressive times, be considered a revolutionary activity. It constitutes an act of rebellion against the linear-minded, time-clock conformity of the System. But so invidious is the System . . ."

"Invidious. I like that. In-vid-i-ous. Why, that's a four-syllable word."

"Shut up and listen, Nick. You're always interrupting. So invidious is the System that it corrupts even such essentially subversive activities as getting stoned."

"Meaning what, Jon?"

"Meaning that even such right-on activities as getting stoned--"

"*Criminal* activities. I think you mean *criminal* activities, Jon."

"As I was saying, even such *right-on* activities as getting stoned are being co-opted by American capitalism's simplistic free market mentality. If we want to sustain a radical approach to our politics, which is to say, to everything in our lives, we've got to free ourselves from our degrading dependence upon our suppliers--"

"Jimmy Bowlegs and Washington."

Arbalest did a second-gear stop the sign at First and Adams, continued down First, the University Medical School to their immediate left, wood frame houses with screened-in porches to their right.

"Precisely. Those two long-haired piranhas couldn't care less about creating social change and bringing down the System. Hell, man, they're profiting by it. All they want is the chance to make a fast buck."

"Them and the guys they work for. I heard Washington wanted to go independent last spring, but they wouldn't let him. I suppose they threatened him with a pair of concrete shoes."

"Yeah, something like that. That's why he carries that pistol around wherever he goes now. I hear he even sleeps with the thing."

"That's one damned cold bed partner, I'd say."

"But I can understand it in his line of work. In fact, Nick, after Kent State, I'm no longer convinced that non-violence will ever do a fucking thing to change the System. Rap Brown was right. Violence *is* as American as apple pie."

"Easy, Jon. You know I'm on the other side on that one. I'll never accept violence as an answer."

"Then you're fucking naive, Nick. We've tried everything-- marches, petitions, teach-ins, even minor league civil disobedience--

and you tell me what any of it's done to stop the war. Nixon and Kissinger were really affected. They expanded the war into fucking Cambodia and Laos. And at Kent State, the war came home with a fucking vengeance. The way I see it, Kent State was the beginning of our own fucking body count."

The light at First and Main turned yellow before Jon reached the intersection. Not wanting to wait, Jon looked quickly both ways and accelerated through it before the light turned red. They started down the long hill that led to the Bottom Road and Old Town. A clearing opened to their right, and they saw two young mothers, one in jeans and a pink tanktop, the other in red shorts and a white blouse, pushing toddlers in kiddie swings (the kind with black rubber seats with holes for the legs and the bars that slid down in front of the kids). Though they couldn't hear the toddlers, Nick imagined them giggling and piping out, "Higher! Push me higher, Mommy! Daddy pushes me lots higher than you do."

"Maybe you're right, Jon, and maybe you're not. That's too apocalyptic for me, though. I still think there's a good chance non-violent resistance will--"

"Oh, for fuck's sake, Nick, how can you still believe in that non-violent Gandhi bullshit? *Satyagraha* won't accomplish a fucking thing. You know why? Because there isn't any such thing as fucking 'truth-force.' Nixon has had his chance to end the war, and despite all the protests and all the marches, he hasn't. I'd say he's made his choice. The question now is what are we willing to do as a response."

As soon as they had moved past the swings, however, a shadow had fallen across the road, and with it a decided chill had come into the air. Past the playground the road bowed left and then right again, following the ravine down between the hills.

Out of nowhere a huge pale white form. Half-transparent, it came toward them dead on, black horns darker than the shadows. Nick stiffened, clutched the armrest, winced as they plowed right through it. He jerked around, looked out the rear window. Nothing. He saw only the two mothers swinging their kids.

"Whatsamatter?"

"Nothing, just thought I saw something run into the road. It was nothing."

Arbalest laughed. "Seeing things and the fucker's not even stoned yet. Which reminds me of how we got off on this."

"Yeah, I think you were leading up to saying that Jimmy Bowlegs and Washington, though criminals, are still puppets of the capitalist system."

"Exactly. Now what I say we do, Nick, is cut those two rattlesnakes out and go straight to the source."

"Not too straight, I take it."

Jon chuckled and slugged Nick on the arm. He veered slightly into the other lane.

"Hey, keep both hands on the wheel." After a short silence, "I don't know, Jon. Somehow, I just can't feature myself in the marijuana production business."

Jon stopped at the sign at the base of the bluff. Sitting to their left, on the corner, was a small log cabin, the oldest schoolhouse in the state, according to a small metal sign tacked to its front. In later years, the schoolhouse would be moved elsewhere, though Nick never learned just where. There were two routes through Old Town to the bridge. They could go straight, across the Bottom Road and the railroad tracks, and then, ignoring the road that veered left and crossed the newer bridge, they could take a right and drive down a paved street past trailers and mostly small houses and an overgrown undeveloped patch by the river, to the old bridge. Or as a second alternative, they could take a right on the Bottom Road, drive west for a little less than three quarters of a mile and simply follow the Road in its bend to the south, the last several hundred yards to the old bridge. A charming feature of the old bridge was that it was hidden from sight until one was nearly upon it, by the dense canopy of cottonwoods lining the banks of the Red Earth River. It was the secluded, secretive nature of the bridge that had made it attractive to Jon and Nick when they wanted a place to get stoned.

Nick suggested that Jon take the Bottom Road. He liked that short stretch of road. They drove by the Farmer's Co-op Elevator. In late July the wheat would be heaped beside it in golden piles, twenty feet high, waiting to be hauled away in railway boxcars, of which three were standing empty nearby on a side track. Just past the elevator was the alfalfa mill, which operated day and night, sending up a continuous white plume of alfalfa particles--making Red Earth an allergy purgatory in the summer.

Off to their right, built up snug against the base of the bluff, small houses began to appear--some neatly kept up and freshly painted, with tiny, close-clipped yards, woven wire fences and metal gates, and little borders of marigolds, zinnias, four o'clocks, nasturtiums, and cosmos; while others were ramshackle, with peeling paint, missing asphalt shingles (some blown off and lying in the weed-smothered grass of what had once been yards), drain spouts hanging, disconnected, rust-eaten old Mercuries and Chevies raised up on concrete blocks beside the houses, hoods up--engines hanging on chains from solid tree branches, and trannies and brake shoes lying about on the oil-stained ground.

These last houses made the pretense of being down-on-their-luck farms, since on their sides and in the rear they had wire, wood, and sometimes even snow-fence, pens of various sizes, quality of construction, and states of repair, that held chickens wild as crows; black, white, and spotted rabbits; pigs that kept escaping through decrepit fences only to find (as their human owners no doubt had years before) that they had nowhere to go; and goats, permanently pregnant, milk bags swollen.

Lean, middling big dogs of no discernible breed slept on the cracked concrete of porches or in the dirt by the gate-less gap in the front fences--which fences were themselves overgrown with wild morning glory, its brilliant blue flowers an incongruous touch of color and beauty amidst the general dilapidation; or they had tansy, ragweed, and violet-headed musk thistles poking through. For some reason, perhaps because they reminded Nick, in the way of some illegitimate second cousin, of his family's own farm, those broken-down, dead-ended, spiritually bankrupt houses--which seemed to hold on only by some mean-spirited, spiteful, prickly pear persistence--were among the things he liked best about Red Earth.

They parked the car in a pull-off by the bridge and made their way through dense grass, foxtail, and sunflowers down below, where, on a flat spot, they sat on two old broken pieces of concrete, the irregular rocks of the riverbank at their feet, and fired up a joint. The area under the bridge was dim and dank and smelled of mold and algae.

They sat in the bridge shadows and in the deep, cricket-singing shadows of the tall cottonwoods. The trees' big leaves shivered in the late afternoon breeze, clattered, changed silver to green, green to silver. Passing the fat joint between them, Nick and Jon fell momentarily silent.

Nick thought about Elizabeth Prescott. Where was she right now? What was she doing? Would they see her that night? What color were her eyes? He couldn't quite see them. But something about the color of her eyes led him to become absorbed in the flowing waters--black-green in the shade--of the Red Earth River, which at that point was about twenty-five feet wide and, in the middle, six or seven feet deep. The little river was not fast, like the Missouri, but it had the virtue of constancy, and inspired by it, Nick began to picture the grand cycle of water--continuously flowing in springs and trickles and streams and creeks and brooks and rivers, flowing and evaporating and congregating in mists and vapors to make clouds, and then pouring forth onto the earth and sinking into the soil, or standing still in pockets and sloughs and bigger depressions, or rilling off and rolling down the incline of the land until it fed into the river again--drops joined to drops joined to drops, ever flowing, ever changing. Nick was somewhere in the middle of the upward part of that cycle, feeling himself collecting about dust particles and forming, in time-lapse fashion, a congeries of clouds, dusky-gray and black streaked, somber with their burden of rain, when Arbalest spoke, his voice startling, as if Nick hadn't been aware of his presence till that moment.

"Now I want you to give this idea a chance, Nick. We can go over to the railroad tracks along the Bottom Road right now, and in half an hour's time, we can pick enough grass to hold us all of next year."

Jon's words became those first big, splattering drops of a shower, which fell, gravity-impelled, through the long expanse of air, little parachuters, to strike at last on the rocks at Nick's feet and splash outwards in a curved, cupped silver burst. But through some process Nick could not quite grasp--the way in a dream one cannot quite comprehend how it is that one is doing something--Nick translated the raindrops instantly back into words as they broke.

"Well, don't just sit there staring. What do you think?"

"I don't know. I mean, local weed, Jon?"

"I told you, that's not a problem. It's all in the curing, and Washington told me just how to do it. He says the main thing is to hang the plants upside down to dry so the THC collects in the leaves." The rocks at Nick's feet were wet and beginning to drip.

"Yeah, but is this even the right time? I heard from somebody that you're supposed to harvest the plants when they're mature. Something about just after they've come into flower . . . or was it just before they come into flower?"

"Nick, have you seen those plants? They must be at least six feet tall, some of them. If they aren't mature now, they never will be."

"But have they flowered?"

"What do I look like, a fucking botanist?"

"And there's something else . . . I can't recall it exactly . . . something about how you're only supposed to pick the leaves of the female plant. Or is it the male plant? Or maybe it's only the female plant that flowers."

"Shit, Nick, how am I supposed to know if it's a fucking male or a fucking female plant? Here I am, ready to go harvest us about two or three kilos of dope and you're babbling shit--flowering plants this and female plants that. I say, the only important thing is, are we going to do this or are we not?"

Rain was striking the rocks by Nick's feet in a downpour, streaming off, running away.

"All right, Jon, you don't have to jump down my throat. I was just trying to remember what it was I'd heard. If we're going to do this, don't you think we ought to try to do it right?"

Nick didn't know why he was suddenly including himself in Arbalest's addle-brained project. He didn't really want any part of it. Buying dope a lid at a time and getting stoned two, three times a week, that was one thing. But it was another thing entirely to go out and yank up fistfuls of plants and then have to hide them (upside down, yet!) somewhere until they dried out--which would take an unknown amount of time--and then pull or clip the leaves off and crush them up. And all the while they'd have to watch their backside, have to make sure no one saw them or got wind of what they were up to.

"Nick, let's just go fucking do it. The worst that can happen is we'll find out in a few weeks the shit is no good, and we'll only be out an hour of our time. But, and this is a significant but, we might also find out we've got some dynamite shit, and then we'll be sitting pretty."

Rainwater runoff was rushing in a torrent around Nick's ankles. His shoes, socks, and pants were soaked. Maybe Nick was suddenly taken by Arbalest's idea of a marijutopia, or maybe he simply couldn't, in his present altered state of consciousness, debate the topic any more. Nick looked at his watch, marveling at the contrast between the gold of the metal rim encircling the face and the gold of the numbers and hands and the black of the band. He looked at his watch, knew it was a timepiece, but for the life of him, he couldn't make sense of it. Had he put it on upside down or something? He turned his wrist to see, but it was still a cipher. He shrugged, deciding it didn't matter what time it was. Time would take care of itself.

"OK, I give in."

"All right, reason dawns at last! Let's do it!"

Nick winced. The only other significant time he could remember Jon saying "let's do it" had been just before they'd marched, with five or six hundred other people, over to the Blake Gymnasium and occupied the ROTC headquarters. Nick wondered why it was that whenever someone of his generation wanted to close an agreement to take action, he or she inevitably said "let's do it." To mouth such a phrase bespoke, it seemed to Nick, a certain poverty of imagination.

So, with that wrenchingly off-key note gnawing at his eardrums like an ant, Nick struggled to his feet, and slogged and splashed behind Jon through a calf-high puddle (odd that Jon didn't appear to notice, much less mind, that, slopping through the puddle, he had become drenched). Sliding, slipping like a shaky cross-country skier every couple of steps, bogging down in quicksand, his shoes squirting out water, squeaking, Nick fought his way up out of the clay mud and mire, and, grabbing at fireweed and quackgrass and sunflowers, up the now thoroughly soggy, frog-and-toad-spawning clay bank, to Jon's Impala.

Chapter 8
Arrestes

As Nick slid into the passenger seat, he felt the stifling closeness of the air inside the car. He also saw a large fresh white-gray deposit of bird dung on his side of the car hood. He leaned forward and saw, perched on a cottonwood branch directly above, a crow, whose round eyes stared unblinking back into his. Against the broad-fanned green cottonwood leaves, rippling silver in the breeze's eddies and backswirls, the crow was a piece of midnight sky cut out and set in the tree, a spill of oil in bird form, a black rupture of nothingness into their space and time. Nick felt his marrow freeze, as if his bones had just been injected with liquid nitrogen.

"What are you looking at?" Arbalest asked, settling himself behind the wheel.

He saw the dung, followed Nick's gaze, saw the crow.

"Goddamned crow. Shit on my car, will you?"

Arbalest lay on the horn, three blasts, trying to scare the bird. It sat looking at them through eyes so calm, they might have been black glass. Arbalest started the car, popped it into gear, pealed out, fishtailing on the gravel.

As they drove by the small houses that backed on the bluff, Nick saw an old man he recognized, standing, in his osteoporotic way, beside an old Ford Fairlane, with a gallon bucket in one hand and a four-inch paintbrush in the other. He had just finished painting the car's left front fender and was working on the driver's side door, painting it with a thick layer of fire truck-red house paint!

"Would you look at that!" Nick said, pointing across Arbalest's chest at the agelessly ancient man, who looked Nick in the eye, grinned with a surprised happiness, and lifted his paintbrush in salutation.

Nick felt the old man's warm, candid look become eyebeams stabbing him through the neck and chest like rusty hacksaw blades. The man stood there, big-boned, his broad brow sweating, smiling--but Nick wasn't willing to swear he was flesh and blood.

"Look at what?" Arbalest asked impatiently, his sideward glance having revealed nothing noteworthy about the oldtimer and his old car.

"Old Frank is painting his car." Of course he's flesh and blood. For Christ's sake, it's just Old Frank Atkins.

Arbalest twisted his head around to look, since they had passed the man by.

"So what?"

"Can't you see, Jon, he's painting it with *house paint*."

"So? That should be pretty strong paint, right?"

"Wrong. Jon, there's a reason cars are spraypainted--first with primer, and then with real auto paint."

"Nick, who gives a shit? Who is this 'Old Frank', anyway? He's a creepy looking old fart."

Arbalest was referring to the fact that the old man had a long grizzled-brown beard and greasy hair that snarled its matted, tangled way down past his shoulders, wore a faded blue-and-white checked shirt (with not one button buttoned, and his untanned pot belly sticking out), held his threadbare black pants up with a piece of twine instead of a belt, and wore lime green thongs on his feet. A half-full Schlitz bottle grew up from the dirt at his feet like some brown extra-terrestrial plant.

"Oh, he's all right," Nick said, though at that moment he wasn't at all convinced of that. "He's just an old guy. I didn't know he lived down here. He walks around downtown, with this big staff-like walking stick. I've seen him in the health food co-op and in the head shop in town a few times. The freaks who run the stores joke around with him. I suppose he gets lonely down here by himself."

Arbalest uttered a terse, noncommittal "hm" in response.

They drove by the alfalfa mill and Nick saw a shell-burst of phantasmal translucent white, twenty yards ahead. A vague form, the outline of shoulders, boss, head, horns. It walked straight toward the car that made straight for it. Nick flinched, sure they would collide. The buffalo evaporated as they struck it, moved like white smoke plumes past windshield and windows. Nick looked back: vacant air.

They passed the grain elevator. They drove through the intersection with First Street and the Airport Road, keeping to their eastern course, the grass-weed-and-tree-overgrown bluff on their left, the railroad tracks running molten silver on their bed twenty feet below.

A white blast, eyeball-scalding, not ten yards in front of the car, black eyes big as softballs racing toward Nick, black scimitar horns aimed at his heart. Everything else undifferentiated. A second searing explosion, the world a mass of white flame, then, retinas burned, humors dried up like ponds in drought country--black--bright--obsidian blackness.

By the time Nick could open his eyes without pain, Arbalest was parking the car in a grassy triangle formed by the conjunction of the Bottom Road and Tenth Street, which ran in a south-southeastward diagonal down the hill from town, splitting in two near the bottom, one fork bending east and the other west to join the Road. Arbalest said he had seen other cars parked there, so he didn't figure the car would attract attention if they left it there. To be certain, though, he raised the hood, so it would look as if someone had had car trouble and had walked into town for help. They were alone on the Bottom Road.

They started down the twenty-foot bank to the level of the railroad tracks. The bank was overgrown with sunflowers, Queen Anne's lace, fireweed, cheatgrass, and marijuana plants, which, indeed, often did hit six feet or more, just as Arbalest had said. The county usually mowed in eight feet or so on either side of the road, but they had obviously been occupied somewhere else for a while. A few yards the other side of the tracks, the ground sloped fairly steeply down another twenty feet before it leveled off and gradually fell away to the Red Earth River, which, cottonwood-and-sumac-lined, ran along, maybe two hundred yards to the south, for a while parallel to the tracks before bending southwards to flow toward its union with the Missouri, three miles away.

They walked along the tracks a quarter mile east, waited for a brown Dodge DeSoto to drive past and out of sight on the Bottom Road, then clambered down to the second incline, grabbing at marijuana plants to keep from slipping. Grasshoppers flung themselves out of their way. Invisible crickets chirped.

They set to, wrenching marijuana plants out of the ground one or two at a time. It had not rained for over a week--and then only an eighth of an inch--so they were difficult to pull up. When the big plants came free, dry earth showered off dull white roots in powdery dirt and hard tiny clods. Almost instantly, their tennis shoes became dirt-engrimed, as did their jeans from the knees down.

They laid a group of twelve or so plants in a single pile on the incline, tips downward, amidst a dense growth of other plants, where they would be obscured from sight unless one stood virtually on top of them. They smoothed over the holes left by the uprooted plants, stripped off fireweed leaves and sprinkled them about on the ground so it would look relatively undisturbed. The humidity had become stifling as soon as they had begun to exert themselves, and sweat was running down their backs and chests and dripping into their eyes. When they raised hands to wipe the sweat away, they left dirt smudges on their faces.

They walked another three hundred yards east before picking more plants. They yanked up another twelve or so and took the same precautionary measures. Their one concern was whether or not they would be able to find the plants again in a few weeks, after they'd dried out. Ravenous mosquitoes appeared--what was it attracted them? the smell of flesh?--and their arms and necks soon bore red stinging puncture sites. They walked into flurries of gnats--like stepping into ground clouds that moved with them--and they constantly had to sweep the innocuous irritants away from their faces.

They walked east a third time, through somewhat shorter grasses and weeds: wild brome, blue stem, mare's tale, ragweed, field pennycress, burdock, foxtail, even a soapweed or two in bare, eroded places. Arbalest kept his eyes trained on the ground directly ahead, to avoid cockleburs. Nick alternated between looking for burs and looking for cars on the road above--though they were far enough down, it would have been difficult to see a car unless it was right above them, on their side of the road. They stopped, harvested another big armload of plants.

By that time they were six hundred yards east of the car. They thought that was far enough in that direction, so they climbed back up to the tracks and walked until they were two hundred yards west of the car. While they were walking along, trying to appear as if they were merely out for a leisurely late afternoon stroll down the railroad tracks, just two hippies out admiring the scenery, a new Chevy pickup (an In-transit sticker still in the rear window) and a Mustang drove by, the pickup headed east, the car west.

Walking along the tracks, Nick felt safe because he was no longer engaged in a criminal act--nobody could prove he had done anything--and because walking down railroad tracks was a relatively unsuspicious thing to be doing. Young people did it all the time.

"Jon, this'll be the last time, OK?" Nick said as they made their way back down the second bank again.

"Yeah, this is getting old."

Their hands were stained yellow-green and their shoes were such a filthy black-brown it was doubtful they would ever come clean again. Their T-shirts hung out and were dirty where they had wiped their hands. Their pants were dusty, dirt-streaked, weed-and-grass-stained.

Nick bent over to pull up a singularly tall plant and Jon tried, at first unsuccessfully, to jerk out a handful of somewhat shorter plants from the ground.

"Do you boys have a license to pick those plants?"

"What?" Nick said, looking up, startled. Two blue-uniformed cops stood above at the level of the tracks, each training a .38 revolver on them. Nick saw the gun barrels streak down the incline at knee level, like strange, hard pipes being furiously laid by viewless hands, but growing bigger round all the time. When the barrels reached a point a yard before them and rose up, like cobras, to eye level, Nick and Jon found themselves staring into steel-encircled black holes the size of cannons (though Jon seemed oblivious to this).

"I *said*, do you have a *license* to pick those plants?"

The cop who spoke was about forty-five and beefy--maybe six-two and two hundred forty pounds. He wore brown tortoise shell glasses, with lenses thick enough to make his face seem curved in through their distortion. His voice was a thick, deep bass, and because he spoke clearly, enunciating each syllable as if he loved nothing better than to hear himself talk--because his voice was so clear and forceful, Nick could credit it with reality. The voice forced him to accept that this was really happening, that those men were cops, that he and Jon had been caught, well beyond any reasonable doubt, engaged in an activity that was not only criminal, but feloniously so.

The second cop was younger by about ten years, much shorter, maybe five-eight, and skinny in what Nick thought was probably a salient-ribbed way--though, he noticed, the deeply tanned forearm of the man's gun hand was a tight, vein-bulging rectangle of defined muscle. The younger cop looked like the kind of guy who went in for the martial arts and who took their nearly ascetic discipline very seriously. Both policemen wore blue hats that matched their suits. Neither Nick nor Jon could make his tongue function.

"If you don't have a license, then you are in violation of the ordinances prohibiting the harvesting and possession of a controlled substance, and you'd better step on up here. Place your hands over your heads and walk on up here, slowly, very slowly."

Wordlessly, Jon and Nick did as they had been told, though the steepness of the bank didn't make it easy to climb up without using their hands. Nick saw the black gun barrels loop around and follow them up the hill. At the top, standing between the tracks, Nick noticed the cops' nameplates, pinned across the tops of the pockets over their left breasts. The big cop's name was Walters, Schering the shorter cop's.

Walters told them in a clear, mellifluous way that seemed more friendly than hostile, to keep their hands well up over their heads, and then he asked Schering to pat them down. Schering's gun retracted to regulation size and he holstered it and performed the pat-down quickly, with a light touch. Either he was deftly efficient or he found the task distasteful, perhaps both. Schering stood back, said they were clean. He took his gun out again, pointed it toward them.

"OK, now, do you young men have any identification on you?" Walters asked. They answered yes. "All right, I want you, one at a time, to take your left hand and slowly pull your identification out of your pocket and hand it to me."

Nick's black leather billfold bound a bit in the back pocket because of the sweat-dampness of his pants. He didn't know how he was going to be able to take his driver's license out of the billfold using just one hand, so he held the billfold out to Walters. But Walters told him to use his other hand to remove his driver's license. Walters had laugh lines around his acorn-brown eyes, and what could be seen of his buzz-cut hair was gray. Schering had short, sandy-blond hair (which

Nick would later see was cut in a flat-top) and oddly placid gray eyes. Walters took their IDs and, without being told to do so, they raised their hands again over their heads.

"So, let's see who we've got here. One Jon A. Arbalest and one Nicholas B. Larkin." Walters had kept his pistol pointed at them, though he balanced the plastic licenses against it in a casual sort of way. "OK, now I want you two to turn around and slowly put your hands behind your backs. Dennis, would you cuff them?"

Jon and Nick followed Walters' instructions. Nick heard Walters slip his cuffs from his belt and hand them to Schering, who must have holstered his gun again with a practiced agility since Nick didn't hear him do it. Schering cuffed first Nick, then Jon.

Watching magicians on TV variety shows escape with relative ease from police handcuffs had given Nick the impression that it wouldn't be terribly difficult to extricate himself from them if he wished to do so. But the cool, intransigent steel enlocking his wrists-- firm but not circulation stoppingly tight--quickly demonstrated the falseness of that impression.

Walters read them their rights, then asked, "Is that one of you guy's Impala parked in the triangle up the road?"

Arbalest said it was his. Walters nodded, asked Schering to recover the evidence (the plants they had just picked), told them to come along. They climbed the embankment to the level of the road and walked in silence back to Arbalest's car, beside which a blue-and-white police cruiser was now parked. The Impala's windows were unrolled and Nick saw a huge fly buzzing around on the inside of the windshield. He thought of Dickinson's poem, "I Heard a Fly Buzz When I Died," which seemed mordantly appropriate.

Walters asked Arbalest where the registration was in the car. Arbalest told him the glove compartment, and Walters asked Schering to get it. Walters kept his gun on them even after Schering handed him the pink slip. Walters studied the paper a moment, then told them to get into the back of the cruiser. Schering held the door open for them, his pistol pointed at Nick's midsection. It was an awkward business, getting into the cruiser, with cuffs on. Schering closed the door behind them, put away his gun, and got into the front seat of the patrol car.

They had to sit sideways a bit to keep from crushing their hands against the back seat. The car had been kept scrupulously clean. There was not a single speck of lint or sunflower seed shell, not one bit of gravel or piece of dirt on the maroon carpet or on the vinyl seat. Wire mesh separated the front and back seats, and through it, Nick's eyes fastened on the sawed-off shotgun jutting up beside the police band radio.

With the heavier Walters on the driver's side, the car listed slightly in that direction. As Walters started the car, Schering radioed the station, letting them know that the "suspects" had been "apprehended" and asking them to check out the Impala's VIN. Then Schering got out and put Arbalest's pink slip back in the glove compartment of the Impala; he set its parking break, rolled up the windows, locked the doors, and lowered the hood.

When Schering got back in the cruiser, Walters turned around and drove up Tenth Street's diagonal into town. He drove with one hand on the wheel, the other propped on his open window, as calmly as though this were an ordinary afternoon drive. In a few moments, they parked in front of the Center Street station, a half block north of Main.

Walters held open the plate glass-and-steel door to the small entryway, the black and white tile of which was still wet from a recent mopping. The radio officer, a tall, poplar-slim guy not much older than Nick, immediately unlocked the door to the radio room. They were directed by Walters to the small office back of the radio room. The white letters on the black plastic sign over the wooden door frame read SHERIFF. Nick noticed that the black hands of the large, round wall clock showed 6:40; the red second hand spun around tirelessly in its determinate arc.

The sheriff's office held only a walnut office desk, a matching walnut rolling chair (the green leather on the back and seat was well worn and starting to crack), two five-drawer olive green filing cabinets, and two white-painted wooden straight-back chairs, on which Schering, after removing their cuffs, told them to sit.

"Now, would you young men like to make a written statement?" Walters asked calmly.

Nick and Jon looked uncertainly at each other.

"Don't we need to have a lawyer present before we do something like that?" Nick asked.

"No, but if you want to wait until your attorneys can be present before you give a statement, I guess we'll just have to wait on that."

Walters sounded a trifle put out, as if it were somehow an affront to his professionalism for them to ask to have counsel present before giving a statement.

Nick turned to Jon and asked, softly enough so only he could hear, "What do you think? Do you have an attorney?"

"No. How about you?"

"No, but I think they'll provide one for us. Isn't that right?" he asked, turning to Walters and speaking louder. "You'll provide an attorney for us if we don't have one, won't you?"

"If you want to fill out an application to have a public defender represent you, you can certainly do that, but you'll have to qualify, of course, under the economic guidelines."

Of course. "So, what *are* the economic guidelines?" Jon asked. He seemed to be regaining his equanimity.

"Well, you'll just have to fill out the applications, and then we'll inform you if you qualify." Walters' voice was resolutely neutral, his face erased of feeling. He wasn't about to make it any easier for them. He probably looked with severe disapprobation upon middle class kids like them sponging off the county government, asking for public defenders.

"And how long will it take to make a determination?" Jon asked. He was definitely getting his stride back.

"I really couldn't say. We'll just have to see."

No, he wasn't going to make it one whit easier.

Nick had less than a hundred dollars in the bank, and that had to last him the rest of the month. How could he ever afford an attorney without going to his parents for help. His parents! He couldn't even think about facing them yet. That would have to wait. But perhaps this thing wasn't so serious after all. Maybe the cops were just trying to scare them. After all, that long-haired, wholly Americanized Thai kid, Little Jimmy--which wasn't his actual name but a handle he'd picked up at the University of Miami, where he'd majored in surfing and beach parties before dropping out (just before he would have flunked out) and starting over again in the more conservative, straight-thinking, Protestant-work-ethic-inculcated Midwest--Little Jimmy had been busted with six other freaks just last month, two weeks before finals, and had gotten off with only a warning. The cop who'd caught them smoking--of all places, on the side of the bluff on the west central part of town just below a small children's playground--had ascertained that they weren't holding anything but a few joints and he'd let them off with an admonitory lecture about the unsalutary effects of cannabis usage and how it would inevitably lead to harder drugs. His sermon was a bit late since Little Jimmy and those other heads were zonked on acid or mescaline or speed or hash laced with smack--which had the slick, insidious street name of "green death"--every weekend.

"Could you tell me the exact charges we're being held on?" Nick asked.

Walters smiled, wrinkling the laugh lines around his eyes, for a second or two. "Well, I can't really say yet, at least not officially. The district attorney will have to look at the particulars of your case, and then he'll decide what charges, if any, are going to be filed."

"'If any'? You mean the charges might be dropped?" Nick asked.

"Yeah, you know, we were only out there because a guy at the bar the other night told us marijuana was growing down there along the tracks," Jon added, sounding awfully sincere. "We didn't believe him, so we went down there, you know, to see for ourselves. Hell, it was just a joke. We never meant to break the law."

"But Officer Schering and I both saw you pick some plants."

"We just picked some for fun, that was all," I said. "We were just messing around."

"But what were you planning to do with those plants?"

"Nothing," Jon said. "We were going to leave them lying right there, on the ground."

"Well, now, if you were to write down what you just told me, I'm sure the district attorney would take your cooperation into consideration in assessing your case."

"You mean he might drop the charges?" Jon was still trying to get some kind of definite answer, but Walters wasn't going to commit himself to anything.

"I really have no way of knowing that. But if you want him to consider your side of things, giving a voluntary written statement is the best thing you could do at this point. Unless you're keeping something back from me, of course. If you were keeping something back from me, why, then I could see why you wouldn't want to give a statement."

"We're not hiding anything," Jon insisted.

"Well, OK then," Walters said, nodding approvingly toward us. "You know what I think you ought to do, but you'll have to decide for yourselves. Officer Schering and I will step outside and let you consult for a moment." He closed the door behind them.

"What do you think, Jon?" Nick asked softly.

"I don't know. I still think we ought to have lawyers here before we say anything. But if there's any chance it'll help us with the district attorney, what the fuck, let's do it."

Let's do it. There it was again, that blunt, emphatic call to action.

Nick opened the door. "Alright," he said to Walters, "we've talked it over and I guess we're ready to give written statements."

"Good. I think you boys made the right decision. I'll be right in with the forms."

"OK, Nick," Jon said, whispering, "we write it down just like I told Walters."

"You mean we heard from Washington at Ted's Bar--"

"No, from a stranger, nobody we know."

"We heard from a stranger in Ted's Bar that there was marijuana growing down by the railroad tracks, we didn't believe him, and on a whim we decided to drive down and take a look for ourselves."

"Right. And remember, we never meant to pick anything and take it with us. We just intended to leave it there. We were, in fact, about to leave when the cops appeared."

"OK, sounds good. Say, you don't suppose this office is bugged, do you?"

"Getting a little paranoid, Nick? No, I don't think these guys are that sophisticated."

Walters stepped back into the office and laid a form and a pen down on the green faux leather-sided blotter on the sheriff's desk.

"All right, one of you can sit here, and one of you can come with me into another room."

"I'll go," Jon said, standing up.

Nick sat down in the green-leather-padded rolling chair, at the sheriff's desk.

"I'll be back in a bit to see if you're finished," Walters said to Nick.

Walters caught the door behind him. A long black plastic nameplate mounted on a long piece of walnut-stained wood, angled to face the door, said Sheriff Rodney Stutheit. On the left side of the desk were two eight-by-ten color pictures in a simple glass-and-metal, V-shaped set of frames. One picture was of a handsome, thin-faced woman of about forty-five, whose short, soft-waved hair, though salted with gray, was still shiny brown, and whose large brown eyes were teasingly defiant, as if she were joking with the photographer, or perhaps, with whoever was standing next to the photographer. She wore a strapless scarlet taffeta evening dress, a pearl necklace, and pearl earrings. Her smile looked coy, largely because of the expression of her eyes; or maybe it was the other way around.

The second picture was of the Stutheit family, with the still comely but somewhat older Mrs. Stutheit dressed in a navy-and-white dotted Swiss dress, a silver pendant, with an oval piece of what might have been onyx set in its center, hanging on a silver chain from her neck. The sheriff, a broad-browed, big-nosed, round-cheeked man with brown eyes and dark brown hair, slicked up in a pompadour (with Brylcream no doubt), was dressed in a navy blue blazer, navy pants, white shirt, and narrow, blue-and-white-striped tie. Of the three Stutheit kids, the two boys were dressed in suits--dark blue and gray pin-striped--while the girl was dressed in a white blouse with frills around the neck and down each side of the front buttons, a forest green scarf, and a forest green wool skirt; she wore a gold broach above her left breast. All three kids looked to be in their late teens, about Nick's age. Everyone in the picture was fairly beaming with familial high spirits.

Nick felt a mallet strike his chest as he remembered the photograph taken of his own family at Christmas, eighteen months before, halfway through his senior year in high school. From the warm, sheltering bosom of middle America to jail, in little more than a year. Nick had never felt more scared, more alone, more angry at himself. In short, more desolate. How would he ever be able to face his parents? Or Judith, who didn't smoke dope herself and who had several times this past year blown up at him for "doing something so completely predictable, so petty minded, so uncreative"? Ever since Judith had become a painter, she had been holding forth on such things as bringing creative passion to bear on all parts of one's life--as if creativity were as much an active attitude as a gift--so that one's whole life became an overarching work of art, albeit one ever in process and perhaps ultimately unfinished (the risk implicit in every life). When he had responded that that was fine for her, she was an artist, she had nailed him with his writing.

He was so dumbfounded, and so embarrassed, he couldn't respond, could only blush, against his will, and listen. He had never told her--he had never told anyone; hell, he wasn't sure he had even told himself--he was serious about writing, but only that he was thinking about taking a writing class next year and that he was keeping a journal. But she had known--as she had always known things, with that matter-of-fact, Cassandra-like certitude that was arguable only as an exercise in futility (when it came to such things, she was *never* wrong, at least not in his experience)--she had known that, like her, he had already made his choice, and that, like her, he would never be happy or at peace in this mutable world unless he could become somehow the artist he knew, with his own trans-rational sense of unerring conviction, it was in him to be. And today, damn it, today, he had felt himself getting closer to learning exactly what kind of artist he might be. He had *felt* it, strong as lust, no, even stronger, far stronger, had felt it while lying on his bed, watching the film images his mind projected on the blank white wall.

Judith had even succeeded, after many scores of hints and reasoned persuasions and challenges and blunt accusations--and to be honest, an ultimatum or two--and cajolery and blandishments and encouragements, and after many months, in getting Wolfram Kohles to abandon pot and the occasional hallucinogen in favor of the straight creative life with her. Wolfram had even cut his drinking down to the infrequent beer or glass of wine. When he was around Judith, he simply had no interest in the stuff. That was all there was to it. No interest. And his music was going better than it ever had. He was composing all the time now, in the car, in the shower, while playing a gig, when he was with Judith, when he wasn't--and not just blues and rock, but complex jazz arrangements, with instrumentation he could hear in his head but that he had never attempted before. Nick knew there was no way, absolutely no way he could ever explain to his parents or to Judith why he had been out there picking marijuana plants by the railroad tracks. He wasn't sure he knew why. Simply being stoned and having the opportunity didn't explain it, couldn't explain it. And it could never ever excuse it.

No, he was of an age now, struggle against it though he might, when he couldn't expect to have his actions excused by others, when there were no more excuses possible, when there were only choices, the choices *he* had to make, he and no one else. And then, having made them, he'd have to find a way to live with them, or, if he was lucky, by them. But why had this choice been so stupid, so impossibly, unforgivably stupid? He wasn't stupid. Far from it. He usually thought of himself as Judith's intellectual equal, and he knew no one brighter than Judith. Except maybe Mike Red Horse, to whom everything came easily, literally everything.

And why did the results of his choices have to be so unyieldingly, so unmitigatedly awful. It had been so with Annie. It was so now. He clenched his hands into fists and strained every muscle in his arms, chest, back, and legs as hard as he could against itself He turned red, then felt a flash of pain in his back, an inch below the right shoulder blade. He unclenched. The pain persisted, pierced him when he shifted in the chair. He knew he'd strained a muscle. More stupidity.

A small gold sticker, placed inconspicuously in the lower right part of the Stutheit family photo, said Saltzberger Portrait Studio. Nick knew the place. It was a studio and camera shop in the middle of Main Street, only a block away, between a bakery and a Sears catalog order store. Nick had walked or driven past it dozens of times but had never had reason to go inside. There was no sticker on the picture of Mrs. Stutheit; it must have been taken elsewhere.

The form Walters had set on the desk had a line of instruction at the top and a great deal of blank space for Nick to tell his story in. It required only half a page to tell the version he and Jon had agreed upon. Nick signed and dated the form in the appropriate blanks at the bottom of the page.

He looked about the room but there was nothing much to catch the eye: a couple of five-by-seven pictures of Sheriff Stutheit proudly holding up some fish he'd caught--a fifteen- or twenty-pound muskie in one and a stringer of rainbow trout in the other--and a wildlife calendar, featuring this month a painting of a white-tail buck, arrested in mid-flight as it sprang over a scrub oak.

Schering came in to see if he was finished. Nick handed Schering the statement, and Schering took him back out to the entryway and then through a locked metal door at the other end. They entered a much larger room with a couple of big tables pushed together in the middle (bright aqua plastic chairs pushed in around them), Coke and Pepsi machines against the right wall, and a small table against that same wall. The table held a hotplate, a percolator coffeepot, and two metal trees, from the branches of which dangled coffee cups of various sizes, designs, and colors. Walters was seated at one of the tables, a steaming cup of coffee and a chocolate chip cookie, on a white paper napkin, before him.

Jon was having his mugshots taken in the camera area at the rear of the room. Behind him on the wall was painted a two-inch-wide, red, vertical line, calibrated with black hash marks, each representing an eighth of an inch, with somewhat bigger marks every half inch and somewhat bigger marks yet every foot. The top of Jon's head was even with the six-three-and-a-quarter mark.

Nick was directed to a tall, narrow table at the right rear, where two sets of his fingerprints were rolled, one finger at a time, onto two forms, by a short, freckle-faced, redheaded cop whose nameplate said Burns. Then Nick and Jon switched places and Jon had his fingerprints rolled as Nick had his front and profile shots taken. As Nick turned this way and that, he noticed the anti-drug posters on the wall, including one directed at parents, telling them the warning signs of drug use to look for in their children, and another that listed the known negative effects of marijuana usage, the first listed being that it inevitably led to the use of harder drugs. How strange: Getting busted on a felony rap didn't even make the list.

Thompson, the young, dark-haired cop who had taken their mugshots, sat down at the table with Walters and Schering and helped himself to a cookie. Burns directed them to a sink on the right wall, five feet from the Coke machine. They used a bar of Lava soap to scrub clean their inky fingertips.

When they had finished, Burns had them empty their pockets into two large manila envelopes, with their names already written on them in black marker. He asked them to take off their belts and remove their shoe laces; he rolled the belts up and slipped them and the laces inside the envelopes, which he sealed. Then Burns took them through the locked metal door in the middle of the rear wall. The door opened onto two barred cells on the right and a row of tall, wide green metal lockers on the left. Some of those lockers, those toward the far end had names taped on them, but none of the nearer ones did. One of the nearer lockers was partly open and Nick saw in it, in two long, clear plastic bags containing the plants they had been caught picking, little clods of dirt still clinging to their roots. Burns opened the barred door to the first cell with a long silver key and motioned for them to enter. They stepped in and he locked the door behind them.

"Is this going to be on the news tonight?" Nick asked Burns before he left. "I mean, they said the district attorney hadn't decided yet if he was going to press charges."

"Sorry, you're askin' the wrong guy. You'd have to talk to the district attorney about that."

"Well, is he here? Can we ask to have him come talk to us? Just for a minute?"

Nick thought that shouldn't be too much to ask, especially since they had been so nice and cooperative about giving written statements.

"No, he's not here right now. I don't expect he'll be coming in tonight."

"So there's no way we can find out now if charges are going to be filed against us?" Jon asked.

"I can ask up front, but I doubt anybody up there knows any more than I do at this point."

"Well, can you tell me," Nick asked, "if it's standard procedure to mention an arrest on the evening news before charges have been decided upon?"

"I couldn't really say. I just started here a week ago."

"Do you think you could ask somebody else who might know?" Nick asked. "If it's going to be on the news, I'd like to call my parents and tell them myself. We do get one phone call, right?"

"Can't say I know the answer to that one, either, but I can ask up front about it."

"OK, thanks. I'd appreciate it," Nick said, trying not to let his voice betray the deep disappointment he felt in the answers he'd received.

Burns went out through the metal door. They heard him lock it from the other side. The second metal door, at the back end of the cell block, opened, Nick supposed, onto the station's parking lot, off the alley.

Their cell contained only a commode--with no seat and with a flush button instead of a handle--and two bunks. Nick took the bottom bunk and Jon jumped up onto the top one. There were no windows, so their only light came from two fluorescent ceiling fixtures, one outside each cell. The mattresses were thin and the pillows mere solid wafers, but the bunks weren't uncomfortable. And they couldn't complain about the cleanliness of the cell. Someone was obviously conscientious about keeping it spic-and-span; a faint odor of Pine-Sol rose up from the floor. The walls had been freshly painted, a bright meringue white, a white so white it would preclude sleep. The walls' blankness screamed out, like a fresh snowfield, for marks, for graffiti.

They lay in silence, having nothing they wanted to say to each other. Nick wondered whether the charges would be dropped, and if not, what they would be. And more important, what was he going to do if charges were pressed? He'd have to face his parents and Judith--a thought almost physically painful. There was a kind of clinical impersonality about dealing with the cops that made it easier to talk to them about what had happened. But with his family, there would be no way any of them would ever attain any kind of objectivity. There would be an unremitting rush of feeling that would batter him from all sides, as if he were running a gauntlet blindfolded. There would be unanswerable questions: "Nick, how could you have done this to yourself? What's happened to you, son? Do you realize what you've done to your future?" There would probably be accusations and shouting, but ultimately the questions would be followed by a titanium-hard silence, impenetrable to any attempt at articulation or inner cry of heartsickness and hurt.

Their one hope--and though it was a slim one, Nick was white-knuckling it--was that the district attorney would agree that they'd just been caught on a college student lark and that their continued freedom posed no criminal threat to society. Freedom! That magical word. The word that had winged so forcefully from his lips the past few years, as he had become aware of the struggles of Blacks and Indians and others for the rights he and others like him had always taken for granted. But liberty was no political abstraction now. His lack of freedom was as basic, as irrevocable, as coldly tangible as those three quarter-inch-thick steel bars he couldn't quit looking at.

Outside, he knew, evening's long shadows were falling. But he wasn't free, as he always had been before, to walk out if he chose, to watch the tangerine light metamorphose to mango to purple to ultramarine, to see the clouds, mottled slate and indigo, become an inverted geography, as if in looking up one was in truth looking down at the earth from above, seeing the cool, shadowy waters of bays and inlets and shorelines, and seeing the land, too, dusky and indistinct. Or not to walk out if he so chose. To choose instead to stay inside and read or listen to music or sleep or make love. Or whatever else he chose to do with his time. The important thing, he knew now in a way he had never known before and that he would know the rest of his mortal days, was to be *able* to choose. And he, because of one afternoon's idiocy, could no longer do that.

He had only the one hope, which was looking more dubious by the minute: That, somehow, miraculously, the charges would be dropped, that, like Little Jimmy, he'd be let off with a warning and a stern lecture about the dangers of drug use. There was one danger of drug use that he now believed in with absolute conviction: The danger of losing your personal freedom. Yes, that one he believed in beyond any reasonable doubt.

Nick turned his head so that he looked at the bare, garishly white wall instead of the bars. He stared hard at its chilly lunar vacantness until it swirled, slipped, slid, dissolved, and, cast up by a phantom projector, Judith's face appeared. He saw her call his room again and again, getting no answer. He saw her get annoyed, then angry, then worried. He saw Judith call Arbalest's room; no answer. He saw her check the rec room, Anthony's Restaurant, the library. No Nick. He had vanished. He saw her explaining the situation to the RA at the dorm's front desk and asking him to have the RA on Nick's floor check Nick's room. He saw them waiting, then the desk phone ringing, the RA saying OK and hanging up, telling Judith the room was empty, not to worry, that her brother had probably just gone out for a beer. Judith had nodded and turned away, not bothering to explain that Nick didn't drink.

Nick saw himself and Jon walking along the railroad tracks by the Bluffs Road, saw them stop and walk down the hill for the last time, saw them begin to jerk the plants out of the ground, and then that bass voice, like the voice of the Almighty, and those blueblack gun barrels streaking down the hill toward them, growing bigger and bigger, till Nick stared into the merciless cylinder of a cannon. He saw the cannon go off and his body standing there headless, like some hapless Civil War soldier in a charge on the enemy's line. He saw them searched, handcuffed, marched away. He saw these scenes over and over, in a continuous loop.

Nick saw his parents relaxing, his father on the couch, reading *U. S. News and World Report*, his mother sitting in an overstuffed chair, tatting, the ten o'clock news just starting. A solemn-faced anchor saying, "Good evening, Channel 11 News has just learned that two university students, Jon A. Arbalest, and Nicholas B. Larkin, were arrested earlier this evening near the town of Red Earth for the harvesting of marijuana and possession of more than an ounce of marijuana, both felony charges." He saw Lena blanch, drop her tatting, say, "Oh my God, Roger, that's our Nick." And Roger go white, set his magazine on the coffeetable, and go to her without a word, and take her into his arms. Over her shoulder, he saw tears falling from Roger's eyes. Nick didn't remember ever having seen his father cry before.

That did it. He swung out of the bed, walked to the bars, and called several times for an officer. A while later, the metal door opened and Burns poked his head in.

"Everything OK in here?"

"I just wanted to know if the DA had decided whether he was going to charge us yet?"

Burns stepped in, shook his head no. "Haven't heard a word about it."

"Well, then, do you think I could make that phone call we talked about?"

"Yeah, duty officer said you could each call one person."

Arbalest said there was nobody he wanted to call. Burns unlocked the cell and Nick followed him out to the bigger room. The clock there said nine-fifty. Its blood-red second hand spun unceasingly round.

Nick tried Judith's number at the dorm. He let it ring fifteen times. No answer. He tried again, no answer. He asked if he could make a long-distance call if he called collect. Burns said yes and Nick sighed and dialed the operator and gave her his parents' number. The operator let it ring ten times, and then said, "Sir, there's no answer at that number. Would you like to try again at a later time?" Nick thanked her and said yes, he would try again later. He remembered. Wednesday was the night his mother's garden club met, each time at a different member's home; it was also one of the nights his father went to the gym to work out.

"Not having much luck, huh?"

"No, could I try again later?"

"Sure. Bound to reach someone sooner or later."

Burns escorted Nick back to the cell. Standing at the locked door, holding onto the bars, Nick looked at the tall plastic bags containing the marijuana plants. The evidence against them. If he could only get out of the cell, grab the two bags, get out the back door, somehow, and abscond with the evidence. Bury it, destroy it, burn it--no, not burn it. That wouldn't be too smart.

Nick turned away from the bars, lay down on his bed. No amount of wishing was going to make those bars melt, thaw, and resolve themselves into a dew. He was 'behind bars'. He'd never known how that word "behind" would be able to hurt him, starting at the crown of his head and racing like a shooting star all the way to his footsoles. He tried to turn his cell wall into a movie screen and project upon it scenes from films he liked, but it was impossible. Nothing came. He closed his eyes, knowing it was futile. Sleep was a long, long way off.

Part IV

December 1959 - July 1963

Chapter 9
Temperature Readings

The Larkin twins knew exactly when it was they became human emotion thermometers: their ninth birthday party, one o'clock Sunday afternoon, December 12, 1959. Their mother Lena set the chocolate-frosted white cake, with multi-colored sprinkles, its yellow candles ablaze, down in the middle of the dining room table at the farm, and they made their secret wishes--the same wish, of course--and they blew at the candles in a crosswind that extinguished them instantly.

When they looked up, they saw that the kids at the party had become different colors. Sheila Wilcox was a warm peach-rose; Bobbie Wilcox a flickering sunburst orange; Linda Schneider a cool aquamarine; Jimmy Van Buren a translucent gold; Larry Schumacher a slightly diluted paint-box blue. They knew just what the kids were feeling, how excited and happy or bored and disinterested they were, just by looking at them. They looked at each other, saw nothing unusual. It was only other people whom they saw as colors. Judith reached over and felt Nick's forehead: normal, as far as she could tell.

Their father Roger said, "Why don't you open the presents now?" He was a steady sunny yellow. They looked at their mother Lena: a bright apricot. The twins opened their presents--sets of jacks, 200-piece puzzles, paddle balls, and Crazy Eights and Authors card games from the kids; a silver snow saucer and a five-foot, hard plastic toboggan-like sled, ice skates, and books from their parents--which made them happy, especially since they knew there would be even more at Christmas. But the thing they remembered the most about that birthday was looking up through the swirling candle smoke and seeing that everybody had become a different color.

* * * * * * *

Early the next July the Larkin family moved from their farm in north-central South Dakota to the LaPointe community airport, in the Nebraska panhandle, on a spur of the Pine Ridge. Roger had been hired to manage the airport, which was exactly the sort of change Roger had been looking for. He had flown jets on reconnaissance missions in

Korea and had felt a self-confidence and exhilaration in the air that he had never known anywhere else, except perhaps in Lena's arms. He would probably have made a career of the service except that its regimentation cut against his grain.

Going back to farming had been a return to familiarity, but it hadn't paid as much, even in good crop years, as it might have, and it had also been somewhat flat after OCS, pilot training, and daily communion with a machine of immense power but exquisite sensitivity. For those reasons Roger had bought a Piper Cub two years before, had converted the north end of his erstwhile sheep shed into a hangar, and had started a crop-spraying business. A small, hand-propped plane with a boom under each wing and a belly tank full of water and herbicide wasn't like piloting jets, but at least it was flying.

When Roger had heard about the LaPointe Airport manager's position, he hadn't had to think long before deciding to apply. The city council had been impressed with his credentials and had hired him after a brief interview. So, he would be around planes, and the men who flew, guided, and repaired them, every day. Also, he and Lena could take classes at the state teacher's college in town and maybe finish their degrees.

* * * * * * *

The day Roger moved his family to the airport, everything that could go wrong did. It was hot, he was driving his old green Ford pickup, and though both he and Lena had their windows down, the breeze that blew through was hot and of little help. The twins sat between them, and where bodies touched, it was uncomfortably warm and sweaty. Three hours into the trip, their passenger side front tire blew, making the pickup lurch abruptly to the right. Roger fought the wheel and got the vehicle stopped on the shoulder of the road. Strips of black rubber, his erstwhile tire, shredded and now looking like a family of snakes, lay in the road throughout the last sixty feet.

Roger cursed when he discovered that his spare was almost flat. The twins saw his face spark the yellow of an acetylene torch when first lit. The pickup had come to rest in a flat place but Roger, always cautious, set the emergency brake. He blocked the wheels, loosened the lug nuts, jacked up the truck, and took off the slightly bent wheel. He hoped that whomever he bought a new tire from in the next town would be able to hammer the wheel back into its proper rondure. Roger had to wait twenty minutes before someone came down the road. It was fifteen miles to the next town but it was over an hour before he returned--with a new tire and a shiny new wheel. Nick and Judith were happy to see him; catching grasshoppers, throwing pebbles hopelessly at gophers, and watching red-wing blackbirds and meadow larks could only fill so much time. Lena, a calm nectarine color, thought it better not to ask what the tire and wheel had cost them. They had started with enough cash to pay for their gas and not much more; now there wouldn't be enough for that. Lena had packed a picnic lunch, so they wouldn't have to buy food.

Sure enough, they ran out of gas about forty-five miles north of LaPointe. They were also out of money. Without saying a word, his color not changing, but becoming lambent, Roger parked alongside the road, got out and hand-pumped several gallons of aviation fuel into the pickup from the tank back of the cab.

"Roger, can you do that?" Lena asked when he got back in.

He turned the key and the engine started. "Sure. It's not a good thing to do for long distances, but it'll get us to the airport with no problem."

* * * * * * *

When Roger unlocked the forty-foot trailer he had bought in LaPointe and had brought out the week before, the twins ran in to look over their new home, a job that required only a minute since it was so small. Still, it was new and they liked it.

Around four that afternoon the Larkins were finished unpacking and settling in. They had had to leave most of their belongings at the farmhouse, bringing only clothes, dishes, cleaning supplies, a few toys and books, a small TV, a radio, and not much else. Roger had already picked up a used couch and a couple of used easy chairs, so they hadn't had to bring any furniture.

"Nick, Judith, you two take this garbage out," Lena said, handing them each a box, one containing several empty boxes and the other a few boxes and the remains of their picnic lunch.

"Where do we take it," they asked together.

"Your dad says there's a barrel out back."

The twins carted the boxes outside, walked through the grass, through the elms bordering their yard, and across a dirt driveway to an old thirty-gallon barrel. Heat from many fires had faded, blistered, and blackened its red paint. The twins threw down their boxes and ran back to Lena.

"Mom, there's already--"

"a bunch of garbage in the barrel--"

"and there's no room--"

"for ours," they said, finishing each other's sentences, as they sometimes still did.

"The Snodgrasses must have left that," Lena said, thinking of the previous manager's family. She opened a cupboard, took out a box of wooden matches. "Here, burn their garbage and then you'll have room for ours."

The twins' eyes got big: They had never been trusted with matches before; the trip must have made their mother really tired. Her color *was* a bit tepid.

"Should we burn ours, too?" Nick asked.

"Yes, those boxes will take up too much space otherwise."

Back at the barrel the twins tried to light the Snodgrass' garbage--without much luck. The waxy half-gallon milk container wouldn't catch fire and what paper things there were buried under a bunch of smelly, rotted produce, coffee grinds, and eggshells.

"So what do we do," Nick asked his sister.

"We've got to get this fire going. This is the first time Mom's let us do this."

"Yeah, we don't want to blow it."

"I know, we'll pump some aviation gas from the big tank in the pickup into this coffee can." Judith managed to dislodge a pound-size Butternut can from the mess in the barrel.

"Are you sure, Judith?"

"Sure I'm sure. Haven't you seen Dad do it before at the farm."

"Yeah, but I know he wouldn't want *us* to do it."

"Well, then we won't tell him, will we? Come on, scaredycat."

Judith started toward the pickup, which Roger had parked on the west side of the trailer to make it easier to unload. Nick worked the handpump while Judith held the nozzle into the can. It didn't take long to pump out a pint; Judith told him to stop. At the barrel Judith unceremoniously dumped all of the gas in and told Nick to light it.

"What? Me light it? You're crazy. Light it yourself."

Judith sighed, mumbled something about having to do all the work around here, and took the box of matches from him. She stood a yard away from the barrel, struck a match, and tossed it in. Whoosh! the flames leaped up two feet above the top of the barrel. Judith jumped back beside her brother and they watched the fire in delighted fear. But the flames soon subsided and began to consume the garbage at a fast rate.

"There," Judith said proudly, " I told you the gas would work."

"I knew it would all the time," Nick said.

"Yeah, sure."

"I did. I just thought you were getting too bossy."

"Yeah, well, you need bossing sometimes."

They watched gray and black smoke rise from the barrel, watched the heat make the air quiver around it. They heard two sharp pops as something glass broke and they heard cans clink dully together as the fire burned everything combustible and the remnants settled. Halfway down the barrel, the fire hit a mass of newspapers and quickly flickered out.

Judith looked in and saw the problem. "There's a bunch of newspapers clogging up the barrel. Run and get some more gas."

"Bossy, bossy," Nick complained, shaking his head as he grabbed the
coffee can and walked, not ran, to the pickup.

When Nick returned, he dumped the gas in a circle over several weeks worth of the Sunday editions of the *Omaha World-Herald* and *Denver Post* papers.

"You light it this time," Judith commanded, holding out the box of matches.

Nick took the box, stood well back from the barrel, held his breath, struck a match and flung it fast at the barrel. But the match flew over the barrel and he had to run up and stomp on it before it set fire to the tawny, dried-out grass encircling it. It had evidently been a while since they'd had rain in western Nebraska.

"You dummy, what are you trying to do?"

"Shut up. I threw it too hard and missed, that's all."

"I guess--missed by two yards at least."

"It wasn't any two yards. It was only a few inches."

"Do I have to do it to make sure it's done right? I didn't miss, you know."

"Stand back or you'll get your hair singed. I've had about enough out of you."

Nick lit another match and threw it into the barrel. The fire took all right, but this time before the flames died down, several big, burning, black-edged pieces of newsprint floated up, were snatched by the light breeze, and landed in the grass in places from five to twelve feet away. Instantly the dried cheatgrass, brome, and sandburs caught fire.

Nick and Judith ran up and started stomping on the grass, but it had caught in too many places and was spreading too fast. They ran in and told their mother, who looked out the trailer window, saw the fire, and ran into the white, concrete block Airport Office building next door to get Roger, who was talking about hangar rent to three brothers who'd just bought a new Cessna. Roger ran out, looked at the blaze, which had left twenty feet or more of grass charred in a ragged fan shape around the far side of the barrel. Though his face looked pale, the twins saw his color turn the scarlet of a burning bush in fall.

"Lena, grab me a blanket. Nick, run over to the FAA and get their fire extinguisher."

"But, Dad, I don't know where the FAA is."

"Oh, shit," Roger spat out, the words sparking red comets, as the twins saw it. "Lena, forget the blanket, " he called over his shoulder as he sprinted across the grass and then the concrete apron toward the FAA station.

He was back almost instantly with a big red fire extinguisher. The twins watched in amazement as he pulled the pin and ran around aiming the black, cone-shaped nozzle at the fire. The extinguisher made a noise like a vacuum cleaner when you put your hand over the end of the hose, a noise like what they twins imagined a dragon would make. A gray fog came shooting out of the nozzle, smothering the fire. When the fire was out, they saw that it had left a black patch that stretched thirty feet, all the way up to the barbed wire fence separating the airport property from the highway ditch.

The fire had attracted an embarrassingly large crowd: the three pilots, one of the men from the FAA station, a ticket agent from the Western Airlines Office, and an old man and his wife who had been in the process of purchasing tickets when the agent had seen the fire and run out.

"What were you two doing," Roger accused the twins, "trying to burn down the whole goddamn airport?" He was glowing red as a hot coal. The twins hung their heads. "How did this happen, anyway?"

"I told them to burn the trash because the barrel was full," Lena said.

"Didn't you use the grate?" Roger asked the twins.

For the first time Nick and Judith noticed the big square of wire mesh lying a few feet away from the barrel.

"No, Dad, we didn't see it," Nick said.

"Didn't see it. But it's in plain sight. Even so, I don't see how this fire could have gotten out of hand so fast."

The twins looked at each other and at the coffee can on the ground. They wished it had burned up in the fire. Roger saw their look, picked up the can, held it to his nose.

"You used gas on this fire?" Roger was flabbergasted. More spurting comets.

"We had to," Judith said. "We couldn't get it to start."

"Where did you get it?"

"We pumped aviation gas from the tank in the pickup," Nick said, a rich tone of defeat in his voice.

Roger couldn't help but admire their resourcefulness. At the same time he was shocked at their daring. He resolved to get a lock for his tank of aviation fuel. Should have bought one before.

"I don't want you two to *ever* start a fire with gas again--you hear me?" They nodded, seeing that his color was cooling, orange-red, then orange, then orange-yellow. "I hope you've learned a big lesson from this." They nodded again. "You see that big white tank of airline fuel?" They looked at the huge tank, roughly thirty yards away, and big enough to take two big tanker trucks to fill. "I'd hate to think what would have happened if this fire had reached that tank. You'd have killed us all. Do you understand what I'm talking about? We'd all have been dead, and they wouldn't ever have found our bodies because there wouldn't have been anything left to find."

The twins gasped. They remembered the exploded farmhouse their family had driven out to see two winters ago. One leaky propane valve and the whole house had gone up. Nothing left but rubble. Roger saw that his words had found their mark. No reason to stretch this out.

"Well, I hope you realize now how dangerous fire can be." They mumbled yes. "OK, I want you to promise me you'll never do this again."

The twins promised and Roger sent them back into the trailer with their mother, while he went to the FAA station to return the extinguisher. That evening, as the twins played in their bedroom and Lena fixed dinner, Roger sat at the kitchen table, sipping a Schlitz.

"Lena, wouldn't you agree this has been one hell of a day? We blew a tire and the spare was flat, I had to buy a new wheel, and to top it all off, we weren't here more than an hour before the kids damn near torched the place."

Lena laughed. "You have to admit, we make a big first impression. Did you see the looks on those men's faces?"

Roger laughed. "They looked like they'd all gone into shock." He chuckled. "I thought I was going to lose my job before I'd even started."

"Oh, Roger, they wouldn't fire you just because your kids set a few square yards of grass on fire."

"I know, but I don't imagine the city council will be very understanding if it happens again."

"Then we'll just have to make sure it doesn't."

"I don't think it will. Did you see how shamefaced they looked?"

Lena nodded, turned back to the stove. That night, in the double bed that took up most of the back bedroom of the trailer, in Lena's embrace, Roger found a way to forget the day's troubles.

****

A week into September, when the days were still pleasantly warm but the nights were cool, Roger met the twins' school bus--actually a big tan station wagon with three seats, which ferried, besides the twins, six farm kids into town for school. Nick and Judith liked riding in the car because Mr. Van Horn, its owner and driver, who had retired from the Union Pacific Railroad after thirty years but who hadn't wanted to sit around home all day, was kindly and patient, and unlike many adults, soft-spoken.

"So, how was school today?"

"Pretty good," Nick said, "Mrs. Mortenson is really nice."

"Yeah," Judith said, "she lets kids from the class design one of her bulletin boards each month, and she chose Nick and me and Kim Barnes to do the first one."

"Nick, buddy, it sounds like they've got you outnumbered--two girls to one."

"It's OK, Kim's nice."

"He likes her because she told everybody she thinks he's cute."

"I do not."

"Don't worry about it, Nick," Roger said. In a few years, you'll be ecstatic when girls like Kim notice you."

"What's 'ecstatic'?" Nick asked.

"You know," Judith said, "it's what happens to the radio when the weather's bad."

Roger laughed. "No, honey, that's 'static'. 'Ec-static' means very happy. Here, why don't you guys come into my office. I've got a surprise for you."

"Really? What is it?" they asked, running through the door their father had opened.

At the sound of the turning knob, a black female Labrador dog had
leaped up from the throw rug where she had lain in front of an old couch and come running over, tail wagging.

"A dog!" the twins said together, petting the Lab's head and letting her lick their hands.

"Yep, I got her this morning from Bill Jeffries, who runs the Gamble's store in town."

"What's her name?" Nick asked.

"Bill's been calling her Betsy--yes, baby, that's you, no, no, don't jump up, I warned you about that. See, she knows her name, so we'd better stick to that."

"How old is she?" Judith asked.

"A year and a half?"

"She's a hunting dog, isn't she, Nick asked?"

"Yep, Labradors are great retrievers. Lots of duck hunters use them because they love the water. But I'm going to use her to hunt pheasants."

"Does she know what to do yet?" Judith asked.

"Sort of. Bill has trained her a little, but I'll have to work with her these next couple of months before hunting season starts." The twins could see that their father's normal sunny yellow had become bright-beamed.

Roger spent an hour nearly every day working with Betsy, teaching her not to walk too far ahead, not to chase rabbits, and not to bite too hard when retrieving the bird. She was a smart dog and learned quickly. The whole family fell in love with her and she responded to their affection with even more of her own. Indeed, her well of love was bottomless and never less than brimful. If no one was paying attention to her and she wanted to be petted, she would walk up to where Roger or Lena or one of the twins was sitting and nudge-nuzzle their legs or hands with her snout. Looking into her eager round brown eyes, it was impossible to deny her a pat or an ear-scratch, a side-thump or a belly rub.

Unfortunately, Betsy did not restrict her affections to humans. Roger hadn't realized she was in heat, hadn't even thought about it in fact, he was so absorbed in preparing for hunting season, when one afternoon in the last week of September the twins burst into his office.

"Dad, come quick! Betsy's stuck to another dog!"

"What the hell?"

"Their rear ends are stuck together," Nick said.

"Sonofabitch! Did you try to get them apart?"

"We tried, but they wouldn't budge," Judith said.

"Where are they?"

"On the other side of the big hangar," Nick said.

Roger found them in the shadow of the hangar, still stuck together.

"Shit!" Roger said, his face brightening like a struck match, red sparks flying. He was barely able to constrain himself from kicking the male dog, which was a brown-gray, short-haired, droopy-eared, big-boned, strawberry-spotted mongrel, who at that moment seemed a mite done in. It might have been a cross between a collie and a German shepherd, with an indeterminate number of other breeds thrown in for seasoning.

Roger tried to separate the dogs, to no avail. He ran over to the hose the FAA used to water their two squares of grass (divided by a sidewalk and flagpole). He disconnected the sprinkler, turned on the water full bore and sprayed both dogs till they were soaked and the ground beneath them was muddy. Either that worked or nature decided the time for Betsy's pleasure was over, because they parted inside a minute, the scruffy mutt trotting off eastwards, and Betsy padding through the mud to Roger and presenting herself for petting.

After that Roger practically kept Betsy under lock and key in his office, but inside of four weeks, his worst fears were confirmed: Betsy was undeniably, indisputably pregnant. It was bad enough that the father was such a scrubby, godforsaken, mixed-breed canine fiasco; that would make it doubly hard to get rid of the puppies. What was worse was that between her pregnancy and her nursing of the puppies, Betsy would miss the whole pheasant hunting season. All of the time he had spent training her had been for nothing. They would have to wait another whole year. The day that he knew for sure Betsy was pregnant, Roger decided that as soon as the puppies were weaned and it was safe, he would have her spayed. It was expensive, but he'd be goddamned if he was going to go through this again.

* * * * * * *

Nick and Judith had taken to airport life, finding it ever fresh and interesting. But of the many things they found to do, nothing could begin to compare with climbing in the rafters of the big hangar. This idea had suggested itself to Nick one day when he and Judith were sweeping the hangar with big push brooms. Once a month, on a nice day, Roger would tow all the planes out of the hangar, tie them down, and hire the twins to sweep the hangar. Nick found that the glamor of sweeping the big concrete floor of the hangar soon wore off and the job became simply tedious. It was the blessing (though others would occasionally curse it) of the twins' lives that when they became bored, their ever-fertile imaginations took over and improvised some way to change dullness to excitement.

So it was that as Nick paused a moment in his sweeping, he heard sparrows chittering above and looked up, trying to see them. He had heard his father complaining about all the sparrows in the hangar and how hard it was to get rid of them. He squinted because it was darker up in the rafters, but he managed to see a half dozen of the small gray birds perched on a rafter twenty feet overhead--and that was when it came to him. He and Judith could have a great time climbing around up there. The horizontal boards were all two-by-eights, so they would be easy to walk on, and there were lots of crisscrossing support boards to hang onto. It would be wonderful.

Nick waited to tell Judith until they had finished their work and their father had pushed all the planes back into their spaces in the hangar and gone back to his office. They were alone in the hangar, much darker now that the big sliding doors had been shut.

"Great, but how are we going to get up there?" Judith asked.

"I think I've figured out a way. Follow me."

He led her to the corner of the back room of the Western Airlines office--an eight-by-fifteen foot area housing their teletype, two desks, some shelves, and some file cabinets. There was a space about fifteen inches wide between the Western Airlines wall and the exterior wall of the hangar, a space for the hangar door to slide back into.

"See, there's plenty of room for us to crawl up," Nick said.

"You mean on those cross boards on the hangar door?"

"Yeah."

"But they're only two inches thick."

"What's the matter, are you chicken? Are you afraid you're going to fall?"

"Hell no."

Judith slid into the gap and began to crawl with the sureness of a spider up the wall of the hangar. It was, in fact, easy, just as Nick had said it would be. In a minute she was standing on a rafter overhead. Nick started to climb, but she didn't wait for him. By the time he was up, she had crossed to the very middle of the hangar.

To Nick's eyes the rafters at the top of the hangar were another world. Walking over the wings and fuselages of the planes parked at angles below made him feel like a high-wire artist in the circus. He learned it was easy to keep his balance on the two-by-eights, especially since it was only three steps or so to the next cross beam he could hold onto. Nick saw dozens of sparrows now. They scattered, chirping when he came toward them. The bottoms of his tennis shoes became white with their dry, chalky dung.

That first time, he and Judith explored every rafter in the hangar. They were sitting in the middle, dangling their legs over the side when a man in a white shirt and narrow black tie--Dick Jones--came out of the FAA office, walked down the north side of the hangar, and went into the door of a storeroom. Quickly the twins drew their legs up and lay down on the rafter, barely peeping over the edge. Jones came back out with a mop and bucket and a bottle that, given its shape, could only be Mr. Clean. The twins held their breaths until he went back into the FAA office. Safe. He hadn't seen them.

They hurried over to the place where they had crawled up, figuring that was the best way down, too. It was a little trickier going down, though; it was dark in that corner of the hangar and they had to feel where to put their feet. But in a short time they were standing on the concrete below. Judith and Nick thought climbing in the rafters was far and away the most exciting thing to do at the airport, so they did it every day for a while and then at least two or three times a week after that. They found that the hangar was shut up and empty of people most of the time, so they didn't have to worry about being discovered.

The second week in November Roger flew out on a charter to Denver. He was to be gone four days. On the second day of his absence, Nick and Judith went climbing in the rafters, as usual. This time, though, as they were starting down, Nick's left foot slipped and he fell down straight and fast as a big rock dropped off a bridge.

Nick went feet-first right through the roof of the Western Airlines back room--smash--and landed upright (somehow keeping his feet) atop the teletype. Johnny Walston, who had been sitting reading the information printing on the machine, flung his hands up in the air--sending his freshly filled fountain pen flying like an arrow out into the other room, dead center into the back of Raleigh Jones' white shirt. Jones, who had just finished weighing and tagging some luggage, shouted "Jesus!" and propelled himself backwards on his roller chair, into George Calhoun, who had a sheaf of papers in his hand, papers which instantly became airborne.

Nick stood, dazed and trembling, on the teletype, a litter of plaster and broken ceiling tiles everywhere around him. He looked up through the hole in the ceiling and saw Judith scurrying down the wall, a fly with a purpose. As she came in the door of the Airlines back room, Johnny Walston was helping Nick down from the machine. Raleigh Jones and George Calhoun stood a few feet away, still white with amazement, speechless.

After they had determined that Nick was unscathed, Raleigh looked up through the hole. Nick looked at the blot of black ink in the middle of Raleigh's back. He looked like some kind of human target.

"Good God, Nick, what happened?" Raleigh asked.

The twins had spent considerable time in the Airlines office, and so, were on a first-name basis with all of the agents.

"I fell through the roof."

The three men laughed at that; they were the warm yellow of a wood fire. George said, "We know that, but what were you *doing* up there."

Nick's guard wasn't up, so he told the simple truth. "We were playing in the rafters and I slipped climbing down."

"You gotta be kidding," Johnny said. "You and your sister up and decided it would be fun to romp around in the rafters? Is that right?" Nick nodded.

"We've done it lots of times before," Judith said defensively, "and this is the only time anything's happened."

"Oh, 'lots of times', huh?" Raleigh asked. He had become aware that his shirt was sticking to the center of his back and he was trying to feel with his hand to see what was the matter. "Hey, I'm not bleeding am I, guys?"

Anyone could have told him the truth, but they waited for him to bring his fingers back around and see their ink-stained tips. "Shit, it's ink. It's from that damned fountain pen of yours, Johnny. If you'd use a ballpoint pen like a normal person, this wouldn't have happened." Raleigh had become woodpecker red.

"Don't blame me," Johnny said, turning rust, then brick red. "I'm not the one who fell through the roof."

"Well, this is a new shirt," Raleigh said, "and it's probably ruined. I don't think anything will get this ink out. Somebody's going to have to buy me a new shirt."

"Like I said, *I'm* not the one who fell through the roof."

George looked up through the hole and said, "Speaking of falling through the roof, all I've got to say, Nick, is that you're one damn lucky boy. If you'd straddled one of those ceiling rafters on your way down"-- he chuckled-- "well, let's just say your future wife wouldn't like it much." All three men laughed, Raleigh and Johnny having cooled back to a squash yellow.

Nick knew what George said was true. He'd seen the two-by-four rafters of the Airlines back room many times from above. The rafters were eighteen inches apart. It had been a miracle that he'd fallen exactly between two of them.

Nick didn't feel so lucky, however, when his father's plane landed two afternoons later. The moment he had been dreading every waking hour since his foot had slipped off the hangar door had come. After his father had tied down the plane and settled his business with his charter in his office, Nick came up to him (watched intently by Judith) and said, "Dad, I've got something to tell you."

Roger was feeling ebullient. He had just been handed a fat check for his four days' work, he was glad to see his kids, and he was looking forward to the homecoming welcome that only Lena could give him.

"Dad, Judith and I,"--his sister scowled at him--"we were playing in the rafters of the hangar and I slipped crawling down and fell through the roof of the Western Airlines office."

"What?" Roger was stunned. He couldn't find words. "The rafters? You fell through the roof?"

"Yeah, I landed on the teletype."

"Are you all right?" Roger quickly scanned his son for abrasions.

"I'm fine, but I knocked a big hole in their roof."

Roger sat down on the edge of his desk, started to turn rose, then cherry tomato red. "My God, I'm gone for four days, and you guys start destroying the place. Trying to burn the airport down wasn't good enough for you?" Nick looked hangdog. "And what in the hell were you two"--he looked around but Judith had vanished--"doing horsing around up in those rafters?"

Roger waited but Nick said nothing. "I'd like an answer to that, Nick."

"It's just something fun we like to do."

"You mean you've done it before!"

Nick nodded.

Roger pounded the desk, said, "Dammit, Nick, I thought you had more sense than that. How could you have ever done such a stupid thing? You're lucky you didn't fall onto that concrete floor or onto one of the planes. If you had, you wouldn't be standing here talking to me now. Do you understand that?" Nick saw that his father was cooling rapidly, cardinal to coral to salmon to ocher, to pumpkin, to canary.

"I know, it was really stupid. I won't do it again, I swear."

Roger sighed, slapped his hands on his thighs. "I guess we'd better go take a look at that hole."

"They covered it with a piece of plywood till you got back."

Roger started toward the door, visions of newly earned dollars slipping through his fingers to pay for patching and painting the Airlines office roof. Nick was right behind him. Fear of a much greater expense suddenly shot through Roger, who stopped so fast his shoes skidded on some gravel.

"Nick, you didn't break the teletype, did you?"

"No, it's OK. But we're going to have to buy Raleigh a new shirt. The one he was wearing got a big ink stain in the back."

Roger flared saffron, shook his head, started to walk again. "An ink stain? Nick, I think you'd better tell me the whole story. Start at the beginning."

It wasn't long after Roger finished fixing the roof of the Airlines office that Betsy gave birth to ten puppies. She simply disappeared to have them, but the twins found her under the trailer, way at the back . It became their chore to crawl back there twice a day with food and water. It became Roger's chore to bend the arms of people to take the dogs. And it took some truly heroic arm-bending to get rid of all of them.

* * * * * * *

The same month that Betsy's litter was born, the city council contracted with Anders Olsen, an airplane mechanic, to run the shop at the airport. He moved his trailer in next to the Larkins'. Olsen was about five-ten, but solid and muscular as a wrestler. He wore western clothes and oiled his black hair up in a tall pompadour. His wife Julie, a cheerful red-headed flibbertigibbet, was short, flat-chested, and square-faced. Anders and Julie, married five years, already had three daughters, Sandra, Linda, and Martha, all too young to be good playmates for the twins.

Judith and Nick kept their distance from Anders Olsen. He was always a hard, icy blue-green, hardly ever melting, even when he was with his family. When he got irritated, his color didn't redden, but instead got darker, until, when he was really angry, he became a deep, scary purple-black, the color of an eggplant. Lena complained to Roger about Julie's adoring obsequiousness toward Anders. For her part, Lena decided early on she didn't like Anders Olsen. She told Roger that Anders was "a know-nothing who thinks he knows everything." He could never admit it when he was wrong or own up to a mistake. Lena took pleasure in criticizing or embarrassing Anders--as when that winter and spring she bested him at archery target-shooting. (Everyone in the Larkin family had gotten fiberglass bows for Christmas, and in January Anders had bought himself one. He and Roger planned to go bow hunting for deer the next winter.) Lena and Roger had taken an archery class at the college, but Anders had thought it a waste of money. Lena relished making him eat his words.

It didn't surprise Lena, but it angered her when Anders, who was almost beside himself with attraction to her sultry, sexy southern looks

(Roger had met her while stationed at the Air Base at Valdosta, Georgia), finally made a pass at her early the next June. Roger was away from the airport for several weeks, flying for a big crop-spraying outfit in Devil's Lake, North Dakota, and for part of that time Julie and the girls were visiting her parents. When Anders knocked at her trailer door about ten-thirty one night, a time when he thought the twins would be asleep (they weren't--they were in bed, with the lights out, but they weren't asleep), and asked her if she'd like to have a drink with him in his trailer, she let him have it.

"Anders, I don't know what kind of tawdry seduction fantasy you've got going here, but you can forget it. It's not going to happen. I love my husband." He started to sputter in protest, but she went on. "If you don't leave right now and stay away from me the rest of the time Roger is gone, I'm going to tell Julie everything as soon as she gets back."

She slammed the door in Anders' face and locked it. She flicked off the lights inside, but when she walked by the twins' room, she burned with her own lava-red light. Anders stood stockstill outside, unable to believe what had happened. A few seconds later he heard her lock the back door as well. Sighing and shaking his head, he trudged off. As soon as he rounded the front of their trailer and appeared on the side the twins' beds were on, they felt a deep, blue-black, smoking cold penetrate their wall, as if it were caked with ice. Anders proceeded to down a pint of Johnny Walker and fall asleep, slumped over his kitchen table. But the twins shivered from the cold all night, though they got winter blankets from the high shelf in their closet.

Lena didn't tell Julie what had happened, but she did tell Roger the night he returned. Roger was shocked at his friend's betrayal. The twins felt heat emanating from their parents' room, as if a fire were raging inside. Roger told Lena she'd handled the situation correctly.

"Does that mean you're not going to say anything to Anders about this?"

"What's the need, honey? You already tromped all over him. He's not about to try it again."

"What are you, afraid to confront him just because he's your friend? I'd say he's a pretty pisspoor friend."

"OK, so he's a lousy friend, but I still have to work with the guy every day."

"It's that kind of attitude that forgives the neighborhood boys when they go out and rape some girl, and then say she asked for it." The twins' felt a sudden shock of heat and their door began to glow.

"Lena, what are you talking about? Anders didn't try to rape you."

"And what if he had? I suppose you'd still be best buddies with him, just because you 'have to work together'."

"Lena, you know I wouldn't."

"Then go knock on his door and tell him off."

"I can't do that."

"Then you can't sleep in this bed."

"What?"

"You heard what I said. Go sleep on the couch." She shoved him off, thump, onto the floor.

Roger picked himself up. "Jesus, Lena, what's gotten into you? Can't you be reasonable."

"I *am* being reasonable. You can sleep on the couch until you decide to confront that sleazeball mechanic friend of yours. And you can cook your own meals, do your own laundry, and iron your own shirts."

"Lena, this makes no goddamn sense at all," Roger said, grabbing his pillow and heading for the couch. When Roger opened his bedroom door and walked down the hall past the twins' door, Nick and Judith saw their door bow in and turn crimson. Any second, they expected it to burst into flames, like those of a Perseid meteor.

The next afternoon, Roger had a talk with Anders, who'd been anxious since Roger had returned, worried what would happen when he found out. Anders paled, though the twins, from their hiding place, saw that he really turned black as old engine oil. Anders and Roger had little to say to each other the next few months, until Anders' contract ran out and he departed for another airport.

* * * * * * *

Of course, the most wonderful thing about having a professional pilot for a father, the twins thought, was that he would take them flying. By their twelfth birthday, the twins had flown thousands of miles, scores of hours. At Thanksgiving, Roger would fly the family up to Spearfish, at the northern edge of the Black Hills, to visit their grandparents. But he would often take the kids flying just because he knew how much they loved it.

Roger would allow Judith and Nick to take the semicircular controls of the Comanche and guide them on a flight out over farmland or the LaPointe State Park (a few miles southwest of town) or the barren, eroded buttes several miles east of town. Roger taught them how to bank the plane into a turn, how to make it climb and descend, speed up or slow down. He taught them how to work the radio. He told them he would give them regular flying lessons when they got into high school.

High in the air over a landscape plotted and pieced as any quilt, their hands on the plane's sensitive controls, the twins felt incomparable freedom. Flying was pure elation. Once the noise of their plane put a whole herd of antelope to flight--twenty-five or thirty pronghorns leaping--so beautifully--across the prairie. Another time they scared a bunch of coyotes. One time, flying over LaPointe, they saw a group of kids flying kites five hundred feet below. Though Nick and Judith liked to fly kites, too, they felt that day that a kite was a pitiful thing compared to a plane. After all, if you wanted to be connected to the air, to fly, you had to really get up there, into the sky.

Chapter 10
Infinity

Sometime in the spring of the twins' twelfth year, they began to turn over and over in their minds, like someone spading the earth of a garden, the idea of infinity. All one of them would have to say is, "You know, if time is infinite. . ." and the other would keenly await the new idea.

"You know, if time is infinite, then everything we do could happen over and over again--" Nick started,

"because there would be time for everything to happen exactly the same all over again," Judith finished.

"That's right. Right down to the exact movement of little brown ants through the grassblades--"

"or wind through tree leaves--"

"or someone blinking their eyes--"

"or wrinkling their nose."

"And if time were infinite, it would also mean that *everything* would happen, every possible combination of events," Nick said.

"In one time, a person might live to be a hundred."

"And in another, they would die at the age of ten."

"One time two people would fall in love and live happily all their lives together."

"In another, they would never meet."

"They might pass, but on opposite sides of the street--"

"not even noticing each other."

"Or maybe they would meet--"

"but wouldn't like each other, would become enemies for life."

"In one time, you and I would be twins--"

"and in another, we would be born into different families--"

"thousands of miles apart."

"I might be born in China--"

"and I might be born in Africa."

"Or maybe we would be born centuries apart."

"Or maybe I would be your mother or your grandmother," Judith said.

"Or maybe you'd be a boy--"

"and you'd be a girl."

"What if everything that happens to you is just a big dream?" Nick asked.

"You mean, what if there isn't really any world or other people or anything?"

"Right, everything is just a big dream."

"A dream that never ends."

"Or that ends when you die."

"And then there's nothing?"

"I don't know. I haven't thought about that."

"But God would still be there."

"Maybe. But he'd be a pretty lonely God."

"That's why God would never let everything end . . ."

"You mean everything in your dream?"

"Yeah, God would never let everything that you've been dreaming is real your whole life end when you die," Judith said.

"Yeah, it wouldn't make sense. Then God would be all alone. And if He were going to be alone, then why would He have made you in the first place?"

"So, if there is a God, that would mean everything in life couldn't be a big dream?"

"No, if God were going to invent all that stuff to happen to you in your dream, He might as well make it all really happen."

"Unless God is playing a huge trick on you," Judith said.

"I don't think God would do that."

"Why not?"

"Because God would have to be evil to play a terrible trick like that on somebody."

"What if God were a woman?"

"What difference would that make? She would still have to be evil to play such a bad trick on you."

"No, "I'm not talking about that now. Just what if God were a woman?"

"Well, what if?"

"Don't you think things might be different?"

"Like how?

"I don't know, maybe men would have babies and stay home with them and women would go to work everyday."

"And the president would be a woman."

"And all the admirals and generals would be women."

"Would we still have wars?"

"I don't know, I think we probably would."

"So everything would be the same as it is now, only women would be in charge."

"Yeah, and queens would be more important than kings."

"If time were infinite, then in some times women would be in control--"

"and in others men would be--"

"and in others no one would be."

"Yeah, if time were infinite, then . . ."

* * * * * * *

By early June of their twelfth year, the twins had known Hugh Link for some time. They weren't sure how he had met their father since he didn't fly. Maybe Roger had crop-sprayed for him (Hugh owned a farm near Gopher Hole, Nebraska, sixty miles south of LaPointe). Maybe they had met through hunting or fishing, since Hugh worked as a game warden for the Nebraska Game and Parks Commission. Anyway, he had been coming by their trailer at the airport to visit every couple of months or so for almost as long as they had been living there. And their family had driven down to Gopher Hole several times to visit his family.

One thing that was different about those visits was that during them Roger and Lena didn't drink, out of deference to Hugh and his wife Shirley, who were teetotalers. The Links were devout Missouri Synod Lutherans. The twins remembered the first time Hugh had stopped by the airport. He and Roger had talked for some time in the office, before, noticing the hour, Roger had invited Hugh to lunch. At lunch, Roger had offered Hugh a beer. Hugh had smiled and said, "Nope, I don't touch a drop." He went on to explain that it went against the principles of his church. He asked Roger and Lena what faith they were.

They looked at each other, and Roger said, "Why, Hugh, I guess not much of anything right now, though we've attended the Methodist Church in the past." He gave Lena a wry look.

"Well, why don't you come to church with Shirley and me some time? You never know, you might like what you hear."

"I don't know Hugh, it's a good hour's drive down to Gopher Hole from here."

"Oh, I didn't mean go to church in Gopher Hole. I'm a lay pastor in the church and I often travel to different churches in this area to talk."

"What do you talk about?" Lena asked.

"I mainly give testimonials to Jesus' power to redeem the lives of even the worst of sinners. I many not seem like it now, but I was a real hellion when I was a kid."

"Really?" Roger asked, his interest piqued.

Lena kicked him under the table. Roger looked at her as if to ask, "What did I say?"

"That's right, I ran with a wild crowd and we drank a lot."

Roger was on the verge of asking Hugh to elaborate when Hugh continued, "Yes, I was a wild one. I was sliding down a big chute, on a one-way trip right into hellfire"--the twins' eyes got big--"when Jesus took pity on me. He reached right down from heaven, grasped my hands firmly, and pulled me back up. I changed my ways and changed my friends. A few months later I met Shirley, we got married, and she's helped me stay on the straight and narrow path ever since."

"So she didn't know you when you were a hellraiser?"

"Oh, she knew who I was, but she wasn't interested. She was a good Lutheran girl. She wouldn't have looked twice at me back then."

Roger was still hoping to hear more of the details about Hugh's life of sin, but while he was trying to think of a way to ask about it that didn't seem too obvious, Hugh said, "Anyhow, all this is a roundabout way of saying that we've attended the church in LaPointe many times. So, any time you and Lena want to go with us, you just let me know, and we'll be right here on Sunday morning to pick you up."

Roger didn't quite know what to say, so Lena said, "Thanks, Hugh, that's a kind offer. We're not looking for another church right now, but some day we might go with you. I've never been to a Lutheran service before. It might be interesting."

"How about you, Roger?"

"Sure, why not."

"Like I said, you might hear something you like." Hugh smiled at them.

"You never know, I might," Roger said, "but I still enjoy a good beer. I'm not sure I'm quite ready to give that up yet."

Hugh laughed. "You're beginning at the wrong end, Roger. Faith and salvation come first. Once you gain faith and are saved, you wouldn't mind giving up beer and liquor at all. Take it from somebody who knows."

"Maybe so, maybe so, but I sure hope you don't have to give up sex."

"Roger! Not in front of the kids!" Lena said, a cloud darkening her brow.

Hugh laughed again, hard, ending it by slapping his knee. "I can promise you, Roger, you don't have to worry about that. If you did, I'd probably be a sinner yet." He and Roger laughed. The cloud beetling over Lena's brow blew away.

The twins had met Hugh when they could still see people's feelings as colors. He had always been a rich carrot orange. They felt the air warm in a pleasant way around him. Their ability to see the secret colors of people had faded over time, but they still felt warm and steady around Hugh. He smiled a lot and they had never known him not to be cheerful. They knew that lots of other people seemed cheerful on the outside; but Hugh Link was the real thing, a genuinely happy man.

The twins liked him, and they figured their father and mother did, too, because he knew how to tell funny stories about catching people fishing without a license and the lies they would tell, trying to get out of the fine. Or he would catch people who'd bagged more than their limit of ducks or geese, or who'd shot a deer out of season. Hugh loved to tell about catching poachers of all kinds.

Hugh also told stories about his past as a saddle bronc and bull rider--he had competed several times against Casey Tibbs--and after he'd quit riding, as a rodeo clown. The twins had seen his medals and trophies and had seen pictures of him taken during his rodeo years, so they figured those stories were all true. In fact, the difference between Hugh's stories and those of other tale-tellers they had known, like Big Bill Burdette the combiner, was that Hugh's stories, though humorous, always seemed as if they had probably really happened. Judith and Nick had hardly ever believed a word Big Bill had said--though he was by far the most entertaining storyteller they had ever heard--but they never doubted Hugh Link.

Hugh and Shirley had three kids--Tim, three years older than the twins (enough older not to be interested in them), Ron, a year and a half older, and Sharon, their age. When the Larkins and Links got together, the twins spent all their time with Ron and Sharon. Usually they played card games or badminton or passed a football around. But that day in June, while they were exploring the loft of the Lakes' barn, Ron surprised them by asking if they'd ever looked at any other kids naked.

"Do you mean when we were naked or when the other kids were naked?" Judith asked.

"Either way," Ron said, kind of half grinning. "Have you?" he asked, looking right at Judith.

Nick was astonished. Was this what Lutheran kids did? He was sure Hugh and Shirley wouldn't approve, to say nothing of his own parents. Of course, that made it even more interesting.

Judith looked right back at Ron. "Do you really want to know, or are you trying to get me to do it now?"

Ron chuckled. "Do you want to?"

"Do you?"

At that moment, Sharon interrupted. "Come on, Ron, leave her alone."

"Let her speak for herself," Ron said, still looking Judith in the eyes. "Do you want to?"

"Tell him to get lost," Sharon said to Judith. "He's seen me plenty of times, but that's not enough for him. He has to see every girl there is."

"Why don't you just keep your big mouth shut, Sharon?" Ron said.

"You mean you've shown yourself to your brother?" Nick asked, amazed.

"Sure, and he's let me see him lots of times, too. Haven't you guys ever done that?"

"I've seen Judith," Nick said, "but only accidentally, you know, like when I've walked into the bathroom, not knowing she was in there."

"And have you seen Nick?" Ron asked Judith.

"Of course, you can't live in a trailer house like we do and not see each other."

"Well, you still haven't answered my question," Ron said. "Do you want to take your clothes off right now?"

"I will if you will first," Judith said, startling her brother.

"It's no good unless everybody does it," Ron said. "How about you two, are you game?" he asked Nick and Sharon.

Nick looked quizzically at Sharon. She said, "I will if you will." Nick hesitated, then nodded yes.

"OK, then, we're all going to do it. Why don't you girls go first? Then Nick and I will go."

"Ron, you're full of shit," Sharon said, shocking the twins.

"I said I would if *you* went first," Judith said, smiling.

"All right, all right. Just to show you that we're good sports, Nick and I will go first. Come on, Nick buddy, it's time to drop your drawers."

Nick was a bit embarrassed, but he was already lagging behind Ron, so he began to unbutton his shirt. By the time he got his tennis shoes off and had unzipped his pants, Ron was standing nude before them. He didn't seem affected at all by Judith's and Nick's stares. He had little dark brown tufts of hair at his groin. Nick paused before pulling down his underwear. Sharon's eyes were fixated on them, and he knew he had no black curls there to match the curls on his head. But he stripped them off anyway.

"OK, now it's you girls' turn," Ron said, smiling.

"Judith, let's climb down and leave them like this," Sharon said, smiling, touching Judith's arm to guide her to the hole at the edge of the loft floor where they had climbed up on a wooden ladder.

"No way!" Ron said running to intercept his sister. He grabbed her and said, "Nick and I did it, so you guys have to, too."

Sharon twisted, but Ron was stronger and she couldn't get away.

"Lemme go, I was just teasing."

"Sure, just teasing."

"I'm not lying. Lemme go and we'll do it, won't we Judith?"

"I said I would if he went first," Judith said.

Ron let Sharon go, and she and Judith took their clothes off. They went no faster than they had to, but it wasn't too long before they both stood naked before the boys. Nick noticed with interest that Sharon had two small breast buds and the bare beginnings of a delta of pubic hair. He was even more surprised to see that his sister, whom he hadn't had occasion to see for a while, also had little beads of breasts and the fuzzy black beginnings of hair too.

"Nick, it looks like you're the only one without hair," Judith said, and Ron and Sharon laughed.

"Shut up, Judith."

"Make me."

"OK."

"Hey, cut it out now," Ron said. I'm sure it won't be long before Nick sprouts out. After all, you guys are so alike it's scary. It shouldn't take him long to catch up with you. And I don't think Sharon here cares if he has hair or not. Just look at her. She's all eyes."

"I am not," Sharon insisted, punching Ron in the arm.

"Oh, Nick, help me," Ron said, "I'm hurt, I'm hurt." He clutched his arm as if it were a mortal wound and staggered a few steps. Nick and Judith laughed.

"Say, Judith, have you ever been touched by a boy down there?" Ron asked, pointing to her groin.

"No, have you ever been touched by a girl?"

"Sure, I've let Sharon touch me lots of times."

Sharon got red-faced and punched him again, a glancing blow on the chest.

"Sharon, stop hitting."

"Then stop talking like that."

"But it's true."

"No, it isn't. And even if it was, that doesn't mean you have to talk about it."

"Don't be such a prude. I don't hear you telling me to stop when I touch you."

Sharon was about to give a fierce reply when Judith asked her, "Do you like it when he touches you?"

"What do you mean?" Sharon asked, suspiciously.

"You know, does it feel good?"

"Why don't you ask him if it feels good. He gets a boner and starts to moan." She parodied a boy *in extremis*.

Ron laughed and was about to say something when they heard their mothers calling them. The voices called again, closer to the barn.

"Quick," Ron said, "get your clothes back on. They'll kill us if they catch us."

There was a storm of summer clothes. When they were just about dressed and their mothers were right below them, Ron called out, "We're coming, Mom, we'll be right down."

The four kids climbed down the ladder one at a time.

"Didn't you hear us calling you?" Shirley asked.

"Sorry, Mom, we didn't," Ron said.

"What were you kids doing up there?" Lena asked.

"Just exploring and playing hide and seek," Judith said, not daring to look at Ron or Sharon, for fear of giving herself away.

"Well, come on, it's time to eat," Shirley said.

They followed their mothers to the house.

After supper, the grownups dropped the kids off at the roller skating rink in town. Tim found friends of his to skate with, but Ron paired up with Judith and Sharon with Nick. By the time the "sweetheart skate" came along, it seemed natural for them to hold hands and skate round the rink in the semi-dark. Then it was time for the Larkins to drive home.

Outside in the parking lot, perhaps prompted by watching the way the kids had got on together, Hugh asked Roger and Lena if they'd mind if the twins went with his kids to church camp the Tuesday after next. It was going to be in the pine-covered hills of LaPointe State Park. The Lutherans had a camp there. Lena asked the twins if they'd like to go, and they said yes, enthusiastically. They'd been to the park several times on picnics with their parents and they liked it there. Roger and Lena agreed, and Hugh said he'd be by late Tuesday afternoon to pick up the twins. He'd bring them back again after lunch on Sunday.

BINARY STAR

* * * * * * *

Hugh Link was as good as his word. He picked up the twins and by five-thirty they were pulling into the grounds of the Lutheran camp--two dorms plus outhouses, a minister's cabin, a tall-steepled chapel that could seat one hundred and that had a cafeteria in the basement, a supply shed and an outhouse behind the chapel, a flagpole in front, and a softball field to one side. All the buildings were fresh-painted, a white that in bright sunshine made the eyes smart. After registering and making up their bunks in the still stuffy dorms, the Link and Larkin kids went outside, where the air was cool and shadowy and heavy-laden with the smell of pine. There weren't that many kids at the camp, twenty boys and twenty-four girls, ranging in age from twelve to sixteen. The kids divided neatly by gender, playing opposite each other at volleyball and alternately at tetherball while waiting for dinner, and they would remain divided for the better part of the week. Nick and Judith already knew about a third of the kids because they were from LaPointe. The first night at the camp Nick had trouble falling asleep, as he had every night since he had seen Sharon Link naked. Her image was as clear to him as if it were being projected on a movie screen in his brain.

Within a day, everything had become a routine of flag-raising, morning services, meals, classes, crafts, recreation, and prayer circles. Nick and Judith won prizes the first two mornings for having the neatest bunks in their dorms, and other days for memorizing the most Bible verses. Everything about the church camp was new to the twins, so they had fun.

A surprising thing happened to Nick on Friday afternoon. He went to the outhouse and was followed by Ron (Nick decided later that they had not met by accident). After they had finished peeing and left the building's close quarters, Ron asked Nick if he had been saved.

"What?" Nick asked, stopping.

"Have you been saved?"

"What do you mean? I've been baptized, I think."

"No, not baptized. Have you accepted Jesus Christ as your personal Savior and invited him in to sit on the throne of your heart?"

Nick thought about that for a moment. He had never considered his heart as having a throne in it. He tried to picture it.

"What do you mean by personal Savior?"

"Believing that Christ died for your sins and that by conquering death he won immortal life for you and all other sinners."

"And what was that about the throne?"

"After you believe in salvation through Jesus, you have to invite Jesus to sit on the throne of your heart."

Nick was still trying to get his mind around that idea. He pictured a tiny throne in one of his heart's chambers and a tiny Jesus walking up and sitting down in it.

"What does that mean?"

"That you humble your pride and bow down before the throne of Christ."

Now Nick was really confused. How was he supposed to bow down before a throne that was in his own heart?

"Where is this throne again?"

"It's in the hearts of all those who believe in Christ and accept Him as their personal Savior."

"Is there one throne or a whole bunch of thrones?"

"There's one in every believer's heart, but it's all the same throne, really."

"What?"

"The throne is Christ's throne in heaven, and when somebody believes in Jesus, they bow themselves down before that throne. It's the same as inviting Christ to sit on the throne of their hearts."

Nick's perplexity was such that he hardly knew what to ask next.

Ron and Nick started up one of the hiking trails through the hills.

"Could you explain to me again that stuff about the throne?

"The throne is just a metaphor, Nick. You know what a metaphor is?"

"Yeah, we studied them in school."

"OK, then, the throne is just a metaphor for accepting Christ as your Savior."

"So he becomes sort of like the king of your life."

"Yeah, something like that. I guess from all of your questions that you haven't been saved yet, huh?"

"No, I guess not. Does that mean I have to go home."

"Of course not. You can stay till the camp's over. How about Judith, has she been saved?"

"Not that I know of."

"Well, would you like to be saved?"

"You mean right here and now?"

Ron hesitated. "Uh, no, that wouldn't be right. I might mess it up. But if you want to, I can talk to Reverend Singleton and ask him to talk to you tonight."

"I don't know. I don't want to be the only boy who has to talk to the minister."

"You won't be. Danny Beltz talked to him last night."

"Is that why he was late getting back to the dorm?"

"Yeah, didn't you see how happy he looked."

"I didn't notice."

"How could you miss it? He was beaming."

"I guess I wasn't paying attention." Nick didn't know what else to say about that. There was a long pause. "So Danny felt a lot happier after he got saved, huh?"

"That's right, and so will you."

"OK, I guess you can ask if I can meet with him."

"Great. You'll never regret this, Nick."

"What about my sister?"

"Don't worry, Sharon's taking care of her."

"You mean you two had this all planned?"

"Not exactly, but don't worry about it, Nick. Some day you'll thank me."

* * * * * * *

By eight o'clock that night it was already getting dark in the camp. Nick wound his way to the minister's cabin. He was feeling miserable about having to talk to Reverend Singleshot--which was what the kids called him when there were no adults around. He didn't know what he was supposed to say. He would have turned back, except he knew the minister was expecting him. If he didn't show up, the minister would probably come looking for him, would call him out of the dorm in front of everybody. He wished he had never told Ron he would do this. He wished Ron hadn't asked him those questions about being saved and thrones and all that confusing stuff. Seeing as how he had no other choice, he sighed and knocked softly on the minister's door.

"Come in."

Nick opened the door and stepped inside.

"Hello, Nick, right on time. The Lord likes punctual people. Have a seat."

The cabin was small and had only a bed, a dresser, a desk and chair, and two easy chairs for furniture. It's only decoration was a crucifix on the knotty-pine wall over the bed and a picture of a long-haired, seraphic-eyed Jesus on the wall over the desk. He'd seen another one just like it on a wall in the cafeteria.

"That's a nice picture."

"Thank you, I like it myself."

Reverend Singleton was a lean, balding man in his late forties. He wore a light blue shirt, khaki pants, and oxblood leather shoes. He had removed the blue-and-gray-striped tie he'd worn throughout the day. He was kindly and cheerful, and he made Nick feel comfortable.

"How did the artist know what Jesus looked like? There aren't any pictures from his time, are there?"

Reverend Singleton cocked his head and looked at Nick more closely. These weren't the usual questions he got from twelve-year-olds.

"No," he said chuckling a bit, "there are no extant pictures of Jesus, so every artist has to draw or paint the Christ he sees in his imagination. Over the centuries, artists have had literally hundreds of different ideas about what Christ might have looked like."

"So there's no way to tell if this picture's anything like the real Jesus or not."

"No, but every once in a while an artist paints a picture that large numbers of other people feel in their hearts is the truth, that captures the majesty but also the humility of Christ. Da Vinci's "Last Supper" is one such painting. This is another. But you didn't come to talk to me about paintings, did you."

"Um, no, I guess not."

"Well, what did you want to ask me, then?"

The last thing Nick wanted was to go round and round again about thrones, so he asked a question he'd thought a fair bit about.

"Do you believe in infinity?"

The minister looked at him quizzically. "Why, I suppose I do. An almighty God is certainly capable of creating an infinite universe." Before he could redirect the conversation with a question of his own--something that, as a minister, he was particularly adept at--Nick asked another question.

"Don't you think that if there are an infinite number of stars, there must be other planets with life on them?"

"Well, I don't know about that."

"Doesn't it just make sense?"

"I don't know. But what I do know is that Jesus Christ lived and died and was resurrected from the dead for the salvation of people on *this* planet."

Nick went on as if he hadn't heard the minister. "What about time? Do you believe that time is infinite, too?"

Reverend Singleton looked relieved. "The answer to that is a definite no. We know that all time will end when Christ returns. The Day of Judgment will be the end of time."

"But how can time come to an end?"

The minister was surprised. The boy seemed innocent, but the questions he asked were tinged with, well, evil. There was no other word for it.

"When Christ returns, the world as we know it will cease to exist. There will be a new heaven and a new earth. All men will be judged and the good will exist with Christ forever after in His Kingdom."

"But wouldn't time still go on? I mean, if good people continued to exist with Christ, wouldn't that mean they were existing in time?"

"No, they would be in eternity," Reverend Singleton said confidently.

"What's that?"

"Eternity is the end of time."

"What does that mean?"

"It means our souls live forever and ever in spiritual communion with Christ."

"Doesn't forever mean infinitely?"

"Well, yes, it does, sort of, if you want to quibble about words," the reverend said, growing exasperated. This verged on impertinence. "But it's not at all the same thing to a believing Christian." He looked hard at Nick, trying to shame him, but Nick's blue eyes stared mildly back at him.

"OK, so say we exist forever. Doesn't that mean that anything could happen?"

"What?" The minister was startled.

"Because forever is long enough for the whole universe to re-shape itself again and again. And each time something different could happen."

Reverend Singleton felt a vexation of the spirit, then a chill. What was this boy, a devil sent to test him? He had never seriously entertained thoughts of devils, but he certainly believed in *the* Devil. No, that was ridiculous. This was just a boy with a big imagination, a boy who hadn't been brought up right.

"Christians don't believe that will happen, because this world as we know it will cease to exist after the Second Coming. A new world will be created, a world that Christ will rule as King forever and ever."

"When will Christ return?"

"No one knows for sure, but a lot of us feel the world is getting so bad that it will have to be soon."

"How will we know it's happened?"

"What?"

"When Christ has returned."

"Believe me, Nick, we'll all know."

When Nick left the minister's cabin a half hour later, he left with his mind whirling like the gas clouds after the big bang. Reverend Singleton was in a similar state. It was almost time for lights out, but Nick walked slowly, unhappily back to his dorm. He knew Ron would be disappointed when he told him that he had not yet been saved. He knew he had already let the minister down badly. He hadn't meant to. He had tried hard not to. But there seemed to be nothing he could do to stop it. The questions just kept popping into his head. And he hadn't had all of his questions answered, either. Not by a long shot. It was as if he and Reverend Singleton spoke different languages. It was impossible for them to understand what the other was trying to say most of the time.

Nick was afraid what his parents would say when they found out. He feared that this would be even worse than the time he'd fallen through the roof of the Western Airlines office. His father hadn't punished him that time, other than making him work off the cost of repairing the roof. But not being saved seemed a lot worse. Who knew what his dad would say about something like that?

****

The next day Nick wanted to avoid Reverend Singleton, but the minister was waiting at the chapel door, welcoming everyone to morning services. Nick put himself at the end of the line of kids going into the chapel, hoping the minister would choose to go in before he got there. But he didn't. Nick gritted his teeth but Reverend Singleton was warmer and kindlier in greeting him than he had been with anyone else. Who could understand it?

Since that night was the kids' last at the camp, the counselors had arranged a party in the cafeteria area. Nick had scarcely spoken to Sharon since the evening they had arrived, so he was surprised when she came up to him an hour into the party and asked him to slip out and meet her on one of the trails in ten minutes. As Nick left the building, he saw Judith ahead of him. He wondered at that, but when she turned off to Reverend Singleton's cabin, he recalled that she had a meeting with him that night to talk about being saved.

Sharon soon joined Nick on the path, and they walked through the pine-perfumed air over another hill, until they stood under the shadows of a clump of tall trees at the edge of a moonlit clearing. The pine needles were springy under their feet. They were alone.

"We can only stay here a minute," Sharon said, "or they'll notice we're gone and we'll get in trouble."

"OK," Nick agreed, not sure why she wanted to talk to him, but enjoying standing close to her.

"Nick, do you remember what we did in the barn?"

"Yes." How could she have thought he'd forgotten?

"You haven't told anybody about that have you?"

"No."

"Nick, you've got to promise me you'll never tell anyone what we did. If our parents ever found out, we'd never be allowed to see each other again."

"OK, I promise."

"Good. That's a relief. I already got Judith to promise, and I know Ron won't tell. He's too afraid of what I might tell people about him. Well, we'd better go back now before they come looking for us."

Nick was deeply disappointed. "Is that the only reason you asked me to meet you?"

"No, Nick, um, I was going to tell you this later, when we took you and Judith back home."

"Tell me what?"

"I can't be your girlfriend. We live too far apart and we don't see each other enough. It would never work out."

Nick stood silently, reeling from this punch out of nowhere.

"Is that OK, Nick?"

"Yeah, you're right. I guess it wouldn't be very smart."

At that moment Nick didn't care if it was smart or not. He just wanted the hurt to go away.

"We can still be friends, though," she said.

"Sure, we can still be friends."

"All right, we'd better go back now. I'll go first. You wait a couple of minutes before you come so nobody'll see us walking together."

She disappeared into the dark. Nick felt sadder than he had for a long time. He'd thought she had asked to meet him so they could hold hands and kiss. How could he have been so stupid? If she'd wanted to do that, she'd have asked him to meet her earlier in the week. Suddenly he was in a hurry to go home. He could hardly bear the thought of spending another night and morning in the camp.

As he was about to start back down the path, Nick looked across the clearing. The moonlight became suddenly brighter. It intensified as if a floodlight had been turned on above it. Then, in a magnesium-white flash that nearly blinded him, he saw the buffalo appear in the middle of the clearing. It was huge and its hide was the color of moonlight. It was only thirty feet away and it stared straight at him, out of round eyes black as the dark side of the moon.

Nick, afraid at first, held his breath. When he let it out, his fear whistled out with it. Big as it was, the buffalo was not threatening. If anything, Nick felt comfortable with it, as if it knew him better than he knew himself. The buffalo gave a little snort and stepped slowly toward Nick. On its fourth step, it vanished. Nick saw through the place it had been to the grass of the clearing behind, lit dully by the moon. Nick waited a long while, hoping the buffalo would come back, then started down the trail to the camp.

* * * * * * *

The next morning, Reverend Singleton seemed distracted, as if he was in a bit of a daze. After lunch, he greeted all the parents as they arrived to pick up their kids. As Hugh Link was loading the twins' bags into the trunk of his 1961 emerald green Pontiac LeSabre, the minister thanked him for bringing them. He said he and they had had some remarkable conversations.

"Oh, really? What about?"

"Oh, a host of different subjects, but mainly about the difference between theological eternity and scientific infinity."

Hugh raised an eyebrow. "Sounds like pretty heady stuff."

"Yes, they asked the most interesting questions. Well, Hugh, it's been good seeing you, but I'd better go say goodbye to the Hinkleys." They shook hands and the minister walked away.

That night Nick's father and mother took the twins to the drive-in movie to celebrate their return home. Nick and Judith felt they were back where they belonged. *Lawrence of Arabia* was showing and watching it, something awakened inside Nick. H had already seen hundreds of movies by this time in his life. In fact, the art nouveau-style movie theater in LaPointe was probably his single favorite place outside of his family's farm and the airport. He loved sitting in the back or in the balcony of the theater. And when the houselights went down, leaving only the faint lights at the end of each row of seats visible, he felt at once both calm and excited. When the movie started, he never took his eyes off the screen. He was wholly in another reality. Judith and he loved the drive-in, too. Every weekend in the summer they begged Roger and Lena to take them to the drive-in. *Lawrence of Arabia* was a long movie, but it didn't seem like it to Nick. He wished it was longer; he didn't want it to end. Driving home, it was all he could talk about.

    That night Nick had a hard time getting to sleep. He kept playing and replaying scenes from the film in his head. The one he replayed the most was from where a rider slowly appeared out of the heat distortions of the desert air. There was something about the way the rider materialized that reminded him of the appearances of the white buffalo. At the near edge of sleep, the two appearances merged into one.

Part V

June - September 1970

Chapter 11
Elizabeth Prescott

The tall grandfather clock was encased in cleanly cut outline in dark walnut wood. The clock was situated in that short piece of wall between the doorways to the dining room and the kitchen, and it was just tolling eight o'clock when Elizabeth Prescott stepped into the living room, pausing to switch on a lamp. Her bare feet sank into the ivory-white carpet.

Alone in the room, she seated herself on the bench of the baby grand, which stood before the first of the two bay windows in the living room of the house, looked idly through a book containing Beethoven's piano sonatas. She had quit taking piano lessons two years before, when she had been seventeen, when the pressure of simultaneously completing her senior year of high school and beginning, on a full scholarship, her first year of college, had left no time for musical pursuits.

Though she had said she understood, her piano teacher of ten years, Mrs. Connie Gunderson, a widow who had devoted herself almost exclusively to her pupils, had been disappointed and hurt. Elizabeth had been by far her most promising student, one who might have had some kind of future in music. The slow, moodily repetitive opening bars of the *Moonlight Sonata* measured out before her eyes and she heard them in her mind and felt in her mind the movements of her fingers on the keys, her feet on the pedals. But the keys were covered, shut from view. She set the book back on its stand and walked over to the free-standing shelves that dominated the far wall.

Those shelves held a Zenith color TV, a stereo component system, and several shelves of albums. Elizabeth selected a recording by Vladimir Horowitz of Beethoven's *Moonlight*, *Appassionata*, and *Pathetique* sonatas. As the needle placed itself at the beginning of the record, she sat down on the beige, firm-cushioned, L-shaped couch, facing, not the stereo, but the dark stone fireplace that occupied the wall opposite the second bay window. She heard the same slow, meditative opening bars of the sonata she had just heard in her mind.

Her sister Laura had gone to a movie and her brother Eric, fourteen now, had gone to a friend's for pizza and nine ball. Her mother

Elaine was out at a Unitarian meeting, and her father was in his study in the far corner of the house doing, well, whatever it was that he did there--and had done for so many nights the past four years. She knew very well what he did there--read, thought, wrote notes for lectures and papers, prepared articles, worked on his book on Heidegger's metaphysics. She couldn't help resenting, however, that he spent so much of his time in self-imposed seclusion, to the bitter deprivation of the family.

How her mother had gone patiently, forbearingly on, as though her husband had not severed their relationship in every way but legally, as though he had not quietly but resolutely withdrawn his affections (they no longer shared a bedroom and there were no nocturnal visitations, so far as Elizabeth knew), was more than she had been able to fathom. As much as she loved her father, Elizabeth knew that she herself would have left him--no, forced him to leave--within the first year of his aberrant self-absorption.

Aberrant because it had not always been so. She remembered her father as the man who had always been there, for the few hours after dinner before their bedtime--playing with her and her sister and brother, helping them with their homework, reading magazine articles aloud to their mother (sometimes, if it was a narrative piece, in dramatic, declamatory fashion) as she knitted or did crossword puzzles. She recalled that her father liked dramatic series like *East Side/West Side* and *Playhouse 90* presentations, but he'd also enjoyed the Jackie Gleason, Ed Sullivan, and Gary Moore variety shows, and even a few situation comedies.

Then, in the spring of 1966 he had begun to keep to his study, pleading work at first and then later not bothering to make any excuses. To be fair, he did not always confine himself to his room, but came out sometimes to watch a baseball or football game with Eric or to talk to Laura about Drama Club or Student Senate or one of her other many activities, or even to talk to Elizabeth about her art.

Elizabeth knew, in a clear and distinct way, as Descartes would have it, that there were strained feelings between herself and her father, and she knew equally as clearly and distinctly that the origin of those feelings, on her father's side, lay in his unbending non-acceptance of her sexuality.

She had fallen in love, deeply in love she had thought, for the first time when she was scarcely sixteen. Bob Vanderneck had been a year ahead of her in school, a senior; but he had lived in the next state. They had met at a Unitarian LRY--Liberal Religious Youth--retreat one September, had spent all of their free time together talking . . . oh, about simply everything . . . and then, before they'd had to pack up into separate cars and leave for their separate homes, Bob had kissed her and told her he loved her. Naturally, they'd written letters, her every day, him two or three times a week, and at Elizabeth's suggestion, her mother had invited him for Thanksgiving vacation. Then his family had invited her for New Year's Eve.

At the end of January they had met at another LRY retreat, in someone's home, and they had managed to find a private place (an upstairs bathroom as she recalled), and, in hot, flushed, breathless fashion, only half-undressed, they had made love for the first time, her for the very first time. It had been somewhat painful and she had bled a little, and the pleasure, what there had been, had been mainly in the fevered kissing and caressing and unbuttoning and touching before, and not in the consummation itself, which had lasted two minutes at most.

Since she had not expected things to progress as swiftly as they had, she had not used any birth control; and being a typical boy of the time, Bob hadn't bothered with protection, either, saying it was like taking a shower in a raincoat, or something like that. But immediately afterwards she had begun to worry about becoming pregnant, though she had kept her fears to herself, not wanting to spoil the good new feeling they had found their way to, had, as it were, discovered almost by accident: Intimacy.

Intimacy. How connotative of warmth and tenderness and adulthood that word had seemed to her. Intimacy. How adult, yes, how . . . sexual. What else could it be called? Her period had always been irregular, sometimes with four, sometimes six, and sometimes eight weeks between. Her last period had been two weeks before they had made love, and she had waited anxiously as day after exasperating day went by, hoping, praying, and finally, trying to will herself not to be pregnant (though she knew, in her moments of rational clearheadedness that was superstitious and absurd).

In the meantime, her daily letters to Bob had become ever more sweet and tender--replete with affirmations of her continuing love--and more confiding, more intimate, telling so much more about her thoughts, desires, and dreams than she had ever told anyone else. But she had not been perfectly confidential. No, she had not confided to him her fear that she might, just might, be pregnant. Elizabeth felt it was impossible to speak of that, even in a letter, though the fear was always just below the surface of her thoughts and broke through incessantly, like the rocks in a riverbed, which were visible below the plane of the water in one place but which ten feet further burst through, driving the swift water into a lather.

It was the first thing she thought about upon awakening and it was the direction her mind's compass ineluctably spun round to, no matter what other direction she tried to move in. It was the final thing in her mind before she lapsed, at long, fretful last, into unconsciousness at night--not to find the dearly wished for oblivion but to be tormented night after night by the same dream. Another being growing inside her, growing, growing, no matter how much she willed it to stop, until she could no longer keep it concealed and she was found out. Everyone she knew--her parents, her sister and brother, her grandparents, her teachers at school, the Unitarian minister Mr. Hampton, Bob's parents, Bob himself--all wore the same look of shock, dismay, anger, and censoriousness.

And in her dream that wild thing within her continued to grow and grow, uncontrollably, until she felt big and shapeless as an Airstream camper. And then her body began to heave, to shake in the grip of contractions, laceratingly painful, until she found herself lying on an operating room table, feet spread and elevated, klieg lights above, nurses beside her on both sides, the doctor reaching between her legs, and then a pain like shark's teeth, ripping and gripping, and ripping at her again, until . . . she woke, alone, in her own bed, in the middle of the night.

Then she would start to worry again, and it would feel like hours before she could fall asleep again, only to have the alarm clock ring in her ear--oh, that idiotic, madding clanging--as soon as she had. After a week of that dream, she began to dread going to sleep. But when she wakened each morning, anxious, irritable, foggy-brained with fatigue, she wished for nothing but to go back to sleep.

She was unable to speak of her fears to anyone, not to her friends at school, not to her sister, not to her parents--certainly not to them!--and not to Bob, either. She remembered that in one of his first letters to her after that first time, he had asked, bluntly, "You're on the pill, aren't you?" So, how was she to tell him, how was she to confide in him? Perhaps worst of all was that his letter mocked her sweet daydream of intimacy, ripped it to shreds like an old school note before her startled face. What vicious things were disappointed dreams. But she couldn't let herself think about things like that. She had no one to rely on, to lean on, no one but herself. She had to wait this thing out, hour by hour, alone.

Seven weeks and three days after she and Bob had made love, her period had started. Oh, the consoling spotting of blood. How her mind was cleansed by the returning tide of her body's blood. The first thing she did was go to her mother that same morning before school and ask her to call Dr. Hall that day, that morning, and ask for birth control pills for her (since the law at that time did not allow girls her age to be prescribed the pill without parental permission). She fully expected her mother would be horrified--after all, hadn't she been so in her dreams those many nights?

So, it was a shock when her mother said, "All right, Elizabeth, I've been expecting this. I'll have Dr. Hall call in the prescription, and you can pick it up at Rexall Drug after school."

"Oh, Mom, thanks for being so understanding. You're such a good mom. But do you think you could pick it up for me?"

"Elizabeth, if you're adult enough to need them, you'll have to be adult enough to go and pick them up yourself."

And so she had. And everything was wonderful after that, wonderfully safe. The pill made her periods regular, and she never had to worry about becoming pregnant again.

Yet that did not prove the end of worries. Her father wasn't quite so modern about it all. Though he spoke only rarely those days to her mother, she had obviously spoken to him about the fact that Elizabeth was on the pill. He began to be gratuitously irritable and acerbic to Elizabeth, and more than once had left the room when she entered, pretending to look at some papers or a book in his hand, or just at his feet or at the floor, anywhere but at her. He would not meet her eyes.

Of course, Elizabeth felt hurt and confused. Whatever had happened between her mother and her father--and she had begun to suspect what it might have been--she herself had always been his "beautiful, smart little girl," whom he had unreservedly showered pride and love upon. And then to have found him possessed of reservations, and to know, without having to be told, that they had been over that new experience in her life, about which she was already so unsure, about which she felt both excited and frightened--it was all so confusing and alarming.

Once, when he had risen from the reclining chair by the fireplace when she had come in and sat down on the couch, wanting to talk to him daughter to father, wanting desperately to straighten out whatever it was that had become ensnarled between them--he had simply risen and walked out of the room and she had begun to cry. What had she done to her life? Everything had gotten so out of control. A few hot, hungry, harried moments in a bathroom--for God's sake, in a bathroom!--with a boy she thought she loved and who she thought loved her, and she'd been put through months of pure, unadulterated hell. What should she do? What *could* she do, about any of it?

She and Bob continued to write, and in March they attended another LRY retreat. That time they snuck up into the attic of the house while everyone else was sleeping, and they made love three times--each time more sustained, less ferociously ardent, more deliciously pleasurable, especially for her.

Then one night at dinner she asked her parents--since dinner was the one time her father and mother diplomatically called a truce in their silent war--if Bob could come stay with them one weekend soon. That had done it. Her father had pushed himself roughly back from the dining room table, thrown down his napkin, and said, "Hasn't this gone far enough? Now you expect us to let him spend the weekend?"

"But, Daddy, his parents invited me for New Years and you didn't say a thing."

"I don't give a good goddamn what his parents did. I suppose you'll tell me next that they didn't even bother with a guest room but just let you sleep in his bedroom. Is that what you expect us to do,

Elizabeth, let him sleep in your bedroom?" And he couldn't help but add under his breath, "As if he'd get any sleep."

"Daddy, you have no right to speak to me like that."

She felt his every sentence as full-handed, burning slaps across her face.

"No right! No Right! Who the hell are you to lecture me about rights? I'll tell you about rights. I damn well have the right not to have my daughter go off on some religious retreat and come back a goddamn slut. I have the right--"

But Elizabeth burst into tears, leaped up from the dinner table, and ran down the hallway and down the stairs to her bedroom, where she threw herself on her bed and broke into great choking sobs.

Her mother came downstairs after her and sat on the bed and held her. "Please, Elizabeth, don't cry. You father didn't mean what he said."

"Yes he did. He meant every word. Oh, I hate him, I hate him! I'll never speak to him again!"

Her mother rocked her gently, as she had when Elizabeth was a little girl and came running into the house, in tears, with some new scrape or bruise. Her mother rocked her, saying, "It'll be all right. You don't mean that, either. Believe me, it's going to be all right."

Elizabeth never knew what her mother said to her father when she went back upstairs, demanded that he accompany her into her bedroom (where he hadn't set foot in some time), and slammed the door after them. But her father came down to Elizabeth's room a bit later, asked more than a little timidly if he could come in, and proceeded to apologize to her, meekly, sincerely. He said he'd behaved inexcusably, that he hadn't meant what he had said, that she was infinitely precious to him, and could she ever forgive him, and of course her boyfriend could come stay with them some weekend soon.

Bob did come to visit and he slept in the guest bedroom upstairs. Several times that weekend he managed to get Elizabeth alone for a moment and kiss her--open-mouthed, heatedly--and touch her. He asked her to sneak off with him some place; he asked her to come to his room; he asked her to let him come to hers. Each time she had said no, firmly. Not at her parents' home, not that weekend. Maybe the next time they were together--there was another retreat coming up in less than a month. And he asked what was wrong, and why not, and she kept repeating not that weekend, not in her parents' home.

Bob was severely put out by her stubborn refusal; he accused her of being a tease and said she'd given him "blue balls." He was noticeably cool when he left on Sunday afternoon, kissing her only on the cheek. It was two weeks before she received a letter from him, though she wrote to him every day, as always. The letter she received was short and to the point. He said he had thought about it and decided their long-distance romance wasn't working. He was sorry but he thought it was best to end it. He said he would always remember her and the special times they had had together, and he hoped she would remember him, too.

Her heart was savaged. His letter hurt her so much it was a week before she could write a response that wasn't so sarcastically abusive that she immediately tore it up. When she was able finally to compose a letter that both expressed what she wished to say and preserved her dignity, she sent it. She told him she was sorry he didn't have faith enough in their love to think it could withstand the temporary inconvenience of mere physical separation, and that she thought their times together had been special, as he had said, but that they had been special because of the particular closeness they had felt when they were able to share all of their confidences with each other, because, even though there had been physical, there had been no emotional distance between them. She had felt almost like they were one person, and not because they had had sex together. If sex was what had made those times special to him, then she had been deeply mistaken about what kind of person he was, and she was grateful to him for ending their, as she saw it now, impossible relationship. She knew now he was not the sort of person she could be truly interested in, not the sort of person she wanted to continue seeing.

Their relationship was in the past now, and, as far as she was concerned, that was where it would stay. There was so much more she wanted from her life. There were so many other interesting people to know, and perhaps to love, people who, she was sure, had some concept of intimacy beyond mere intercourse. Love, Elizabeth. She wondered about closing with "Love," but she figured why not; it made her better than him.

Because that first side of the album ended with the second movement of the Pathetique, the soft adagio, Elizabeth didn't notice at first that Horowitz's piano had ceased to sound from the speakers. She turned the record over, sat down in the recliner. She propped her feet up and looked out the window. The tall red oaks in front of the house and the big elms bordering the park across the street threw down long, dense shadows. The light that had been yellow was now filtered green. The evening was still, the twilight cool. A squirrel ran down one of the park trees and then, by cautious starts and stops, across a span of grass and up another tree. Was that progress, as a squirrel saw it? A crow swooped down onto their front walk, hopped nearly up to their steps, and then, with an abrupt flare and flurry of wings, flew off.

Bob Vanderneck was succeeded by Rick Campbell, who was succeeded by Gary Saunders, who was succeeded by Steve Morris, who was succeeded by Tim Farley, who was succeeded by Jim Snow, who was succeeded by Brad Burton, who was succeeded by Ray Johnson, a black linebacker on the University football team, her only boyfriend of color, who was succeeded by Tom Morgan. In each of these young men she had sought a depth of intimacy and love that, one by one, each of them had showed himself, either incapable of achieving, or of sustaining.

Why was the love she wanted so difficult to find, or if found, to keep? Perhaps she had never truly found it, though a few times she had certainly thought she had. With Tim, with Brad, and with Tom. She winced thinking of Tom. She wasn't over that yet. It had ended too weirdly. She wasn't sure she'd ever be over it.

Watching a last sunbeam break through the clouds and set the window adazzle for a moment, she believed Plato was right. Love *was* like a ladder. She had climbed that ladder in total darkness, unable to see the rungs, having to search them out with her hands. With each new rung, she had felt certain dawn would break at last on the bleak horizon of her world, that she would pull herself up into the full blinding blaze of the sun. But it had never happened. No matter how many men she had shared her hopes, her dreams, her secrets with, no matter how many bodies she had pulled herself up on, no matter how many men she had let pull themselves up on her body, they had never emerged from all those the frenetic nights into the warm, healing, permanent light of day. What kind of fool, she asked herself, kept climbing such a ladder in the dark. This was more absurd than Sisyphus rolling his rock forever and ever.

And what of her parents? Why hadn't two good people like them been able to sustain their love? Her mother had had a short-lived affair four years ago and her father had never been able to forgive her for it. How stupid, she thought, how banal, on both their parts. Elizabeth wouldn't have thought of defending her mother's infidelity. To begin to think that one's life had become too prosaic, too ordinary, to find the husband who had devoted so much time and care and love to the family--who had seemed to see their marriage at times as a marriage of five, not two, who had always been thinking in his restless way, of what the family could do this weekend or where the family could go next summer--to begin to think of that man as too conventional and of her marriage as lacking in freshness and blood passion, that was too easy. She had expected more of her mother; and she knew her father had expected more.

But she wouldn't have thought of defending his four years of wound-licking seclusion, either. Granted, he had been cruelly surprised, grievously hurt, and by the one person of whom he had felt absolutely confident, of whom he had never entertained a single doubt. But what was one supposed to say of his behavior afterwards? Was one supposed to be grateful he hadn't beaten her up or gone out and bought a shotgun--for he had never owned a gun in his life--and blasted them both straightaway to whatever ring of hell was reserved for adulterous lovers, down there with Paolo and Francesca. Elizabeth didn't feel she could be grateful for that. It was the least, the very least, she expected of him. He was a philosopher, after all, an erudite man, not some semi-literate redneck. She expected him to be civilized.

No, the manner in which he had chosen to react, not to leave but also not to stay, to simply withdraw in wordless protest--didn't that smack more than a little of moral cowardliness, of bad faith? It was painful for her to think of her father, whose moral courage she had admired all her life, as a coward, ultimately, when it came to the complications, perplexities, and ambiguities of love.

There was no such thing as stasis, though. The world we woke to this morning was not the world we left to enter sleep's clean blackness.

Heraclitus was dead right about those rivers. Of late something had begun to change between her father and her mother. Some thawing, at first imperceptible, had come, some spring melting had arrived. She felt her father had finally found the desire to see beyond broken faith and crippled pride. On her return from California, she had noticed they were actually talking--not merely taking part in family conversation, where they wouldn't necessarily have to be speaking to each other, but actually talking together, the two of them, when there was no one else in the room, when there was no television set or stereo on to distract two people from speaking their honest thoughts and feelings to each other. This was promising.

Elizabeth had walked in on them several times since she had come back, and she had quickly walked on through the room, as though she were preoccupied with her own affairs and had noticed nothing unusual. But inside she had danced and leaped wildly and cried out. It was what she had been hoping for these past four years, what she had, truth to tell, given up hoping for. Evidently something had happened during her five months in San Francisco. Something more than mutual outrage at their oldest child's continued obstinacy and waywardness.

Eventually maybe two souls really could pull themselves up out of the darkness of willfulness and hurt and into the strong-beamed sunlight of forgiveness and trust. She herself thought she had begun to see daybreak, real daybreak when she had met Tom Morgan. Not the fluorescent lights of her other loves but authentic sunshine. It had been so good, so very good, at first.

They met at the Kansas City Art Institute, which they were both attending on scholarship. He spoke admiringly of her painting, she of his sculpture. He had more self-confidence than any other student artist she knew, more than most of the teachers. He knew, with a bedrock certainty, he was good. And yet he was charmingly non-self-aggrandizing, sweetly non-arrogant. With the other students he could be amazingly empathetic, amazingly tolerant of their unending self-important posturing, of their affectations and limitations. He spent hours at a time in the studio, sometimes staying all night, but he was always willing to drop everything and go to a bar and rap about art, or politics (in which he had little interest), or religion (in which he had no interest at all), or sex (well, let's just say he was always interested), or one of his favorite subjects, like modern sculpture or Ken Kesey and the Merry Pranksters.

Tom Wolfe's *The Electric Kool-Aid Acid Test*, of which he owned a well-thumbed, cloth-bound copy and several paperback copies (which he kept buying to give away to friends), and Kesey's own two novels were for him such objects of fascination and zeal that one wouldn't have gone far wrong to have said he invested them with the meaning and approached them with the veneration usually reserved for sacred texts. Tom loved to rap about Mountain Girl and Cassady or about being on the bus or off the bus or about Kesey and the Hell's Angels or the Pranksters and the Unitarian ministers (Tom enjoyed twitting her about her Unitarian upbringing) or the acid tests. Or about McMurphy and Chief Bromden or Hank Stamper and the godalmighty, steel-sinewed Wakonda-Auga River.

Tom spoke of San Francisco as *the* new center of American culture, as the city on the far western edge of the continent where the frontier had only appeared to end, but had in fact shifted ground, inside one's own cerebral cortex. There, with LSD or mescaline or whatever psychedelic drug one had at hand, one could keep pushing out beyond the boundaries reached the day before, beyond Edge City, further and further into the infinite intergalactic reaches of the self. He seemed not to have noticed that the Pranksters had supposedly "graduated" from acid. It was a perhaps intentional oversight.

Tom liked some poets too, not only the dada, surrealist, or beat poets that one might have expected (Appolinaire, Breton, Kerouac, Ginsberg, Ferlinghetti), but also Blake and Shelley and Dylan Thomas, whom he called spiritual forefathers. Tom frequently gave his sculptures allusive titles: "Mind-Forged Manacles" and "Binding with Briars My Joys and Desires," or "Asia's Song," or for a dyptic, "Time Held Me Green and Dying" and "Though I Sang in My Chains Like the Sea."

Tom felt it was a waste of life force, effort, and time for him to continue his work in the Midwest. How could he become inspired by its flat land and its even flatter culture? He said certain people were meant to live in certain places at certain times in history. It was their karma. And Kansas City was *not* his place. Even if one dropped acid in the Midwest, it would still be the Midwest. A hallucinated cornfield was still a cornfield. What else could it be? But San Francisco! The name became his mantra, his koan. It was a place where real psychic magic could happen, where one could trip out and discover the infinite, intricate byways--more intricate than any mandala--of the self. The city itself was psychotropic. There one could at last be an artist, a real artist.

Tom had proselytized about California all autumn of last year. But that he never spoke of what California might mean to Elizabeth, that he never considered for an instant what it might mean for her to give up her scholarship at the Art Institute, that she was never anything but ancillary in his plans, that she would simply be moved, as one moves some piece of necessary equipment, say a stereo or TV--never occurred to her, or rather, did occur, but more as a faint premonition, ambiguous and easily dismissed, than as a thought to give her serious pause. Sitting in the recliner, Elizabeth couldn't understand how she could have been so ill advisedly self-abnegating. Love was her only excuse. But what kind of love was it that allowed one to punish oneself so unmercifully?

Tom promoted his *idée fixe* all fall, and finally, after she returned from Thanksgiving at her parents' home to the small apartment she and Tom shared in Kansas City, she consented. But she asked for two things.

First, that they wait until the end of the school term before they left. Tom groused a little about that; he was all for packing up and leaving the next day. He kept saying that his artistic apprenticeship was over, that he didn't need teachers any more, that teachers only taught because they couldn't make it as real artists, that they kept students feeling dependent on them just so they could rationalize their existence, that they were, all of them, scared one of their students might be better than they were might possess true genius. Nonetheless, he agreed to wait; it wasn't that much longer. He quit going to classes, though, telling Elizabeth he had withdrawn from all of his courses. It wasn't until months later that he let slip that he had never formally withdrawn, but had just disappeared from his classes. For her part, Elizabeth finished her courses in typically exemplary fashion. Her professors commended her on her development that semester, saying her work and growth--especially as a colorist--not only lived up to the early promise that had led to her being awarded the scholarship, but surpassed their expectations, high though they had been. Elizabeth knew from talking to the other students that such praise was not universal. She was pleased with herself.

The second thing Elizabeth demanded was that Tom come to her parents' house for New Years to help her explain their move to San Francisco. Then they could pack up and go. Tom resisted that second condition, saying they didn't need to ask anyone's permission. She said they weren't seeking permission but simply informing people who were important to their lives of their plans, out of common courtesy and respect. He said he didn't give a fuck about courtesy, that it was just part of the bullshit game the older generation played to keep young people under their thumbs. And further, she could call it informing or discussing or consulting, or whatever she wanted, but it all amounted to the same thing, little kids coming to the big parent authority figures and begging permission. Elizabeth had to realize, they were no longer kids. She should have realized that the first time they had made love. They were adults now. They had the right to make their own decisions about whatever they wanted to. But Elizabeth said if he didn't do this, he could go alone. So, after endless grumbling and complaining, he agreed.

And it turned out about as she had feared it would. Her mother thought it an awful idea to quit mid-year, to sacrifice their scholarships. Why couldn't they wait until next summer and then go to California for a few months to see if they really wanted to make a permanent move? That way, if they found San Francisco wasn't everything they hoped, they could still return to the Art Institute. Their scholarships would still be there, waiting.

But her father had been against even that compromise. He said they both needed to finish school. He said it was ridiculous to think that two students could just pack up and move and expect to be taken into the San Francisco art world with open arms. Did he have to remind them that neither of them had participated in a single show yet. Besides, even discounting the patent absurdity of the move on artistic grounds, what about the hard economic facts? How were they going to support themselves? He hoped they weren't so naive as to think they'd be able to live off their art. Nobody bought the work of unknowns, and if they did, they paid next to nothing for it.

Elizabeth could see Tom becoming more and more furious throughout this lecture, well intended though it was. Still, he managed to ride the crests of the waves of his anger, perhaps out of residual respect for her father (Tom had told her that he admired her father's moral courage in opposing the war). Tom said he knew someone who ran an avant-garde movie theater, a place that showcased the films of young, independent filmmakers, and that the guy had invited him to come out to San Francisco several times, so he was sure he could get a job working at the theater. It would be just the chance he was looking for because he thought film was the art form of today and he'd been thinking for some time of switching from sculpture to film. At the theater he'd get to meet lots of people on the cutting edge of the film world. And what could be better than learning from real artists working in the medium?

Her father countered that he had been under the impression that that was what they had been doing at the Art Institute, learning from practicing professionals. Which had led Tom to exclaim that Kansas City was an artistic backwater, that if their professors were really any good, they'd be in New York or San Francisco themselves, making their living from their art. And her mother had responded. And Tom had said in his defense. And her father had lectured. And Tom had argued emotionally. And so it had gone, back and forth, back and forth.

At last Elizabeth broke in to say that, whether her parents liked it or not, she and Tom were going, period, so they might as well accept it. Her father said, knowing her, that didn't come as a surprise. And she'd asked what's that supposed to mean? And he'd said she'd never listened to him in her whole life, so he didn't know why he'd expected her to start behaving rationally now. He wouldn't let her respond, but angrily rushed on to say she'd always done exactly what she'd wanted, without considering what anyone else might think or feel about it, she was completely self-centered, and everyone knew it.

Her mother interrupted, tried to salvage things by asking everyone to sleep on it, to talk about it all again tomorrow, after they'd all had a chance to cool down. There was no need to decide this today.

But Elizabeth said, no, Mom, we've already decided. We're going. We only consulted you out of courtesy and respect. But she could see now her father couldn't appreciate that, that he'd always been opposed to her doing anything on her own, that he'd never had any faith in her, any confidence that she might, just might, do the right thing once--at least the right thing for her. He'd never been able to accept that she was her own person, who had thoughts, feelings, talents, and ambitions of her own, and that she couldn't go through life trying to please him, doing what *he* wanted her to do. She was an adult now. She had to make her own decisions, right or wrong. And what she had decided was to go to California. He could approve or disapprove, but she was going.

And her father said, in that case, he wanted it clearly known that he disapproved, that he thought this was a perfectly absurd idea, just the sort of half-baked thing he should have known she'd come up with. And her mother said, Bill, really. And Elizabeth said, I have nothing more to say to you about this, then. We're leaving for Kansas City tonight, to pack. And her mother said, Elizabeth, please, there's no need to leave, stay the night, at least. But Elizabeth said, no, we're going, Mom, I won't stay here any longer and listen to how much Dad disapproves of me. Come on, Tom, let's put our suitcases back in the car.

By the time they were ready to go, her father had calmed down. He said he was sorry about the things he'd said, he was angry, that was all, and he wanted her to know he and her mother loved her and that if it didn't work out as she hoped, she could always come back home, she'd always be welcome. Elizabeth shook his hand, kissed her mother goodbye, got into Tom's old red Corvair, and left. She cried half the way back to Kansas City.

And so she and Tom had left that first week of January for the golden land of California. The Corvair's heater barely worked, so they had to wrap up in blankets to try to keep warm (unsuccessfully) and keep stopping to scrape the ice off the windshield. But they made it to San Francisco, a little frostbitten perhaps, but they made it.

And much as she hated to admit it, her father and mother had been right. Nothing had worked out the way they had planned. There was no job for Tom at the movie theater. The man who ran the theater hadn't been able to make a go of it showcasing independent filmmakers, so he'd taken to showing sex films instead. He shrugged and said it was a living. Elizabeth found a job clerking in a restaurant on Fisherman's Wharf. Her check paid the rent on their roach-infested, one-bedroom walk-up and bought enough groceries to keep life in their bodies, and paid for Tom's grass and hallucinogens.

Tom didn't get a job. He said it was good the theater job had fallen through because he had all these new ideas for sculptures and needed time to get them down. He said he knew now that filmmaking had just been a passing whimsy, that he didn't know what he'd been thinking. It was impossible for him to work in their apartment, but he kept busy drawing, planning the sculptures he'd execute when he could afford a studio. He worked all day on his drawings while she was at work, but he wouldn't let her look at them. After a few weeks of this, she got up one night and looked through his notebooks. She couldn't believe it. The sculptures he was planning were monumental in scale, fifty, eighty, a hundred feet tall. What on earth was he thinking? No one could construct any one of them without an astronomical commission, the kind that went only to nationally known sculptors. Even if he could get a studio, which wasn't likely since he didn't seem to have any plans to get a job and earn the money for a studio and materials, he couldn't create any of those monumental pieces. She had a hard time getting back to sleep that night. In fact, she battled insomnia just about every night, worrying about how they were going to live and what Tom was going to do.

But Tom began to sleep plenty. During the day as well as at night. He stopped drawing and began to sleep all day while she was at work. Then he wanted her to spend every evening writing down his dreams. He was obsessed with dreams, saying they were the only true reality, that everything else was an illusion. And his dreams were frightening. Elizabeth being stripped, and beaten, and forced by two men into every imaginable form of trio sex, while, hearing her screams, Tom ran down hallway after hallway, up and down staircase after staircase--as if he were trapped in some Escher etching--but was unable to find the room she was in. At last he found himself inside a room where he could look through a one-way window at what they were doing to Elizabeth-- handcuffing her facedown, spreadeagled, on a bed and whipping her-- but could not reach her. Then he was the one with the whip in his hand. And he was striking her fiercely, using all his sculptor's strength, demanding that she beg for more. Then he woke up and found the bedsheet wet by his groin.

Tom dictated dozens of variations of this and a few other equally vicious scenarios. But Elizabeth saw quickly that they were all more or less the same dream and she became more and more anxious. They never went out anywhere. Some nights he didn't say anything at all to her, not even in response to direct questions. He acted like she wasn't even there. If on those nights she made the mistake of asking him what was wrong, he'd grab her by the shoulders, shake her, and shout that NOTHING WAS WRONG. WHAT COULD BE FUCKING WRONG? He never hit her, only shook her. Then, immediately afterwards, he would be so contrite, begging her again and again to forgive him, he hadn't known what he was doing, he was so sorry, he loved her more than anything. He would be charming and nice the rest of the evening, they would have great sex, and she would go to sleep thinking everything was going to be all right.

But, of course, it wasn't all right. Nothing changed. The whole cycle would start all over again. Elizabeth finally faced facts: Tom was totally dependent on her, he deeply resented his dependence, he wasn't going to get any better, he wasn't going to get a job, he wasn't going to get serious about his art. When he finally got tired of their rationing of her bi-weekly check and asked her to go panhandle to get some money quickly, she knew she had only one choice. She had to leave. If she stayed, she would become as crazy as he was.

In late May, she returned to Red Earth, to the home of her parents, who were genuinely happy to have her back. So here she was. What was she going to do? The yard was full of shadows, no birds flitted about. It would be dark soon. What was she going to do?

Tom Morgan had shown up in town two weeks ago--remorseful, beseeching her forgiveness, begging her to go back to California with him. This time everything would be different. This time he'd get a job--he already had some prospects--and they'd get a studio, where they could work together at their art. Everything would be different. They'd be better lovers than ever.

She didn't believe it. She'd heard similar promises before. Besides, in the time she'd been back in Red Earth, she'd gained some much needed perspective on their relationship. She didn't want to try again. She wanted it to be over. She was no longer the victim of his charm and talent. She no longer felt for him what she once had. It was over. She didn't love him any more. So what was she going to do about it?

She decided to bike over to the Art Studio and work on the painting she was doing for class. At least her art was going well. She'd probably never get her love life to work out, but she was getting new ideas about color and shape all the time.

The Art Studio was a long, army barracks-looking building that had been built sometime in the thirties. Its paint was faded and dingy inside and out; it was cold in the winter and hot in the summer. The decrepit window air conditioners couldn't begin to keep up. The building began to cool off when the sun went down, which was why Elizabeth usually went there in the evening. She often worked till two or three in the morning. She loved to ride her bike across the campus then, when the only sound to be heard was the sound of water sprinklers, and when water dripped off the leaves of maples and oaks, and the old-fashioned lamps lining the sidewalks made gentle pools of light, softening but not eliminating the darkness. She felt unthreatened, entirely safe. Though the next school year two women would be raped on campus and strings of new lights would spring up on aluminum stalks, wearing pointed hats which made the lamps look like props from a science fiction movie. The whole campus would become so well lit that not even the biggest, broadest oak or spruce would cast a shadow.

The lights were on in the painting studio, as they always were. But Elizabeth stood in shock in the doorway. There, standing before an easel and a fifteen by eighteen-inch painting, with his back to her, his long black hair caping his shoulder blades, was the boy she had met that afternoon. Oh, what was his name? Jack? No. Rick, that was it. No, that wasn't it, either. Oh well, she could ask him again. She thought back. Yes, she had mentioned that she was taking painting this summer, but he had said nothing about being a painter himself. That was strange. She thought about walking up and saying hello, but seeing how intently he was working, she decided she'd better announce herself first.

"Hey, why didn't you tell me you were a painter?" she called from the doorway.

"What?" a somewhat distracted Judith asked, turning half around.

Suddenly, behind the young woman Judith saw a flame-bright snowburst. Light flooded into the studio like water over a spillway, setting everything adazzle. The great familiar beast stood in brilliant clarity behind the young woman a second, dwarfing her. Then, just as suddenly, the only illumination was from the fluorescent bulbs hanging from the ceiling. There was only darkness behind the woman in the doorway.

"You know, when we met this afternoon," she said, walking towards Judith, "it wasn't very fair of you not to tell me you were a painter, too."

"What are you talking about?" Judith asked, standing, small, pointed, white-watercolor-tipped paintbrush poised in her right hand. Judith was wearing a paint-splattered blue work shirt, with the first two buttons undone; it was not tucked in but hung loose over her bottom.

Elizabeth faltered. What had happened? He'd seemed so friendly earlier.

"Don't you remember? We met this afternoon, on the sidewalk east of the Union. I was on my bike. Remember? I was giving my raccoon a ride. And you were with Jon Arbalest."

"Oh, you must mean my brother."

"What?"

"Believe me, if it was Jon Arbalest, it was my brother you met, not me."

"You mean . . ."

"Yeah, I have a twin brother. His name is Nick."

"That's it, Nick. I'm sorry, you really do look so much alike."

"Don't sweat it. It happens all the time. My name's Judith, Judith Larkin," she said, transferring her brush to her left hand and extending her right."

"Elizabeth Prescott," she said, smiling and taking Judith's hand, surprised at the firmness of the grip.

"Elizabeth. Do you shorten that up to anything."

"No, just Elizabeth."

"I don't go for nicknames, either."

"I wish I could find a good nickname. I've never much liked Elizabeth."

"Why not? It's a pretty name."

"I might like it better if my mother hadn't told me she named me after her favorite Jane Austen character. She's got this thing for nineteenth century novelists."

"It could be worse. What if you were named after some movie star or something?"

"You're right, that would be worse."

"What did you say you were doing with your raccoon?"

Elizabeth laughed. "Taking him on a bike ride. Say, why haven't I seen you in here before?"

"This is the first time I've come over at night to work. I've been coming in during the afternoon, but today the heat was just oppressive."

"I'm in an upper-level painting class. What about you?"

"Lower level. I just finished my freshman year. But you must have gone somewhere else last year. I'm sure I would have seen you around if you'd been here."

"Yeah, I did one semester at the Kansas City Art Institute."

"Why just one?"

"It's a long story."

* * * * * * *

Judith and Elizabeth comparing paintings:

Judith's was a deep-textured, impassioned painting called *Moonrise*. Four trees, three on the left and one on the right, occupied the middle ground. Behind them, just right of center a huge vermilion moon, shot with gold, rose through steaming white-purple-violet clouds. The foreground was dappled with purple-red and gold and slate-blue flowers, was white-dotted with others that rhymed with the white dots of the stars, seen through the blue-black sky and filtered through the gold-red edges of the clouds. The hues were rich and vibrant, the mood intense.

"Is this a real place, somewhere out in the country around here?"

"Not really. I started with this image of the moon in clouds. I added the trees and everything just seemed to flow from there."

"You're using watercolor but how did you get this texture and this intensity?"

"I used different things. Watercolor, watercolor crayons and pencils, blue and black India ink, and spray paint."

"Spray paint! That's how you did the clouds, isn't it? You started white and then spray-painted red over them."

"Yeah."

"I like it. And you sprayed the red and this gold up here above the clouds and down here in the foreground, too."

"See these flowers. Guess how I did them."

"I don't know, it looks like some kind of template."

"I spray-painted through the lacework on an old nightie."

Elizabeth's painting was much larger; her canvas has been stretched over a four-by six-foot frame. The painting was oil, maybe three-quarters finished. Smoky swirls of a hundred shadings of indigo and rose, slashed with thin, jagged blades of obsidian-black and nightmare emerald. The canvas pulsated with color energy; but it was an energy constrained and shaped by thought, barely perhaps, but constrained nevertheless. The painting was a visual oxymoron: pensive storminess.

"I like this," Judith said immediately. "It has the colors of the Fauves, it has a kind of Kandinsky-esque feel to it."

"Yeah, I like Matisse and Derain--and Kandinsky, too."

"I'm no good at abstraction myself, so I tend to have inordinate respect for people who are."

"Your painting's representational, Judith, but it's not realism. It reminds me of that statement of Georgia O'Keefe's, that all good representational painting is really abstract."

"What'd she mean by that?"

"That the painter has to find the abstract forms within the flower or the nocturnal cityscape or the cow skull in order to render those things with force and power."

"I'll have to think about that. What're you going to call this, anyway?"

"I don't know. I'm lousy at titles. Any suggestions?"

"How about *Vision in Indigo and Rose?*"

* * * * * * *

Sometime later, Judith on her recent life with Wolfram:

"And so this producer who heard him play at the Vietnam Vets Against the War march in Washington told him he should make a demo and start sending it out. The producer had given him the names of some contacts in Minneapolis, so Wolfram got ahold of them and arranged some bookings in that area for June and July. He figured while he was up there playing, he and the band could cut some demo tracks.

"He called me yesterday and said they'd reserved time in a studio next week. He won't be able to get back here before the beginning of August. So he wants me to come up there.

"Isn't that just like a man? He can't get away, but I'm supposed to just drop everything and come running up there to be with him. I'd get mad at him if I didn't miss him so much. I don't know, I think I might drive up after this summer session is over."

* * * * * * *

Still later, Elizabeth and Judith discussing Elizabeth's attempt to leave Tom Morgan.

"So he's followed me here. He can't accept that it's over. I can't believe I was so stupid as to go to California in the first place. I think I just didn't want to admit that my parents were right."

"I've done things like that. They usually didn't work out very well."

"I wanted to make my own decision, right or wrong. OK, I can see now it was the wrong decision, but what am I supposed to do with this guy? He just keeps hanging around."

"Where's he staying?"

"He's crashing out at the Freedom Farm, smoking their dope and eating their food. From what I hear, all he does is sit in a room and get high."

"Why do they let him stay?"

"I heard he told them he was my boyfriend, that we'd had a little misunderstanding, but we'd be getting back together soon."

"Will you?"

"Not a chance. I have no feelings for him at all any more."

"You need to tell him that."

"I thought if I just went about my own business and ignored him, he'd get the idea and go away."

"Maybe, but he'll probably stick around as long as he can keep sponging off people who know you."

"I don't think they'll put up with him much longer."

"Then he'll find another place to crash at. He can keep that up indefinitely."

"So you think I need to confront him once and for all."

"Don't you?"

"Yeah, but I have another problem."

"What?"

"No transportation."

"No problem. I have a car."

"No, I can't ask you to drive me out there?"

"I said it was no problem."

"All right, then, let's go."

* * * * * * *

As Judith drove through the intersection of First and Main and started down the same long hill Nick had driven down earlier that day, she saw the huge beast moving ahead of her in the dark, blinking on, then off, like a neon sign. A blaze of white, then darkness. She glanced at Elizabeth. No, she saw nothing. Further on, another blaze of white, then darkness. It moved at the same pace as the car, staying a hundred yards ahead.

Judith crossed the railroad tracks and the newer bridge and then headed out on the blacktop Airport Road. The beast blinked into darkness for the last time. Above the engine noise she heard the whining of crickets, an insistent, sheared-metal drone. Beetles crawled across the road and the air was full of flying insects that flew into the headlights and wrote their deaths on the windshield. Dead gophers drew flies where spinning tires had left them, crushed and bleeding.

Crosby, Stills, and Nash's "Ohio," their new song of outrage at the killings at Kent State, came on the radio. The night was clear, the breezes slight, and the heavens over-seeded with stars. Hercules strode above; she picked out Lyra, Ursa Major, and Sagittarius, her and Nick's birth sign. What was Nick doing now? She hadn't heard from him all day. Probably reading that fat novel for his English class.

Wouldn't Nick be surprised when he found out Elizabeth Prescott had mistaken her for him. Judith knew Elizabeth was the type Nick went for--smart, articulate, independent, pretty. She was all the more beautiful because she didn't seem aware of her beauty, didn't seem to be trying to impress anyone with it. But Elizabeth wasn't ready for anyone new in her life. She had to get straight with herself first. Besides, Judith was discouraged by Nick's behavior in the six months since he'd gotten that final kiss-off postcard from Annie. He'd spun from bed to bed, satisfying, or trying to satisfy, something in himself, and leaving hurting women littered around the campus. She'd tried to talk to him about it, but he'd told her to mind her own business. No, Elizabeth certainly didn't need Nick right now. Until he changed, no woman needed him.

Elizabeth had little to say. A half mile past the airport, Judith turned left at the Uncle Sam mailbox, into a driveway that led to a big white farmhouse. She parked halfway up the drive, as it was already full of cars and motorcycles. The high, ethereal opening of the Rolling Stones' "Let It Bleed" was heard from the stereo in the house.

The front yard was full of long-haired guys and women in braids, tank tops, and jeans. She recognized the lanky form of Willow. His black handlebar mustache stood out from his face. He gestured animatedly as he told a story to a big group sitting on the grass around a keg of beer, drinking, laughing, passing joints. Elizabeth and Judith made their way through the crowd on the porch and into the house, where the stereo was easily twice as loud. In the living room people sat on the couches and chairs and around the walls on the floor, talking and passing pipes and joints. An old upright piano, painted psychedelically, stood against one wall; a guy with long, frizzy blond hair was standing in front of it, pretending to play along with the music. Elizabeth saw that he didn't know the first thing about the piano. Still, a couple of girls that looked about sixteen stood, beers in hand, at one end of the piano, looking on appreciatively.

They started across the room when a skinny guy with an acne-pitted face and long, greasy, straight brown hair grabbed Judith by the hand and the waist and began whirling her toward the middle of the room, where four or five other couples were dancing. "Come on, darlin', let's you and me dance." Judith extricated herself and she and Elizabeth stepped into the hallway that led back to the kitchen.

The hallway was also full of people, standing, leaning against the walls, sitting. Halfway down the hall, a door opened onto the stairs that went up to the second floor. Elizabeth asked someone she knew where to find Tom Morgan. She was told to look in the third floor attic. Judith and Elizabeth threaded themselves dexterously through the people on the stairs, and then through the crowd in the second floor hallway.

Elizabeth knew the way to the third floor was through a pull-down staircase in the back bedroom, the door to which stood open. Nine or ten people were sitting on the bed and on the floor there, passing around a joint. The walls were plastered with dozens of overlapping posters of rock stars. Judith sat down on the floor, saying she'd wait for Elizabeth there, and to call her if she needed her. Somebody handed Judith a joint that she passed straight along to the next person.

Elizabeth emerged headfirst into the attic. A strobe light, mounted on the ceiling was the only light source in the room currently in use. It took Elizabeth's eyes a moment to adjust. When they did, she saw a queen-size waterbed at the opposite end of the room. Two guys and two women, sat in a cozy circle on the rag rug before the bed, sharing a hash pipe. Tom saw her and stood up. The strobe made it seem as if he was walking toward her in slow-motion.

"Hi, babe! I really need to talk to you."

Morgan moved to embrace her, but she pushed his hands away.

"That's why I'm here, Tom, to talk to you." She was surprised by the coldness in her own voice.

"Uh-oh," a woman said. "Guess we'd better be leaving."

The other three got to their feet, filed past Tom and Elizabeth, and clumped downstairs to join the party below. They took the pipe with them.

"Why so unfriendly, babe?"

"Don't call me babe."

"OK, sorry. Come on, have a seat."

"No, what I want to say is better said standing up."

"All right, suit yourself." He sat down on the rug, cross-legged. "I thought you might show up tonight. Have you thought about going back to San Francisco?"

"That's why I'm here, to talk to you about that."

"Great, so you've decided to come with me! I knew you'd come around eventually. Elizabeth, I know you grew up here and so have some sentimental attachment to this place, but I'm here to tell you, this is one of the draggiest towns I've ever spent time in. Ok, I'm ready, lay 'em on me."

"What?"

"Lay 'em on me. I know you've got a whole bunch of conditions for going back with me. I'll agree to anything you say."

"Look, Tom, I don't have any conditions."

"Really? Well, OK, come over here and give me a kiss."

"Tom, I'm not going anywhere with you. You're going to leave, but I'm staying here, in my hometown."

"What? Are you serious?" Morgan sounded as if she'd walloped him with a two by four. "Come on, tell me you're kidding."

"No, I'm not kidding. I want you to leave tomorrow. The only reason you're hanging around here is because of me, and that's over for good."

"Think about what you're saying, Liz. You've got to give me another chance."

"No, Tom, no more chances. You used your last chance up a long time ago. I want you out of my life. Now."

"Honey, you don't mean that. Come on, give me a chance to explain."

Morgan got up and started toward her.

"I don't want to hear any more explanations, Tom. I want you to leave. Tomorrow."

"No, Elizabeth, you've got to listen to me."

Morgan gripped her by both shoulders; his sculptor's hands squeezed her tight.

"Let me go," she said, trying to throw off his arms.

Morgan gripped her more tightly.

"Elizabeth, stop this, settle down." She continued to struggle. "Stop, now. You've got to listen to me."

"I'm through listening to you, you bastard," she said, struggling to free herself.

"Elizabeth, stop now," he commanded. "I said stop all this."

Morgan gripped her hard as he could and began to shake her. It looked in the strobe light as if they were doing some strange dance. Elizabeth tried with all her strength to throw off his arms, but it was useless.

Tom pulled her to him. "All you need, Elizabeth, is a good fuck."

He forcibly kissed her clamped-shut lips and began pushing her toward the bed. Without thinking, Elizabeth shot her right knee up hard and fast as she could--though in the strobe it looked slow--straight into his groin, a move she'd seen in a movie. Morgan yelped and bent over double, clutching his crotch. He collapsed onto his knees.

"I told you the last time you shook me, you son of a bitch, never to do it again." Morgan groaned, rocking on his knees. "Now, I'm going to say this just once more. I *never* want to see you again. This is *my* hometown and you have no business here. Tomorrow you're going to clear out. And you're *never* going to bother me again. Is that *clear*?"

Morgan moaned, said breathlessly, "What the fuck, Elizabeth?"

"I *said*, is that *clear*?" Elizabeth became aware she was almost yelling.

No answer, then, softly, "OK, I heard you. I'll go. But, Elizabeth, you're making a big mistake."

"No, the mistake I made was going with you in the first place."

Elizabeth turned and descended the stairs. Judith stood up and they walked together out of the house. As they opened the doors to Judith's car, someone changed the music again. Rod Stewart's "Maggie May" came shouting out of the old farmhouse.

Driving back toward town, Elizabeth noticed for the first time all the stars overhead. The Milky Way stretched out in a luster and made her feel happy, as if it were her own personal star highway to freedom.

Elizabeth touched Judith on the shoulder, said, "Thanks for your help."

"Don't thank me. You did it all yourself, Elizabeth."

"But I wouldn't have gone out there and done that if you hadn't pushed me."

"I didn't have to push very hard. You wanted to do this. I was just the taxi service."

"You were more than a taxi, Judith. You were a friend."

Judith turned, looked into her eyes, smiled. "I like that. Friend sounds good."

As they drove the short distance back to town, under the bright winking and twinkling of the stars, Judith saw the huge beast, moving ahead of them in the dark, appearing incandescently and then disappearing again, like--like what? Something from her distant past. She had it: the airport signal beacon. She felt the buffalo's presence as a blessing.

After she dropped off Elizabeth, Judith thought of Nick. She'd call him as soon as she got back to the dorm. He could interrupt his reading to hear about her night. She drove happily down the lamp-lit streets. Yes, she felt blessed.

Chapter 12
Dialogues

When Nick returned to Red Earth and the University in September, he had been chastened considerably. His parents had come home five minutes after he had tried to call them from jail, and, switching on the ten o'clock news, had learned of his arrest in the manner he had feared. Lena and Roger had nonetheless been generous, putting up a thousand dollars as a retainer for his attorney John Holst's services.

Holst told them the bad news was that Nick was being charged with a felony count of harvesting marijuana; the potentially good news was that there was a case slated to be heard by state Supreme Court the first week of September, a case which challenged the constitutionality of the state's controlled substance laws. Holst felt the laws were wretchedly written and would be found unconstitutional by the higher court. In that event, Nick and everyone else who had been arrested under those laws in the four years they had been in effect would have their cases dismissed, or, if applicable, their sentences terminated. All records of arrests and convictions would be destroyed. The slates of all those individuals would be wiped clean. Holst said that if the court threw out the laws before they came to trial, he would refund half the retainer.

Holst, a shrewd man possessed of a tragic vision of life, was right. The State Supreme Court found the laws unconstitutional the week before Nick went back to school. He was a free man again. Holst congratulated him on the timing of his arrest, saying he would certainly have been convicted if the case had gone to trial. Holst said the best Nick could have hoped for was a suspension of imposition of sentence, which meant that though convicted, he would not have a sentence imposed by the judge, but instead, would serve a period of probation, upon the successful completion of which, the record of his arrest and conviction would be erased. Holst said the law allowed for this to give the judges discretion when dealing with people who may have made a mistake but who were not criminals, who needed a bit of legal correction perhaps, but also a second chance.

An incredible period of anxiety, fear, grief, and nauseating regret thus came to an end for Nick. But his euphoria was tempered by the knowledge of the great hurt he had inflicted on his family. His parents were hard-working, law-abiding people, but more important, they were good people--thoughtful, self-sacrificing, compassionate. They didn't deserve to have anything terrible happen to them, but most especially not at the hands of their son, the young man with whom they had unstintingly shared their love and time and humor and wisdom, their lives, in short.

The thought that he had betrayed his mother and father so brutally, that his thoughtless and irresponsible act had brought them such pain, was enough to drive Nick into paroxysms of self-loathing and remorse. Sometimes he got so angry and sick from self-hatred that he vomited, the loss of whatever he'd recently eaten (followed by wracking dry heaves) leaving him weak, shaken, and sore-ribbed. At such times he wished he could simply cease to exist.

He saw that Judith had been right. He had been behaving for several years in a wholly self-centered way, greatly concerned about the gratification of his own needs and desires, but very little concerned about anyone else's. Growing up, he had always hated to admit that his sister was right about something and that he was wrong. It had been difficult, if not quite impossible, for him to do. But he had no trouble now. He was so manifestly wrong this time, and she was so undeniably right that, far from being hard to do, it was easy for him to admit that she had been right. Indeed--and wasn't this the strangest thing?--he felt somehow grateful to her for being right, for having had the clarity of moral perspective to be able to judge things so correctly.

But his arrest was not the only thing Nick was tortured by in those months. He learned near the end of the second summer session, about five weeks after his arrest, that Jon Arbalest was dating Elizabeth Prescott. After their release from jail, Nick and Jon hadn't seen much of each other. It was as if they both felt that whatever friendship they had had was over, as if its artificial closeness--more a matter of shared anti-war politics and having no one else to hang out with during summer school than anything else--had been shattered, like a wine glass, on the granitic boulder of THE ARREST. That was how Nick always thought of it: THE ARREST. Then one day, Nick heard a loud, impatient knocking at his door. He knew before his hand even reached the door handle that Jon was standing on the other side.

Jon had a lascivious grin on his face, a grin that Nick later remembered as repellent.

"Well, Nick, you smartass, all I've got to say is I told you so."

"What are you talking about, Jon?"

"Elizabeth Prescott."

"What about Elizabeth."

"I've been going out with her for the past two weeks, and last night I balled her."

"Yeah, you're full of shit, Arbalest."

"You'd like to think so, wouldn't you, Nick. You didn't think I had a chance with Elizabeth, but I told you I'd get into her pants. Of course, that sister of yours wasn't much help."

Nick didn't know the whole story, but somehow the same night he and Jon had been arrested, Judith had met Elizabeth, and after that they'd quickly become best friends.

"That's because Judith knows what kind of a shit you are with women."

"Yeah, well, I love her too. She tried her fucking best to poison Elizabeth's mind against me, but the old Arbalest charm won out, just as it has a hundred times before."

"Like I said, Jon, you're full of shit."

"It's hard to admit when you're wrong, isn't it, Nicky boy? And I'm telling you, she's was one hot bitch in bed."

Jon's grin was really starting to get to Nick. If he didn't wipe it off his face real soon, Nick would wipe it off for him.

"Whatsamatter? You have plans to get into her pants, too?"

Nick felt flame come into his face.

"Yeah, sure, Arbalest. I look at women the way you do."

"You know, that's what I can't stand about you and your sister, Larkin. You've both got this fucking superior attitude about sex. But you're no different. You like getting laid just as much as I do."

"Jon, I've got work to do. If that's all you came to say--"

"No, I just want to say one more thing. I'm gonna fuck Elizabeth again tonight, and again tomorrow, and every day for the foreseeable future. Because when you get into some really good pussy like that, you just don't turn away from it till you've had your share and more. Lots more."

Jon laughed and walked off down the hall. Nick closed his door and lay down on his bed. He felt like he was going to throw up. Waves of revulsion shuddered through his body. He clenched his hands so tightly into fists that his fingernails left indentations in his palms that lasted a couple of days. He slammed his fists over and over into the mattress. He got up and paced around the room, kicking his wastebasket, his basket of clean and neatly folded laundry, his book bag. He kicked a drawer hard shut on his desk. He knocked all his books and notebooks off the desk with one big swipe, and then he kicked them, fast and furiously as he could, across the room. He looked around and when he couldn't find anything else to kick, he kicked the bed frame--so hard he thought he'd broken his toe.

But he didn't care. All he could think about was the grin on Jon's face as he told him he'd fucked Elizabeth. He should have smacked that grin right back through Arbalest's teeth, knocked it down his throat till it clogged his windpipe. He felt like running out and tracking Jon down and smashing his face in--beating him so he'd never grin again, so no chick would ever be interested in fucking him again. Nick picked his pillow up and belted it to the floor again and again, imagining each time it was Jon's face. But it was no good. Hitting a pillow was worthless. So he turned and lashed out at the door to his room. He hit it hard smash with his right fist, hard smash with his left, hard smash with his right, until he'd bruised and bloodied the knuckles of both hands. It must have sounded to someone walking down the hallway as if someone was knocking--no, hammering--on the door from the inside.

Nick threw himself down into his chair and put his face in his battered hands and clenched his long hair into knots. And so the torture went on for the next two days. Until, in a moment of irrational anger, he called up Judith and verbally assaulted her.

"Judith, how could you let this happen?"

"What, Nick?"

"Don't give me that. You know very well what. "

"Nick, I don't know what you're talking about."

"How could you let Elizabeth Prescott go out with Jon Arbalest? You know what kind of a bastard he is."

"Well, it's good to finally hear you say so, Nick."

"And after you told me not to ask her out because 'after her last relationship, she needs time to heal.'" Nick's last words were drenched in wasp venom.

"Now just a minute, Nick. I was right about that."

"Well, then how come she's been going out with Arbalest?"

"Look, Nick, I did everything I could to talk Elizabeth out of that. You know how much I detest him."

"Then why didn't you stop her?"

"Nick, I know you're pissed off and don't want to hear this right, but Elizabeth is her own person. I gave her my opinion, but she made her own choice."

"He fucked her. Did you know that, Judith? He fucked her."

"Is that what he told you?"

"Damn straight. He came to my room just to rub my nose in it."

"He's lying, Nick. Elizabeth's gone out with him a few times but she said nothing happened, and that she didn't plan to let anything happen."

"You believe her?"

"What kind of question is that? Of course I believe her. Do you believe that asshole, Arbalest?"

"Yeah, maybe you're right. But you didn't see him. Didn't see how full of himself he was as he grinned and told me how he'd balled her."

"And I suppose you've been goading yourself with this ever since."

Nick didn't want to admit it, but he knew Judith would see through him if he lied. His voice dropped to a raspy whisper. "Yeah, it's been bad."

"I didn't know you cared that much, Nick."

"I didn't, either."

"Well, I'm sure Arbalest is lying, but if it'll put your mind at rest, I'll talk to Elizabeth. She needs to know what that prick's been saying about her."

"Thanks, Judith." Nick slowly replaced the receiver.

Judith called him back a few hours later. "Nick, Arbalest is a lying sonofabitch. Elizabeth told me nothing happened between them, that she closed him down fast every time he tried to make a move. Nick? You there?"

"Yeah, I'm here."

"And Elizabeth was furious that Arbalest had been going around spreading these lies about her. She went over to break it all off with him."

"You don't know how happy this makes me, Judith."

"Nick, I want you to promise me something."

"What?"

"That you won't ask Elizabeth out."

"How can you ask me that, Judith? After what I've been through these last two days."

"Nick, whatever you've been through, Elizabeth has been through a lot more. Not just with Arbalest, but with that last bastard she lived with, Tom Morgan. Elizabeth really does need time to heal, figure out what she wants for herself, before she gets involved with another guy."

"You're asking too much, Judith."

"Nick, you owe me."

"Yeah, but this is too much."

"Nick, I insist."

"Insist all you want. You have no right to ask this of me."

"I do have the right. I'm Elizabeth's best friend."

"What about me? I thought you were my friend."

"Nick, we're more than friends. We always will be. And that's why you're going to do as I ask."

"You presume too much, Judith."

"No, I don't, Nick, and you know it. Now tell me you're going to do as I asked."

"This isn't going to be forever, is it?

"No, just till Elizabeth has time to get her balance back."

"So how long's that going to take?"

"I don't know, but it won't be forever."

"OK, Judith, I won't ask her out--for one month.."

"Nick, that's not long enough."

"One month, that's all I'm going to promise."

"Three months, Nick, three months."

"Two."

"OK, two."

They left it at that. Nick was grateful to Judith and he respected her request. It burned him like lye soap to admit it, but he knew his sister was probably right.

The twins went home for the few weeks between the end of summer school and the beginning of fall classes. All that time, Nick began to see his sister with fresh eyes. They talked a lot, and Nick enjoyed it. He hadn't realized how much he'd missed that closeness, that special intimacy they'd once had. He regretted the distance they'd allowed to grow between them the last several years.

They'd probably never again be so close that they'd know each other's every thought and dream each other's dreams. To be that close they'd have to give up some large part of their separate identities, and neither of them wanted to do that. They each liked themselves very much the way they were. But they could become close again, very close. That prospect pleased Judith immensely, and it made Nick feel more and more grateful to have her as his sister. He told her as much as they sat over coffee one late September Saturday morning, at a booth in the Student Union.

"Do you still see things?" Nick asked. You know, things other people don't see?"

"The day you got arrested I saw the white buffalo."

"I did, too, but not distinctly. It was a pale phantom."

"Not for me. It was bigger and brighter than ever."

"Then it must have been my fault I didn't see it whole."

"What difference does it make? At least you saw it."

"No, don't you see, it was fading. I was losing my connection."

"You can get it back."

"I feel as if I've desecrated something incomparably beautiful."

"That's too strong, Nick."

"Maybe, but it's how I feel."

"You made a mistake. There's no need to torture yourself.

"Lately, that's what I've excelled at, self-torture. But let's change the subject. I want to ask Elizabeth out."

"I don't know, Nick. Given your recent record with women, are you sure you're the best guy for Elizabeth."

"Come on, Judith, you're supposed to be my friend."

"I'm also her friend."

"So what are you saying, you have to protect her from me?"

"No, she can protect herself." Judith looked at him intently. Her eyebeams could cut glass. "Nick, tell me you're sincere, that you're not just trying to get Elizabeth into bed. I'll know if you're lying."

It was difficult, but Nick returned her stare. "No, I'm not just trying to get her into bed. I haven't been able to get her out of my mind since I first met her."

Judith stared hard--hard--another half a minute. Her look almost gave Nick physical pain, but he endured it without averting his eyes.

"All right, what are you doing today?"

"Nothing till tonight."

"What's tonight?".

"You know, the second film in the Welles series?"

"What is it?"

"*The Magnificent Ambersons.*"

"OK, how about this? Wolfram and Elizabeth and I are going to Sioux City this afternoon." She looked at her watch: eleven a.m. "I'm supposed to pick up Wolfram in half an hour. We'll meet you in front of the Union at noon and then we'll go pick up Elizabeth."

Nick was ecstatic.

* * * * * * *

Nick refilled his coffee and opened his journal. He wanted to finish the poem he'd started the night before. It was a collection of images, half-remembered, half-imagined, from his childhood on the farm. He read what he'd written so far, the words choked with crossings-out and both inter- and extra-linear additions. He was pleased with the accretion of detail in the lines, but he was worried that the reason he'd stopped last night was not because he'd been tired, but because he hadn't known how to finish the poem. He thought a moment, then quickly added six lines, then three more. He read them over twice. That was it. Done.

Since school had started, Nick had written several poems for his writing class, all of them about the farm. It was as if he couldn't move forward in time until he had come to terms with his childhood experiences at the farm. At midterm, they were supposed to switch to writing fiction, but Nick had already approached his teacher--a thirtyish, freckle-faced, red-headed woman named Kate Winfield--asking if he could write a screenplay instead. He knew that she had a background in theater and had written plays before turning to novels, so he'd expected her to embrace the idea enthusiastically.

Instead she had frowned, sighed, and complained to the air, "Why doesn't anyone want to write books anymore? What happened, did you see *Midnight Cowboy* and get blown away by it or something?"

Nick smiled. "No, *The 400 Blows*."

She arched one thin eyebrow, looked at him as if seeing him for the first time. He didn't know it, but he'd stumbled onto one of her favorite films.

"Did you identify with Antoine? Somehow you don't strike me as the scrappy street-kid type."

"No, I didn't identify with him. My life's been completely different."

"Did you have a happy childhood?"

Nick knew this was a grave artistic sin, but he felt dishonesty with her would have been a greater one.

"Yeah, I guess I did."

"And you grew up on a farm, right?"

"We lived on the farm till my sister and I were about ten. We spent our summers there for several years after that."

"Your sister is your twin?"

"Yeah, her name's Judith."

She turned her head slightly sideways, as if changing angles might make Nick come clearer for her.

"Judith? Have you read Virginia Woolf?"

"No, why?"

"Oh, never mind, it's nothing. Tell me, does your sister write, too?"

"No, she's a painter."

"A visual artist. Do I see a trend here?"

"If there is, it's accidental."

"Does your sister paint farm scenes?"

"No, but she does tend toward landscapes."

"Is she a realist?"

Nick thought of the peculiar vibrancy of Judith's paintings. "No, not exactly. Her work is representational, but it's pretty intense in its use of color and light."

"Sounds interesting. You'll have to introduce me to her some time."

"Sure."

Nick began to see Kate Winfield's features become softer, gentler. He saw her face begin to glow, felt the Platonic warmth radiating from her. He felt wholly relaxed, comfortable. The temperature in the room rose a couple of degrees.

"So, tell me, Nick, why do you want to write a screenplay?"

"I grew up watching a lot of movies, mostly with my dad. Last year I attended the film series at the Union, and I was amazed by the storytelling possibilities of film. I guess I'm a fairly visual person."

"I can tell that from your poems. You have a strong aural sense, too, but you might do more with touch and smell, especially smell. That, by the way, points up one distinct advantage writing has over film."

"What's that?"

"Writing is more sensually capable. Film can make you hear and it can make you see. I don't think it can make you smell or taste or touch."

"No, I think it can. It can present an image with such graphic intensity or with such jarring juxtaposition of editing that a kind of synesthesia occurs. You imagine that you smell the thing you see."

"That may be true of reeking garbage on city streets or other disgusting things, but I doubt film can suggest the more beautiful, intoxicating smells."

"Sure it can. Through lighting and editing, the aromatic potency of a rose garden can be suggested, or the smoke of incense rising through shafts of light in a room, or even the perfume of a woman."

"Even if I concede that--and I'd have to think more about it before I did --what about the mimetic potential of writing, the ability of the writer to create a sense of felt life through the accretion of hundreds and thousands of details? Film can't begin to match that."

Kate Winfield had glowed peach, then saffron. Nick felt the light from her face like a warm breeze. The air temperature climbed another degree.

"I think it can." Nick's voice took on a new charge of enthusiasm. "In fact, that's where film has the advantage, because it's made of the pieces of the actual world, not of words--which are only the symbols of things."

"But in selecting which things to film and how to shoot them and then how to edit them, doesn't film turn those things into symbols? And, think about it, Nick, the things we see up on a screen in a theater are not the things themselves. They're two-dimensional representations of those things--modified by lenses and lights and filters and a lot more."

"Yes, but there is a sort of, oh, I don't know what you'd call it-- existential? I guess that's close enough--anyway, a sort of existential quality film has that makes it at least one remove closer to the thing itself. Film may not actually be the thing itself, but it is closer than writing can ever be since it captures what most people would agree is the very likeness of the thing itself."

"Then why does almost every film adapted from a novel fall so far short of the book? Not only do they not convincingly ground us in the characters or the setting, but often they seem merely to point back to the book, as if to say, see, here is Anna Karenina, or this is Heathcliff or Pip or Ahab?"

"That's probably because of the economics of filmmaking. It simply costs too much to put on film an *Anna Karenina* that is as long and complex as the novel. But if the money could be had, and if time were not a concern, I think a film version of *Anna Karenina* could be made that would be just as dramatically powerful as the original."

"Sort of the 'world enough and time' argument, huh?" She smiled at him. She was enjoying this. How long had it been since a student had walked into her office and challenged her thinking so much? Not recently. "But isn't money always going to be a limitation? And time, too. No director, no matter how talented, is going to be allowed to make ten- or fifteen-hour movies because the theaters could never arrange enough showings to make back the cost of the films."

Kate Winfield turned an irradiant pink, then a lustrous rose. Nick basked in her light. Her office felt so completely peaceable.

"Well, that may be true, but one thing I've noticed about the little fiction writing I've done is that it takes me forever--pages and pages--to fully set up a scene, to describe the place and the characters. Film can show you the place and the people, in all their detail, in seconds. It's much faster than writing because its images are at least one step closer to real life. So, maybe it doesn't need all those hours to achieve the same effect as a book."

"But that's the real problem, Nick. The effect of a film can never be 'the same' as the effect of a novel."

"But they both work with the same elements, don't they--characters, setting, plot?"

"But the way those elements are used can never be the same. The writer uses words, rhetorical devices, various figures, and dramatic structure to create atmosphere, mood, and the feeling of significant events happening to distinctly real human beings. It takes so much time to do that with words because it takes time to build a world that will strike us as congruent with our world, as true. And the more time spent by the writer, the deeper the felt truth of the portrayal, the more complex the human reality that can be revealed."

A solar prominence flared from her brow, like a massive static electric charge built up by the firings of her neurons.

"But isn't it more than a matter of time and detail? Doesn't imagination play a role here? And can't the filmmaker possess just as much imagination as the novelist?"

"Of course, but film will always lack one thing that all literary works have."

"What's that?"

"The ability to excite imaginative participation by the reader."

"You mean that a film by Bergman or Fellini doesn't excite the viewer's imagination?"

"Sure, but our view of the characters is always determined by the fact that real actors play those characters. We'll always see Bergman's knight as Max Von Sydow, Fellini's strong man as Anthony Quinn. And the same thing goes for place. The Swedish countryside will always be the setting for *The Virgin Spring*, Paris will always be the setting of *The 400 Blows*."

"But isn't Mississippi always going to be the setting for *As I Lay Dying*, and Algeria for *The Stranger*?"

"No, it's different, Nick. Truffaut's Paris reveals itself, in the most graceful, spontaneous way, with a literalness that the most realistic of novelists cannot begin to approach. But Faulkner creates his Mississippi through a series of verbal suggestions that cause his readers to fill in all the missing details--the details photography must necessarily reveal--through a complementary act of imagination."

Another solar prominence looped into space from her hairline, like a strand of hair gone wild. She had become magma-red and was glowing so brightly it was hard to distinguish her features. Sitting near her, Nick felt as if he possessed incredible energy.

"When a writer says a character has dimples, or pimples, or a mole on his chin, though, the writer is limiting the reader's imagination."

"Not so much limiting as guiding. A certain amount of guiding is needed to activate the imagination. But no matter how mimetic a writer is--and writers differ vastly on how much they want to guide the reader--he or she cannot begin to create the literal surface factuality of the filmed image. Charles Foster Kane can only be Orson Welles."

"Thank God. No one else could even come close."

Kate smiled. "Of course, but you see what I mean, don't you?"

"Yeah, but I'm not sure that film makers don't use the symbolic nature of film images to suggest and prompt the imagination in ways similar to the ways writers do. I'm going to have to think about this."

"Why don't you tell me the story you were thinking about for your screenplay."

Nick felt charged with energy. He outlined as quickly as he could the basic series of stories he saw making up his plot--events drawn from his and his sister's lives (without the visions; he had never spoken of the visions to anyone but Judith), incidents connected and carried forward not so much causally as thematically. When he was finished, Kate thought for a time before responding.

"Yes, I can see this as a film. It all has a nice fluid, visual feel to it. But I can also see it as a novel, and I would suggest that it might be better for you to go in that direction with it. Today everyone wants to see films about urban culture, films that reflect the huge changes our culture is going through. People want to read about that, too, but I think you'd have a better chance with a book set on a farm than with a film set on one. And you can always write a screenplay for your novel later."

Nick felt himself bathed in rivers of light.

"I guess that's something to consider."

And so Nick had started to turn some of his journal entries into stories, chapters actually. He had extrapolated from the incidents, at first modestly, and then wildly, learning in the process that very little was needed in the way of a 'real-life' incident (much less than he had ever thought) to serve as the point of origin, inchoate and mysterious, for a story. And the more he actively re-imagined the real-life incidents, the more he augmented, dilated, distorted, distended--in short, the more he fictionalized--the more he enjoyed the writing. Ever after it would be the act of imagination, and not the reportage, that would make writing a thing of joy for him. That this process ran exactly counter to the way most people thought of writing was of no concern to him. For Nick, the exercise of the creative imagination became writing and writing became what he did--his way of being in the world.

* * * * * * *

Nick heard the door of the snackbar open and saw Jon Arbalest walk in and make straight for him, his blond locks cataracting down over his olive-green Army surplus jacket. Nick had hardly spoken to him since the day Arbalest had come to his room and bragged about sleeping with Elizabeth Prescott--a lie Judith had caused him to eat with a vengeance.

"Nick, my partner in crime, how goes the revolution?"

"I think it's stalled out."

"Yeah, no matter what that fucking Nixon does, the American people just seem to take it. Sometimes I think Nixon might be half right about the silent majority."

"I think people are worn out by the war. They don't want to listen to a bunch of college kids' fantasize about some Woodstock nation."

"I hate all that 'give peace a chance' bullshit."

"Well, peace *is* still our goal, isn't it?"

"You know as well as I do, Nick, that 'peace and love' is just naive fucking bullshit. There's never been peace on this planet and there never will be because the world is full of motherfuckers like Nixon and Kissinger. Once we realize that, we can clear our heads of all that 'love is all you need' bullshit and commit ourselves to the struggle."

"Struggle in the Marxist sense."

"Struggle to spark the revolution and bring the fuckers down."

"Sounds like you've been hanging out with Kathleen Doyle and the People's Revolutionary Committee."

"Fucking A. They're the only people around here who've seen through the bullshit and committed themselves to doing something about it."

"So, you going to take part in the march next week?"

"Fuck no. Do you really think this fucking country pays any attention at all to a few thousand college kids marching through the streets whenever they have nothing better to do?"

"Gandhi believed that persistence slowly wears away at the resistance of the oppressive force and breaks it down."

"Fuck Gandhi. That son-of-a-bitch is dead. And so is Martin Luther King. The only thing you're going to wear down by persistence is your own sense of purpose. You don't know what you're up against. Every bank in this fucking country has invested up the asshole in the very companies fueling the war machine. The whole economic system of this country is dead set on continuing this war. Can't you see that?"

"I see you've read Marx and Marcuse without asking a single question."

"Shit, Nick, the time for these nitpicking philosophical arguments is over. All we have time for now is action."

"And what action is that? Blowing up buildings?"

"Maybe so, maybe so. Time is running out fast here in America. It won't be long before they send the tanks down our streets and start the round-ups. I'll bet those motherfuckers are building the camps right now."

"Jon, this is paranoid bullshit."

"Laugh if you want, Nick, but you won't be laughing when they send in the fucking Marines. We've got to spark the revolution now. It doesn't matter if we have to burn down every city in America to do it."

Nick rolled his eyes, and as he did so, he saw Jon change into a cobra, risen to eye level before him, swaying slightly, hood opened, its tongue forking out to sense the air, frozen black eyes staring at him, round and unfeeling as ball bearings.

"You don't want peace, Jon. You want power."

"Fucking A."

"You and the Kathleen Doyle only want to bring down the government so you can take over. You're a bunch of frustrated totalitarians."

The cobra swayed more. Its eyes shot deadly cold into the air, its tongue darted in and out, its fangs shot poison into the bloodstream.

"And you know what, Nick, you and all your bullshit peaceful protesters are just tools in the hands of the system. They're letting you march and make your little speeches because it makes them look so democratic and fair. And all the while they're bombing the shit out of Hanoi and Cambodia. Before you know it, they're going to send in the fucking tanks and round up all you pacifists. They'll string you peace-and-love types up on trees and lightpoles all over this country."

Amazement leaped from Nick's eyes. "I've got better things to do than listen to any more of this shit." Nick grabbed his journal and his jacket, slid out of the booth.

Jon grabbed his arm as he walked by. "Some of us are going to be fighting 'em on every street, Nick. You should think real hard about joining us. I'd hate to see you and that pretty sister of yours hanging from lightpoles downtown."

Nick wrenched his arm free. "Fuck you, Arbalest. Who're you to tell me what I should do?" Nick walked away, his bootheels tapping on the tile floor.

"Fuck you, too, Larkin. You peace-and-love types' days are numbered."

* * * * * * *

Just as Nick stepped through the glass doors on the west side of the Union and into the sunny-cloudy day, Judith drove up in their Chevy II. Wolfram got out the passenger door and let Nick into the back seat.

"What's wrong, Nick?" Wolfram asked.

"Nothing."

Judith put the car into gear and they set off to pick up Elizabeth.

"It doesn't look like nothing," Judith said.

"Oh, Jon Arbalest just pissed me off so much I walked out on him."

"Jon Arbalest. Say no more," Judith said.

"He was saying some pretty scary shit."

"He's been hanging out with Kathleen Doyle," Judith said, "so I suppose he gave you the Maoist party line."

"Yeah, but it was all paranoid and apocalyptic. He was talking about the government sending tanks into the streets and lynching war protesters."

"Nick, you should stay away from him," Judith said.

"Hey, it's not like I went looking for him. He came into the snackbar and sat down at my booth. He was talking about setting fire to every city in America to spark the revolution, or some such shit."

"That's one sick mother," Wolfram said. "And probably dangerous. You know, guys like him are really just fascists. They want to impose their will on everybody else."

"I told him something like that, but it just set off more ranting."

"Well, let's hope he leaves you alone now," Judith said. "He's brought enough grief into our lives."

"After today, I don't think he's going to be seeking us out. He prefers Kathleen Doyle and the PRC."

"Why doesn't that surprise me? Have either of you ever spent ten minutes talking to Kathleen Doyle?"

Nick and Wolfram said no.

"Well, I have," Judith said, "believe me, *she's* dangerous. I've never seen anyone get so ecstatic about planting bombs or go into such raptures about 'offing the pigs'. I think she derives erotic pleasure from fantasizing about blowing property and people into a million bits."

"The Weathermen's Joan of Arc," Wolfram suggested.

"Sort of," Judith agreed, "though she wouldn't like the religious overtone."

"People like her and Arbalest do more to undermine the war resistance movement than anybody else," Wolfram said. "If the movement doesn't keep the kind of spiritual discipline King demanded from his marchers, it's never going to stop the war," Wolfram said.

"You're asking it to keep 'keep' discipline when it never had any to begin with," Judith said.

"Maybe so," Wolfram said, "but a lotta organizers go back to the days of civil rights."

"I think Arbalest's idea of 'sparking the revolution' is a lot like inciting a riot," Nick said. "He wants to set this destructive frenzy in motion."

"I know for a fact Arbalest could never envision the course that frenzy would take or what a post-revolutionary society might look like," Judith said.

"No," Wolfram said. "He and Doyle can't see past executing the powers that be and setting themselves up in power."

"This is like some surreal cartoon of a revolution," Judith said.

"At the first hint of a real armed insurrection, Nixon would call in the Marines," Wolfram said. "The Jon Arbalests of the world would get mopped up in short order. Guys like that have no idea, I mean no idea at all, what they're up against."

Judith pulled into a driveway across the street from Lewis and Clark Park. A hundred yards or so into the park's elms and locusts and pines was the city water tower (which always seemed to Nick like some alien craft from *War of the Worlds*), a drained swimming pool, and a playground.

"On that grim note," Judith said, getting out of the car, "I'm going to get Elizabeth."

* * * * * * *

Judith held the seat forward and Elizabeth said hello and climbed into the back. As Elizabeth looked toward Nick, the sun sent warm shafts of light into the car, making the green parts of her hazel eyes flash. Hazel, Nick thought, answering a question of his from several months ago. Her eyes are hazel. Elizabeth's perfume smelled vaguely mideastern.

Nick thought Elizabeth looked stunning in her red-black-and-brown peasant blouse, her big, dangly, gold, Mexican-looking earrings, her black jeans, and her jean jacket. The sunbeams flooding the car filled her long auburn hair and his long black hair with winking lights, as if hundreds of fireflies blinked amorously in their tresses. Elizabeth turned her eyes toward the front seat. Judith backed the car out and set off down the street.

"Judith's told me so much about you Nick," Elizabeth said, "I feel like I know you already."

"I'm not sure I relish being known by Judith's representations."

"Didn't tell her anything but the truth, Nick."

"That's what he's afraid of," Wolfram said, laughing.

"Judith said only good things about you," Elizabeth said. "You're lucky to have a sister who cares about you so much."

Nick smiled. "Tell me more."

* * * * * * *

In Sioux City, Wolfram bought everybody lunch, and they spent the afternoon shopping for records, sheet music, books, and clothes. The four of them talked happily non-stop.

At the record stores they visited, Nick and Elizabeth discovered they shared a passion for Beethoven--Elizabeth's long-held, Nick's newfound. Elizabeth bought a boxed set of the late quartets, Nick a record with the Seventh Symphony on one side and the Eighth on the other. Wolfram, a little more flush with cash, bought records of Ali Akbar Khan, Mississippi John Hurt, Elizabethan songs, baroque trumpet, Mahler's Ninth, as well as John Mayall's "The Turning Point" for himself--and Judy Collins' "Whales and Nightingales" as a gift for Judith.

At the bookstore, Judith bought a copy of Lama *Govinda's Foundations of Tibetan Buddhism* and *The Way of the White Clouds* for herself and Alan Watts' *Psychotherapy East and West* and *The Way of Zen* as a present for Wolfram, who was into Watts of late. Elizabeth bought paperback copies of the seven volumes of Proust's

Remembrance of things Past, a novel she said she'd wanted to read since high school, and Nick bought a book containing four Bergman screenplays.

They also went to several clothing stores (buying shirts, blouses, vests, belts, and pants). This shopping took the most time, and Judith noticed that at about the second clothing store, Nick and Elizabeth had begun to hold hands--as naturally as if they had been going together for months. Their last stop was the Army-Navy Surplus Store, which Wolfram refused to enter on principle, saying he had already had all the Army clothes he ever hoped to own in this lifetime. He waited for them in the car.

Wolfram noticed that when Elizabeth and Nick got into the back seat afterwards, they exchanged a quick kiss. He looked at Judith, who'd also noticed, and she raised her eyebrows. Somehow it felt right, though, that there were no longer just the two of them.

* * * * * * *

After dinner and the Welles film, which Nick was rapturous about, the four of them went to Wolfram's apartment to listen to some of the music they'd bought. As Beethoven's Seventh, that bright paean to spontaneous, overspilling joy, played in the background, Elizabeth and Nick sat on the couch, holding hands, and Judith and Wolfram sat on the loveseat.

"You know, Nick," Wolfram said, "Judith and I have been together almost a year now."

"A year next month, Wolfram," Judith said, smiling at him.

"So, I'm pretty certain," Wolfram continued, "that I know Judith's ideas about love. But what about yours? Do the twins think alike, or do they just look alike?"

Everyone looked at Nick.

"OK, I'll try to answer the question. A few months ago, I would have said that my views of love were about as different from Judith's as different could be."

"What was your view then?" Wolfram asked.

"I never put a lot of thought into it, but I'd say that I believed in romance, in love as overwhelming attraction for another person."

"You mean physical attraction?" Elizabeth asked.

Nick looked down and shook his head yes. "Sure, though I wouldn't have been able to admit that to myself then. To me it was all one huge feeling--all terrifically exciting."

"For years that was my view of love, too," Wolfram said, "all red-hot sexual attraction."

"Lust, in a word," Judith said.

"Yeah," Wolfram said, "'that's a good word for it."

"An honest word," Judith said.

"Lust must be the view of love held by every man in this country," Elizabeth said.

Wolfram laughed. "Don't expect me to disagree."

"Nor me," Nick said.

"You enjoying this, Elizabeth?" Judith asked with a smile.

"Yeah, but it's too easy," Elizabeth said. "Who expected them to capitulate without a fight?"

"So, if that was the old Nick, what's the new Nick like--you know, the reformed rake?" Elizabeth asked.

"Better to be a reformed rake than never to have been a rake at all," Nick said, laughing. "But seriously, I'd say that now, instead of seeing love as the drive to feed the body's wailing hungers, gaining a temporary satisfaction, only to be driven back out again to the endless hunt, I see it as a search for the self who complements us. I think everyone is basically incomplete--woefully imperfect and suffering for it every day--and that we find completion and release from pain only in the lover who is our perfect complement."

"You mean everybody's searching for their other half, as Alcibiades speculated in the *Symposium*?" Elizabeth asked.

"Only I don't think we were once one creature that was sliced in half."

"Yeah, if you believed that," Wolfram said, "then Judith would be your other half--literally."

"That's it," Judith said. "I'm going to insist that we maintain an elevated discourse here. We'll entertain no theories based in incest and no Egyptian brother-sister marriages."

"No, I'm not talking about incest," Nick said, "but about the idea that for each of us there exists someone who complements us--who is strong where we're weak, rational where we're unthinking, perceptive where we're blind, and so on."

"And is there just one perfect complement for each person?" Elizabeth asked skeptically.

"No, that'd be absurd. The odds against finding the one perfect match would be hundreds of millions to one, and no one would ever find fulfillment in love. I really don't think there's any way of knowing how many complements there may be for each of us. But one thing is certain. We wander the world perennially grieving and wretched, leaving broken love and promises in our wake, until we chance upon one of those people who is our complement."

"Then you're saying that love is the source of meaning in life?" Elizabeth asked.

"I don't know, I suppose for some people there could be other sources. But for me, love is it."

"For me," Wolfram said, love is the beginning and the end."

"Now what is that supposed to mean, darling?" Judith asked, teasing.

"It means--and realize I'm talking here as a bluesman--that love is the life source. We are conceived in love, nurtured and brought to term in the womb of love, and then delivered into this world, into the tender care of those very lovers who conceived us. But the world we grow to maturity in is often indifferent and chilly toward us, and sometimes downright hostile. It's a place where we experience mostly the lack of love--which we then try to make up for with sex, or drugs, or booze. But whatever we try just takes us deeper into the blues. And who can say they haven't known the blues, the real downhearted, lonesome, body-and-soul-hurting blues. Love is the only true, once-and-for-all healer in this lonely world."

"What about your music, Wolfram? Doesn't that heal you? Doesn't that give meaning to life?" Elizabeth asked.

"Sure, but just playing music is incomplete. It has to be shared with others to be a healing force."

"And don't you share every time you play in front of an audience?"

"I used to think so. But there was always the problem that, if you were only fully alive onstage, what did you do with the rest of your life? You can't live onstage. When I met Judith--"

"Pay attention, here comes the good part," Judith joked.

"That's right, baby. You *are* the good part. So, when I met Judith, I found someone I could share, not only my music with, but everything else I am as a person. And not just for the few hours a week I'm onstage, but all the time. That's what love is to me--a complete sharing. The best, the worst, and everything in between."

"I think that deserves a kiss!" Judith said, embracing him.

"Ooh, Mama, that feels fine!"

"There's more where that came from."

"Judith, please," Nick mock-pleaded.

"Don't worry, we're not going to turn this into an orgy. Elizabeth, your turn."

"Well, my ideas about love have undergone a real metamorphosis in the last several months. I used to believe in some kind of transcendental unity of two lovers, who found the deepest intimacy possible with each other. An intimacy that might have begun with the sharing of their bodies, but which ended with the sharing of their whole selves. There would be no secrets, nothing held back. Lovers were the ultimate confidantes. I saw this sharing as a lifelong process of mutual discovery and deepening appreciation. I still believe that's possible, but I don't think it's a given that everyone, or even most people, are going to find it. I tried for years and I came up empty-handed."

"But the mismatches we make prepare us the better for the person who is our true complement," Nick said. "All our mistakes bring our souls to ripeness."

"And 'ripeness is all'?" Judith asked, making quote marks with the first two fingers of each hand.

"It is when two lovers finally find each other," Nick said this looking directly into Elizabeth's eyes.

"Elizabeth, you said that's what you used to believe," Judith said. "What do you think now?"

"I no longer see the love between two people as the only meaningful love."

"So, how many people do you want?" Wolfram teased.

Elizabeth narrowed her eyes and made a mock-frown. "No, I believe that even if two people are lucky enough to serve as perfect complements for each other, as Nick believes, or to share everything and so redeem the pain of living, as Wolfram thinks--even if they're that lucky, I don't think that will be enough for them."

"What else do they need?" Judith asked.

"Two people being all in all to each other seems too solipsistic to me," Elizabeth said. "I think they have to go beyond the intimacy they share, into the larger world of ideas and of action based on those ideas."

"So you're talking about social activism," Nick said.

"Yes, active engagement in the mitigating of the suffering caused by selfish politics, greed, unjust systems, and so on. We have to find an idea that speaks to us of a reality larger than ourselves and devote ourselves to making that idea a living, organic part of our progress through this world."

"You mean something like the antiwar movement." Wolfram said.

"It can be."

"Then I know what you mean. I never felt better about myself than when I worked for Vietnam Vets Against the War."

"And that was because?" Elizabeth asked, leading him.

"Because I believed in what I was doing, but also because it was unselfish, something I did without any thought of my own gain."

"I think that's the important thing," Judith said, "doing something selflessly, to alleviate human suffering."

"Only it doesn't always have to be a cause," Elizabeth said. "It can be any conscious acts of kindness or generosity or justice."

"My ideas are similar to Elizabeth's," Judith said. "Only I believe what we're talking about is more than trying to ameliorate physical suffering. I think all pain, all suffering, originates in the soul. So for me, the healing of that pain must also originate in the soul. I believe all human beings are intimately connected with each other's welfare."

"Even if we're unaware of it?" Nick asked.

"Even if we deny it," Judith said. "We always have the choice of contributing to or diminishing the spirits of people we meet each day.

Love may begin with the physical, or it may have progressed to the social and political."

"But you don't think it should stop there?" Nick asked.

"No, like Socrates," Elizabeth said, "she believes in a ladder of love, the lower rungs being love of physical objects and self--"

"Yes, and then rising to love of one other person--and then to love of and service to all humanity."

"And then?" asked Nick.

"You sure you want to know?" Judith asked.

"Why not? We've followed you this far."

"OK, my personal view is that then we rise another rung of self-transcendence to love of the Great Maker, Whose mystery and spirit we share, and Who has fashioned each of us out of love and, without our knowing it, tenderly--with infinite patience--guided us through these successive stages of love, till we have risen, all of us together, spirits ablaze, with flaming hearts of love, at last to blinding, blessed reunion with Herself."

As Judith had spoken, the other three had suddenly seen a great spirit ladder appear before them, stretching from a bottom infinitely far down and rising to a height infinitely far above, and they had ascended with Judith, rung after rung, almost flying upwards, until, kindled, they caught fire and burst into pure burn, selfless fulgurance, like a comet whose orbit brings it close to a star and which flames out in a long tail of sparking light. They shared momentarily her vision, and the four of them became simultaneously four flames and a single blaze, distinct identities and an indistinguishable unity. A great eye-searing flashpoint of white burst through the room--brilliance between two curved jet horns--and though blinded, they felt the presence of a force infinitely greater than themselves, eclipsing their ability to comprehend. They felt consumed in but unconsumed by a love they had never known before, a love out of which universes could be born and into which universes could collapse again.

It was some time before any of them spoke.

Part VI

August 1967 - December 1969

Chapter 13
Invisible

At sixteen, but for Nick's much shorter hair, Judith and Nick still looked identical. They were nearly six feet, slender, and, in an epicene way, pretty. Judith was the second tallest girl in the high school, but unlike many tall girls, she didn't stoop, trying to hide her height. She always walked with her spine straight as a saber, and she looked people right in the eye, though she had to look down to many people to do it. Though she and Nick had once been so close they dreamed the same dreams, those times were, but for a few strange, exceptional hours and days, past.

Indeed, the twins had over the past couple of years perfected the art of invisibility. Their first attempts had been predictably awkward and amateurish. What good was it after all to walk about with everything visible but one's fingertips or eyebrows or earlobes? They improved in time, but they still couldn't very well stroll around the house with no apparent elbows or ears or cheekbones. They felt self-conscious when their buttocks, belly-buttons, or ankles became viewless, even if these were already hidden from sight.

But slowly they mastered the dynamics of their art and became capable of disappearing at will. Lena would come into a room she had just heard them laughing in and find--emptiness. They were gone, though there was no other exit but the door she had entered by. Or Roger would come in from outside, see them sitting listening to records or reading, turn his back for a few seconds to hang up his coat, and turn back to address--no one.

This new ability meant that Nick and Judith got out of a lot of chores, missed a number of parental lectures, and had the sinister pleasure sometimes of flummoxing their parents. Of course, Lena and Roger had often been perplexed or confused or mystified or simply left blank with incomprehension by the twins. They weren't startled or shocked any more, but they didn't adapt easily, either.

Over time the twins began to disappear to each other, too. That was harder to do. Their first experiments were crude botches, all the more frustrating since they had become quite adept at becoming invisible to their parents. Nick and Judith weren't sure why they wanted to be invisible to each other, but as they got older, they felt it increasingly necessary--and sometimes imperative. Of course, unlike their parents, they knew exactly what was going on when one of them disappeared, and that made the vanishings vexing as a sliver in a finger or a blister on a heel. As if daily life weren't bothersome enough, their twin, their duplicate, the closest thing there was in the universe to another one of them, had to go and make things harder. It frosted one, it really did.

* * * * * * *

None of Nick's basketball buddies or their girlfriends had to work the last Saturday in August. They planned to spend the whole day and evening on the river. The Larkins had moved to the town of LeBeau, a central South Dakota town on the Missouri River, a little over a year before. LeBeau was about an hour's drive from their farm, which they now leased out to a neighboring farmer.

Nick, Bill Matthews, Bruce Baker, and his foster brother Mike Red Horse, planned to go scuba diving at eight above the massive earthen dam a few miles west of town (they would meet the girls later for a picnic lunch). It hadn't rained in ten days and it hadn't been windy lately, so the underwater visibility would be about as good as it got on the Missouri--fifteen to twenty feet.

Bill pulled his white '64 Renault into Nick's driveway at seven-thirty. Bill, Nick's best friend, was six foot, had short red hair, and sleepy, heavy-lidded eyes. Like Nick, he played forward, and in track he ran the quarter and the half. Nick had on his wrap-around shades and had a chocolate donut between his teeth and a quart of orange juice in one hand when he met Bill at the door.

"Hey, where's my donut?" Bill complained. He hadn't had breakfast.

"Hold on a second."

Nick returned with the whole dozen his mother had bought the night before. He tossed the bag to Bill.

"OK, let's load your gear."

When they arrived at the place they had dived once before, about a half mile above the dam, no one else was there. They didn't want to get any closer to the dam because they were on the same side of the river as the hydroelectric generator's big intake openings. They knew that fish and logs and debris of all kinds got sucked onto the mesh traps on the intakes, and they didn't want to add four divers.

"Bruce probably overslept again," Nick said as he lifted his black Aqualung tank out of Bill's back seat.

"I hope not," Bill said, taking his wet suit and weight belt out of the trunk in the front of the car. "I've never known anyone harder to wake up than Bruce."

"Yeah, when he's out, he's out."

They carried their equipment through the grass and the prickly pear down to the small shale beach. It was a warm, sunny day and the sky was pale blue and cloudless. By the time they had put on their wetsuits, Bruce had driven up in his red Mustang and parked beside the Renault.

"You're late," Nick called, good-humoredly.

"Says who?" Bruce replied, getting out. "You guys are early. You're always early. If we didn't let you get here first, you'd probably get mad and go home."

Bruce and Mike lugged their equipment down to the beach.

Bruce had short brown hair, was six-four, and played center. His looks were a study in incongruity: He had a football-shaped head, high cheekbones, big round brown eyes, slender eyebrows, a cleft chin, and a dimple on the right side only. Looking in a mirror a few years before, he'd concluded he'd have to make it on his personality. So Bruce had become a clown and one of the most popular kids in the class. His father was a lawyer and he was by far the richest kid in the group. The Mustang had been a sixteenth birthday gift from his parents the previous October.

Mike was five-ten, muscular, quick, and agile. He played guard and had been the only sophomore to start last year on the varsity. He was lean-faced and had dark eyes that at first glance seemed all pupil. They looked deep inside one (he'd never lost a stare-down contest). He wore his hair in a flat-top. Mike and Bruce had developed a fast friendship in kindergarten and it had only deepened through the years. Mike had lived with Bruce's family since the previous December when his parent's had been killed--three days before Christmas--in a one-car accident caused by glare ice. Mike had no other living relatives, and the state had placed him with the Bakers, on their request.

****

They spit in their masks to keep them from fogging over, rubbed the spit around, rinsed it out with lake water. They fitted their masks to their faces. The water was cold. They dippered it with their palms into the legs and chest area and arms of their wetsuits, so their bodies could begin warming it. They zipped up and walked out, taking big awkward steps with their flippered feet. When they were chest-deep, they sank into the water. The shale bottom had already become mud. It sloped gently downwards for twenty-five feet, then dropped straight down for fifteen feet. Their weight belts gave gravity the advantage over the natural buoyancy of their bodies. The four divers, trailing bubbles from their mouthpieces and kicking evenly with their flippers, felt like they were gliding downwards--around two water-logged trees (whose few remaining bare branches wore rusting red-and-white-striped and solid-colored spoons with triangle hooks, hula poppers, six-inch artificial worms with two or three hooks, and other lures, each trailing a leader and a wisp of monofilament line), and then around a boulder.

They started across a plateau, saw a school of gar, which quickly darted away. They kicked harder, to chase them, but the fish swam much faster and soon slipped past the edge of their vision. They swam along, past spineless plants and dead trees. Mike was in the lead; he stopped and pointed. Ten feet away they saw two northern pike, three pounders, sleeping on the bottom. Mike and Nick swam slowly over, taking pains not to move suddenly and waken the fish. When they were just above and a little behind the fish, Nick raised one finger, two, three: They grabbed the fish just behind the gills and lifted them. The northerns snake-squirmed and shot out of the boys' hands like two speedboats suddenly thrusting into forward gear.

The four divers swam along, following the curves and slopes of the bottom. They tried to catch other sleeping fish, but the fish saw them, shooshed their tails, and shot away like crossbow bolts. The bottom fell away precipitously and they followed it, swimming down a sheer earth wall, the light growing dimmer as they dived.

Fifty feet down it was considerably darker, but they could still see a short ways. They took turns leading. The three following stayed close, usually within half a body's length, never falling more than a full body's length behind. They swam along at that depth for a while, seeing a couple of crumpled beercans, a rusted tin can, a single tennis shoe, filled with clayey mud, its tongue hanging out like a hanged man's, a slanting, rotted wooden fence post that came apart in their hands when they dislodged it, and some big rocks. They tried moving one, but couldn't budge it.

Nick was leading when an immense shadow-black shape--as if the murk itself had solidified, congealed into swimming, shovel-nosed life--crossed a body's length in front of him, turned, and angled towards the four of them. They froze, floating like dead men, holding their breaths, panic screaming in their eyes. Nick tried to become invisible but couldn't. The fish swam slowly past. First the spade-like snout, the recessed mouth, the four sensory barbels underneath. Then the body, with its rows of bone-hard plates--a body nearly as long as theirs but bigger in girth. Then the long tailfin, too reminiscent of a shark's. Keep going, they prayed, needing to breathe but not daring to. Keep going. It did, vanishing silently, sleekly into the darker depths.

They breathed again as they swam smoothly, steadily upwards. They broke the surface together and swam hard for the shore. Clumsily, they ran, still wearing their flippers, from the water, yanked masks off, collapsed on the shale, gasping for breath. They tugged at flippers, began to remove weights, tanks.

"Did you see that thing!" Bill said.

"I thought we were goddamn fish bait for sure," Bruce said.

"What in the hell was it?" Nick asked.

"I think maybe it was a sturgeon," Mike said.

"A sturgeon! You gotta be kidding," Bruce said.

"No, I think maybe Mike's right," Nick said.

"But that fish was six feet long," Bill said.

"They can get that big," Mike said. "Every few years somebody snags a big one like that."

"Well, I'm not gonna dive or swim in this damned lake ever again," Bruce said.

"You don't have to worry," Mike said. "They're bottom-feeders. They shovel food out of the mud."

"That's why you can't fish for them with bait," Nick said. "You have to snag one to catch it."

"You telling me that mother was harmless?" Bruce asked.

"That's right," Mike said. "Sturgeons can't hurt anything, and nothing else will try to hurt them."

"How can you be sure that's what it was?" Bill asked. "It was dark down there. We could barely see it."

"Yeah," Nick said, in a teasing tone. "I've heard stories of hundred-fifty-pound catfish in this lake, and giant northerns--big enough to take off a man's leg in one bite."

"That's right, remember those divers hired by the state two years ago to clean the debris off the intake traps?" Mike asked, catching Nick's tone. "They came back up and refused to go down again. They said they'd seen a pike down there big enough to take a man apart like that." He smacked his hands together.

"Yeah, yeah, sure," Bruce said. "I've never heard of a northern bigger than thirty pounds."

"Those are the ones you can catch," Nick teased him. "You can't catch the really big ones."

"But they can catch you," Mike added.

"All right, enough of this bullshit," Bruce warned, half-seriously. He got up and began to gather his gear. "What are you guys trying to do, make sure I never dive again?"

"Course not," Nick said, "We still have twenty-five minutes on these
tanks."

"You're nuts," Bruce said, "if you think I'm going back in that lake today."

"Well, if you're not going, I guess there's not much point in the rest of us going without you," Nick said. He and Bill and Mike got up.

"Yeah, we'll have to quit, too," Bill said.

"You talked me into it," Mike said.

"I just want everyone to know," Bill announced as they lugged their equipment back up the hill to the cars, "the only reason I'm not going back in the water is because I'm starving and Nick brought a bag of chocolate donuts."

"Yeah, Bill," Bruce said, "and the six-foot fish had nothing to do with it."

"Where's the donuts?" Mike asked.

"Bill already ate half of 'em," Nick said. "Let's get dressed and go out for breakfast."

They stowed their equipment and drove back up the looping dirt trail, the Mustang in the lead, both cars making little dust clouds that lingered in the air a few moments and then settled to earth again.

* * * * * * *

The sun was three hours past the meridian when Bill and Bruce pulled their cars onto the dirt road that ran down from the new Missouri River highway bridge, turned under the old highway bridge, ran beneath the railroad bridge, and continued down the south bank of the river. They parked in a pulloff by the railroad bridge, and eight kids, four girls and four boys, dressed in swimming suits, spilled laughing from car doors and trudged up the short, steep hill to the bridge.

The new highway bridge, which rose on squat concrete columns only twenty feet above the water and which had no girders that rose above the road level, was a quarter mile downriver. The old highway bridge was the tallest of the three bridges, rising fifty feet above the water on its numerous thin green pillars. The high, steep angles of its girders, which rose another thirty or more feet, made it look as if it had been built with an Erector set. The land on either end of the railroad bridge was undeveloped, and tall stands of cottonwoods grew there, stands cut through with a few car trails. The trees were much thicker on the north side of the river, making it a preferred parking place at night for teenagers.

When they reached the first big concrete footing supporting the bridge, they hung their towels on the short bridge rail, took off their shoes, climbed over the rail, and jumped upstream. It was about twenty-five feet to the murky, green-brown river, which flowed swiftly past. The water was cold and they didn't have a chance to get used to it the short time they were in it. They let the current carry then to the steel ladder attached to the downstream end of the concrete footing. As they climbed from the water, the sun felt good on their tanned wet skin.

They walked to the upstream side of the footing and jumped or dived off again, and again. Sometimes they would climb up to the trestle level and jump, but Mike was the only one who would dive from the trestle. When they got shivery-cold, they would lie on their towels on the footing. There was a lot of horseplay, laughing, giggling, and kissing.

After a while they went climbing on the bridge's girders, which rose in three gently sloping staggers to long flat sections on top. The thick rusty-brown girders had rows of round-headed rivets running down both sides. It was easy to grab the warm girders with both hands and half-run up them. Coming down was easy, too. There was room in the space between the rows of rivets for people to squat on their tennis shoes and slide the length of the girders.

They were following each other around on the bridge when five guys they knew walked down the bridge to the first footing.

"Kathy, could I have a word with you?" Ron Kuntz asked in a way that was half command.

Ron was big as a grizzly bear, and about as handsome. He wore his blond hair in a crewcut. He was a tackle on the football team and had gone steady with Kathy Schoemer during the last school year and the first two months of the summer. Then she had dropped him for Mike Red Horse.

"I have nothing to talk to you about," Kathy said.

"Kathy, I said I'd like a word with you. Now are you going to come down or am I going to have to come up and get you?"

"I said I have nothing to talk to you about."

"Why don't you leave her alone, man?" Mike said. "She doesn't want to talk to you."

"Butt out, Red Horse. This concerns just Kathy and me."

"Nothing about me concerns you, Ron," Kathy said. "It's over between us."

"What if I don't want it to be over?"

"That doesn't matter. It's still over."

"Are you saying you prefer that prairie nigger to me?"

"Hey, what did you call him?" Bruce yelled out. "You watch your mouth, you sonofabitch. He's my brother."

"Let me handle it, Bruce," Mike said.

"I called him a prairie nigger. And if you're his brother, Baker, that makes you a prairie nigger, too."

"And what does that make me?" Kathy asked.

"I guess it makes you a red nigger's squaw."

"Kuntz, I want you apologize, to Kathy, to Bruce, and to me," Mike said, his words coming slow but sharp, like flint knifeblades.

"And what if I don't? You think you're man enough to come down and make me?"

"I'll help him," Bruce said.

"And so will I," Nick said.

"Me too," Bill said.

"Go ahead. We're ready. The five of us'll pound the shit out of you guys."

The other guys with Kuntz were football players, also. They were probably big enough to make good on Ron's boast.

"Nobody's coming down to fight you," Mike said. "We don't come down to fight ignorant bastards like you."

"Then we win. Send the squaw down and we'll be on our way."

"No, you come up."

"What?"

"I said, you come up."

"You want to fight me on the bridge? What are you, fucking crazy?"

"No, we're not going to fight. We're going to climb up to the very top, just you and I, and we're going to have a diving contest."

"Shit, Red Horse, you're even crazier than I thought you were. Nobody's ever dived off this bridge before."

It was true. No one had ever dived off the bridge. There was one story about a guy who had successfully jumped from the top of the bridge on a dare, but the story was so old it no longer had even a name attached to it.

"Then we'll be the first . . . if you're brave enough, that is."

"Mike, I don't think this is such a good idea," Bruce said, a worm of worry in his voice.

"Mike, don't do it," Kathy said.

"It's all right, I know what I'm doing."

"Somebody's going to get hurt," Bruce said.

"Better listen to your friends, buckskin," Ron said.

"Nobody's going to get hurt," Mike said. "I'm going to make a perfect dive off this bridge and Kuntz is going to chicken out. Then he's going to admit he's a coward and apologize to Kathy."

"Coward, my ass, prairie nigger. I'm coming up."

"I'll be waiting for you on top."

A minute and a half later Mike, Bruce, Nick, Bill, and Ron stood on a girder atop the bridge.

"Nick, would you watch upstream to make sure no logs or pieces of wood are coming?" Mike asked. "Tell me when it's clear."

Nick looked down at the green-brown water flowing fast and steady sixty or more feet below.

"It's all clear," he said a moment later.

That instant Mike leaped out from the bridge in a swan dive. He shot down like a fishing eagle and entered the water perfectly vertical. His friends held their breaths till he surfaced, fifteen yards downstream. They cheered and the girls below cheered. Mike swam toward the south bank, and Kathy ran down the bridge to meet him.

"OK, asshole, he did it," Bruce said. "Now let's see you do it."

Kuntz stood there, looking down at the swift, muddy water.

"It's all clear," Nick said.

Ron stood still as a bridge pillar.

"Come on, dive, Kuntz," Bruce said. "Or are you a fucking coward, like Mike said?"

"It's all clear," Nick said.

"Dive, Kuntz, or go back down and apologize."

Kuntz stood another half minute looking down, then said, "Only a crazy fucker would dive off this bridge."

He turned and began to climb back down.

"You won, Mike," Bruce shouted, waving at his brother, who had just crawled up onto some big rocks along the shore.

Mike waved back. Kathy ran down to meet him, threw her arms around him.

When everyone was re-assembled on the trestle, Ron looked at his feet and tersely apologized to Kathy, Bruce, and Mike. Then he and his friends left. They spun the tires on Kuntz's '58 Chevy and raced back down the dirt road, making a big dust cloud. When the dust had settled, they were gone.

* * * * * * *

At eleven that night, Nick sat on a blanket with his girlfriend Linda Prine and his sister Judith and her boyfriend Steve Van Arsdale, at the edge of nearly four dozen kids, who were either standing about or sitting on blankets. Bill Matthews and Nancy Sheridan, Bruce Baker and Karen Heffler, and Mike Red Horse and Kathy Schoemer were sitting near Nick and Judith.

The kids were having an end of the summer party on LeBeau Island, a mile-long, three hundred yard-wide strip of wooded land in the middle of the river, directly south of the town. Many had reached their location in the center of the far side of the island by boat; the Larkins' sixteen-foot boat and the Bakers' twenty-two foot cabin cruiser were parked next to half a dozen other boats. Jeff Richards, Darrell Sorenson, Dan Fuerst, and Randy Bouska had brought the beer kegs by boat. About half the kids, though, had parked their cars at the end of the causeway the town had built connecting it to the island, and walked to the party site. Ducts through the causeway allowed fresh river water to continue to fill the quarter mile gap between the town shore and the island, but prevented the bank's erosion by the swift current. The causeway had allowed for a swimming area with a sand beach to be built on the town side of the river, at the edge of a municipal park.

The revelers had lights, music (a Beach Boys album was playing on a battery-operated stereo), food, and three kegs of beer. Neither Nick nor Judith had touched beer since that summer night years before when they had become sick-drunk on beer and visions. They drank the Coke and Fresca they had brought with them in a cooler. They were almost the only ones not trying to get inebriated.

The boys relived for the twelfth time, at least, their encounter with the sturgeon and Mike's victory over Ron Kuntz, in his elegant swan dive from the top of the railroad bridge. Nick had been afraid

Kuntz would show up at the party and that they would have trouble again, but he hadn't. Only one of Kuntz's friends, Eric Borth, had shown up, and he had kept quiet about the incident. He'd nodded to Nick and the others when heÕd arrived but had kept his distance all night.

"California Girls" was playing when Nick went into the tall cottonwoods to relieve himself. He walked far enough away that the party lights could be seen in the distance but the music was muted. He looked up at the sky as he peed, expecting to see stars. It had been clear all day, but now the sky was black with low clouds. He was just about finished when he heard Judith call his name, right behind him. It was too late to turn invisible.

"Good God, Judith, I'm taking a piss," he complained, finishing in one long, forced burst. He zipped up.

"Done now?" she asked.

"Yeah, I'm done. What do you want?"

"Nick, I want to talk to you about Linda."

"I shoulda known. How many times do I have to tell you, Judith, I don't need any of your advice?"

"Yes you do."

"Look, Judith, you have your life and I have mine, as I've told you many times before. Do I ever give you advice about your boyfriends?"

"You don't have to."

"Oh, yeah, sure, like all your boyfriends have been real prizes."

"Steve's nice."

"Of course Steve's nice. He's one of *my* friends."

"Nick, you have nothing in common with Linda Prine but sex."

"Sex! Jesus, Judith, I haven't laid a hand on her. But what business would it would be of yours if I did?"

"Get off it, Nick, she was all over you tonight."

"She was not."

"She was practically lying on you the whole last hour."

"Judith, you're exaggerating."

"Oh, and I suppose it doesn't turn you on when she rubs herself all over you like a cat in heat."

"Is that what you're worried about, that I might like it?"

"No, I'm trying to stop you from making a stupid mistake."

"Judith, why don't you worry about your own mistakes."

"I'm not the one who's going to get some girl that I could care less about knocked up."

"Oh yeah? Well, I happen to like Linda."

"Sure, just like you liked Jill and Barb and Joan and Kim and all of your other girls-of-the-month."

"Listen, just because you stick your nails into some guy and hang on forever doesn't mean everybody has to."

"I don't 'stick my nails into' anybody. Maybe some of us are simply more capable than others of long-term relationships with the opposite sex."

"And maybe some of us don't really care what you're capable of."

"I think you do care."

"Think what you like."

"I will. And what I think is that you're afraid to stay with any girl longer than a month."

"Oh yeah, why?"

"Because you're afraid of the responsibility that comes with a real relationship."

"And why would I be afraid of that, dear sister? Come on, tell me."

"Because you're only comfortable keeping things on a simple physical level."

"And just what does that mean?"

"You know what I'm talking about."

"Why don't you spell it out for me, Judith."

"Nick, just keep your cock in your pants and --"

"What? Keep my what in my pants?"

"You heard me."

"I think I've heard more than enough. Nice talking to you, Sister." Nick pushed past her.

"Nick, I'm just trying to keep you from wrecking some girl's life," she called after him.

He ignored her and walked back to the party.

* * * * * * *

Steve and Linda and the others wondered at the odd new chill between the twins, but nobody said anything. Nick and Judith fought as much as any brother and sister, but their fighting never meant anything. They'd usually forgotten it by the following day.

In the next half hour, the heavy clouds, black as smoke billows from an oil fire, slipped lower and lower, as if sliding down a series of terraces in air. They grumbled and growled and lightning half-lit their glowering faces. Nobody seemed willing to move, though. Maybe there would be a lot of light and commotion and noise, but no rain. Maybe it would all blow by. A thick, dirty-white fog rolled in off the water, filled up the spaces between boats, trees, bushes, people. Jefferson Airplane's first album was playing on the stereo but the music seemed muffled.

As if some kind of consensus had been reached, all the people who had been sitting down stood up and began to mill about as if they were trying to decide what to do. A few began to pack up their things.

Then blinding flashes from all sides, bright as lightning strikes.

"All right, everybody stand right where you are!" a deep voice announced on a loudspeaker. "Don't move!"

"It's a bust!" someone yelled.

Shrieks, yells, people running in all directions through the fog and the brilliant light. One boy ran smack into a tree and knocked himself cold. Someone bumped into the stereo, sending the needle skid-scratching back and forth. It settled halfway into "White Rabbit." Two girls tripped on a blanket and fell over each other. Policemen grabbed at kids, forced them to the ground, face-down. Two policeman grabbed Eric Borth and handcuffed him to a tree.

When the flood lights had been snapped on, Judith and Nick had seen silhouetted for only a second in the flash a great beast whiter than the fog, more dazzling than the lights--as if its sun would put out their stars. Its hooves and incurved horns were black as anthracite. It was there, it was gone. The twins knew what to do.

They caught their friends before they could run, told them to stand still, join hands, and follow them. Kids ran by them, scared, shouting. Cops ran by. They could have easily seized them, but for some reason they ran after kids farther away.

"What's happening?" Bill asked, half whispering.

"They act like they don't see us," Steve said.

"It's like we're invisible or something," Linda said.

"Quiet!" Judith said emphatically.

Nick and Judith led their group through the noise and chaos, toward the boats. They were almost there when three cops came charging right at them, but veered off to chase other kids.

Nick and Bruce pushed their boats out into the water, climbed in, and started the engines. A cop shouted, "Hey, someone's getting away."

"Stop those boats now!" the loudspeaker barked. "You can't get away!"

"Oh, yes we can," Nick said under his breath.

Bruce and Nick slammed their boats into gear and hit the throttles. They disappeared into the fog. They took the boats five miles downstream, waited till nearly dawn, then drove back and hauled them out of the water.

Before they got into their separate cars to go home, Mike took Nick aside and asked, "What was that animal we saw in the trees when the cops turned on the lights?"

"What animal?"

"Come on, Nick, I know you saw it."

"I don't know, a deer maybe."

"It was too damn big to be a deer. It looked more like a buffalo or something."

"Maybe it was a cow."

"What would a cow be doing out on the Island?"

"Well, what would a buffalo be doing out there?"

"Nick, we were invisible, weren't we?"

"Sure, Mike, 'invisible'," he said, gently mocking.

"It's the only possible explanation."

"Just be happy we got away, Mike."

"And leave it at that?"

"And leave it at that." Nick clapped Mike on the back and they walked to the waiting cars.

Chapter 14
Annie Thurston

A year later, near midnight on a warm Friday in mid-September, Nick parked his and Judith's three-year-old Chevy II on the street in front of his friend Bill Matthews' house. Getting out, he heard a stereo playing loudly three houses down, the house with all the cars parked in the driveway and along the street. Somebody was having a party. He decided to have a look before knocking on Bill's door.

Nick stood under a red maple and watched people come in and out through the open front door. Nick liked the house, a big, two-and-a-half story, white-painted frame home, with a wrap-around front porch, full of drinking, talking, laughing, smoking people. The house reminded him of one his parents had rented when they'd first moved to LeBeau. Bridal veil bushes lined the front of the porch. Every light in the place was on, windows were open, and an old Beatles album was playing on the stereo. Nick was about to walk away when a dark-haired man in his late thirties came outside, a half-full drink sloshing in the plastic glass he held unsteadily. The man joked with some people sitting in the porch swing, then, noticing the boy, walked wobblingly down the steps.

"And who's this, come late to our party? That's right, you by the tree. Come out here so I can get a better look at you. Jesus, you're a good-lookin' kid.. I'll bet you've got the girls lined up just waiting for you? Am I right? Am I right?"

The man, whoever he was, had had a few too many shots of Old Granddad or vodka screwdrivers or gin and tonics or whatever it was he was drinking. But as drunks went, the man was genial enough, so Nick didn't wave him off and leave.

"Say, I got a wonnerful idea. I got a really wonnerful idea. Come in and dance with the other kids. They're your age. Come on. Nope, I won't take no for an answer. This is a night to celebrate."

The tipsy man opened the screen door and taking Nick's arm, guided him inside. The smell of cigarettes and beer and booze hit Nick like a slap. He saw twenty or thirty people standing around in groups talking, milling about, filling up paper plates with the food on the dining room table. Twelve couples, at least half of them Nick's age, were dancing. He recognized Brad Bailey, Mary Sample, Rich Stromm, and Linda Rasmussen from his school--which set alarms jangling in his head: These were friends of Ron Kuntz. Since the day over a year before when Mike Red Horse had swan-dived off the railroad bridge and humiliated Kuntz, there had been bad feelings between Mike and his friends and Kuntz and his.

The man called across the room, "Annie. Annie." He made a couple of big hook-swings with his right hand, motioning someone to come to him. Because of the crowd of dancers, Nick couldn't see whom he was signaling to.

A girl sighed, got up from a couch, and came toward them. Nick saw her and felt his heart being ravaged by a flaming, barb-headed arrow. It pierced him, was ripped out, was thrust into his chest again. Annie Thurston was tall, but what was arresting about her was her hair. She had thick, straight dark brown hair that had never been cut. It hung down shiningly to her knees, like a roquelaure, and while she could easily sit on it, she never did, as it tugged at her scalp and tended to catch her up short when she leaned forward. Nick had never seen anyone with hair like hers. It was as if Rapunzel had walked out of a book of fairy tales, a flesh-and-blood girl. Annie's hair pulled at him with a force like the gravity of Jupiter.

After her hair, Nick noticed Annie's eyes. They were almond-shaped and startling because she wore contacts that made them violet. She also wore blush and a light purple-violet lipstick on her small, thin-lipped mouth. Her face was moon-like and softly pale, its roundness emphasized by her slim brown eyebrows, her small chin, and her slim, graceful nose. Her ears each had a wrinkle in the lobe, as if a sliver had been cut away and the gap sewn back together.

"Annie, this is, uh, what'd you say your name was, son?"

Nick hadn't given him his name, but he said, "Nick."

"Nick, this is my daughter Annie. Nick and I've just been having a wonnerful conversation out on the porch, I mean a wonnerful conversation, and I said, 'Son, you shouldn't be talking to me. You should be inside dancing with kids your own age. And I've got the perfect dancing partner for you.' So, go on, Annie, take Nick out there and make him feel welcome. Go on now, before this song gets over."

Annie turned to Nick and, lookin straight into his eyes, asked, "Would you like to dance?"

Nick felt embarrassed. He could scarcely work his tongue to say, "Yes." Annie led him to a spot on the other side of the room from her father, and they began to dance, though Nick was having a difficult time catching his breath. The song ended, but instantly someone picked up the needle and set it down at the beginning of "I Want To Hold Your Hand," driven by handclaps and George Harrison's fifties-style rock guitar. Annie smiled at Nick and the flaming dart pierced his breast again. He thought he might black out, but he danced instead.

Annie danced freely, with a cervine sleekness, shimmying, twisting, moving from her ankles to her shoulders, tossing her head from side to side. Waterfalls of hair fountained down her body, streamed, rippled, flowed around her. Her hair caught the light in a thousand purls, riffs, swirls, cascades, rapids, and cataracts, and glistered as if a thousand tiny flints had been struck, no, as if a thousand stars had fallen into those wild waters.

Nick wanted to dive into those darkling currents, to be carried away in their surge and force. He wanted to struggle in their deluge and gush and undertow, to feel the spill wash him, tumbling, along, thrust him under, to flail vainly in the flood, and then to accept, submit to drowning, and find that in his submission he could breathe freely.

After that song someone picked up the needle again. In a few seconds "She Loves You" swept through the dancers like the storm of flaming cinders and sparks after a forest fire's explosion. Everyone danced harder, like people burning up, but painlessly so. Annie saw no one but Nick, tall, muscular, wide-browed, straight-nosed, full-lipped. His dark brown hair hung in gentle waves over his ears and down his neck. His eyes glinted like a raptor's.

Suddenly the wall of the house gave way, lay down flat as if it were on a hinge, and the boards of the hardwood floor they were dancing on slid sideways, extending themselves. They were dancing alone, in a space like the yard--a bur oak's thick branches hung over them--but not the yard. Family and friends had vanished. Only Nick and Annie and the music remained. When that song was over, another album was put on, but neither Nick nor Annie was aware any longer what songs were playing, only that their arms and hips and legs were impelled by percussive rhythm, urged by insistent melody, only that song succeeded song.

Then, in the pause between album changes, Nick and Annie heard someone ask with sudden anger, "What's *he* doing here?" The floor boards instantly retracted, the wall rose back into place, and they were once again in the smoky room, filled with the chatter of milling people.

Nick turned and saw Ron Kuntz standing by Rich Stromm and Brad Bailey, not ten feet away. Nick quickly asked Annie if she wanted something to drink. She said yes and they walked into the kitchen to get some lemonade.

"He came while you were out in the back yard," Brad said.

"He's got some fucking nerve," Ron said, "crashing our party."

"Annie's dad brought him in," Rich said.

"Yeah, he acted like they were old friends," Brad said. "Then he made her dance with Larkin."

"*Made* her dance?"

"Yeah, he called her over and asked her to dance with him," Brad said.

"OK, here's what we'll do. When they come back, I'll ask her to dance. Then you guys show him the way out. And make sure he knows not to come back."

The needle fell into the groove of Cream's "Spoonful." Kuntz exhibited surprise when Annie wouldn't dance with him.

"Whatsamatter, Annie, you too good to dance with your own cousin now?"

"No, I've been dancing a lot," Annie said precisely. "I prefer to sit this one out."

"What you mean is you won't dance with anybody but Larkin."

Annie smiled at Kuntz. "If you say so, Ron."

Kuntz walked away, muttering under his breath. He and his friends went outside.

"Ron Kuntz is your cousin?"

"Yeah, lucky me, huh? We moved here because my parents both have lots of family here. Ron's dad is my mom's brother. He called my dad last month and said there was a management opening at the Chevy dealership he owns. Dad jumped at the chance. That's my uncle Jerry over there."

She pointed out a big paunchy man on the other side of the room. "Most everybody here are my relatives."

Annie and Nick danced again, and again the wall gave way and the floorboards they stood on shot outside. They saw only each other, and they could not stop looking. Every time they paused to get something to eat or drink, the floor slid back and they re-entered the noisy, smoke-filled room. The party broke up about three in the morning and the floor slid in for good.

Annie wrote her number down on a slip of paper and walked Nick out onto the front porch. They wanted to kiss each other, badly-- but there were too many people around.

"Call me tomorrow, OK?" Annie asked, squeezing Nick's hand.

"Sure," he said, squeezing hers back.

Annie went inside and Nick strode down the walk and into the darkness under the red maple tree. He drifted upwards, a helium balloon in the shape of a boy, until his head nearly banged the branches arching over the sidewalk. Nick saw no sidewalk, saw no branches, indeed, saw no trees. He saw only Annie--Annie talking, Annie laughing, Annie dancing, her body swaying lithely, her long hair swinging wildly. He floated, a lost balloon, through the darkness.

Then Nick saw his car. He ran into the street to look at the other side. All four tires were flat. Nick looked for but saw no puncture sites. Kuntz and his friends hadn't slashed the tires, just let all the air out.

"That bastard, I'll kill him," Nick said to himself.

"I hope not."

Nick turned, saw one of the men from the party, walking home with his wife.

"What's wrong, son?"

"Somebody let the air out of all my tires."

"All of them? Really? You'll have to get a compressor from a service station tomorrow. Why don't we give you a lift home?"

"No, that's OK. It's late, I don't want to inconvenience you."

"No inconvenience. We'd be hap--"

"No, thanks anyway. My best friend lives in that house"--Nick pointed--"I can spend the night with him."

"You sure?"

"Yeah, no problem. Thanks again."

"OK, suit yourself."

The couple crossed the street and turned into a gate several houses up. Nick was surprised that they'd offered to take him home, but glad he'd refused. It *would* have been an inconvenience to take him most of the way across town. It was way too late to ring the bell at the Matthews house. He'd go round to Bill's room and knock on his window.

In the Matthews' back yard it was so dark Nick tripped over a croquet stake and fell face-first onto the grass. He lay still, afraid he'd made too much noise. But there was no noise from the house. He saw a light go on several houses down. The Thurston house? It must be. What other house would still have a light on at this hour?

Nick found his way to the alley without tripping again. Not asking himself why, he walked down the alley till he stood at the privacy fence behind the Thurston house. Their back porch light was on but he heard no sounds. He reached up, grasped the tops of the fence boards, chinned himself. The house was dark but Annie sat on a chaise lounge on the big back deck. No one else was there. Nick felt warmed, as if he'd just seen the sun rise. He dropped to the ground, found the gate to the privacy fence. He was in luck, it wasn't locked. He let himself in.

Annie sat with her arms encircling her knees, her hair, picking up gleams from the light, caped about her, obscuring all but her face. She said something but he couldn't catch it. He stole closer, but she saw movement in the yard and jumping up, said, "Who's there?"

"It's me--Nick," he said in a loud whisper, walking toward her straight across the back yard.

"Oh, Nick, I'm glad it's you," she whispered back. "You scared me."

"Sorry, I didn't mean to. I'll go if you want me to."

Nick had reached the bottom of the steps that led up to the redwood deck. He looked up at her face, which had risen moon-like over the deck rail.

"No, don't go. Wait a minute."

Annie walked back into the house. The porch light went out. Nick saw her dark shape appear above him, heard the soft sound of her bare feet on the steps. He started up.

"I'm so happy you came back, Nick. I was thinking about you, wondering if you'd call me, or if my family and I had scared you off for good."

"You don't think I'd scare that easily, do you?"

Nick took a last step and closed the gap between them. Annie took his hands in hers.

"No, I guess a boy who'd come to a party at a strange house and dance for hours with a girl he'd never met before wouldn't be the timid type."

Nick put his hands under her hair, rested them on her shoulders. "Would the timid type come back to see you like this?"

Annie put her hands up on his shoulders, pulled him into her embrace.

"I'm not the timid type, either." She kissed him.

After a long moment, their lips parted, still burning. "No, you're not."

"Too forward for you?"

In answer he kissed her hard and pulled her tight to him. Their lips were liquid fire, their tongues licking flames. The lilacs and apple trees in the yard suddenly broke into full and unseasonable blossom, densely perfuming the air. Tulips, iris, and sweet William bloomed again of an instant. Half-dead roses shot into full-petaled, velvet richness and added their odor to the night. Nick and Annie parted breathless, half-scorched.

"Guess not."

"No, you're exactly the girl I've always wanted."

Annie leaned back in his arms. "So you want me, do you? Are your intentions honorable or are you just trying to see what you can get," she teased.

"You decide," he said, preventing her response with his mouth.

Green life pulsed into sere, withered marigolds, pansies, peonies, and daisies, into columbine, lilies, cowslip, and lavender, into violet, buttercup, primroses, and Maltese cross. When they separated, her tongue had second-degree burns. She could scarcely talk.

"Definitely dishonorable," she said huskily.

"Then honor's just a word and love's a lie."

"So, you're saying you love me now."

"I'll say it all night if you want me to."

"There's not much night left."

"Then all day--as you'll stand here and listen."

"I'll stand and listen as long as you'll say it. But time's short and you can put those pouty lips of yours to better use."

"Pouty? I always thought of them as--"

Annie stopped his tongue with hers. Asters and hosta, delphinium and dianthus shot up in super-fast time-lapse photography: sprout to stem to bud to full-headed bloom. Hundreds of nightingales--yes, nightingales!--suddenly broke into song on all sides. Sweet-trilled melodies filled the lovers' ears. Flames raced through their tight-laced bodies as though fanned by hard wind gusts.

"Annie," a voice called through the screen door separating the kitchen from the deck.

"My mother," Annie whispered.

Nick sprang back as if he'd touched a live wire, flew down the stairs, darted under the deck.

"I'm here, Mom," Annie said.

Her mother switched on the porch light, stepped out on the deck

"Annie, what are you doing out here? Don't you know what time it is? You should be in bed."

"I know, Mom, but I wasn't tired when the party got over. I'm starting to feel sleepy. I'll come in soon, OK?"

"OK, but be sure you lock the door. Goodnight, sweetie."

"Goodnight, Mom. Oh, Mom, would you turn the light off. It hurts my eyes."

The deck dropped into blackness.

"She's gone," Annie called over the railing. "You can come up now."

Nick took the steps two at a time, trying to be quiet. They embraced again.

"Nick, I've got to go. Call me first thing tomorrow."

"You mean today?"

She smiled. "Guess I do."

Annie started towards the door, stopped in midstep, rushed back into Nick's arms. Nick wished he could hold her and never let her go. She pulled away.

"Bye, Nick."

"Bye."

She started to walk away.

"Annie."

She stopped. "Yes?"

"I meant it when I said I loved you."

"Oh, you . . ." She ran to him again, kissed him, arc-welding her lips to his.

"I love you, too, Nick," she said when their lips broke apart.

She slipped in through the screen door. Nick walked back through the yard, let himself out the gate. He spent the rest of the night at Bill's, and in the morning Bill took him to get a compressor.

* * * * * * *

Annie soon charmed all of Nick's friends. Judith also took to Annie right off. As editor of the school paper that year, Judith was able to give Annie, a year her junior, some plum assignments. Annie appreciated the faith Judith had in her abilities and performed exceptionally well. She also quickly became a star on the debate team and the chess club. Teachers smiled approvingly when they saw Annie and Nick walking down the halls, holding hands.

Annie's parents, Paul and Helen, found much to be happy with in Nick and nothing to blame. He was cheerful, courteous, smart, funny, handsome, and genuinely interested in other people. They couldn't believe their daughter had chosen a boyfriend who would actually take a few minutes to listen to what adults had to say. They frequently invited Nick to stay for dinner. They treated him like a member of the family.

Nick's parents, who hadn't been able to keep track of his other girlfriends since they changed so fast, were pleased to see a girl who was able to live in his affections for more than a month. They thought Annie was sweet, polite, intelligent, good-humored, and pretty. They were surprised that she didn't mind spending time with them. In fact, she seemed to enjoy it--a marked departure from Nick's past girlfriends. So, the two families accepted the sweethearts.

All but Ron Kuntz. Ron's impatience with his cousin, who could not be made to see the folly of her choice, turned into hot-browed anger. His dislike for Nick turned into black malice. Ron connived with Nick's old girlfriends to attempt to arouse Annie's jealousy. Those girls presented Annie with old notes Nick had written them, passing them off as recently penned. But Annie believed none of them. They spread rumors about Nick and other girls, but she laughed at them. Ron had other football players tell Nick they'd slept with Annie, but he refused to take them seriously. Nick was duly supplied with forged lovenotes, supposedly written by Annie to various boys, and even with one of Annie's monogrammed handkerchiefs (supposedly found in Bruce Baker's locker). But Nick scoffed at them all, especially the last. He laughed, said he'd read *Othello*, and walked away. They didn't get the reference.

When none of his machinations worked, Ron resorted to a more blunt approach. He and his friends began to bait Mike Red Horse again, leaving him anonymous notes--in his notebooks, in his gym bag, in his brother Bruce's car--featuring the words 'bucksin' and 'red nigger' and 'big buck' in a variety of threats. Then one Tuesday night, six of them, wearing ski masks, waited outside the school until Bruce and Mike's student government meeting was over, and attacked them, beating them viciously. Bruce had a broken nose and Mike had severely bruised ribs on both sides. Both had cuts, abrasions, and blackeyes. Bruce's parents sought recourse from the school and the police, but because the identities of the assailants couldn't be proven (though the boys were certain they knew who'd done it), the police took statements but said there was nothing further they could legally do.

Nick had kept an equable temper in the face of everything else Ron had done to separate him and Annie, but when his friends were beaten up, he became filled with wrath, as a sail is bellied out with wind. His choler rose and raged, a banked fire. Livid, he flamed and flared, spit sparks, blazed: Nicolo Furioso.

Nick challenged Ron the Friday after Mike and Bruce had been beaten up. Ron had no football practice because there was a home game that night. They met after school on the practice field, surrounded by dozens of their friends. Some of these, like Bill Matthews and Brad

Bailey tried to talk them out of fighting, but blood-eager with hate, they didn't listen.

They circled each other, two pumas searching for an advantage. Then Nick stepped in and smashed Ron in the mouth with his right fist and in the chest with his left. Ron socked Nick hard in the left side and uppercut him on the chin. Nick fell back a few steps. Ron charged forward but Nick kneed him in the stomach, stopping him dead. They circled, moving less cat-gracefully and more horse-tiredly. They bled from their cuts, breathed through their mouths. Ron swung and missed. Nick bashed him alongside the head. Ron fired back a blow to the right eye and two to the chest. Nick swung, missed. They circled.

Two months of annoyance and frustration and anger surged in Nick, drove him upwards, a young tree after a month of rain-heavy days. He leaped to eight, ten, twelve feet. His arms grew oak-knot-thick with muscle. His skin became oak-bark hard. Ron right-hooked him in the shoulder, then fast, left-smacked him in the gut. Pain shot through Ron's hands--as if he'd struck a tree trunk. Nick hit him, sock, sock, in the chest, he slugged him in the nose, he haymakered him on the chin. Ron flew back off his feet. He was dazed, woozy. He felt as if he'd run headfirst into a tree branch.

Their friends ran between them. Ron rolled to his side, pushed up onto hands and knees. Nick returned to normal size, breathed heavily. Both boys' faces ran with blood and sweat.

"He's had enough," Rich Stromm said.

"He's done, Nick," Bill Matthews said.

"All right," Nick said, "but if you lay a hand on one of my friends again, Kuntz, I'll give you worse than this."

Nick turned to leave, but walked right into Principal Henderson and Mr. Myers, the football coach--who'd heard of the fight and come running.

After hearing much prejudiced testimony from both sides and accusations and counter-accusations from the young pugilists themselves, the principal took them to his office and called their parents. When they arrived, Mr. Henderson informed them both boys had been equally in the wrong, and so they were both were suspended from school for three days.

"Now wait a minute," said Coach Myers. "You can't suspend Ron. We need him for tonight's game."

"I not only *can* suspend him, I *am* suspending him. You'll have to pull somebody off the bench to replace him."

"But he's our star halfback."

"Well, as of now, he's your suspended halfback. Both boys are suspended from school for three days. And if either of them gets into a fight on school property again, he'll be expelled."

After three days, Nick and Ron returned to school. Each acted as if the other had ceased to exist. Ron also snubbed Annie. Nick regretted having given in to his anger. He apologized to Annie, to his parents, and to the Thurstons. He privately vowed that he'd never strike another person.

* * * * * * *

The first weekend in November, Annie's father went out of town on a business trip and her mother went with him. Nick told his parents he was spending Friday night with Bill. Annie and Nick made love for the first time on Annie's twin bed. Her bedsprings creaked and squealed and whined and keened for hours with the passion they had somehow kept subdued all fall. They went to sleep with "I love you" on their lips, Annie with her back flush against Nick, his arm around her, his hand cupping one of her breasts. Nick spent Saturday night with Bill, too.

A week later the lovers had a scare. They were in Annie's second-floor bedroom. Nick had taken off Annie's bra and begun to caress her breasts and
Annie had unzipped Nick and rubbed him into tumescence when they heard a car door slam outside.

"Oh, no, it's my mother!"

"Quick, get dressed!"

They threw themselves together and ran down the stairs and into the kitchen. They had scarcely made it to the table, where their schoolbooks lay in two piles, when Helen Thurston walked in the front door. She heard them giggling and made straight for the kitchen. Nick, still erect, was glad a maple table lay between Mrs. Thurston's gaze and his crotch.

286

Judith did catch them once, in Nick's bed. Not thinking he was home, she'd entered without knocking, looking for the Joan Baez record she'd loaned him.

"Oh, I'm so sorry."

Flushing with embarrassment, Judith put her hand over her mouth, lowered her eyes, backed out of the room, and pulled the door closed. Later, though, when Nick was reading before bed, she came into his room to talk to him.

"Nick, do you know what you're doing?"

"Yeah, I think I do, Judith."

"You're making a big mistake."

"Well, thanks for that unsolicited opinion, Judith, but I've--"

"Stop it, Nick. Respect me enough to hear me out."

"OK, Judith, say whatever it is you came in here to say."

"Nick, you're my brother, and I wouldn't say anything at all if I wasn't worried about you. I think it's wrong for two kids who are still in high school to jump into bed together."

"We didn't jump anywhere."

"You said I could speak my mind."

"All right," he sighed, "go on."

"I think it's wrong because I feel love should come first, before sex. Then sex can deepen two people's tenderness, deepen their love."

"So there's no problem. We're in love."

"Nick, how can you say that? You've only known her a few months."

"I love her, Judith, and she loves me."

"How do you know it's not just another of your infatuations?"

"It doesn't feel like that?"

"How do you know it isn't just lust?"

"So, you're trying to convince me by insulting me."

"No, Nick--oh, you're not listening to me."

"Sure, I'm listening, but do you hear what you're saying? It's damn insulting."

"I'm sorry, OK? Just tell me that you're doing something to protect Annie."

"You mean from getting pregnant?"

"Of course that's what I mean."

"As if that's any of your business, Judith. But if you must know, we're using protection. Now, are you quite through?"

"I've said what I wanted to say."

Judith left his room.

* * * * * * *

A few days later Helen Thurston was cutting salad vegetables on a pullout cutting board in her kitchen. Its wooden surface was scarred by innumerable knife slices, and where vegetable juices had seeped into the scars, it was permanently stained.

Annie sallied into the kitchen for a glass of chocolate milk.

"What's for supper, Mom?"

"Pork chops."

Annie wrinkled her nose.

"I know you don't like them, Annie, but your father loves them. He grew up eating them once a week. If I don't make them once in a while, he starts to pout."

"I don't mind. What else are we having?"

"Peas, mashed potatoes, and"--she gestured with her knife--"tossed salad."

"Anything good for dessert?"

"Cherry pie."

Annie looked. "Good. Supper sounds wonderful, Mom."

"It's just an ordinary meal, Annie. No need to sound so cheery about it."

"What's wrong with being happy?"

"Nothing, but I'll bet it's Nick who's put that smile on your face and not my dinner."

Annie blushed slightly. "Mom, really."

"You've been going out with Nick, well, practically since we moved here. He comes over every day and--"

"I thought you liked Nick, Mom."

"I do like him, Annie. All I'm trying to say is that a person can't help but notice how close you two have gotten, that's all."

"I don't understand. You don't think Nick and I should be close?"

"I'm just saying you might want to slow things down a bit. You don't want to do anything foolish."

"You mean like get pregnant? Are you trying to tell me to take precautions?"

Elaine colored. "Oh, Annie, has it gotten to that point?" Annie stood mute, neither acknowledging nor denying. "Well, I don't really know. We, uh, didn't really have this problem as much when I was a girl."

"Mom, please. This is too much. Look, you don't have to worry. Nick uses protection."

"Are you sure that's the best thing?"

"You'd rather he didn't?"

"No, of course not. It's just, well, I read in a magazine that those, uh, are not always effective."

"Rubbers, Mom, they're called rubbers."

"Annie, I don't care what they're called. The question is, do they work?"

"Are you suggesting I take the pill?"

"No--yes--I don't know. Wouldn't that be better?"

"Sure it'd be better. But the drugstore won't just give them to me because I ask, Mom. You'll have to give your permission to Dr. Anderson before he'll prescribe them."

"Uh, well, all right. I mean, I guess if that's what's required, then I'll call him tomorrow for an appointment."

Annie suddenly hugged her mother tight. "Mom, I never thought-"

"What?"

"That you'd be so understanding."

"Would you set the table, dear? Everything's ready now."

* * * * * * *

That Christmas Eve, Annie and Nick gave each other matching black-and-white-striped sweaters. He gave her a carved wooden chess set and she gave him two Creedence albums and a bottle of Brut. The day after Christmas, they drove out to the Black Hills with Nick's parents, to go skiing. Lena and Roger Larkin couldn't believe the change in their son. An often self-centered and sometimes irresponsible boy had become all sweetness and consideration, not only to Annie, but also to them and--this was most surprising--to Judith.

Observing Nick and Annie as (trying to execute the skiing tips he had just given her), she fell, knocking them both over, laughing--Judith said to Lena, "I guess there's no denying she's been good for him."

"You'll get no argument from me. He even helps around the house now without being asked. That's what I call a major improvement."

"At first I just thought Nick was infatuated with her."

"And now?"

"I really think they're in love."

"I'm afraid I do too."

"Why 'afraid'?"

"No mother's ready for her son to fall in love when he's still a senior in high school?"

"Mom, Nick and I just turned eighteen."

"I know, and in my opinion that's too young to fall in love."

"But, Mom, all over this country eighteen-year-olds are being sent to
fight in Vietnam."

"I know, I know."

"And how old were you when you had us?"

"Eighteen. OK, you're right. It's just hard for your father and I to get used to the idea."

"I thought Dad approved. He's always talking with them and joking around with Annie."

"Oh, he approves. He likes Annie a lot. But they aren't even in college yet."

"Mom, you talk like they're going to get married before they're even out of high school."

"Don't think your father and I haven't talked about that possibility."

"You don't really think? Mom, what would you and Dad say if they asked?"

"I don't know what we'd say. We'd try to talk them out of it, of course, but if their minds were made up, what could we do? We wouldn't want them to elope."

"Well, I think they're just having a good time together. I don't think marriage has even crossed their minds."

"You're probably right."

* * * * * * *

But Judith wasn't right. Marriage had definitely crossed Annie's mind. She had broached the subject with Nick many times in the past month, always as if her interest were purely hypothetical. Their last night in the Hills, standing alone on top of the mountain in the frosty air, watching clouds slip across the face of the half-moon, as silently as Annie's nightgown slipping from her shoulders (at least that was how Nick saw it)--that last night Annie spoke more directly about marriage.

"Nick, do you love me?"

"What kind of question is that? You know I do. Don't I tell you I do every day."

"I know, but I mean do you *really* love me?"

Nick looked her in the eyes, said solemnly, "Annie, I love you as deeply as it's possible for one person to love another. Do you love me?"

"Nick, you know I do. So why don't we think about getting married?"

"What? Married? Are you serious?"

"Don't I sound serious?"

"Annie, we're not even out of high school yet."

"So what? We're in love. Really in love. And when two people are really in love, they get married."

"Why do you want to rush things? I'm happy the way things are going now. Aren't you?"

"Of course I'm happy. I've never been happier. But that's my point. When people feel this happy together, the next logical step is marriage."

"But that isn't something you should just leap into, Annie?"

"Nick, love is a living thing. If it doesn't keep growing, it wastes away and dies."

"Our love isn't wasting away, Annie."

"Maybe not now, but it will if we don't do something to keep it growing."

"How can you say that?"

"It's like this. Love begins in a single room, but it soon grows and becomes too big for that room. So the lovers open the door into the next room, to give it space to grow. But if it's real love, it quickly becomes too large for that room, too, and then for the next--and then for the whole house. If the lovers don't open the door to the outside, their love will be stifled--like a root-bound plant. The door to the outside, Nick, is marriage."

Nick had no idea what to say. "I don't know what to say, Annie, except I don't feel stifled. Do you?"

"I don't know, yes, sometimes I think I do." She clutched him. "Nick, what's going to happen to us?"

"Nothing, Annie. We'll be fine."

"How do you know you won't feel differently next week or next month? How do you know what we have won't start to die?"

"That won't happen, Annie. Trust me, we won't let it happen."

Nick kissed her, as if that could convince her where his words had failed. She returned his kiss.

"Nick, promise me one thing."

"Anything, but first kiss me again."

She did.

"Promise me that you'll think about what I said."

"Sure, I'll think about it."

"You'll think seriously about it?"

Nick smiled at her. "Yes, I'll think seriously about it. Now let's start down the mountain."

* * * * * * *

Two weeks later Annie asked Nick if he'd given any more thought to marriage. She received much the same response she had that night at the ski resort. Two weeks after that she asked him again.

Then, the night of Valentine's Day Roger and Lena went to a party and Judith went out to a movie. So Annie and Nick had the

Larkin house to themselves. They exchanged gifts and made love twice in Nick's bed.

Lying next to him afterwards, Annie asked, "Nick, will you marry me?"

"Sure, we'll get married someday."

"That's not what I mean."

He looked at her, confused.

"Nick, you don't understand. I'm proposing to you. You have to give me an answer."

"What? Proposing? But, Annie, we've talked about this dozens of times before."

"I know, and I'm tired of talking. I need to know, Nick. Will you marry me or not?"

"Annie, please, I love you. You know I love you. Isn't that enough?"

"Not any more. I want to know, Nick. Will you marry me or not?"

"Annie, please, it's Valentine's Day. Let's not fight."

"This isn't a fight, Nick, it's a proposal. So, please, give me your answer."

A look of sudden pain, as if he'd been slashed with a straight razor, came into Nick's eyes. "I can't give you an answer. I'd like to say yes, I really would. But I'm just not ready yet."

"I'll take that as a no, then."

Annie flung herself out of bed and began dressing, rapidly. Nick sat up.

"Annie, this isn't fair. I didn't say no. I just said I need more time, *we* need more time."

"I don't."

"Annie, is it such a crime to want to wait?"

"No, it's not a crime. It's the usual thing. But I expected more from you, Nick, than the usual thing. I thought we had something special."

"We do have something special."

Nick got out of bed, began to walk toward her.

"Correction, Nick, we did have."

Annie grabbed her coat and hat and turned to leave. Nick jumped to stop her but she left fast, pulling the door shut behind her. He opened the door and ran naked down the stairs after her, but she was already out the front door. He grabbed a raincoat from the entryway closet, but he got out onto the porch only to see her screech away in the new Camaro her parents had given her for Christmas.

* * * * * * *

Nick called Annie. She wouldn't talk to him. He went over to her house. She refused to see him. The next day, she made an appointment at the beauty shop her mother went to and had all of her beautiful long hair chopped off. Her hair ended now in a little flip just above her shoulders. Her new bangs accentuated the roundness of her face. She looked just as pretty as before but radically different. In school on Monday Nick couldn't have been more shocked if he'd stepped into a bear trap.

"Jesus, Annie, what have you done?"

Ignoring him, she hurried away. She snubbed him resolutely all day, all week.

* * * * * * *

The next weekend after Valentine's Day, Annie went out with Brad Bailey. They doubledated with Ron Kuntz and Karen Simmons. Ron had a fake ID and he bought them two six-packs of Michelob and a fifth of Everclear. Ron, Karen, and Brad drank the beer, but Annie took long pulls from the Everclear bottle. It tasted to her a little like rubbing alcohol at first, but that sensation soon went away. Annie took slug after slug. Inside an hour, she'd drunk more than half the bottle.

"Shtop the car--ohhh ohhh--I'm going--ohhh ohhhhh--to be shick."

Ron hit the brakes. Brad opened the back door on his side, hopped out, and was going to help Annie out--when she fell out into the snow. She crawled a couple of feet and threw up. She heaved and heaved, stopped. Brad helped her up. She walked a few steps with his help, then threw up again. She fell to her knees and heaved, hacked for a long time in the hard, body-racking seizures of dry heaves.

"Ohhhhh," she moaned. "Ize shick, 'elp me, shumbuddy 'elp me."

Brad tried to help her stand up, but she was dead weight.

"Ron, give me a hand. She can't stand up."

"What's the matter with her?"

Ron hooked her under one armpit and Brad under the other. They pulled her up.

"She's really sick. She drank most of that bottle of Everclear by herself."

"You gotta be kidding me. How could she?"

"I don't know. Let's see if we can get her to walk. Maybe she can walk it off."

Annie's feet were syrup. She could stand if someone held her but she couldn't walk a step without collapsing. Her head flopped down like a cabbage. She was out. In a few seconds she lifted her head, then passed out again.

"Ron, she keeps passing out. We gotta get her to a hospital."

"No fuckin' way. We might as well just hand ourselves over to the police. Let's take her home and put her to bed. You know, let her sleep it off."

"Ohhhhh--ohhhhhhh."

"No, Ron, we're gonna take her to the hospital. If we don't, she might die."

"OK, OK, settle down, let's get her in the car."

Ron drove fifty-five miles an hour in thirty-five zones, ran red lights. Brad held Annie in his arms in the backseat. He kept saying, "Stay awake, Annie. Come on, you've got to stay awake. Come on Annie, talk to me. Talk to me." They reached the hospital emergency entrance in less than ten minutes. They carried Annie in, and two paramedics ran to take her. They put her in a wheelchair, and with one of them holding her in and the other pushing, they rushed her away.

After a few questions, the doctor on duty began to give orders. He told Ron, Brad, and Karen to go back out to the waiting room and call Annie's parents. Helen and Paul got there while the doctor was still pumping Annie's stomach, and a nurse asked them to wait outside the room until they were done.

Two hours later, Annie became aware enough of herself and of her surroundings to talk coherently (she had passed the stage where she would shake her head sharply, as if that could clear it, and bug her eyes trying to focus them). Dr. Anderson said, "Young lady, that was a close call. If your friends hadn't brought you right in, well, I'm afraid you'd have been in a great deal of danger."

Paul and Helen Thurston stood on either side of Annie, each holding one of her hands.

"Annie," her father said, a hairline fracture of fear in his voice, "Ron said you were the only one who drank the Everclear and that you drank a lot of it fast. Were you trying to hurt yourself, honey?"

"No, Dad, I wasn't."

"Then why?" her mother asked.

"I was just so sad about breaking up with Nick and I was so mad at him. I couldn't think about anything else. I thought if I drank enough, I could make that feeling go away."

"Oh, baby, you scared us so badly," her mother said, beginning to cry.

"We were afraid for a while there that we might lose you, Annie," her father said, his voice catching.

"I'm sorry, I'm so sorry, I wasn't thinking."

"As soon as I get home, I'm going to call up Nick and give that little bastard a piece of my mind, and then I'm going to talk to his parents."

"No, Dad, no," Annie said as firmly as she could, tightening her grip on his hand. "It's not Nick's fault. I'm the one who broke up with him and I'm the one who drank the Everclear. Please, leave Nick out of this."

"OK, if you insist. But that goddamned cousin of yours is another story. He bought the stuff you drank and he and Jerry are going to hear about it."

* * * * * * *

Paul Thurston proved true to his word. The next morning he lost his temper with Ron and Jerry Kuntz and ended up losing his job as well. Annie did not return to school, but by the end of second period

Monday morning the whole school knew the story of how Annie had almost died of alcohol poisoning.

Nick left school as soon as he heard the news. He walked straight out the front door and ran down to his car.

Paul Thurston came to his front door, but as soon as he saw who it was, he said, "Don't you think you've done enough to this family?"

"Please, Mr. Thurston, I know how you must feel."

"No, you can't begin to know how I feel, you little sonofabitch. I almost lost my daughter."

"I just want to see her for a minute, Mr. Thurston. Please."

"Get the hell off my property. Get off now before I call the police."

Paul Thurston slammed the door in Nick's face. Nick remembered Valentine's night, when Annie had stormed out. He'd jumped, but she'd already shut the door. He felt the same helplessness he'd felt then. The February air, which had been warming for the last forty-eight hours, froze instantly around Nick. He was so cold his clothes cracked as he walked. His pants chafed him so badly it was torture to walk the thirty feet to his car.

Nick couldn't get warm all day, even when he turned the thermostat up to eighty and piled four blankets on his bed. He felt weak, he thought he could hear his blood running in slush through his veins. He had a headache as if he'd eaten ice cream too fast. Every half hour he struggled out of bed and through the keening Arctic winds of the house, downstairs to the phone. Fearing his fingers would snap off, he dialed the numbers. The dial spun sluggishly, but at last the phone was ringing on the other end.

The first time Helen answered. When she found out who it was, she said, "Nick, you can't talk to her. Please, do us all a favor and forget you ever knew her." She hung up.

The second time he called, Paul answered, cursed, and slammed the phone down hard. After that their phone was permanently busy; they must have taken it off the hook.

Nick tried everything he could think of but was unable to see Annie. He even stole into the Thurstons' back yard one night and climbed up to Annie's window. The shade was drawn, the window locked. Annie didn't respond to his knocks, if she was even in the room. Nick felt as if the Thurstons had shoved a long thick icicle--a stone-hard lance of ice--through his breast. The rest of his body returned to a slightly chilled normal, but nothing could warm the frozen ventricles of his heart.

A week later the Thurstons moved. One day they were there, the next they were not. Rumor had it that they'd gone back to Arizona. A sympathetic friend of the Thurstons, feeling the lethal cold emanating from Nick's chest, finally took pity on Nick and gave him the Thurstons' forwarding address.

Nick wrote Annie a letter every day until the end of the school year (when he graduated). He wrote at least twice a week up through July, and once a week for some time thereafter. He received no answers to any of his letters, but slowly his breast began to thaw. The more he wrote the more the cold leaked away from him and gathered elsewhere. By August he was confident that his heart was indeed pumping blood again, if sluggishly and many degrees cooler than normal.

But the blue mailbox he dropped his letters into had become so oppressed with cold, its slot had frozen shut, and he had to wear leather gloves just to touch it. By the time he and Judith left for college in September, it required all his strength to force the depository open. At the university, there were complaints that his dormitory's mail drop slot was always iced shut. Nobody could figure it out. The blue mailbox a block away was iced over, too. The postal workers chipped the ice away all fall, so they were shocked to find that, in the middle of the winter, when the temperature had dropped into the teens, the ice covering the slots had suddenly melted--never to return.

Only Nick knew that he had received a postcard. "Dear Nick, I read all of your letters but felt it better if I didn't write back. I'm only writing now to ask you not to write me any more. It's hard to intercept the letters before my parents see them. I've had a boyfriend since the homecoming dance this fall, and we're very happy. We'll graduate in May and we're going to be married in June. With affection always, Annie."

Part VII

October 1970 - May 1971

Chapter 15
Europe Is the Less

On Saturday, October 16--he would ever after remember the date--Nick sat in an out-of-the-way carrel on the third floor of the University Library, working on the opening chapter of the novel Kate Winfield had persuaded him to write. He'd had breakfast and two cups of coffee at the Union, then walked over to the Library. It was about ten. He had ideas he'd been spading over in his head the past week, and he was anxious to get started. He had a short piece of description that had flowed spontaneously from its first image. He read through it again, to see if it satisfied the criteria he'd decided, for him, was the single most important. He'd found it in Keats' letter to Shelley of August 16, 1820--" . . .be more an artist, and 'load every rift' of your subject with ore"--and copied out on a three-by-five card, to set in front of him whenever he wrote. He read over what he'd written the way he read his poetry--aloud. Which was one reason he'd chosen that solitary carrel. He read, softly but with feeling:

"The wind had snow in its throat and ice in its heart. It flew straight out of the Canadian Arctic and flung itself, bluff and blustery, against the house, was rebuffed, and screamed past the windows, a wounded cougar. It wailed, hissed, swirled away, subsiding to as dead, sub-zero stillness. There was no moon, no stars, There was only the cold black funeral of the February sky."

He read the next paragraph, describing the power and sound of the wind. And then he connected the description to his young protagonists.

"Like that wind, death came, startling and strange, into Johnny and Billy's life that winter of Johnny's seventh year. It was like profoundly original music heard for the first time."

Nick felt it was a decent enough start. It created the atmosphere he wanted. He imagined Billy as a year or two younger than Johnny. He smiled to think what Judith would say when she found out she'd been demoted to the role of younger sibling. It'd serve her right for boasting all these years that she'd been born first. And a boy sibling to boot. But it held true to something they both believed--that the significant thing was not the autobiographical foundation of art, but the way the imagination extrapolated creatively from the autobiographical. Art was not history, despite the attempts of eighteenth century novelists to make their fictions palatable to their new middle-class audience by passing them off as historical narratives.

"Here you are."

"Wha--" he said, looking up to see Judith quickly closing the gap between them. Her face looked pale and somber. Her eyes were red, as if she'd been crying.

"Nick, I've been looking all over for you. Mike told me you might be here."

"Judith, what's wrong?"

"You haven't heard?"

"No."

"Jon Arbalest's dead."

"What!"

"He and all the members of the People's Revolutionary Committee who lived in that farmhouse southeast of town."

Nick dropped his black flair-tip marker. "What happened?"

"They were making bombs and something went wrong and they blew themselves up."

"When?"

"Yesterday, about noon."

"The news mentioned Jon by name?"

"Yes, him and Kathleen Doyle, Mike Jensen, Sam Waters, Lance Hendricks, and Rodney Chase. They said there were maybe five other bodies they hadn't identified yet."

"'*Maybe* five others'?"

"You can imagine how it was. The farmhouse was reduced to splinters."

Nick wiped tears from his eyes. "Remember the day we went to Sioux City, how I said I thought Jon had gone over the edge?"

"Looks like they all did."

"Jon thought I was naive because I didn't believe in violent confrontation."

Judith nodded, impatiently wiped away a tear of her own. "Well, I guess he showed us what not being so naive leads to."

Nick ran his hands through his hair.

"I couldn't tell whether Jon was all talk and bluster or whether he really wanted to blow up some symbol of the establishment."

"Now we know."

"I could vaguely half-imagine Jon and Kathleen Doyle attempting to bomb the ROTC headquarters or something. But I really thought Jon was just sounding off, you know, the way he usually does."

"Did," Judith said softly.

"Yes, did." A tear streaked down Nick's left cheek. "I didn't imagine this. I never imagined this."

"No one did."

Nick took out his handkerchief, dabbed at his eyes. "But don't you see, Judith, I should have done something anyway. Just in case he *was* crazy enough to do something stupid like this."

"Nick, that's ridiculous. You can't possibly blame yourself."

"But, Judith, I was one of the only people outside the People's Revolutionary Committee that Jon talked to. Maybe the only one."

"Nick, you know as well as I do that Jon was always railing about this or that. And if he hadn't moved into that farmhouse, he'd probably never have done anything but talk."

"But I should have known his joining the PRC meant trouble."

"That's absurd, Nick. How could you be expected to have known? Nobody thought the PRC would ever do anything but talk, either. Remember how you told me once you thought they were nothing more than a group of revolutionary dilettantes?"

"That's true, but I should have done something just in case."

"What could you have done, Nick?"

"I could have talked to Jon."

"And do you think, after your last little chat together, he would have listened? You said yourself he was completely irrational."

"But I could have tried anyway. If that didn't work, I could have gone to the police."

"The police! Nick, the police would have thought *you* were the crazy one. Have you forgotten they arrested you just last summer on a dope charge?"

"I could have made them listen."

"I don't think so, Nick. Nothing Jon said to you was incriminating. It was just a lot of apocalyptic political wind."

"Judith. I feel so bad." Tears ran freely down Nick's cheeks.

Judith, weeping herself, took him in her arms and held him tight.

"I do too, Nick, I do too." She patted his back. "You can't blame yourself for the way things turned out. There's nothing you could have done. You've got to believe that."

"I know, Judith, but--"

"Nick, the Jon Arbalests and the Kathleen Doyles of the world are always going to do what they're going to do. They and they alone are responsible for their acts. Not you or I or anyone else. It's on their consciences only."

"It still hurts, Judith. It hurts so bad."

"I know, Nick." She hugged him tighter.

* * * * * * *

The next Thursday a memorial observance was held in the University's Chamberlain Auditorium for the eleven students--seven men and four women--who had perished in the explosion. The local and national media--reporters for at least a hundred big-city and regional papers, writers for fifty or more magazines, and correspondents for the three national networks and ten or twelve television stations from the immediate four-state area, had arrived on Saturday, giving the local economy--motels, restaurants, bars, and liquor stores an unprecedented boost.

The explosion of the People's Revolutionary Committee farmhouse was the biggest single instance of violent death in the war protest movement. The fact that it had occurred in a small town in the geographic heart of America made it seem somehow all the more tragically significant. Members of the press had fanned out over the campus, trying real hard not to bump into each other, and begun to interview students, faculty members, administrators, clerical staff, library, cafeteria, and snackbar workers, and almost anyone else they could snare.

Judith, Elizabeth, Wolfram, Val Burroughs, Mike Red Horse, and Bruce Baker were all interviewed more than once. Nick laid low. He knew that once the press learned from the Red Earth police that he had been arrested with Jon Arbalest the previous summer, they would try to make something of it, and he would be plagued with obnoxious, reporters who cared everything about their story, but nothing about him. By dinner time Saturday, the press was prowling every floor of Nick's dorm--some with bigger budgets had even paid students who knew Nick to scout around for him–so it was impossible for him to return to his room. He called Elizabeth from a phone booth in a gas station downtown, and she told him to stay there, she'd pick him up. He could stay in her parents' guest room until all this had blown over.

The president of the University, Dr. Hugh Miller, had said that this tragedy had been, "the work of a tiny group of radical extremists, who--let everyone be very clear about this--in no way represented the students of his campus, who were as bright, dedicated, ambitious, wholesome, and law-abiding a group as he'd ever been proud to know." Then why was it, a reporter for *The Des Moines Register* had asked, that they had stormed and occupied the ROTC headquarters in the wake of the Kent State slayings the previous May. Miller had fulminated that that meant nothing, that such occupations had occurred on hundreds of campuses nationwide, that it was a short-lived response to an almost unbearable tension in the country at the time, and that that particular incident was now history.

Is that right, a reporter for *The New York Times* had asked? Then why was it that scarcely more than a month into the fall semester eleven students had died trying to make bombs that were undoubtedly going to be used to advance a war protest agenda? Miller had tried to fall back on his earlier statement that the People's Revolutionary Committee was a small group of extremists, who were in no way indicative of the students of this University, but by then he had lost his credibility with the press--and after they had filed their reports, with the public at large. The members of the Board of Regents would unanimously vote at their meeting the first week of November to ask for Miller's resignation.

Bob Barnes, a senior business administration major, a member of Sigma Nu Fraternity, and the president of the student body, said he'd had a great time at the University all three years he'd been there and that he thought agitators like the People's Revolutionary Committee were part of an almost invisible radical fringe on campus and that most students shared his lack of concern about the war. Asked what they were concerned with, he smiled and said that, other than having a good time, most were concerned with getting a good job after college and settling down and starting a family. Barnes thought that Kent State rally, at which half the campus had shown up, had not really been about politics at all, but about getting out of class and having fun on a warm spring day. He didn't think there were more than a small handful of students--and Jon Arbalest and Kathleen Doyle had been prominent among them--who had gotten all bent out of shape about the deaths of the four Kent State students. Halfway through Barnes' comments, the reporters had begun to give each other knowing looks and begun to think about other prospective interviewees.

The people of Red Earth were asked what they thought of the incident, and opinions ranged widely. Rich Langford, the manager of the town's biggest grocery store said he'd been serving the students of the University for twenty-five years and that he thought the University's students were a great bunch of kids--well-mannered and full of hope and idealism. A pharmacist in the Rexall Drug downtown thought that the political disease that had infected universities across the country had finally been caught here, and that he was afraid some other student lunatics might try to blow up buildings on campus. A clerk in a hardware store on Main Street seconded that opinion and thought the governor ought to call out the National Guard before worse violence broke out.

The governor, Burt (Buddy) Murfin, said a day later that all the intelligence accumulated thusfar indicated that this was an isolated, freak incident, highly unlikely to be repeated, and that he had no intention of mobilizing the National Guard. His speech didn't play well across the state, and many would later say his decision not to call out the Guard was the major reason he lost his bid for re-election a few weeks later, in November.

A Red Earth Presbyterian minister thought the incident was evidence of the loss of spirituality in America. He said that if those kids' parents had made sure they went to church every week, they would never have considered making bombs a meaningful way to indicate disapproval of their country's war policy in Indochina.

The head pastor of the United Campus Ministry, Reverend Darryl Spenser, disagreed, saying he'd never known a generation as spiritually minded as the present one, that he'd personally counseled hundreds of students, and that all of them were intently seeking to live more creatively spiritual lives. They were, in their own ways, ardently searching for spiritual truth and peace. In fact, he believed that, led by its young people, America was in the midst of a profound spiritual revolution that might, by calling into question all the shibboleths and false idols and hypocrisies of their parents' generation, redirect this country back to the spiritual ideals upon which it had been founded. Reporters sighed loudly from boredom.

The principal of Red Earth High School said that he wouldn't be surprised to learn that the students who'd destroyed themselves were activists from out of state, maybe from California or New York. He could say without a moment's hesitation that the kids in his school were as patriotic a group of American youth as could be found anywhere, and that they found the actions of that radical-liberal campus group absolutely repellent. In fairly short order, however, it was learned that the dead students, to a person, had been state residents.

Reporters then scavenged after the families of the deceased, mothers, fathers, brothers, and sisters. Dan and Sally Jensen, a dentist and legal secretary from Aberdeen, said their son Mike (twenty), a political science major, had long been committed to peaceful protest against the war, and that they were certain he had been guilty of nothing more than being at the wrong place at the wrong time, that he had probably only dropped in to visit a friend, and that he had been an innocent victim in this awful tragedy. When told that, no, he had in fact been living in the farmhouse in question, they said it must be some mistake.

Bill and Irene Chase, an electrician and homemaker from Sioux Falls, said their son Rodney was a good boy, who had been confused lately about things, as a boy his age (nineteen) was bound to be. A reporter's question elicited the information, only grudgingly given, that Rodney hadn't been home since the previous Christmas, though Sioux Falls was only a fifty-five mile drive from Red Earth.

Louise Doyle, the mother of Kathleen, was discovered at the State Hospital at nearby Yankton, where she was midway through a treatment program for alcoholism. Mrs. Doyle was currently unemployed, though her last job had been as a clerk in a grocery store in Huron. She had been divorced from Jerry Doyle, an insurance salesman and Kathleen's father, for eight years and no longer knew where he lived. Mrs. Doyle remained in the hospital and would not make herself available to reporters.

Ralph and Lucinda Arbalest, a banker and junior high teacher from Rapid City, could scarcely speak of the loss of their only son Jon, so hard was their grieving. They said Jon had taken his political idealism seriously, and they admitted that he and his father, a supporter of Barry Goldwater in '64 and George Wallace in '68, had had several heated arguments in the past two years about the war and about the American capitalist system. Still, they could never believe he would have been able to accept violence as a solution to the problems that divided this country. At heart he had been a good boy.

And so other parents had said of Sam Waters, of Lance Hendricks, of Mary Fletcher, of Sharon Murray, of Linda Snow, and of John Franklin. They had all been good boys, good girls, at heart.

* * * * * * *

By nine o'clock Thursday morning, an overflow crowd of more than three thousand had assembled at the Chamberlain Auditorium for the memorial observance. Elizabeth, Judith, Wolfram, Bruce, Mike, and Nick (wearing sunglasses and a hat) had entered as unobtrusively as possible and taken seats in the last row of the balcony. The huge crowd had heated the air in the auditorium and the witches' brew of scents--deodorant, cologne, perfume, and yes, rogue whiffs of body odor--had risen with the warm air to the balcony.

The families of the dead students sat like untouchables in the three front center rows, which had been roped off for them. The orchestra pit was filled with members of the media and the accouterments of their profession. The top of the large wooden podium at center stage had become a hydra-headed microphone monster.

President Miller thanked the families for their willingness to share this sad occasion with the University family. He thanked the faculty in attendance and he thanked the members of the student body for turning out to express their grief at the terrible loss of eleven of their peers. (He didn't thank the media for choosing to be present.) His speech after that was decidedly brief, speaking of the healing of divisions and saying that if this could be achieved, they would have the solace of knowing the eleven students would not have died in vain. Reverend Spenser spoke next, and he also kept his remarks brief, and unwontedly general, as he had been informed at some point in the past few days that the deceased had all been atheistic Communists. Student body president Bob Barnes gave a speech that, for him, was unusually sober and earnest, if littered with bromides.

Dan Jensen spoke on behalf of the grieving families, saying he was sure they joined him in saying how very grateful they were to their sons' and daughters' fellow students for sharing this observance with them. Mr. Jensen kept looking at notes he had scribbled on a small notepad. A few sentences into his talk he had to wipe a tear from his eye. His tears flowed almost non-stop after that. He removed the handkerchief from his suitcoat pocket and dabbed his eyes continuously. He kept valiantly on and was within three sentences of the end of his scripted remarks when his voice cracked and he broke into sobs, and, burying his face in his handkerchief, walked off the stage.

Bill Prescott was the last to speak. He had been asked by the president because of Prescott's well-known sympathies with the student war protesters, but also because he was known to be a reasonable man, someone who would speak temperately and not bring scandal on the University--especially not before all those members of the media. Bill Prescott wore a navy-blue suit, a white shirt, and a navy-blue tie. He looked grave but calm. When his turn came, he walked deliberately to the podium. He spoke as he lectured to his classes, without notes, in a clear, warm, resonant voice. Those who heard him knew they were hearing something genuine and heartfelt.

"Like those who have spoken before me today, I want to say how very gratified I am to see so many of our student body in attendance. I am told that many hundreds are standing outside in the chilly air of this autumn day, listening to this observance via loudspeakers. But I am particularly grateful that the members of the families of the eleven students we have so tragically and unexpectedly lost have consented to be with us today. I only hope that this great outpouring of sympathy in some way lightens their terrible burden of grief.

"I speak to you today, not merely as a professor at this university, but also as the father of two university students and as a man who has dedicated no small portion of his time these past several years to talking to our many, many students who are morally offended by our country's continued involvement on a massive scale in what can only truthfully be seen as a civil war in a tiny sliver of a country halfway around the earth, a country of no imaginable strategic threat to the United States. I have shared innumerable cups of coffee in our Student Union discussing the war with individual students and with groups of students. I have shared a podium with them at teach-ins and rallies. I have marched with them peaceably through the streets of this town. I knew personally all eleven of the students whose lives we have come here today to commemorate--some well, some only as acquaintances, some as students in my classes, some only through informal rap sessions and demonstrations against the war.

"I am a pacifist, so I have never embraced violence of any type as a morally acceptable means of redressing wrongs and injustices. As a man who has dedicated his life to peace and to the pursuit of peace through non-violent means, I cannot tell you why these eleven students decided on the course of action that led to their untimely deaths. I cannot speak to the motives and reasons that led them individually to their tragic ends in a rented farmhouse a few miles from this building.

"But I *can* tell you of the incredible sense of frustration and impatience they must have felt when they saw our elected leaders time and again mouth empty political slogans and turn their backs coldly on any suggestion of withdrawal from our 'police action' in Vietnam, when they saw our newly elected president speak of pursuing peace and then order the unremitting aerial bombardment of Hanoi, and when they saw the war illegally, but nonetheless purposefully, strategically, expanded into neighboring Cambodia. And I can tell you of the moral horror they felt when they saw four students shot down in cold blood last May on a college campus in Ohio, four students guilty of nothing but protesting what they felt to be an indefensible war.

"I *can* tell you of the righteous indignation and anger and bitterness they must have felt at that ruthless betrayal of democracy by the forces of their own government. I can tell you because I felt those things too. And while I cannot justify to my mind or conscience the path these eleven students took in response to that or any of the other outrages of our government, I can say that I understand what might have led them to it. As I have said, I am a pacifist, and I find all acts of violence unethical and repugnant. I believe that as rational creatures it is our responsibility to reason together, to consult together to find peaceful solutions to our problems. To me, neither the magnitude of the problem, nor the seeming hopelessness of peaceful, rational solution ever--I repeat, *ever*--justifies resorting to violence. I believe that to do so not only undercuts one's own moral position, but also forestalls peace and pushes further away the hope of a just solution.

"So, I cannot and I will not sanction the course of political action that these eleven students dedicated themselves to and that led to their deaths. But I *can* say to their grief-stricken families, and to the students of this university, about which hangs an almost visible black pall of sorrow, that these eleven students were idealists who, because of the impenetrably bellicose mentality of their elected leaders, leaders stubbornly impervious to reasoned moral argument, had reached the end of idealism. They were activists who had reached the conclusion that all of their previous actions had been futile, for naught. They were human beings who, in the face of moral outrage and atrocity, had reached the absolute end of patience. I wish they had not. How very much I wish they had not.

"If only we were gathered together today to celebrate the end of this unjust war, and not to commemorate eleven more of our war dead. I wish these eleven students had held on, had persisted in the path of peace, no matter how hard, no matter how frustrating, no matter how seemingly impossible.

"For I believe from the deepest core of my being that the path of peace is the only path that can ever put an end to war. And I believe that, no matter how dark and disordered, even deranged, the times may seem, no matter how fruitless our endeavors in the path of peace may seem, no matter how weary and disillusioned and dispirited, how bitter and depressed and angry, we may become while walking the path of peace, we must hold on. Because one day, maybe soon, maybe not, the victory *will* be won. Peace *will* prevail. Light *will* banish darkness. And we will be joyous and we will weep with gratitude. For we will know that our actions have not been for nothing. We will know that righteous actions lead inevitably to righteous results. We will know finally, once and for all, that only peace can beget peace. I can tell you, as sure as I am standing here today, that I believe that day is coming. It *will* arrive. And when it does, when that day finally dawns, we will all wonder how we could ever have doubted that it would."

Bill Prescott paused a moment. Silence held sway in the auditorium. He began again.

"But today is not that day. Today we are gathered, broken-hearted and morally chastened, to mourn the loss of these eleven students. They have been taken brutally from us, snatched violently away, before their times. Their ages ranged from eighteen to twenty. Not one of them was even twenty-one years old. We can truly say their lives were ended before the promise of their lives had begun to be realized, before their potential as individual human beings had been made manifest. In this overwhelming tragedy, that is perhaps the single most tragic thing. As I said, I speak to you as a father. My oldest daughter is twenty--of an age with these eleven. I know what I would feel if her life had been cut short, as theirs have been. I know what I would feel, and that puts an even sharper edge on my grief today."

He paused again for a few seconds.

"You might well ask what possible comfort we can find today in the face of this tragedy, this loss. I can speak only for myself. I am a professor of philosophy, but it is not to Socrates that I turn, Socrates who felt that it was unreasonable for us to fear death, because our entry into death was an embarking upon an adventure into the unknown. Socrates believed it was irrational to fear the unknown, since it could as well turn out good as ill. Socrates was a brave man, a great soul. But it is not to him or to any other philosopher that I turn on this day.

No, when I was walking from my home this morning to the auditorium, I found my thoughts turning to a poet who lived almost four hundred years ago, a poet who also wrote some of the most memorable prose in English. John Donne's "Meditation 17" tells me that whenever the deathbell tolls, it tolls for me as well, because, as he said, 'No man is an island, entire of itself; every man is a piece of the continent, a part of the main. If a clod be washed away by the sea, Europe is the less, as well as if a promontory were, as well as if a manor of thy friend's or of thine own were. Any man's death diminishes me, because I am involved in mankind . . . .'

"I know that each of you is here today because you too feel diminished by the death of these students, because you too are involved in mankind. Though these deaths have hurt us terribly, we can yet take solace in our feelings for our fellow human beings, in our shared humanity. Sadly, it sometimes requires death to reawaken us to our knowledge of the deep bonds of kinship that tie each of us inextricably to the other, that unite every man, woman, and child on this planet in an indissoluble bond. I cannot say that this lessens our pain or knits up our wounded hearts, but I can say that it helps us feel closer, not only to the dead, but also to the living, with whom we must find a way to go on. May all of you go now in peace and brotherhood."

Bill Prescott turned from the podium and walked off the stage. Everyone in the auditorium began to file slowly, soberly, through the several exits. The reporters were happy. Prescott's speech would play well.

As Elizabeth walked out, hand in hand with Nick, she felt, though mourning, almost elated. She had never been so proud of her father. She felt moved, and she knew that everyone in the audience had felt moved, by his words, whether or not they agreed with his politics. Today her father had given her an incomparable gift. She would thank him for it when she got home.

Chapter 16
Spirit Mound

The Saturday after Thanksgiving, Judith and Wolfram walked in Lewis and Clark Park, amidst the denuded trees. The sinuosity and sleek angularity of the leafless trees appealed powerfully to Judith's eye, began to set sparklers spraying jewel-bright through her brain and spinal cord, the sign that she had already begun in her mind to make a new painting. No children swung, slid, whirled round, or teeter-tottered on the playground equipment. Most of the leaves had been ground up by the city's lawnmowers, but a few shapeless brown relics remained. They sat on benches by the tornado slide.

"I look forward to bringing our kids to this park to play," Judith said.

Wolfram, who had been a bit distracted, watching the gusty southwest wind drive big gray-bellied cumulus past the branches of a big elm, said, "I'm sorry, what?"

"I said I look forward to bringing our own kids to the park to play."

"Kids?"

"Yeah, you know, the little two-legged creatures you see everywhere."

"You want kids?"

"Of course. Don't you?"

"I've never thought much about it."

"Really? I've thought about it as long as I can remember."

"I guess that's the difference between men and women."

"What do you mean?"

"You know, girls are taught from day one, by their mothers and everyone else around them, by TV and movies and advertising, to think of themselves as future mothers."

"OK, so we absorb the feminine mystique through our every pore. So what?"

"I'm just saying that guys aren't prepared like that. So the subject always takes us by surprise."

"Oh, come on, the world around us is rife with messages of two-parent families, of fathers doing this and that with their children."

"Yeah, but it's nowhere near as strong as what women are bombarded with. Besides, we get other messages, too."

"Like what?"

"Like stay single and unentangled as long as you can, because as soon as you get married, your freedom is over. Like having kids means having to provide for a family, having to put food on the table and pay the bills. Like having kids means the grind of a job, day-in, day-out, the rest of your life."

"So the only thing that's supposed to be important to a man is to satisfy the hunger in his groin and move on. Is that what you're saying?"

"I'm telling you all men get this huge message–'preserve your freedom at all costs'."

"And wives and kids are just so much unnecessary baggage."

"Hey, I didn't say this was my view. I'm just saying that society gives guys really contradictory messages."

"OK, so what are your views, Wolfram?"

"I knew you were going to ask that," he said, chuckling. "I don't know. I guess I like kids all right--"

"Can you see yourself as a father?"

Wolfram, alarmed, "Well, sure but not in the near future. This is a new idea for me."

"How far in the future?"

"Well, I'm not in any hurry. I think the married couple have to have a really stable marriage first."

"What does that mean?"

"It means just what I said--really stable. The couple should be completely comfortable with their relationship, should be at a point where they're ready to invite someone else to share it. And they should have stable incomes. I don't believe a couple has any business bringing any kids they can't support into this world."

"Do you think we have a 'completely comfortable' relationship?"

"Well, yeah, of course. But hell, Judith, we haven't even gotten married yet."

"Will you marry me, Wolfram?"

Wolfram's eyes got bigger, then narrowed to study her face. She stared calmly back, as though she had just asked him to go to the movies.

"You're serious, aren't you?"

"That's right, I'm proposing. Will you marry me?"

"I'll say one thing, Judith, you really know how to surprise a guy." He stood up, looked pensively at the ground a moment, looked up, sought her eyes. "Yes, Judith, I'll marry you."

"You mean it?" she asked.

"I've never been more serious."

"Oh, Wolfram!" Judith exclaimed as she jumped up and hugged him.

They kissed each other as if all life had been compressed into lips and tongues.

"I love you, Wolfram." She squeezed him tighter.

"Judith, I knew from that first night that I loved you more than I've ever loved anyone. But--one question."

"Yes."

"When?"

"What?"

"When do you want to get married? Next week?"

"Next week!"

"Oh, too late?" he teased. "How about tomorrow, then?"

"Don't be silly. Who wants to get married in November, when it's freezing outside?"

"People do it all the time."

"But not here."

"In Red Earth?"

"No, in this park."

"You want to get to married in this park?"

"After today, doesn't it seem like the perfect place?"

"Sure, but you still haven't said when."

"In May."

"Great." He kissed her. "Judith, the stores are still open. Let's go buy an engagement ring."

"Oh, Wolfram, you make me so happy." She hugged him tighter.

He leaned back and looked into her eyes a long while. He kissed her and put his arm round her waist. They walked through the sodden leaves to the car.

* * * * * * *

Since their early autumn trip to Sioux City with Wolfram and Judith, Nick and Elizabeth had spent all their days and evenings together. Whichever one woke first called the other. They met for breakfast and then walked each other to their separate classes. They had lunch together and studied together in the library. Nick developed a fondness for the battered old busted-springed couch in the art studio, where he sat and read, or wrote in his notebooks, while Elizabeth painted--hour after hour. She accompanied him every week to the films shown in the Union and in the theaters downtown and in Sioux Falls and Sioux City.

Elizabeth's sister Laura and her brother Eric liked Nick, but her parents embraced him in a big way: "Can you believe it, Bill?" "What?" "That Elizabeth finally found such a good boy." "Yeah, he stands head and shoulders over any of her others." "Especially Tom Morgan?" "Yes, over him especially."

Nick spent many an afternoon and evening at the Prescotts' home, listening to music, watching television, playing chess with Bill Prescott. Elizabeth and her parents taught him how to play bridge. Sometimes, though not often, Nick was able to cajole Elizabeth into playing the piano for him (she always claimed she was shamefully out of practice). Elaine Prescott gave Nick a standing invitation to dinner, and more days than not six o'clock found him sitting down with the people who had become his second family.

Elizabeth's family owned two horses, a palomino and a sorrel, that they kept in the small pasture directly back of their property, which they rented from a neighboring farmer. Nick and Elizabeth went riding nearly every weekend, and it was on horseback that he really came to learn and to love the land around Red Earth. They particularly liked to pack a picnic lunch and ride down to the Missouri, where they spent hours riding and walking along its banks. On horseback, Elizabeth also introduced Nick to Spirit Mound, which rose above the prairie a few miles northwest of the town. She explained to him the Yanktonnais Dakota legends about the Mound and its sacred significance; she also told him about Lewis and Clark's unproductive trip to see it.

The Mound was now owned by a farmer who treated it as if it were nothing more than an usually tall bit of acreage. He raised cattle and had built a manure-and-silage-reeking feedlot on the northwest side of the Mound, directly adjacent to his farmhouse. He'd strung a barb-wire fence along the Mound's east side, halfway up, making a pasture between the Mound and the highway, where a big historical marker explained the Mound to interested tourists and pilgrims.

Nick asked Elizabeth if she'd ever climbed the fence and walked up to the top of the Mound. She said that one night when she was a sophomore in high school, she and a couple of her girlfriends, more to do something different than for any spiritual reason, had left their car parked by the road and sneaked up to the top. The problem was that at night one couldn't see very far, so the impact of the Mound's height above the surrounding plains was lost.

* * * * * * *

One Sunday night in January, Elizabeth and Nick sat in an Italian restaurant downtown. They had just finished their spumoni, and were drinking espressos.

"You know, Nick," Elizabeth said, taking his hand, "these last several months have been really happy ones for me. I don't think I've ever been so happy."

She squeezed his hand gently.

"Me, neither."

"Not even with Annie?"

"No, of course not. What I have with you, Elizabeth, is nothing like what I had with her. I was just a kid then, and I was infatuated with her. That's all."

"Good."

"What about Tom Morgan?"

"What about him?"

"Is this like what you felt for him?"

"No, it's nothing like my relationship with Tom."

"How's it different?"

"For one thing, Nick," she said, her hazel eyes staring straight into his brown eyes, "I really love you."

He returned her look. "And you didn't love Tom?"

"I thought I did, but I didn't really know him. I think I fell in love with this idea I had of Tom as an artist. Of course, that idea didn't turn out to be anything like the real Tom. I was younger--somehow I feel like I've aged so much in the past year--and anyway, I guess I was knocked over by his talent. No, it wasn't so much his talent as his attitude. He had this incredible confidence. He wasn't arrogant or condescending but just so sure of himself."

"So he was charismatic."

"Yes, he had charisma. But with him it had this knife edge of defiance and rebellion to it."

"Which you liked."

She laughed. "OK, I'll admit it, I did. But like I said, I was younger then. I don't think I'd fall for it so readily today. My parents certainly didn't fall for it."

"What did your father think of him."

"Tom Morgan rubbed my father's every nerve blood-raw. I think Dad felt something pretty close to contempt for him. I know he considered Tom shallow and pretentious."

"And what did you think?"

"At the time I thought Dad was totally unfair. I thought he was just jealous of Tom?"

"Why would he be jealous?'

"Because here was this overly confident, handsome, avante-garde young sculptor--someone who represented a kind of hipness that my father thought merely faddish. And this brash young upstart was proposing to run off with his first-born daughter. No, that didn't sit well with Dad at all."

"I'd call your father's attitude protective, not jealous."

"I probably would, too, now, but at the time I thought he was just jealous."

"So your leaving the Art Institute and going to California with Morgan caused a rupture in your relationship with your parents."

"Oh, God, yes. With both Mom and Dad but especially with Dad. There was big showdown when we told my parents we were going to San Francisco. I'd never seen such hurt and disappointment in my father's face before. He'd disapproved of a lot of things I'd done since I'd arrived at puberty, and he'd always made sure I felt his disapprobation. But it was nothing like what I saw in his eyes that day. I felt like I had disappointed him so badly I would never be able to regain his trust or approval. I can't think of anything in my whole life as painful as looking into my dad's eyes and seeing his sense of wounded betrayal, and then having to turn away, to leave.

"As soon as Tom and I drove away, I began to cry, and I cried all the way to Kansas City. Tom couldn't understand it. He was feeling great. He had just declared his independence from another adult authority figure, and nothing made him feel better than that. I don't think Tom ever understood what had happened between me and my parents that day. He was simply incapable of comprehending something like that."

"When did your father change his opinion of you? Every time I've visited your house, he's seemed affectionate toward you and completely accepting."

"It was a gradual change, last summer. But I began to notice a real difference when I went out to the Freedom Farm that night with Judith and broke everything off with Tom once and for all."

"Didn't Morgan leave town right after that?"

"The next day. He disappeared and no one's heard anything from him since. Dad was very glad to hear Tom had left. I think Dad was half afraid I might run away with him again."

"Did you consider it?"

"Are you kidding? *No.* I knew when I left San Francisco I no longer loved Tom. And when I saw him again that night at the Freedom Farm, I felt nothing for him at all, except maybe pity. And when he tried to rape me, I felt only hate and repulsion. The sight of him lying on the floor at the end, moaning and clutching himself, literally nauseated me. I despised him."

"Well, I can see now why you didn't seem too interested in me that day I met you for the first time."

"It had nothing to do with you, Nick. It would have been impossible for me to have an interest in any guy then. It took me the rest of the summer to get over my shattered illusions about Tom."

"And Jon Arbalest?"

"He was just somebody sympathetic to talk to. At least I thought he was sympathetic."

"And you didn't feel anything for him?"

"Nothing romantic. And especially not after he went around spreading lies about me."

"So my timing was better that second time we met, when we went to Sioux City with Wolfram and Judith."

She laughed. "A thousand times better."

She looked at him a moment, squeezed his hand. He squeezed back.

"I love you, Nick."

"I love you, too, Elizabeth."

"And you know what, Nick?"

"What?"

"Mom and Dad like you, too."

As Nick looked into her eyes as she said those words, he suddenly saw a man and a hugely pregnant woman walking against the wind that was driving snow into their faces as they walked to their car in mid-afternoon. He saw the man, a much younger Bill Prescott, help his young wife Elaine into the car, saw him start the car, get out, swiftly scrape the windows, and drive off down the slippery street. Earlier that day in the third week of March, the streets and sidewalks had been dry and the grass had been showing green in the yards.

He saw Bill arrive at the emergency room door of the hospital (just three blocks from their house), and help Elaine inside. He saw Bill waiting through the evening and through the night. He saw the nurse come out into the waiting room at three in the morning of March 21st and tell Bill he had a healthy baby daughter. He saw Bill follow her to the operating room, where he stood beside Elaine, who was holding the baby, and despite her exhaustion, smiling radiantly. He saw Bill take the baby, and he saw the incredible pride and happiness in his face. He was beaming like a small sun.

And he saw Bill an hour later walk out into the frozen night air to the parking lot behind the hospital. The storm had long since stopped and the sky had cleared enough for a few constellations to be seen above. He saw Bill stop halfway across the parking lot and look up with wonder and amazement at the sky, where the northern lights were pluming southward in great luminous starts and fits. He saw Bill stand stockstill for several minutes, watching the ghostly lights streaking and shooting in waves halfway across the sky. And he saw Bill's lips mouth just the two words, "Thank you," before walking to his car and driving home.

Nick saw this all in an instant outside lived time.

* * * * * * *

One day in February, Mike Red Horse called Nick and asked if he and Elizabeth would like to go with him that night to a Lakota *yuwipi* ceremony. A holy man, Sam Shoots Ten Arrows, was visiting the campus and the *yuwipi* ceremony he was going to conduct was the kick-off event for the first-ever Native American Culture Week at the University. Specifically, the ceremony was meant to bless the museum and particularly its art gallery, where the Lakota painter Oscar Howe's works were to be permanently displayed.

Mike had begun seriously investigating his Lakota heritage during his freshman year. He was in his second year of Lakota language classes and he lived in a University-sponsored house with five other Lakota students. He was a student senator and frequently introduced matters of interest to Native American students for consultation in the Senate. He also worked on the campus suicide hotline. He had talked two Native students, among others, out of killing themselves. Elizabeth and Nick were agreeable to the invitation.

Judith and Wolfram would normally have gone with them, but Wolfram and his band were in Los Angeles, in an Elektra Records studio, laying down tracks for their first album. Wolfram had sent demos out in the late summer and fall, with no results. No one appeared to be in the market for a rising blues-rock guitarist. Then he sent one to the Elektra offices, on a whim really, and was surprised when he received a call a week later, asking when he and Body Count were going to be playing. Elektra wanted to send a producer out to give a listen. The man from the studio had been utterly flattened by Wolfram and the band's live show, and within forty-eight hours their signatures were on a contract (after Wolfram's lawyer had read it and suggested changes, which the studio had agreed to) and they were on their way to L. A.

Wolfram and Judith talked every day on the phone (usually about dawn, after he returned, exhausted but nervously excited, to his hotel room--after spending all night in the studio). Then last Monday Wolfram had called and asked Judith if she'd consider flying out for the weekend. He'd buy her air ticket. She said yes without hesitation. She missed him badly.

Before the ceremony had begun in the Harper Museum, Shoots Ten Arrows had walked around the building, stopping on each of its four sides to pray and smoke a pipe. Thus had he blessed the building and prepared it for the ceremony. Oscar Howe's works--full of cubist geometry wed to magical mythical swirlings--adorned the walls of a big room on the museum's second floor.

Mike, Nick, and Elizabeth sat on the floor along one wall of the gallery, as they had been directed. All four walls were lined with people. In the center of the room, Shoots Ten Arrows, a short, slim, and slightly stooped man, with a face as time-eroded as the Badlands, sat cross-legged on the floor, holding a gourd rattle. He wore a green and brown plaid shirt, jeans, and scuffed brown boots. He wore his hair in two long braids, each tied at the end with a leather thong. Behind him on the floor were a large star-pattern quilt, a bowl of the transparent round *yuwipi* stones collected from ant hills, several pieces of flint, and four sections of rope. Pieces of sage were strewn all about the middle part of the room. His assistant, a heavy-set man in his thirties, sat next to the holy man. Before the assistant was a drum, which he began to beat as he sang, in a piercing falsetto, starting high and descending, time after time. The medicine man shook the gourd rattle rapidly as the song finished in a flourish of drumbeats.

Shoots Ten Arrows got to his feet, lit his pipe, and offered it to the four directions, to the sky above and the earth below, pausing to say a few words in Lakota and to smoke each time. He made a long prayer in Lakota. Then his assistant explained that in the next part of the ceremony, the holy man would be bound within the star quilt. Shoots Ten Arrows removed his boots and socks and stood calmly in his bare feet as his assistant tied his hands tightly behind him with one piece of the rope. Another piece was tied firmly around his ankles. The star quilt was placed over Shoots Ten Arrows' head and tied snugly to his body with the two remaining ropes. The assistant then lowered the bound holy man to the floor. The assistant explained that the lights would be turned off for a few moments and that when they were turned back on, Shoots Ten Arrows would be sitting, free of his bonds, in the middle of the room.

The lights were put out, leaving the room so dark Nick could not see Elizabeth's face when he turned to look at her. But almost immediately sparks began to be struck off the pieces of flint in all parts of the room. A pause, then irregular drum beats. The gourd rattle began to shake, soft and then hard, and then suddenly it went zinging off across the room. More sparks were struck from flints simultaneously in all parts of the room. More arhythmical drumbeats, only now from the wall opposite the one where Mike, Nick, and Elizabeth sat. Another short pause, then the drum was being beaten fast and steadily in the center of the room, up by its high ceiling (a good fifteen feet above the floor). More sparks and the rattle again went flying across the room. Many quick drumbeats, this time right in front of the three friends.

Then an eye-scalding explosion of light and the white buffalo, almost twice the size of a real buffalo, appeared in the room. Its hide glowed as if illuminated by starlight. Its horns were blacker than the darkness of the room. It snorted and walked to within a few feet of Elizabeth, Mike, and Nick, who each thought that none of the other spectators in the room were seeing it. Had they leaned forward and reached out, they might have touched it. Whole galaxies swam in the buffalo's eyes, which seemed ancient, all-knowing, all-wise. The three friends felt suddenly filled with an inexpressible happiness, emanating from the buffalo. Then another eruption of white light, and the buffalo was gone. The room was again pitch dark.

A couple of random drumbeats twenty feet or so to their right. More sparks, then for two minutes, nothing. Not a sound. Not a spark. Then the fluorescent ceiling lights were turned back on, and around the room everyone began rubbing their eyes. Sitting quietly, cross-legged on the star quilt, in the center of the room was Sam Shoots Ten Arrows. His assistant said the ceremony was now over, and he thanked everyone for sharing it with them. Shoots Ten Arrows began to pull his socks back on as people stood up, pulled on their winter coats, and, began to leave the room. As Nick stood up, he saw the holy man smile at him and turn away. The three friends, subdued, speechless, but with minds striking off questions like the sparks struck from the flints, walked out of the room, down the stairs, and out into the clear, cold late winter night.

* * * * * * *

After dropping Mike off at his place, Nick and Elizabeth felt far too buoyant to return to Elizabeth's house, so they drove out into the snowy countryside, ending up at the boat landing on the Missouri, a few miles southwest of town. They watched the river, frozen on either side, flow fast and black under the moonlight, in its narrow channel. They watched the moon fire with cold silver the edges of black clouds that blew across it, and when covered, irradiate them from behind--and then outline them in icy white flame again as they slid past.

Nick held Elizabeth close.

"I'm so happy," he said.

"Me, too."

Nick's eyes flashed as he looked her in the eye, held that look.

"I know what would make me even happier."

"What's that?"

"If you would marry me."

Elizabeth saw how serious he was.

"Yes, Nick, I'll marry you."

His lips put the torch to hers and they kissed. They held each other close, feeling the bonfire begin to rage between, as the river flowed blackly in its bed and the clouds flew darkly past the moon.

"Nick, I've got an idea. I don't know what you're going to think of this, but . . ."

"Tell me."

"Let's get married the same day as Judith and Wolfram."

"In May?"

"Yes, let's get married with them in the park?"
"They won't think we're crashing their wedding?"
"No, I think they'll feel it's somehow perfect, just meant to be."
"Judith will be back tomorrow. We can ask her when we pick her up at
the Sioux Falls airport."
"She's going to say yes, Nick, I know it."

* * * * * * *

Judith did say yes, and Wolfram too. Families were informed and new enlarged wedding plans were made and everything proceeded apace. Maids of honor and bridesmaids and best men and groomsmen were asked, dresses were picked out and tuxedos ordered, musicians were hired for the reception (which was planned for the covered shelter in the park), the Unitarian minister was asked to officiate, alternative rain sites were chosen for the wedding and reception, guest lists were drawn up, and invitations and cakes and place settings and food for the reception were chosen and ordered.

* * * * * * *

Finding themselves restless near midnight one day near the end of April, Judith, Wolfram, Elizabeth, and Nick decided to make a pilgrimage to Spirit Mound. Along the way they picked up Mike Red Horse. Wolfram parked his car under two cottonwoods just down the road from the historical marker. As they walked up the hill through the pasture, fifty Herefords turned their heads to look at them. The pasture was well-grazed and cow pies were everywhere, so they watched their steps. Halfway up the hill, Judith and Wolfram held the wires in the fence apart so Nick, Elizabeth, and Mike could climb through. Mike and Nick returned the favor.

Walking about the top of the mound, they noticed that the soil there was sandy and eroded in places; they saw several ant mounds and a fair number of gopher holes. Bluestem and buffalo grass, wild oats, and foxtail barley covered the hill. Soapweeds sprung up here and there. Four small chokecherry trees grew on the west side. The night air was cool but not cold and the half moon had risen in the east. The four of them stood looking up at the Big and Little Bears, Lyra, Draco, and Hercules. Hundreds and hundreds of other stars shone in the cloudless sky.

Below, the farmer's house was dark. A yardlight gleamed from atop a pole, lighting the driveway, the barn, the machine shed, two silos, and a henhouse. Scores of cattle stood somnolently in the feedlot, wholly unaware that their fates consisted of much smaller pens, a last walk through narrow wooden corrals, the killing floor.

At that moment one of the pointer stars fell out of Ursa Major, streaked southwest across the sky, turned in a tight arc, and burned straight for the mound, brightening as it came. They stood, mouths open, helpless to move, as if they were in a dream. Two hundred yards south of the mound, the star burst, turning night to day, blinding them. When they were able to open their eyes again, they saw, against the star-filled sky, the white buffalo. It walked toward them on air, stepping as surefootedly and steadily as if it walked on solid ground.

The buffalo stepped onto the mound, walked a few paces, and stopped, not thirty feet away. It snorted, pawed the ground aimlessly, snorted again, and lay down and rolled, smashing the grass flat. It rolled back again. It stood up--moonlight dazzling on its white hide, glinting off its big black horns--snorted, and turned to the east. They looked in that direction and saw the night roll up, like a great black-painted canvas. Another canvas was rolled out for them and they saw it was a bright spring day a long time ago, long before the land was fenced and the highway built.

Two Indians, a man in his fifties and a boy in his middle teens, rode up to the bottom of the hill, hobbled their horses, and walked to the top. They wore breechcloths, leggings, beaded leather shirts, and beaded moccasins. The man wore a single eagle feather tied in his hair, and carried something in a beaded leather case. They stopped on the east side of the mound. The man rubbed himself and the boy with sage, took a carved red stone pipe from the case, rubbed it with sage, then took pinches of *kinikinik* from a leather pouch and tamped it in.

He lit the pipe and offered it to each of the four directions and to the sky above and the earth below, smoking and praying each time. He and the boy walked around the top of the hill, stopping at each of the cardinal points to offer the pipe, to smoke, and to pray. When they returned to the east side, the older man sang a song and offered a long prayer. He offered the pipe to the six directions again and he and the boy smoked a last time. The older man rubbed the pipe with sage and slipped it back into its case. The man and the boy descended the hill, removed the hobbles from their horses, mounted, and rode away. When they had vanished behind a hill on the prairie, the canvas of that day was rolled up and the canvas of night was spread out again.

    The buffalo snorted, pawed the earth, and turned to the south. The night's canvas was again rolled up and that of another day, a hot, sunny mid-summer's day, was spread out. A small party of tired, profusely sweating men appeared over the top of a hill and trudged slowly up the mound. When they reached the top, they walked about for a bit, sat down to rest a few moments, stood up, walked about again, kicking aimlessly at gopher holes and an ant mound or two, and then, after one of them was bitten by an ant that had crawled up his pantleg, left in a hurry. The day's canvas was rolled up behind them and night's laid out in its stead.

    The huge beast turned to the west, where another day's canvas was laid out. A group of people came walking up the hill. It took the five of them a moment to realize that they knew these people. Nick and Judith recognized Gene and Linda Andrews and their two children and Big Bill Burdette, who was carrying a blond-haired fifteen-month-old boy. Big Bill grinned at them and nodded, as if he was pleased to see them again after such a long time. They recognized Lena's grandparents, whom they had met once when Lena had taken them to visit her family in Georgia. And there were the high school cheerleader and her boyfriend, who'd drunk the better part of two six-packs and then accidentally driven his car off the top of the big earthen dam northwest of LeBeau, onto the huge boulders on the north side. There was the girl who had left her car running in her parents' garage, with the garage door closed, after she had learned she was pregnant. There were Jon Arbalest and the other members of the People's Revolutionary Committee.

    Elizabeth recognized a cousin who had died of leukemia at age twelve, her young grandmother (whom she knew only from pictures), who had been in such pain from a brain tumor that she had shot herself.

She saw her great-grandmother on her father's side, who had died of a stroke. She stood by her husband, who had died of prostate cancer. Elizabeth saw the four boys from her high school who had gotten drunk after homecoming one year and, speeding, lost control of their car on the Airport Road and accordioned their car on a tree. She saw a girl she had worked with in San Francisco, whom she had later heard had overdosed on smack.

Wolfram saw his father's brother, who had died of a heart attack at age thirty-four. He saw his mother's father, who had died of lung cancer. He saw his mother's mother, who had died of pneumonia one winter. He saw a high school history teacher who had been electrocuted when he had stepped out of the shower and touched the light fixture over his bathroom sink. And he saw the parade of buddies he had known in Vietnam, and the VC and North Vietnamese soldiers he had killed or seen killed--all magically gore-free and whole of limb.

Mike saw his parents, come back whole from their car crash, smiling at him. He saw his father's parents, standing up straight and solemn-faced, bright colored blankets about their shoulders. He saw a boy from his fourth grade class, who had died while playing in a tire swing in his back yard. He had spun the swing around and around and had gotten the rope wrapped tight around his neck, strangling himself before he could get it untangled. He saw his cousin Joy, who had drowned, at age twelve, while swimming in a small lake. He saw two friends of his, a boy and a girl, both seventeen, who had driven into the country to park, accidentally backing their car's tailpipe into a snowbank. They had died of carbon monoxide poisoning.

All of these people walked up to and past the five of them. And almost all were smiling, their faces lit from within. Then that day was rolled up and night unfurled again.

The buffalo turned toward the north, and a terrible plain of suffering was unrolled before their eyes. They saw people dying by the hundreds and thousands, of war and genocide. The earth ran with blood. Clouds of gray-black smoke rose everywhere from tall heaps and piles of burning bodies. They saw great masses of people dying of starvation and epidemic diseases. They saw people perishing in terrible natural and man-caused disasters. Everywhere they looked they saw the corpses of the dead and the pain-wracked faces of the dying. They knew this was the time they were living in. Then this panorama of agony and torture and death was rolled up and the peaceful night sky unrolled in its place.

The buffalo snorted and turned to the east again. There they saw a beautiful daybreak sky unfurled--the just-risen sun ruffing and ribbing indigo-and-slate clouds with rose-nectarine and peach, with saffron and pollen. They saw people of every race and ethnicity and occupation and religion--a rich, variegated flower garden of humanity, brilliant of hue and redolent of fragrance--living peaceably together on the land and in the cities. And the city streets and air and buildings were clean. No one had to live any longer in soul-desolating, squalid, decaying neighborhoods. Everything had been rebuilt. Trees lined streets and parks were everywhere.

The people of that time did not look that different, but they talked and laughed differently, with the joy that comes from knowing their essential oneness, and from living lives dedicated to the service of others. They maintained their identities as Americans or Senegalese or Thais or Venezuelans, but they also considered themselves members of a great planetary commonwealth. After a time that day was rolled up and the starry night sky spread out again.

The buffalo turned and walked right up to their small group. He looked down on them with great black eyes in which they saw infinite kindness and a love so great they could not begin to comprehend it. They felt the buffalo's breath on their faces, and it was sweeter than any perfume or scent they had ever known. His hide was a field of sparkles and glints and glimmers, a field that seemed to widen and stretch and grow before their eyes. His horns were pulsing with innumerable tiny lightnings. They felt his breath on them, felt themselves lifted up at tremendous speed, high up into a realm of light beyond all imagining.

And then they were standing once more in the dark on the mound. The buffalo rolled in the grass ten yards away, got to its feet, turned, and walked straight off the hill into the night. Suddenly a white flash broke from horizon to horizon and they saw a star streak back into the sky above their heads. The sky became black once more and they stared up at it in silence. Minutes passed before they walked, still in silence, down the hill to their car.

Chapter 17
Epithalamion

      In mid-May, after generous rains,
      When dandelions dotted the grass
      Throughout the park, and crab apples
      Dropped red blossoms, and apples white,
      When bridal veil bushes stood, bright
      Snowbanks, wholly unseasonable,
      And cloud's cool shadows floated past,
      On lush, green land, movable stains,
Bringing but momentary dimness to their sight,

      When robins, blue jays, and blackbirds
      Sang unseen from nests in the great
      Green houses of oaks, honey locusts,
      Elms, and maples, when gray squirrels
      Raced in the rafters or quarreled
      With passersby, when frogs in lust
      Croaked loudly to attract a mate,
      And when poets' heads filled with words,
Then did lovers, from different worlds,

      Two couples, come together, their
      Families and friends assembled,
      To promise fidelity and hope
      For love's sweet increase through seasons
      Unborn, to make declarations
      Before all of love's boundless scope,
      To pledge, as finches' voices trembled
      Above, their dreams and lives to share--
Purely for love's sake, no other reason.

      As lovers kissed, scores of pigeons
      Were released behind the band shell, to
      Fly up and over the trees. "Oh, look!"
      People said, pointed. To the sounds

Of "Ode to Joy"--beyond all bounds
Each heart was pushed--and as the flock
Of pigeons soared, newlyweds through
Friends and families walked. At once
Everyone cheered, then danced for hours on the grounds.

Just as they left to drive (in two
Cars) to Omaha and the Red
Lion Inn, Nick and Judith, Wolf-
Ram and Elizabeth saw a bright
Explosion in the road, the white
Body and head, as light engulfed
Them. They felt hot waves of love flood
Through them. The road cleared and a new
Highway stretched out before: Their cars took flight.

Epilogue

LilyAnn Burdette, after an extended period of mourning for Big Bill, devoted herself to activities in the Razor Strop, Oklahoma, Southern Baptist Church. About three years after Bill's death, she experienced the first of many visitations of the Lord. She returned to her church and said, calmly, before the entire congregation that the Lord had told her that they must integrate their church. After the clamor and consternation had died down, she was interviewed privately by the minister, who could not convince her that she had either had a hallucination or been visited by the Devil.

When she continued to push publicly for the change and met only with rebuke and insults, she resigned her membership in the church and started holding meetings open to all races in her home. For a long time the only white people to attend were LilyAnn and her four sons, Jeremy, Jimmy, Johnny, and Jasper. At first three, then five, then eight, ten, twelve, fifteen, and twenty Black families attended services, prayer meetings, Bible study classes, and social events regularly. Eventually they incorporated as The Church of the Living Love of Jesus, Redeemer.

About a year later, LilyAnn had an especially intense visitation and afterwards told everyone that the Lord had given her the power of healing. She proved it by removing the gout from Eulalie Baker, a sixty-two-year-old grandmother of twenty. She performed any number of healings, never refusing a request, and never accepting any personal material reward for her services. She said the gift came from God and that he did not wish anyone to profit from it except the grateful souls who had been restored to health. She did allow people to make whatever donation they wished, though, to The Church of the Living Love.

It was after LilyAnn began laying on hands and healing that the white citizens of her town, most of whom had thought her insane, began to spontaneously drop by her house--"Well, hi, LilyAnn, we just happened to be in the neighborhood and thought 'We haven't seen LilyAnn in so long. We should stop to see how she and the boys are doing.'" LilyAnn would always take them into her living room, offer them coffee and cookies, and make them feel welcome. Usually, within thirty minutes they had worked up the courage to make their requests: Would LilyAnn be willing to try to heal George of his arthritis, Edna of her "female troubles," Sam of his shingles, Gerald of his emphysema, Sally of her angina, and on and on. LilyAnn always readily agreed. Many people experienced LilyAnn's gift of healing love, thanked her profusely afterwards, and then were never seen again. A few, though, began to attend services at her house.

LilyAnn had to expand, first to a tent, and then to a church. The Baptist church she'd left had in the meantime suffered such an erosion in membership that it could no longer afford its high overhead and was forced to put the church building up for sale. The board of directors of the Church of the Living Love made an offer, which, as there were no others, was reluctantly accepted. Five years after she had resigned her church membership and walked, straight-spined down the center aisle and out the door, LilyAnn held her first services in the church. Her congregation was now two-thirds Black and one-third White.

News of LilyAnn's integrated church had spread, and one Sunday Dr. Martin Luther King, Jr. visited and delivered a powerful homily on the creating of "a new race of man" through the "unvanquishable" love of Christ. LilyAnn and her entire congregation accompanied Dr. King on his poor people's march on Washington and listened to his "I Had a Dream" speech. Dr. King's death struck LilyAnn hard, harder even, truth be told, than had Big Bill's. She cried for what seemed like weeks. But after another intense visitation from the Lord, she led her congregation to rededicate themselves to the cause of racial equality and justice, a cause from which neither she nor they ever veered or swerved.

LilyAnn became a popular speaker on college campuses throughout the seventies and eighties. She talked about racial and women's issues and about social justice. She became a major advocate for the poor and the homeless. In 1990, her autobiography became a surprise best seller. After the rights were sold to TV for a miniseries, she started the Burdette Foundation, to oversee the granting of scholarships to the University of Oklahoma and several Black colleges, as well as other charitable work. LilyAnn said many a time that she would retire only when Dear Jesus called her to her heavenly home.

LilyAnn's son Jeremy became a country humorist, an endlessly resourceful teller of downhome tales that never failed to make his audiences laugh so hard they teared up. He was a regular at The Grand Ole Opry, and he performed at clubs and fairs all over the country. Each of his albums sold better than the last. His *All-Time Best Country Tales of Jeremy Burdette, Vol. 1* went gold, as did *Vol. 2*. He and his wife June and their four kids, Billy, Annamarie, Lisa, and Tim, lived in Nashville.

Jimmy earned an MBA in marketing and went to work for a firm in Houston, where he lived with his wife Maureen ("Reeny"), and their kids Brent, Bruce, and Brad. Johnny married and he and his wife Pam had one child, Christina. Johnny went to divinity school and became the pastor of the second Church of the Living Love, in nearby Potlatch, Oklahoma. Jasper became a computer software designer and lived in Silicon Valley with his wife Linda and their kids Lily and Samantha.

After Big Bill's death, things went progressively downhill for Ray Donovan. He quite combining and his wife divorced him, citing numerous infidelities. He ran a liquor store in a small Texas town for the next seven years. One night two men came in and held him up. One of them panicked and shot Ray three times in the chest. He was pronounced dead at the scene. He had no known survivors.

Roger and Lena had always dreamed of owning a house in the Black Hills, and In 1978, Roger got a transfer to a state office in Rapid City and Lena got an elementary teaching job in Sturgis, South Dakota. They built a large house in the hills between Sturgis and Deadwood. In the early nineties, they retired. Roger kept busy landscaping his property (he turned out to have an excellent eye for design and organic form), and he took up woodworking, something he hadn't done much of since high school shop. Lena filled her basement with half a dozen stations for the different crafts she enjoyed. She also took up watercolor painting.

Bill and Elaine Prescott healed the wound in their marriage and once again became each other's best friend. In 1972, Elaine started a photography studio in downtown Red Earth. She was hired for weddings and individual and family portraits. She made enough at it to pay her overhead and finance photographic shooting trips to every inhabited continent in the world. Bill accompanied her on many of these trips. Elaine closed her business in 1981 to work full time on her photography. Bill retired from the University in 1989. He wrote two books on epistemology in the next five years.

Jim and Melissa Kohles continued to live and work in Sioux Falls, he as a doctor and she as a CPA. Neither of them were quite prepared for the fame their son Wolfram achieved in the early and mid-seventies. They were proud when his first album was released, thrilled when it went gold, and simply astonished when his second, third, fourth, and fifth albums went platinum. They were nearly tongue-tied when reporters from *Rolling Stone, Spin, Time, Newsweek, and The New York Times* called them--called them!--for background and reactions after Wolfram won three Grammies in 1976.

Bill Matthews transferred to the University of Minnesota in his junior year. He studied theater and became one of the most sought-after set and lighting designers in the Twin Cities area.

Bruce Baker and Mike Red Horse both graduated *summa cum laude* (Mike with a 4.00 GPA) from the University in 1973 and both followed in their father's footsteps by entering Harvard Law School in the fall of 1974. Both received offers from New York firms upon graduation, but after one year Mike left to work for the American Indian Movement, who had considerable legal troubles. In 1980, Mike joined a firm in Chicago. By the mid-eighties, both Bruce and Mike had become partners in their firms.

Val Burroughs majored in biology, considered graduate school in everything from zoology to herpetology to marine biology, but ultimately decided to help break a few more barriers for women by going to veterinary school at the University of Iowa. After many years of working for others, she and her best friend from vet school, Joan Burke, started their own small animal business in Des Moines, in 1984.

Wolfram's first album received critical raves for his guitar work, for the tightness of the band and the virtuosity of its individual members, for his writing (particularly for his Vietnam songs), and for his and the band's covers of songs by Muddy Waters, Howlin' Wolf, and Robert Johnson. His song "Vietnam Landmine Blues" made it, albeit briefly, into the top twenty on the *Billboard Magazine* rock chart, and he received Grammy nominations for both for that song and for his album, *Wolfram Kohles and Body Count*. That year he did not win.

Wolfram and the band made an album a year. They toured in

support of the first eight, and sporadically after that. Wolfram's live performances became the stuff of rock legend. He was most frequently compared to Hendrix and Clapton. Judith accompanied him on tour, until their children, Caitlin and Oberon, were born, in 1976 and 1978. After Oberon's birth, Wolfram quit regular touring to spend more time at home with Judith and the kids. They owned a farm near the Missouri River, not far from Red Earth. Wolfram had the barn converted into a recording studio. Whenever he'd have his agent book a concert in the eighties and nineties, it would sell out within hours. He was inducted into the Rock and Roll Hall of Fame the third year he was eligible, in the year 2000.

Judith did a number of groundbreaking mixed-medium rock-and-roll paintings those first few years. Besides becoming a staple of various rock magazines, they were also featured in a some art journals. She continued to work on her intense landscapes, too, and more than once she had shows of her rock paintings in one gallery and of her landscapes in another, in the same city. Her rock paintings were often high-spirited but grittily realistic. Her landscapes were often referred to as "religious," a term she liked, except that she considered all of her work religious.

While Judith didn't mind traveling around the world with Wolfram, she preferred the stability and order of their life on the farm. After the births of their children, she began to speak in interviews of Caitlin and Oberon as her finest works of art. And, yes, she made papier maché animals with them. Those brightly painted animals were displayed all over the house.

Some of Judith's friends couldn't believe that she would trust Wolfram out alone on the road, but she just laughed at the thought of his infidelity. She said she'd chosen her man well and trusted him absolutely. He reciprocated the trust when she traveled to New York or Chicago or San Francisco or Santa Fe for an opening.

Elizabeth went to graduate school in art at USC, after Nick was accepted there for graduate school in film. She began to show her work while still in school. In the late seventies, feeling the need to challenge herself in new ways and to refresh her palette, she shifted to photographic realism and began the series of works that would bring her national recognition. She found that the vanity of most people in the film world made them uncooperative (and outrageously demanding) subjects, so she worked most frequently from photographs she took of ordinary people--on the streets, at work, in restaurants, and in all manner of recreations.

Elizabeth and Nick had two girls, Jane and Sarah. They were--strange coincidence this--born in 1976 and 1978, just as Judith and Wolfram's kids were. Elizabeth was a devoted mother--who took Judith's suggestion and made papier maché animals with her daughters. Jane and Sarah didn't like to model for their mother--"Mommy, it's so boring!"--but she took hundreds of photographs of them and used the photographs, as well as many she'd taken of Caitlin and Oberon, to create a number of paintings.

Elizabeth and Nick lived in L. A. throughout the seventies, but, after spending the first few years of the eighties in London, moved in 1982 to Red Earth, where they purchased the big old house that Wolfram had once live in. Restoring the house took a huge amount of work, but they felt it was worth it.

Nick wrote a screenplay based on the fiction he had written for Kate Winfield during his senior year of college. He used the screenplay as part of his application package to USC Film School, where it seized the attention of the professors on the Graduate Entrance Committee. After graduating from USC, he got gigs directing low-budget genre films for Universal.

After Nick's third film, a noirish detective story, made money hand over fist and was praised by the critics, he was offered better work. His next film, a harrowing treatment of alcoholism and child abuse--he said in interviews he wanted to work on something as far removed from his own childhood as possible--also won praise for its writing and montage sequences. Nick was nominated that year for a Golden Globe for his screenplay and for a Director's Guild Award. He took his losses with a sense of humor.

However, he shocked just about everyone he knew in Hollywood by moving to England, where, in the course of the next three years he directed adaptations of *Twelfth Night* (the play's twins fired his visual imagination), of Austen's *Persuasion*, and of Woolf's *To the Lighthouse. Twelfth Night* and *Persuasion* were virtually ignored in America (though they were praised by some for their lyricism and editing), but the imagination and ingenuity with which Nick had adapted *Lighthouse* could not be ignored. That year he won a New York film critics award for his adapted script. He remained in England during the awards, but his sister Judith accepted it for him--causing everyone's jaws to drop at what appeared, at first glance, to be Nick Larkin in drag.

After Nick returned to America, and he and Elizabeth and the kids had settled permanently in Red Earth, he made films of Ann Tyler's *Searching for Caleb* and *Morgan's Passing*, which showed what he could do with contemporary comic material. Being "small" films, they were mostly overlooked by critics and audiences alike. Disappointed, Nick switched to television. His miniseries of John Gardner's *The Sunlight Dialogues* and Mark Helprin's *Winter's Tale* were both popular and well-received. Film versions of Gardner's *Nickel Mountain*, John Cheever's *The Wapshot Chronicle* and Ron Hansen's *Desperadoes* followed. All were well reviewed, but all performed only middling well at the box office.

Nick decided to try an action film about a spy who was sent to the Soviet Union by the CIA, double-crossed by operatives on his own side, and who had to escape on his own crook. The spook made it out through Afghanistan, which allowed for a number of blow-em-to-smithereens battle scenes in rough terrain. The film garnered tepid reviews--from critics who wondered what had possessed Nick Larkin to return to this kind of genre film--but it won Nick a whole new audience and made enough money that he finally gained a margin of clout with the studios.

And Nick knew just what use he wanted to put that clout to. He took his first screenplay out of a drawer and decided to rewrite it one last time--with psychically linked, visionary twins--but still very different from his own life (for one thing the twins were both girls). He completed the screenplay in three weeks. The first four studios he showed it to were scared off by the 'strange' subject matter and the huge special effects budget the film would require. They begged Nick to consider other projects--especially another action film. At last word, Disney was considering greenlighting the film, with a budget of a sixty million.

And the white buffalo? It continued to be seen by Nick and

Elizabeth and Wolfram and Judith and Mike Red Horse. It was still seen, of course, by visionaries of all kinds--holy men, vision questers, sun dancers--and by more than one madman, artist, and hobo. And of course it was seen by the Larkin and Kohles children, who took the visitations right in stride--as if they had been born to it.

* * * * * * *

There is a water that is night and dream . . .

Printed in the United States
3645